Foolish Beliefs

An April May Snow

Southern Paranormal Fiction Thriller

By

M. Scott Swanson

April May Snow Titles

Foolish Aspirations

Foolish Beliefs

Foolish Cravings

Foolish Desires

Foolish Expectations

Foolish Fantasies

Seven Title Prequel Series

Throw the Bouquet

Throw the Cap

Throw the Dice

Throw the Elbow

Throw the Fastball

Throw the Gauntlet

Throw the Hissy

Never miss an April May Snow release.

Join the reader's club!

www.mscottswanson.com

Author's Note- This is a work of fiction. Character names, businesses, locations, crime incidents and hauntings are purely imagination. Where the public names of locations are used please know it is from a place of love and respect from this author. Any resemblance to actual people living or dead or to private events or establishments is entirely coincidental.

Gonna cuss the morning when it comes

'Cause I know that the rising sun

Ain't no good for me

'Cause you'll have to leave

Luke Bryan- "Don't Want This Night To End"

Chapter 1

During the short drive from my parents' lake house to downtown Guntersville, I'm more nervous than a long-tailed cat in a room full of rocking chairs. I don't know the reason for my angst other than the gut feeling something terrible will happen today.

Given I have psychic abilities, it would behoove me to pay attention to my feelings.

As I rack my brain to identify the source of my concern, I tick off my to-do list. I'm not due in court today. I've completed all my paperwork and finished all the filing at my uncle's law firm, Snow and Associates. Well, not really, but I do have the documents in folders ready to go into the filing cabinets. It's Uncle Howard's fault anyway. Who keeps hard copies nowadays?

My phone rings, and I look down. I see James, roll my eyes, and sigh. There's the dreadful thing due to happen today.

James and I went out on one date. I've been trying to dodge him ever since.

He feels there's a special bond between us because I saved his life when a corrupt evil spirit drowned him. I'm trying to avoid him for the same reason he believes we have a connection.

The less I interact with people who have paranormal energies floating around them, the better.

Plus, James doesn't get my motor running. It's more accurate to say he doesn't even turn the key in the ignition.

I know, why did I go on a date with him? It's a fair question.

If I'm honest, James was a rebound meant to stroke my ego after Shane White unintentionally made me feel undesirable. Shane is my current love interest. Unfortunately, I'm his "friend" interest.

Being relegated to friend status by a guy I'm interested in is a whole new quandary for me. I'm not vain enough to believe I'd be mistaken for a supermodel. For one thing, I have way too many curves for that, and I like my curves. Still, until I met Shane White, I never had difficulty catching the eye of a man who tickled my fancy. If I wanted, I could always gain a man's attention long enough to determine whether they were fascinating or a bore.

More confusing, I technically did catch Shane's eye—at first. That's how he came to have my cell phone number. Then things never really progressed from there, and I wasn't about to throw myself at him. I'm not exactly desperate.

Even if I did consider making my desires overtly evident to Shane on more than one occasion.

With Shane, it's like I changed my shampoo to the "We Can Be Friends" brand. To say our non-relationship has done considerable damage to my confidence is a distinct understatement.

The adult thing would be to answer the phone and explain to James I'm not interested. I should be polite yet direct to the point while giving him the necessary time to comprehend we don't have a future together. I know that's the proper response, but my finger won't press the green button.

Be an adult, April May. But I don't want to be. Being an adult is so overrated.

His call goes to voicemail. Great. Now I feel like a complete heel.

I pull my car in next to Howard's ten-year-old Volvo. As I open the door to the law office, I hear Howard talking on his phone. He's discussing golf. If I were to guess, he's talking with Lane Jameson, our local district attorney, who has an equal passion for the sport.

"April, is that you?" Howard hollers from his office.

"Yes, sir."

"Good morning. I've got a surprise in here for you."

"Good surprise or bad?"

"Like your uncle would bring you an unpleasant surprise."

I let his comment hang in the air. We both know it's a dubious question at best. It's too early for a debate, so I choose to treat it as rhetorical.

Given my low expectations for the day, I should sit down at my desk and get to work rather than humor him. But I have enough curiosity to kill a thousand cats. I can't endure, not knowing.

I trudge to his door, and he continues his phone conversation. I'm treated to his description of what iron he used on the three-par hole number eight.

With a huff, I cock my hip.

Howard notices my motion and mutes his cell phone. "Jasper cooked tenderloin this morning. I saved you one." He lifts a grease-stained, white paper bag off a stack of manilla folders.

"On Monday?" I ask in awe as I accept the bag as if it's a rare artifact.

Howard wiggles his eyebrows at me, returning his attention to his call.

I'm totally wrong about today. Jasper Bell, the defensive coordinator for the Guntersville High School football team and the school's crackerjack algebra teacher, wastes his true gift while working at the school.

The man grills pork tenderloin so perfect it melts on your tongue like cotton candy. Sadly, with his hectic schedule, he only works for Ms. Bell's Meat and Four during the summer months on Friday and Saturday.

I can feel the warmth of the biscuit emanating from the cavernous sack. The scent of spiced tenderloin commingles pleasantly with the fresh biscuit scent of clover honey and cinnamon.

The honey and cinnamon are supposed to be a secret. Ms. Bell would say, "You must be outside of your mind, girl," if I claimed to have guessed the secret ingredients in her biscuits.

Her secret is safe with me. I cheated and used my paranormal abilities to find out the unique ingredients. It is one of my less-proud moments when my curiosity got the best of me.

Besides, everyone who knows me is aware my culinary skills come to a screeching halt after desserts that don't require the use of an oven. No one would believe I solved Ms. Bell's fifty-year-old secret.

I steal back to my desk with the prize sack. I resist the urge to stroke the bag and whisper, "My precious." I know you think I'm joking. You'll never understand until you try one.

The front door opens. A man standing at five foot eight with a forty-eight-inch waistband slams the door behind him. He looks like he's been through three wars and a goat roping.

"I need to see Howard now!"

Yep. Right about the time I thought the day was changing for the better, an over-important man comes marching into the office and screws up my simple pleasure. Is it too much to ask that a girl be allowed to enjoy a free breakfast in peace?

"He's on the phone presently."

"I need to speak to him posthaste."

Who says that? "You can take a seat and wait if you wish."

Tubby braces his arms on the front of my desk. His chin is positioned above my biscuit sack. The man's nose violently twists four consecutive times. "Is that a tenderloin biscuit from Ms. Bell's?"

I pull my precious sack toward me and hold it protectively in the crook of my elbow. "Howard can't be interrupted when he's talking to the district attorney. If you take a seat, I can slip him a message that you're waiting, Mister..."

"Jared Raley." He pulls at the size-eighteen collar that might have fit him fine fifty pounds earlier. His face, a light pink when he entered the office, is now beet red. "I don't see the point in having an attorney if I can't talk to him."

What a baby. "I didn't say you can't talk to him. I said he's speaking to the district attorney." I say "district attorney" exaggeratingly slow and loud in case he didn't understand the first time I told him.

Jared stands up straight. He wipes off the sweat marks his palms made on my desk with the side of his hand. "I'm sorry. I just have a bit of an emergency."

Now that's interesting. "Sir, we do law here. Emergencies are for ambulances and police officers. Nothing happens fast when it comes to the court system. Now, if you'll just take a seat, Counselor Snow will be with you momentarily."

I believe I may have gotten through to him. He relaxes, and the redness eases from his jowls.

"I've already been to the police. They told me there is nothing they can do for me since no criminal act has been committed. Then, I called the prosecutor's office to talk to them, and they corroborated what the police said. The prosecutor's office told me my only recourse is a civilian case."

I'm at a loss for words as I try to determine how a civilian case versus a military trial is pertinent to the conversation. I snort a laugh as I realize the flustered man has it wrong. "You mean 'civil' case."

"Right. That's what I said."

"Of course you did. What was I thinking?" I'm thinking my biscuit is getting cold. This man's stupidity is obviously contagious because I'm feeling stupider by the second.

"I'm actually Howard's assistant attorney, so I might be able to help you." *Did I just say that?* I only need to wait for Howard to quit talking about his golf game to pass Jared and his "civilian" case off. But no, I had to open my mouth.

Jared takes his time weighing his options.

"I'm just saying that unless you're talking about huge damages, in all likelihood, I'll be the attorney assigned to your case anyway." *Shut up already.* Hello, biscuit.

"How much is a man's self-respect worth?"

Who doesn't love questions like that? "How about we start from the beginning, Mr. Raley. Explain to me what happened and tell me what you told the police."

"I've been violated. My wife and my marriage, the sanctity of my home violated, all of it violated."

I nod my head in agreement. Not because I understand what Jared is talking about, but because the deeper red creeping back onto his face concerns me. I feel a little affirmation might help him not have a stroke in our office.

"Okay, I understand your rights have been violated. Now, tell me exactly what took place."

"It's awful. I came home from the lot. It's the end of the month, and we always have a big push to hit our quota. But it has been one of those good months where we hit the quota early the last day.

"I've been working sixteen-hour days all week, and I thought I'd take the opportunity to head on home and catch some sleep."

That's where I've seen this dude. He owns the Kia dealership in Boaz. I've seen his late-night advertisements on the local cable station a thousand times.

I've always thought his commercials odd because he has a really tall, blonde model standing next to him during the advertisement. If I were a man of average height, I believe I'd prefer a shorter woman standing next to me in my ads, so I don't look like a runt.

But what do I know about marketing?

"When I get home, before I head off to bed, I look for Crystal."

"Crystal is your..."

He frowns like I asked the stupidest question in the world. "My wife."

Okay. I was thinking dog. But whatever.

"She wasn't in the bedroom or the kitchen, so I checked out back by the pool."

My curiosity kicks in gear; this is getting juicy. Forget the fact that my favorite breakfast is turning into a greasy mound of mush. I am sitting on the edge of my chair, waiting for Jared to drop the bomb and tell me what he found. My bet is Ms. Raley in the pool house getting the rail by Mr. Pool Boy. This is so much better than reality TV.

"I step out the French doors, and Crystal is asleep on one of the lounge chairs. Only I hear this funny, high-pitched noise. And there it is, a drone flying three feet above her."

Not what I was expecting at all. "A drone?"

"You know, one of those helicopter-things with the circular blades that people fly remotely with radio controllers."

Right, I do know what a drone is. "So, what is the problem?"

"Isn't it obvious?"

Yeah. No. I hate the "guess what my problem is" game. I hold my tongue and refuse to play Jared's silly game.

Jared shakes his hands in the air. "It was in my yard hovering over my wife. To make matters worse, it had a camera strapped to it."

I fail to conceal a grin. "Really?"

"Yeah, so come to find out, my neighbor is taking nude pictures of my wife, and I'm the bad guy."

I shudder in confusion. "What do you mean, nude?"

Jared clamps his lips tightly together, and his color returns to a deep purple as he pulls something out of his coat pocket and tosses it on my desk. "Nude."

Against my better judgment, I pick up the photos he's

printed out. It all clicks when I see the long-legged blonde lady from the commercials.

She must have found the fountain of youth or been surgically improved, as her exposed breasts look like those of a woman at least twenty years younger. "Does she always sunbathe topless?" I feel that's a fair question, given the pictures show a chain-link fence rather than a privacy fence in the background.

"She says tan marks make her breasts look malformed."

Out of courtesy, I flip through the last six photos even though I've seen quite enough. The sixth photo has an unwanted surprise for me. It's a closeup of a woman's bikini bottoms, but they're pulled to the side, and her naked "hamster" is in full view.

"Oh my." I avert my eyes and put the other photos on top of the startling one. "I'm sure your wife had a tough time explaining that one."

"She was simply adjusting. Haven't you ever had a pair of panties bind up?"

Yeah, but I didn't solve the issue by exposing myself for a photo. Surely Jared can't be this dense. "I hope you don't mind me saying this, but I understand why nobody wanted to prosecute this case. It would be impossible to prove your neighbor did anything illegal."

"He was flying his drone in my yard."

"Flying it would be the operative word. If it had been a toy car with a camera mounted on it, we might have something we could work with. As a property owner, you own the mineral rights of everything below the ground and everything to the grass's tip. But you don't own the air. Think about it, if you owned the air, people would be trespassing when they fly on commercial airliners."

"Commercial airliners don't hover over your wife taking pictures."

"No, that's true. Laws aren't perfect, but they must draw the line somewhere. I'm afraid we can't help you because it's not a winnable case. Not even for a civil trial from what you have explained to me."

"But I've had trauma!"

"I believe you. But getting a jury to believe that is a whole different story."

"So, that's it? He gets to take nudies of my wife, and I'm the one who must pay two thousand dollars and do three months' probation?"

"For what?"

"The probation is for reckless endangerment with a firearm and discharging a firearm in the city limits. The two thousand dollars is to pay for the drone."

I'm getting stupider by the second just talking to Jared. "You shot it out of the air?"

Jared's skin color lightens as a broad grin stretches his face. "Who says pistols are inaccurate? I hit it with my first round and didn't even damage the camera."

Even if there were enough evidence to move forward, I'd lost all desire to consider this man's case. I think guns have a purpose. Shooting toys out of the sky in a subdivision is not one. "Like I said, the probabilities of winning anything on this are so low we just wouldn't be interested."

Jared pulls another piece of paper from his pocket, this one smaller than the pack of pictures. He unfolds a check and sets it on my desk with his right pointer finger holding it down.

"I don't care how much it costs. My neighbor has cuckolded me, cost me money, and turned me into a criminal. This can't stand. I must fight back and make him pay.

"This is a twenty-thousand-dollar retainer. I'm willing to go as high as forty thousand before we discuss future expenses."

"Like I said, the probability of winning the case is extremely low, but lucky for you, you selected the right attorneys for the job." I pick up the retainer check.

One of my duties at Snow and Associates, besides assistant attorney, receptionist, coffee maker, and the sandwich runner, is the bookkeeper. Howard makes bank on billings, but he's awful at collections and worse on organization skills. Cash flow is at a premium nowadays at Snow and Associates until I can do some more invoice payment collecting.

"I want him to squeal like a stuck pig."

"Yep, we specialize in making cheating pigs squeal."

Jared likes my statement as he nods his head enthusiastically and adds, "That's why you have a lawyer. Because if you don't, people are gonna push you around, and you don't have any recourse."

The crazed look in his eyes spooks me. I wonder if Howard has ever considered installing a metal detector.

Chapter 2

When I arrive at my parents' lake house, Daddy's truck is the only car in the driveway. My daddy has a perfect look to be a successful bank robber. He's average height, average build, brown eyes, and brown-going-to-gray hair. It would be impossible to single him out in a crowd. He could be half the white male population in Alabama.

His intellectual capabilities aren't average, though. Daddy has a Ph.D. in physics from Auburn. He works at Redstone Arsenal in a job so classified he and his co-workers don't know how the government plans to use their inventions. He's also an adjunct professor at the University of North Alabama.

He's a seriously smart dude.

I pull open the sliding glass door of the lake house. I have the munchies, and I know the small fridge in my apartment over the boathouse contains half a diet Dr. Pepper and two water bottles.

It isn't necessary to go past the first row in my parents' fridge before I hit the mother lode. Somebody made nacho cheese with RO*TEL and Velveeta and kindly left some for me. I warm up my cholesterol treasure in the microwave.

I rummage in the chip basket and find half a bag of tortilla chips while I wait for the dip to heat.

Leaning against the counter, I devour several chips I've used as miniature shovels to fill the hole in my stomach. I relax as dopamine dumps into my brain, eliciting a smile.

Crack! An explosion echoes through the house, causing me to duck behind the counter. It sounded like a rifle shot.

Struggling to remain calm, I attempt to determine the source of the noise. My muscles tense as I realize it came from Daddy's laboratory. All sorts of horrible images flash through my imagination as I race down the wood-floored hallway and slam into his work door.

As the laboratory door flies open, thick gray smoke rolls out, engulfing me. My eyes burn as the smoke detectors wail their alarm—late. The tangy scent of gunpowder hangs heavy in the air. "Daddy!"

"I'm good. I think I just used a few too many grains."

Daddy appears out of the blue-gray smoke, clutching the edge of the countertop, his glasses askew. I'm stunned by the amount of black grime on his face. His gray hair is blown back and standing up in a fabulous Einstein fashion.

"What are you doing? I thought you accidentally shot yourself or something!"

"I was working on a new starting mechanism for my perpetual generator. It works fine with electricity, but I need a different energy source to begin the motion to really market it.

"It's ironic to have a perpetual electrical generator that requires electricity to start it.

"I thought percussion caps would be the way to go. Obviously, four hundred grain is a bit much."

Daddy's usually a man of measured words. If he's this talkative, he came within a frog's hair of killing himself.

"You scared the tar out of me."

He looks at his machine to avoid eye contact. "I'm sorry."

Daddy doesn't handle emotion well. That's why he and the boys have an easier time relating. I try to calm my tone and divert from the apparent close call. "You said it'll actually work now?"

He makes direct eye contact and straightens his glasses. "Hook up one nine-volt battery, and that's all you need to get it started. This prototype generates two hundred amps of one-hundred-and-twenty-volt electricity.

"I ran it for ten weeks during the last test. It would have run longer if I hadn't accidentally bumped it when I was working on the miniaturized battery storage unit."

"That's pretty cool, Daddy." I'm not exactly sure what the amperage and volt thing is, but if his machine can make it, from his expression, I take it to be a good thing.

"I think so. Of course, I've got a long way to go for it to be usable for my real goal."

The older I get, the more I realize I didn't inherit my father's natural altruistic nature. In college, I participated in numerous marches that were supposed to help a variety of worthy causes. Maybe they brought "awareness," but perhaps they didn't; it's tough to be sure.

No. Daddy never marched in any protest. He marched for the Army. A year in the Iraq desert to free Kuwait during Operation Desert Storm.

My daddy is a person of action, not words.

I don't know if he'll ever be able to fine-tune his invention. But his objective of bringing a perpetual energy source that is environmentally neutral to underdeveloped communities around the world brings tears to my eyes. I know I'm rooting for him to crack the code.

"How's the job search going, baby? Any new opportunities?"

I shake my head. "Not since the Louisville interview that I blew."

He gives a knowing frown. "Bad timing for sure. But at least you were there to save your friend Gerald."

"James," I correct him.

"James." He wipes his face with a hand towel.

"You have to believe things happen for a reason. I still

have my money on you moving to either Chattanooga or Birmingham."

"Those aren't major markets, Daddy."

"No, but they're big enough. Besides, you can't blame a father for wanting his daughter to be closer to him." He cracks a grin. "Who's going to check in on me when I get old and decrepit."

"You and Mama never age. Besides, it doesn't matter where I end up. You know I'll be visiting all the time."

"From your mouth to God's ear. It never works that way, I fear."

I frown. "No rhyme intended, I'm sure."

"Your father is a man of many talents, April."

"This I know to be true." I lean forward and give him a kiss on the cheek. He smells of sulfur and smoke. I turn to leave.

"Don't forget, I'm cooking white chicken chili tonight. We'll be eating around seven. I expect you to bring a healthy appetite, young lady."

"I'll be there, but go easy on the gunpowder, Daddy."

My belief today would be horrible was misplaced. Instead of a dreadful day, I'm on a hot roll, the missed call from James notwithstanding. I scored my favorite breakfast this morning. Now, Daddy is cooking one of his most requested meals.

Not to mention things are looking up on the business front. Our client has a severe case of reality denial. His wife is cheating on him.

Still, when I deposited the twenty thousand dollars at the bank, I heard a sigh of relief from the cash flow at Snow and Associates. That retainer will keep us flush for a few more months.

I really am catching on to this business thing. It's not like people hire you just because they like you and you have the right degree. The business must turn a profit so the April May Snows of the world can draw a steady paycheck and pay off their student loans. That's something they don't teach in college, but they should.

Nana Hirsch once said if you have a hot hand in Vegas, you don't walk away from the table. She told me that when I was eight. At the time, I thought it had something to do with burning your hand on a hot plate at the dinner table and not crying from the pain.

I don't think that anymore, but time has not diluted the impact of her words now that I understand them. To take full advantage of my current streak of luck, I decide to check the large firms' recruiting boards worldwide.

Sitting with my legs crossed on top of my queen size bed, I fire up my laptop. I was right. Three positions fit my skill set and desire to a T.

There was only one such ad last month. My pulse quickens as my excitement is over the top.

One position is in New York, one in Boston, and another one is in Memphis. There's a fourth that fits my skill set well in Birmingham.

I shake my head and grin; Daddy always has a way of talking things up. Sorry, Daddy. It's not going to happen.

I tidy up my résumé, including my current employment as an associate attorney at Snow and Associates, a local defense counsel located in Guntersville, Alabama. I also add my recent accomplishment—the successful defense and acquittal of an innocent woman charged with capital murder.

Leaning back onto my pillows, I review my revised résumé. Wow, what a difference a couple of weeks makes.

The ability to add an existing position and some experience has changed my résumé from a desperate plea for employment to a professional inquiry about opportunities that will be mutually beneficial.

The realization of what a different impression my revisions will have on prospective employers has me highly animated as I prepare the inquiries. As I change the headings and addresses on my cover letters, my enthusiasm and expectations grow.

I hit the send button on the last inquiry and laugh like a loon. This is it. All I need to do now is sit back and wait for the three interview requests to come in. My new career and life are going to be here in short order.

It does cross my mind to send the same cover letter and résumé to the firm in Birmingham. I decide not to. Backup plans are for wimps and people who don't believe.

I close my laptop, shut my eyes, and visualize. It's December in New York. I'm walking the streets looking into the large glass retail windows decorated in full regalia for the Christmas season.

The snow falls in large, heavy flakes. I lift my face to the steel gray clouds. A huge snowflake flutters side to side as it treks to the ground. I open my mouth and catch the white ice on my tongue.

It tastes like money. It feels like success. It's a shiny new car and a hundred pairs of uber-cute shoes in April's closet.

My eyes open, and I'm smiling so wide my face hurts. Granny Snow has always preached how important it is to visualize having what you want already in your possession. That's an epically convincing case of visualization by my standards.

Unfolding my legs from under me, I pad to my miniature refrigerator and pull out a bottled water to celebrate my impending career breakthrough.

The tapping on the bottom of the boat dock is so violent the tremor vibrates through my feet. I rush to build a barricade around my mind to keep out the ghost's voice, but it's too late.

"You don't belong here."

I find that laughable. Especially since that's exactly how I feel about it. I unscrew the cap from my water bottle and take a drink.

"Get out."

You know, rather than fight it and ruin a good mood, I think I'll take his excellent suggestion. With a roll of my eyes, I leave my apartment and walk back to the lake house.

I was a normal little girl until the spirit that makes its home in the vicinity of our boathouse grabbed my ankle and pulled me underwater. From that day forward, I've been cursed with the ability to hear the voices of the dead.

My grandmothers and brother, Dusty, call it a "gift." Unfortunately, it's not one I can return for credit on my debit card. Lord knows I would if I could.

Personally, I consider my "gift" to be a royal pain in the butt. In some ways, the most annoying ghost, the scariest, because he was the first that physically touched me, is the one under our boathouse.

It's grumpy, rude, and random with no agenda other than wanting to be left alone. Hopefully, we'll both get our wish as soon as I nail those interviews.

Chapter 3

Daddy's hair is damp from his shower. He's in the kitchen slicing chicken breast for the chili. The white pepper simmering in the stockpot tickles my nose, and my mouth waters in anticipation.

"Need any help?" I ask.

"I've got it all under control. You can hang out and keep me company if you want."

I know Daddy is just being nice. You can't call him a lone wolf, but he works as well in solitude as he does in a group. It's always the task that keeps his interest, not his surroundings or company.

I take a seat at the counter and watch the steady, quick strokes of the chef knife he wields with practiced expertise. Rather than a simple up-and-down cut, he slices the chicken breast at a diagonal. His claim is it makes the chicken more tender in the chili. He's always exacting like that, paying the most exceptional attention to the smallest of details.

There isn't much arguing with the results. Be it Daddy's chilis, soups, or jambalaya, you will be hard pressed to find anyone to compete with his versions.

"What are you working on at the arsenal?"

He keeps his eyes on the task. His hands don't slow. "Solid and liquid fuel calculations again."

"For what?"

"Boosters."

Like I didn't know. "Boosters for what?"

He pauses mid-slice, pushes his lip out, and looks up. "I don't know." He shrugs and slices the rest of the chicken breast.

There's no way I could do Daddy's job. I'd have to know why the government needed the calculations.

Given their similar mechanical aptitude and ability to focus on a task, my older fraternal twin brothers are younger, albeit taller, versions of Daddy. Sometimes I wonder if I weren't the product of a later-life fling by Mama.

"Your Granny called today. She is asking about you."

There you go. I managed to think Granny up.

No, that's not a skill I possess. However, it is my family's belief. If you talk or think about somebody long enough, they tend to pop up. It's just a coincidence. I think.

"Is everything okay," I ask.

"Oh, sure. She'll probably outlive us all. She was disappointed when she heard you were back in town and you had not come to visit yet."

"I've been busy, Daddy." My voice is high-pitched and whiny, and I cringe.

"I explained that to her. She does want you to come out to the farm and see her."

"I don't know. I just got this new case." I exhale loudly when he cuts his eyes to me. "I'll see if I can come up with some time to visit."

"Good. She said she has a surprise for you."

My family is so unfair. They all know what motivates me and use it shamelessly. They all know I can't refuse a surprise. But who doesn't love presents?

There's the thrill of getting something unexpected for free and the satiation of your curiosity once you unwrap the gift. "I'll try to get out there before the end of the week."

"You're a good granddaughter. She'll love the visit."

The glass door slides open, and my brother Dusty fills the

opening. "Better be using the big stockpot today, Dad. I'm hungry, and I brought company."

"It's white chicken chili; it doesn't taste right in the small stockpot," Daddy says with a matter-of-fact tone as if even a five-year-old would know it to be true.

"True that," Dusty agrees.

Dusty's large body blocks my view of his guest. It's all I can do not to roll my eyes when his partner Miles Trufant steps from behind Dusty's girth.

Miles promptly pushes his glasses up on the bridge of his nose with a single finger. "I accepted because of the culinary delights promised. I had no idea the table was going to be graced by such beauty tonight."

"Can it, Miles, or I'll feed you to the catfish under the boat-house," I say.

Miles opens his mouth to reply before thinking better of it and shutting his mouth. He appears to understand I'm not in the mood for his thinly disguised romantic gestures to-night. Miles rarely misses an opportunity to hit on me. I'm not sure if he's incredibly persistent or a masochist. I try my best to ignore him.

He's my brother's research partner. Miles is a theologian professor who spent several years attempting to debunk my brother's research.

Dusty convinced Miles to go on one of his research trips. During that field excursion, Miles experienced a particularly nasty apparition. Ever since, he's worked for Dusty.

"Did you try two-hundred grain?" Dusty directs his question to Daddy.

"No. When I ran the diagnostics on the unit, I realized I fried my I/O board from the first try."

Dusty scowls. "That bites."

"Just another obstacle. The greater the obstacle, the greater the reward."

Two things here ruffle my feathers. Number one, I'm the one who checked on Daddy. I was the one who made sure he hadn't blown himself up. But does he discuss what grain count to use on the next experiment with me? Oh no, he calls my older brother and has a discussion with him about it. He totally dismissed my ability to understand his experiment.

Number two, it irks me to no end that I'm the only one in my family who sees an obstacle for what it is. Something that keeps you from what you want.

There is no high logic in the sky that preordains that a more significant obstacle means a more valuable prize. Obstacles are obstacles. They are a problem and not something you want in your life.

I stay quiet on this point as I am a minority of one in my family.

I'm still seething in my own silent temper tantrum when the sliding door opens again—my beautiful mama steps into the kitchen.

"Hello, Snow clan." Her eyes fall on Miles, and she gives a quick wink. "And Trufants."

She looks at me. "Is everyone playing nice this evening?"

"They better, or I'll be cracking some heads together," my brother Chase says as he enters the kitchen behind Mama.

"There's no violence to report yet. It's probably because I have a knife, and they know I know how to use it."

Mama kisses Daddy on the cheek. "You sure do know how to use it, baby."

Eww. My gag reflex almost kicks in with Mama's double entendre. As I scan the men's faces, I realize it's just my mind in the gutter because I'm the only one who seems to have understood her comment.

Someone steps into the kitchen just behind Chase. A hot sensation flushes my body, and my eyes open wider to take in the sexy stranger.

"Yeah, play nice. I brought company for dinner, and I don't want you to scare him off before I get a chance to look at his seventy-six 'Vette."

Chase puts his hand on the man's shoulder. "Y'all, this is Patrick McCabe. We're gonna be looking at his Corvette tonight."

Patrick shakes Mama's offered hand first, followed by Dusty and Miles. Daddy declines by lifting his hand and explaining he has chicken on his hands. He must have broken the handshaking chain as I'm only offered a nod of the head rather than a shake of the hand.

It's for the best. I might have used my "gifts" to scan for more information and felt guilty about it later.

"Are you the original owner of the 'Vette, Patrick?" Daddy asks.

Patrick shoves his hands into the front pockets of his jeans. He is incredibly adorable. "No, sir. It was my father's."

The silence holds in the air before Daddy broaches the sensitive subject. "When did he pass, son?"

"Just last month, sir." It didn't seem to catch Patrick by surprise that Daddy understood his father was dead.

"Have you ever restored a car before?" Mama asks as she opens the fridge.

"No, ma'am, and I may find I don't have the talent for it. But I just..." His voice cracks.

Mama hands him a beer. "I know, honey. You couldn't fix your daddy, but maybe you can fix up something he loves."

The smile on his face tells me he's happy someone understands, but the liquid pooling in his eyes confirms the hurt is fresh.

Mama continues to hand out beers. "White chicken chili is always best with a cold beer."

"Amen to that," my brothers say in unison.

My stomach continues to swell after dinner. The best thing about Daddy's white chicken chili is it's so delicious you can't stop eating it. The worst thing about Daddy's white chicken chili is you can't stop eating it.

I lie down on my back, still dressed, and groan. I'd think a grown woman could moderate her eating habits. I'm such a failure in that department.

My roommate ghost appears to have taken the rest of the night off. I've not felt nor heard him since I came back from dinner. With any luck, he won't be haunting my dreams tonight.

One thing is sure, Patrick McCabe will most definitely be prominent in my dreams. I know next to nothing about the attractive tall man. But he lit something inside of me that I worried was extinguished for anyone other than Shane White.

I can quit worrying.

My desire is strong. I want to learn more about Patrick and spend some time with him. So much so that I almost offered to help with his 'Vette this evening.

Fortunately, I came to my senses before I suggested something so idiotic. My entire family would have seen right through that ruse for what it was.

Now, I lie on my bed in pain from an overfilled stomach. I'm going out of my mind knowing Patrick and my brother are less than fifty yards away working in the mechanic shed.

The only solace I can take from this moment is the knowledge that tomorrow I can ask Chase questions about Patrick's background and ask where he works. Chase is the only member of my family who might not immediately recognize I'm interested in Patrick.

Chapter 4

I arrive at Snow Associates before Howard. I unlock the front door, and as I open it, the humidity and sweltering heat slap me in the face. I leave the door open and quickly step to the thermostat. Geez, it's hotter in the office than outdoors.

The thermostat is set at seventy degrees. It's reading eighty-five degrees.

I turn the knob to sixty-five, and nothing happens. I set the fan from auto to on. Again, nothing happens. Perspiration beads on my forehead as a lone trickle of sweat runs down my spine onto my panty line.

Fudge biscuit. Maybe today is the lousy day my dream Sunday night foretold.

I call Howard's cell. He picks up, and I don't bother with hello. "Hey, did you know we had a problem with the air conditioning?"

Howard laughs. How do you laugh when you find out you have an expensive repair bill in your near future?

"Well, April, if I did, don't you think I would've had it fixed?"

Yeah, there is that. "It's pretty hot in here. What do you want me to do?"

"Tell you what, if you will, call Cool Breeze HVAC for me. I did some work for their owner a year ago. Let's see if I can't let him recoup some of the attorney fees I charged him."

Howard is one of the biggest believers in patronizing those who hire him. He's the original "you scratch my back, and I'll scratch your back" business owner. "Okay, do you have a number for them?"

"No, but you can Google them."

"Will do."

I do a search for Cool Breeze HVAC, and four locations pop up. They have an office in Birmingham and three in other north Alabama cities, with the nearest being Huntsville. I consider calling one of the closer HVAC companies. Still, it's Howard's decision and money, so I call Cool Breeze's Huntsville shop.

The dispatch explains they're overbooked in Huntsville this morning. She promises she'll call the owner and see if they can get out sooner since it's my uncle's business.

The fact they give special attention to my uncle's needs puts me at ease in the eighty-five-degree sweatbox. With any luck, they'll be by soon.

A few minutes after eight in the morning, Lane comes in the front door.

"Howard's not here right now," I warn him before he walks to Howard's office.

"I'm here to see you."

That gives me pause. Lane has his serious face on, all harsh and hard-like. "I understand you're taking on a civil case for Jared Raley."

It wasn't a question. It was a statement, so I just nod.

"You understand the man discharged a pistol in the general vicinity of his wife, and in the city limits no less."

"More or less."

"I only offered him the probation versus a trial to spare everyone from dealing with the case's stupidity. Now you plan to take up Judge Rossi's time with his absurd civil case?"

"I'm not. Jared is. It's his decision."

Lane's face becomes uncharacteristically colored with a reddish hue. "He has no possibility of winning."

I shrug. "I never said he did."

"Why is it so blasted hot in here?" Lane asks as he pulls at his starched collar.

"The air is out."

"You need to get that fixed," he says.

You think? "I have a service call in."

Lane shakes his head. "This will upset Judge Rossi. She does not suffer fools well, and she'll wonder why I ever cut a probation deal for this idiot."

"Maybe because you felt sorry for him because he's the only one who doesn't realize his wife is boinking their neighbor." The hard twitch of Lane's face notifies me—I said that and didn't just think it. Here I'd been doing such a respectable job of keeping thoughts like that to myself.

"It's not fair that a man gives a woman a life of luxury, and she abuses him in such a despicable manner," Lane growls.

We lock eyes, and I say nothing. I think I did more than enough bruising with my last rude comment.

"Very well, then." He turns on his heels and marches out the front door.

Lovely, nothing like getting under the district attorney's skin first thing to start a day off right.

It's eight thirty, and I have the start of a severe case of swamp butt. When the AC guy gets here, assuming he does, ever, I'll have to go home and change since I no longer have a single stitch of dry clothing on me.

I consider calling Cool Breeze HVAC back and asking if they can give me an estimated arrival time for their technician. If it is later in the day, I can at least transfer the company phone to my cell and go over to the courthouse. As I pick up the phone, the front door opens.

"Hi, is Howard in? Hey, I know you."

My heart stops, and I quit breathing. Talk about talking

someone up.

"Hey," My voice sounds husky like I just ran a mile.

Patrick clasps his hands together. "I didn't put it together last night that you worked for Howard. Now that I think about it, it only makes sense. I feel stupid."

My composure is coming back. "It never really came up."

He looks like he wants to continue the conversation on a personal basis but thinks better of it. He makes a show of looking left and then right. "Where's the unit and the circuit box?"

Good question. "Truthfully, I have no clue. I just started here a month ago."

Patrick gives me a smile that is just short of a laugh. "I'll check around for them if that's okay with you."

As he starts toward Howard's office, I follow him. He gives a quick, cursory scan of the walls and checks behind Howard's door. He comes back out into the reception area and takes a right into the kitchenette.

Patrick pulls open a small utility door I'd never noticed before. "Here it is." Opening the panel, he studies the interior for a moment and flips one of the breakers. "That should cut the power."

I follow Patrick outside. Men are not made for Armani suits and Italian loafers. I'm a firm believer that the masculine body looks best in well-scarred work boots, relaxed fit jeans, black T-shirts, and a well-populated leather tool belt hanging off their hip.

"It's sweet of you, but I'll be okay. You don't have to stay and watch me."

I break out of my trance and realize Patrick is addressing me. I feel a blush of heat start at my chest and run up to my ears. "I'm sorry, I was just curious."

"Well, in that case, stay." He pops the HVAC unit's side off. "Maybe you'll learn enough the next time you can just take care of it yourself."

"No chance of that." Stupid, he was just joking. "I guess

it's just a habit. Growing up, I used to like to watch my daddy and brothers work on stuff. Unfortunately, it never sank in."

Patrick looks over his shoulder. "I'm sure if you had to, it would come back to you. Still, a woman like you could probably always get a man to do it for you."

Yes, it's sort of a sexist remark, but it isn't bothering me for some reason. "Have you been working for Cool Breeze for a while?"

"Uh-huh. About ten years."

Ten years. I hope someday to say I worked for a company for ten years. "Your boss must be okay to work for."

"I think so. Some of the technicians think he's a jerk."

"I suppose you can't make everyone happy."

"Which is why you might as well focus on making yourself happy." He stands and stretches his back. "I'm getting too old for this." He points at the unit. "Just a blown control board; I have one in my truck. I should be able to get you up and running here in just a few."

I watch him saunter off to the service van parked next to my car. From my vantage point, there is a lot to like. Despite all the positive physical attributes and the fact that he is a good guy, it is clear we're from two different worlds.

He is a blue-collar worker in the small town I'm trying to escape. I'm familiar with his type.

They like to put in their forty hours, hard hours, a week and have a little fun fishing, hunting, or even racing cars on the weekend. They marry girls who like to cook dinners, keep the house, and work part-time jobs while the kids are at school.

Men like Patrick have a challenging time living with women who make two or three times what they earn. They also don't transfer to the large city well.

I watch his backside as he opens a couple of cabinet drawers in his van. When he starts back toward the office, I force myself to look down and go back inside.

This really bites. It isn't like I'm looking to get married.

Besides, it isn't my responsibility to make sure nobody gets hurt if we decide to date. That'll be on him if I'm always honest about what my intentions are. Yeah, I can tell myself that, but I don't believe it.

"Are you feeling lucky?"

Patrick's voice shocks me out of my deep thought. "Should I be?"

He chuckles as he struts back to the kitchenette. "No. I have some skill at this, so luck isn't necessary." He disappears through the doorway.

The air kicks on. Instinctively I stand and put my hand toward the vent. Ah, blessed cool air.

"Feels like a cool Arctic breeze."

Patrick stands inches from me, his hand to the vent next to mine. The second heatwave since he arrived flushes my face.

"It feels awesome. I'm so glad the owner and Howard know each other. It would've been a long, miserable day if they hadn't sent you out right away."

"The owner and your uncle have a special relationship. He helped him through a rough time."

"That sounds like my uncle. He's usually helping other folks out."

"That he is. Well, I've got to get. It was a pleasure to see you again. Your brother and I have a lot of work to do on my father's car, so if you see me in your mechanic barn, don't be a stranger."

"You either."

He smiles. He has a sexy "I have a secret" smile.

"Right, I'm going now."

"Okay. Goodbye." I shut the door behind him and lean my forehead against the door. *April May Snow, don't you dare get involved with that boy. You know there is absolutely no way a relationship would work out, and both of y'all would just get hurt,* my conscience admonishes me.

My conscience is right. I'm just not sure I can abide by the wise advice.

Chapter 5

I spend the rest of my morning giving thanks for the advanced technology known as air conditioning that some wonderfully industrious inventor created. I now understand the rise in the southern population over the last half-century is directly related to that person's imagination brought to reality.

Perusing the internet. I find a couple of interesting cases tangential to drones and property rights. I also scan some cases regarding picture taking of a voyeuristic nature. The significant difference between those cases and the Raley case being that the victim, the person being photographed without their knowledge, in every case brought the suit against the deviant photographer.

It's not that I believe it changes the case that dramatically for Jared to be pressing the charges and not Crystal. Nude pictures were taken regardless of who filed the suit. What concerns me more is I have a suspicion Mrs. Raley was a willing participant in the flying-photo escapade.

"Is it a full moon or something?" Uncle Howard slams the door while pulling his tie over his head in one movement.

"It's still daylight," I say.

Howard stops his rant in mid-flow and looks at me as if I've lost my mind.

"What? It is."

He gives a slight shake of his head. "As in 'somebody threw nuts on the floor because all the squirrels are out.'"

Oh, right. That sort of full moon. "Wait. I thought you were in court for the Phipps' lemon case."

"I was. We were supposed to present the settlement to Judge Rossi. But last night, one of Eddie Phipps's mechanics leaked some critical information to the Taylors. It has changed the complexion of the case dramatically."

"I'm guessing not in Eddie's favor."

"The Taylors have withdrawn their approval of the settlement. The case has moved from a three-thousand-dollar settlement to a felony charge. No, it was not in Eddie's favor."

"What in the world?"

Howard's lips grow thin. "Eddie Phipps. I should've known better. This one's on me. That Toyota he sold the Taylors didn't have a bad engine; it had an old engine. Plus, an old transmission, radiator, and everything else on it. The car was a rental with a hundred and ten thousand miles, not the nine thousand miles he had listed on the bill of sale."

That doesn't make any sense. "How did Eddie get by registration?"

"Exactly. Pretty hard to do without a little help from the County Clerk's office. You know what"—he waves his hand —"that's not my issue. Whoever he paid off, I hope they put the extra hundred dollars or whatever he paid them in savings. I suppose they'll need it for bail and or severance pay."

"What about Eddie?"

"I guess we get to defend him against a felony charge now." Howard raises his chin. "I thought you said the air conditioning was out. It feels cool in here."

"Correction, it feels awesome in here. That A/C company you told me to call sent one of their technicians right out. He fixed the unit in just a few minutes."

"Symbiotic relations, April. The best kind of business you

can ever cultivate. Now, if you'll excuse me, I'm going to go into my office and slam my forehead on my desk a few hundred times. Then, I'll attempt to develop the defense for a client who deserves to spend time at the county bed and breakfast."

I can't help but savor the moment. I'm the high-drama person in the office. Howard is never flustered, and this is the first outburst I've ever witnessed from my uncle.

If I must guess, his outburst has more to do with Howard feeling foolish for accepting Eddie's case. Howard knows the scheming character of Eddie Phipps, and he still gave him the benefit of the doubt. Everyone in town knows Eddie is as slippery as they come.

Howard can be a pushover for someone in need. It's not his fault; he's just wired that way.

At eleven, Howard asks if I'm hungry. Like Pavlov's dog, I know this means he's buying.

I offer to pick up sandwiches at Jerry's. After gorging myself on chili the night before, I don't need the heaviness of a Jerry's deli sandwich. But I also don't know if anyone will cook at the lake house tonight.

Even with free rent and no car payment, money continues to be tight, and I have two twenty-dollar bills that I must stretch until Friday. My mind, for that reason, went to the most food for the money.

Jerry's is a local deli catering heavily to the construction workers, first responders, and blue-collar workers from the few factory jobs still left in town. It's known for ridiculously thick stacks of bland luncheon meat stacked on hard hoagie buns at a very affordable price. It's always busy on workdays at lunch.

As I round the corner to enter the town square, I notice a Gadsden News Thirteen van. I give an involuntary shudder as the plastic-like vision of Chuck Grassley pops into my mind.

Chuck covers the Guntersville news stories when there

are any. He's a pompous blowhard who has half the women over fifty in the county absolutely in a hot tizzy. I figure it's time for an excellent ophthalmologist to open in Guntersville because there are a tremendous number of grandmothers who need eye surgery.

Fighting back my gag reflex, I wonder what news we have in town to prompt a visit from the Gadsden news team. They hadn't been in town since last month when the monster truck engine Paul Brant was building exploded and burned his garage down. The sheriff initially recorded it as a terrorist bombing. Once the terrorist theory was debunked, Chuck Grassley took his flat-top haircut and pleather knock-off Italian loafers back to Gadsden.

I order a large New York steamer. If you're not familiar with it, it's a pound of highly processed, warmed-up mystery meat with about another half-pound of cheese dripping over it. There's something on it that makes the bun slide off the meat. I'm not sure if it is a special sauce or if the meat is just self-lubricating.

Howard requests a small turkey and avocado, no mayo on wheat bread sandwich. The lighter sandwich selection by him is a new occurrence that coincides with his return from an ultra-secret, extended weekend trip to Mobile, Alabama, two weeks ago. He's tightlipped about any details, but the family's general impression is that he has a lady friend on the coast.

My number is called, and I pay for the order with Howard's card. The heft of the bag makes me smile as my stomach grumbles with anticipation. I'm ecstatic. As I turn toward the exit, my happiness evaporates. My Guntersville nemesis stands before me.

"Why, I declare, if it's not April May Snow."

"Hi, Jackie," I say through clenched teeth.

Jackie's perfect white teeth are blindingly bright. Her dark, thick hair is shiny enough to make a shampoo model envious, and her red lipstick perfectly placed and blotted on her full lips.

It aggravates me as I imagine what I look like. I'm sure after sitting in a broiling office this morning, my blonde hair is frizzy like I was struck by lightning. The only thing shining on me is the grease on my face after having sweated all morning. I can't stand that Jackie looks so put together.

"Don't you just look spectacular," she says with too much of a smile.

My eyes narrow. I struggle not to punch her in the mouth.

"Randy told me you were back in town a few weeks ago."

I know Jackie only mentions Randy to rub salt in my wound. She stole Randy from me back in high school when I told him we needed to date other people for a little while.

Jackie was co-captain of the cheerleader squad with me, and I never expected her to stab me in the back like that.

"Tell your Uncle hi for me. I hope Mr. Bojangles is doing better now."

I'm out of breath. When did I stop breathing? The room spins, and I know if I don't get out of her immediate vicinity, I'm going to vomit.

Uncle Howard and Mr. Bojangles? They are her patients now? Et tu, Brute? Say it isn't so, Mr. Bojangles. Is there no loyalty left in the Snow family?

"Well, I best place my order now. It's great to see you, April. If you ever decide you want a pet, please come by the clinic. We've always got names and numbers of people who have animals needing to be adopted."

Adopt? Do I look like I can take care of a pet? I can only stare at her gorgeous face. The face that was my best friend for the first seventeen years of my life.

Jackie subtly nods her head and turns her back to me as she gets in line. I consider jumping on her back and pulling her thick hair. But Jerry's is way too busy for me to be able to get away with that. It's Jackie's lucky day.

I slink out the front door of Jerry's.

"You took Mr. Bojangles to Jackie's?" I yell toward Howard's office as I enter the front door.

"Who's Jackie?"

I stand in his doorway and fume as I shake my head. "Playing like you don't know who I'm talking about isn't going to help. Jackie Rains. She works for Doc Tanner at the veterinarian clinic."

Howard smiles knowingly. "Oh, you mean Dr. Rains. She doesn't work for Doc Tanner; she's his partner. She's going to buy him out at the end of the year."

All I can do is close my eyes and simmer. Family simply doesn't stick together like they used to.

"Here's your sandwich." I drop his turkey sandwich on his desk.

"Thanks?"

Chapter 6

At three forty-five, I'm still angry over Howard and Mr. Bojangles' treachery. It's too much to contemplate.

Would it be too much trouble for Howard to drive to Huntsville? They have plenty of veterinarians there, and it's only an hour away.

I gather my backpack and purse as I prepare to leave the den of traitors. The front door opens, and Lane stomps into the foyer. Everyone has the same mood today. Maybe it is a full moon.

"If you're looking to talk me out of the Raley case, my answer is the same," I say.

"Not now, April. I've got something pressing. Is Howard in his office?"

Ouch. Lane's dismissal smarts. "Yes, he's still back there."

After that exchange, my ego wants to finish packing my bags, grab my remaining half a sandwich from the fridge, and disappear out the front door. But of course, my curiosity will override the smart decision. I linger at my desk, picking up and setting down the same three folders repeatedly.

Their voices are just below audible, but I don't dare move closer to Howard's door. The thought of being caught eavesdropping by Lane is a scary proposition.

"I can't go tonight, Lane. I have the Freemasons' meeting,"

Howard says as he raises his voice.

"April."

I drop the files in my hands, scattering them on the floor. "Yes, sir?"

"Can you come here?"

Leaning over, I try to scoop the loose papers in one unsuccessful motion. "Just a minute."

As I enter Howard's office, the discomfort between the two men is palatable. I look to Howard and then to Lane. "What's up?"

"It looks like you're up in the batting order," Lane remarks. He looks less than happy about the circumstance.

I hope the awkward smile on my face isn't as stupid looking as it feels. "How so?"

"We just had our first incident involving the new ordinance commonly referred to as the 'make my day' law."

I may not know how to fix an A/C unit or change spark plugs, but I keep up with my profession. The state of Alabama recently updated a firearms self-protection law. The new statute allows folks the right to protect themselves with deadly force if they feel threatened.

It no longer requires the victim to use a weapon matching the threat. Suppose the attacker carries a baseball bat or a knife. In that case, it's perfectly acceptable for the victim to use whatever weapon they have at their disposal, up to and including firearms.

"The homeowner wants to lawyer up. The police still have him in interrogation," Lane says.

"I have the Freemasons' meeting tonight, and since I'm the president, I can't skip it," Uncle Howard interjects with a frown.

This isn't making sense. "If it was self-defense, why does he need a lawyer, and why is he being interrogated?"

Lane rubs the five o'clock shadow on his chin. "Let's just say it's a little more complicated than that."

Sometimes Lane's ambiguity makes him a jerk. "Let's just

say I need a little more information, so I know what I'm walking into, District Attorney."

He arches his eyebrows then sighs. "Your client is Vance Wagner. He moved to town from Rainbow City three years ago when he married Leslie Mann. Her parents gave them a ten-acre plot from the family land off of Fortress Road, two miles past Rex's.

"They're young; early twenties. They bought a double-wide to put on the property with big plans to build the Ponderosa someday."

Lane falls silent. I can tell something about the case is disturbing him, and he's determining how best to explain.

"Honestly, this is a tough one. Vance is a drywall subcontractor. During the summer, with the heat, his crew starts work at five in the morning and leaves the job site at one.

"He arrived home at one thirty where two assailants attacked him, knocked him upside the head, and shoved him into his trailer. They struck him in the head again, and he passed out."

"Vance sounds like a victim so far."

Howard touches my shoulder. "He's both a victim and a suspect for murder, April."

Lane nods his head. "It's what happened later. When Vance regained consciousness, he found himself zip-tied to a chair. Leslie was strapped to a chair next to him. Her clothes were disheveled, and her face was covered in blood and welts. She had been beaten severely."

I can't imagine what went through Leslie's or Vance's minds in that situation. With events totally out of their control, they had to believe it was their last few minutes alive.

"The attackers kept demanding Vance tell them where he kept the cash in the trailer."

That's odd. "How would they know if there was or wasn't cash in the trailer?"

Lane holds up a finger. "I'll get to that in a second. Vance feigned cooperation. He told them to check the floor vent in the kitchen. There, true to Vance's word, they found twenty thousand in cash."

"Holy moly. Is he dealing drugs?"

"We considered the same thing," Lane says. "Still, we have no reason to suspect that. Besides, everything about this boy tells you he's old school. He was raised by his grandparents, and they had a serious distrust of working for corporations and loathed banks.

"The cash was for his quarterly taxes coming up. At least that's what he's telling us."

"I'm surprised he didn't think they would just kill them once they had the money."

"I don't know what level of schooling Vance has, but I can tell you the young man's deductive reasoning is remarkably high. He explained the two assailants had on ski masks at first, and as long as they kept them on, he believed they would leave once they had the money," Lane says.

"Unfortunately, that's not what happened," Howard interjects.

"No," Lane says. "After they had the cash, both men took off their masks to count the money. Vance explained his belief that the only witnesses that don't talk are of the dead variety."

"When the men left the trailer, Vance was convinced they were getting supplies to dispose of him and Leslie after they killed them," Howard says.

My stomach rolls as I imagine how the thieves would have disposed of the young couple. "That's awful. They had to be scared."

"I'm sure they would have been," Lane continues. "But Vance was past fear since he had freed himself from the cable tie around his wrists."

I'm calling bull malarkey on that. "You can't break cable ties."

Howard laughs. "You don't have to break them if your abductor uses releasable cable ties."

I can't help it. I know it's not funny, but I giggle anyway.

Lane puffs out his chest, obviously offended by my sophomoric reaction.

"The men had twenty thousand dollars, and I'm sure they were elated as they walked out to their car. According to Vance, even after they took off their masks, they took their time leaving."

"Which would have convinced Vance all the more that they were going to make sure there were no witnesses," I say.

"So he claims. Still, it's no excuse for what he did," Lane says. "As the two men walked to their car, Vance ran to his bedroom and grabbed the riot gun out from under his bed."

Whoa. I lean forward as Lane continues his story.

"Vance let the first blast of double-aught fly as he stepped out the front door catching the passenger as he was getting in the car. The driver realized they were under attack and slammed the car in reverse, dragging his partner's lower body down the gravel drive. He was unfortunate enough to be wedged between the open car door and the car's running board.

"Vance jumped off the porch and directed two blasts at the driver's side windshield as he pursued the car down his drive. The driver lost control, catching the drainage ditch on the side of the driveway. The car turned over as the rear hit an oak tree.

"Vance shot a few more blasts in the direction of the men before returning to check on Leslie. He claims it took him forty-five minutes to tend Leslie's wounds before he felt positive she was out of immediate medical danger. He called the police after that."

"Wow" is all I can manage to say as I play the events in my mind. Those poor criminals didn't have a clue they were messing with the reincarnation of John Rambo. "Why didn't he just call the first responders right away to help Leslie?"

"Vance is a hunter," Howard volunteers. "Most hunters will tell you to wait thirty to sixty minutes before you start tracking an animal. That gives it time to bleed out."

A chill runs up my spine. That is so calculating it's intriguing on some perverse level. "Are you serious?"

"With this character, I would be surprised if it didn't at least enter part of his decision process." Lane sighs. "He's claiming he should be cleared of all wrongdoing by the new statute. But as you can see, his actions go way beyond the intent of the law."

"Unless he misunderstood the statute. I mean, if he thought it meant if an attacker was still on his property," I offer. The thought of what the two men did to his wife makes Vance's actions seem warranted to me on a personal level, even though I know it to be a stretch for the law.

"I'm sure he would tell you that. As I said, he's slick. But that also means he is intelligent enough to know exactly where the boundaries of the statute are and that he stepped past their intent. We may approve of the fact he eliminated two thugs, but the law is the law. In this case, we are looking at a minimum of two counts of murder two. We could try him for first-degree murder because he baited them with the cash once he knew his hands were free. Still, I think we'll settle for a second-degree murder charge given the circumstances."

"It's awfully early for all this, considering the crime was reported just a few hours ago, isn't it?"

Lane shakes his head. "This has the potential of being a real mess. Not to mention we could end up with some state and, heaven forbid, national coverage. I need you to talk to him and determine what plea deal we can offer to make this go away."

"Second-degree murder isn't much of a deal for a man in his twenties who was defending his wife," I say.

Lane raises a hand. "It's better than the death penalty. Just see where his mind is at for now."

I want to talk to Vance now. The story is provocative, and I'd love to keep him from spending years in jail over a fight he didn't start.

"Sure, I'll go meet with him this evening," I say.

"Great." Lane takes a pen from the inside pocket of his suit coat and writes on the back of a business card. "This is my cell. Call me tonight and let me know what you find out."

Chapter 7

I'm glad I saved the second half of my New York steamer. I grab a bench outside the police precinct to eat my dinner as quickly as possible.

I know it's not very professional, considering Vance is waiting on his attorney. But I won't be doing him any favors if I can't concentrate. Nobody can be creative on an empty stomach.

One thing is for sure, Howard will need to come off some money if I'm going to keep drawing these capital cases. When I agreed to work for him, I thought I'd be mostly doing wills and contracts. I never anticipated people's lives would be hanging on my professional skill level. It's unnerving, to say the least.

As I finish the last bite of my sandwich, I close my eyes and savor the taste. I focus on New York City. I'm in Central Park, enjoying my sandwich. I just came out of my fancy law office to feel the sunshine. Later this evening, I'll take the subway to my ultra-cool flat. There's a good chance I'll take up painting too since my studio flat is so roomy.

Visualization is of the utmost importance for goals. I can feel the sunshine of New York on my face, I hear the horns of the cabs and people walking to work. When the scent of car fumes commingles with the hot dog stand half a block down, I know my visualization is of the highest order.

Yes, it is only a matter of time, and April May Snow will have a corner office in a New York high rise.

"Are you okay, April?"

I open my eyes. My good friend Jacob Hurley pops my New York bubble. He's blocking the sun with his massive frame as he stands over me.

"Sure."

He tilts his head to the side. "Okay. You just looked troubled."

"No, all good with me." I try not to act disappointed with his interruption.

Like the good cop he is, Jacob continues with his questions. He won't be satisfied until he understands the situation. "What are you doing out here anyway?"

I show him my empty wrapper. "Catching a bite to eat before I go in and see my client."

"Who's that?" His brow wrinkles.

"Vance Wagner."

"The young Walt Kowalski? Whew, good luck with that."

"Walt who?"

Jacob laughs.

Jacob has the sexiest laugh in the world.

"Clint Eastwood. You know Gran Torino"—he twirls his finger—"the vigilante movie where he protects his neighborhood and home against a bunch of gangbangers."

I push out my lower lip and shake my head. I have no clue what movie Jacob is referring to.

"Aw, man. I'm going to have to bring my laptop and some popcorn over so we can stream it together."

His comment makes me panicky for some reason. I shouldn't get nervous. Jacob and I are merely good friends. I mean, he could be considered gorgeous if you happen to be into oversized Greek gods in uniforms. Still, his flint doesn't spark my tinder wood. Mostly. Well, a lot of the time.

"I don't have a television."

"I said we could stream it on my laptop."

"Oh, yeah."

"I can get with you about that later. I'm sure you need to get in there and see what you can do to help Mr. Wagner."

The Gadsden Channel thirteen van has moved from the courthouse to the precinct, and Chuck is set up with his camera at the stairs. The right side of my upper lip ticks up in disgust.

Drawing nearer, I'm surprised to see the News Channel Seven van from Huntsville has arrived as well. Uh oh. That's not good. Huntsville doesn't make its way down to us unless there's a big story and it's been confirmed.

The epiphany hits home, and I roll my eyes. Stupid. I'm the big story.

Or at least my client's actions are causing all the interest. Perfect. No pressure about keeping a lid on this one, April.

I walk as nonchalantly as possible up the precinct stairs. The advantage of being new, well recently relocated, to town is nobody knows my role yet. I'm sure Chuck and the Huntsville reporter would bum rush Lane or Jacob if they walked into the precinct.

My foot touches the first step when I hear a perfectly tuned male baritone voice behind me. "Now that's the most perfect thing I've seen today."

Aw, heck no. Please tell me that isn't Chuck. I seriously attempt to ignore his vulgar comment and continue up the stairs.

But I can't.

I turn and give him my best "I just ate a lemon" stare. "Excuse me?"

Chuck leans back and forms the outline of a rectangle with his hands. "Mm-hmm. I'd love to have that picture framed on the ceiling over my bed."

I'm so shocked I freeze in place.

"Or better yet, put it on a poster. For my poster bed." He raises his eyebrows and points at me. "See what I did there?"

I realize the man is ageless. In the twenty-plus years he's been reporting the news, he looks the same as the day he started.

Odd. Before now, I never considered when I saw Chuck on the news that he appears to have never aged. I step toward him and focus on him closely.

Chuck stands taller and leans toward me. As I continue to stare, he frowns, "What are you looking at?"

What exactly am I seeing? He has tiny scars peppered just below his golden flattop from a less-than-stellar plug job. The creases that should be present from laughing have been replaced by puffiness that resembles wasp stings. If there is such a thing as Botox wasps.

Even if it weren't for the hairline scars and swollen face, his turkey gobbler neck not fully concealed by his collar and tie is a dead giveaway. Man, just how old is Chuck? Seventy?

"You know what they say. Once you sleep with a star, you never go back," he says nervously.

"Nobody says that," I say.

"Sure they do."

"No, it's not a thing."

"It could be. You won't know if you don't give it a chance."

This guy doesn't stop. "Thanks for the offer, but I'm not into charity for old men."

I continue up the stairs. Which is what I should have done in the first place.

Chuck must have short-circuited my digestive tract since my sandwich feels like a steel ball bearing the size of a grapefruit in my gut. Now I'm seriously regretting having dinner before meeting with Vance.

I enter the precinct. The officer on duty takes me back to the interrogation room, which I have become quite familiar with over the last few weeks.

Two middle-aged men in rumpled suits stand just outside

the door.

"Colby, Dorsett, this woman is Mr. Wagner's attorney," my escorting officer says.

"I didn't know you could intern as a high school student," the thinner, white male detective remarks.

"Age is a matter of perspective. Speaking of age, I thought they made detectives take retirement after their seventieth birthday," I say.

The thick, black detective next to him chuckles. "She's old enough to deal with you, Cannon." He sobers and asks, "Seriously, though, young lady, you're not planning to keep this slime bucket from talking to us, are you?"

I'm not sure which of these bullies I'm going to kick in the shin first. They both are such deserving targets.

"We will answer any fair questions that do not harm his defense."

The two men weigh my response. The older white man, Cannon Colby, responds first, "We're game for that." He grins like I'm walking into a trap.

Maybe I am. Maybe he is.

As I open the door, the two detectives are on my heel. I turn and push against Dorsett's chest. "Give me a few minutes alone with my client first."

His eyes narrow. He doesn't seem keen on my request.

"Or I could demand you charge Vance or release him now."

"Don't ask for us to do what we already plan to do. We'll be charging your client soon enough. We have him dead center for two counts of first-degree murder," Dorsett says.

"Hmm. Interesting. If it is such a slam-dunk case, why haven't you charged my client yet?" I put a finger to my lip. "Oh, I know. Because you're not sure you can get a jury to convict a man for defending his wife and home against two men who beat them and threatened to kill them."

Dorsett opens the door. "Five minutes."

"Thank you."

The alert eyes of Vance Wagner scan me from head to toe in a non-judgmental manner. It's as if he's cataloging my look for future reference while assessing my physical abilities. "Are you my lawyer?"

"I am. My name is April Snow." I point to the chair across from him. "Do you mind if I sit down?"

"Be my guest. But I have to warn you, it's not an extremely comfortable chair as you approach the third hour."

"You know some interrogators use a chair that slant, so you're constantly trying not to slide off the seat." I can't remember where I read that, but it stuck with me as it would be incredibly aggravating.

Vance laughs. "Yeah, that level of mind games requires some real working intelligence. Something these two numbskull detectives lack."

He waves his hands as he talks. They are bloody and lacerated as if someone tried to skin him with a dull pocket knife.

I point at his hands. "You need to get those looked at."

The toothy grin he flashes me is unnerving. "I have a high pain threshold. Besides, L made me soak them in saltwater before I called the police."

Vance is not a large man. He's my height, and I'd guess a hundred and sixty pounds after Thanksgiving dinner.

He fits one of the two major categories many men from Guntersville fill. The first category is big, tall, sweet, and thick with a brain that's a little slow to shift out of first gear. The second category of man is average-to-small size, charismatic, and scary smart.

The kind of smart that'll send warning bells through every part of your body and spark spider tingles up the back of your neck. Vance is prototypical for the latter.

I pull a notepad from my backpack. "They may not be Mensa members, but they have a few tricks up their sleeves. Like leaving the microphone on. I'd like to ask you a couple of questions, so I can better understand the case."

"Understandable."

"I want you to write your answers down for me and hold the cover at a forty-five-degree angle so the cameras can't pick up your answers."

His state of agitation dissipates, and he grins. He favors me a quick nod of the head as I slide the notepad and a pen to him.

"Did you know you were going to kill your attackers?"

He sits forward, writes quickly, and turns the notepad to me. He's careful to keep the cover half-closed. **I intended to if I could, or die trying.**

I motion for him to turn the pad back to him, "Did you delay the call to the first responders on purpose?"

He turns the pad back to me. **Absolutely.**

"Okay, last one. Why didn't you just call the police when you freed yourself instead of going after the men with the shotgun?"

He pulls the pad back and writes one word quickly. **Police.**

I nod. "Right. Why not call them?"

Vance shakes his head vehemently and taps the word police with the pen.

"Yes, the—" I catch myself before I speak what Vance has written.

He clicks his tongue. "No, April. They were"—he taps the pen to the pad. "I knew the police couldn't help because the bastards were"—he taps the notebook again.

That's an interesting conspiracy theory. Daddy always says there's a razor-thin line between genius and outhouse rat crazy. A line that can often be blurred during stressful situations.

"How could you possibly know that, Vance? I thought you didn't know them."

"Didn't have to. All of them have a certain body language and a certain cadence to their speech. I don't know where they're from, but they were definitely"—he taps the pad again.

If I could only grab his hand and read him. My need

to confirm proof positive he's telling the truth is intense. Everything about his demeanor backs up the truthful fact, but I still don't know if I can believe his story.

I also now know Lane is only partially correct. Vance isn't just smart; he's off the chart intelligent.

That plays against him. I'm convinced, if he wants to, he can force his body to react correctly while he tells a whopper of a lie. An untruth like his two assailants were cops, so he was justified in not calling the authorities.

The thicker of the two detectives sticks his head into the room. "Ms. Snow. Can we come in now?"

"Aw, did you miss me already, Dorsett? I told you I don't swing your way," Vance jokes.

I ignore Dorsett and turn my attention back to Vance. "I need to know. Do you trust me?"

His left eye squints momentarily before returning to its open state. "Yeah. I trust you, April Snow."

"Good. We're going to fight this, but that means you'll have to stay in jail tonight."

His face twists into a frown. "But L is at the hospital."

"I'll check in on her for you once we're done."

Vance's face contorts in displeasure for the briefest of seconds. Then he masks his emotions. "So, you're gonna leave me here to play with these jokers by myself?"

Dorsett's and Colby's faces are priceless. It's all I can do to restrain a laugh. Yes, Vance is a scary individual at his root. Still, he has a dry sense of humor and a perfect delivery second to none. "Actually, I believe this interview is done."

"Ms. Snow, you did promise we could ask any reasonable question," Dorsett reminds me gently.

"I did say that you can ask any reasonable question that would not affect his defense negatively." I smile sweetly. "Unfortunately, I'm not sure there is a question you can ask my client that won't put his case in dire straits, gentlemen. As I see it, we're done for tonight."

The ghost of a smile flashes across Vance's poker face. It's all the encouragement I need to make an even grander exit than necessary.

I make a show of packing my backpack, and as I stroll to the door, I say over my shoulder, "Y'all have a blessed evening."

Chapter 8

My high spirits fade as I exit the precinct and see the additional news van setting up. The stakes have grown exponentially. My gut churns as I watch the News Two van from Birmingham unpack their gear.

Birmingham news means the entire state will see the broadcast. That also means if the national news catches a whiff of anything interesting, or in the case of Alabama, anything crazy, the national news will pick it up in a flash.

This snowball is picking up speed, fast. I feel like I'm standing in its path at the bottom of the hill.

Fortunately, the three competing station reporters are huddled up and trading notes. I'm able to escape without any questions or, in the case of Chuck Grassley, additional propositions from vain grandfathers.

I try not to feel sorry for myself as I drive to the hospital in Albertville. I fail miserably.

This is all Howard's fault; I shouldn't even be in this position. A young, unseasoned attorney has no business defending someone charged with murder. If Howard weren't so socially conscious, he'd be taking care of this case instead of chairing the Freemasons' meeting.

Well, that may be shallow on my part. It's not like Howard's golfing or running off to Mobile again on another top-secret trip. Freemasons do a lot of good for children in our community.

Ugh. Now I feel bad for being so petty. My emotions are all scrambled, and my self-doubt is blaring. I don't like feeling this way.

As I pull up to the hospital, my stomach cramps in earnest. I hope it's from the day's stress, including dealing with two hard-headed detectives and eating on the run, and not that something was wrong with the second half of the steamer I ate. The perspiration droplets accumulating on my chest make me fear it's the sandwich.

This is no time for food poisoning, April.

Despite my discomfort, I brighten upon entering the hospital. My luck is turning to the positive as Wanda Neil is working the admissions desk tonight.

"April May? I heard a rumor from your brother you were back in town. I suppose your mama and daddy are happy to have the Snow clan complete once again."

"It's just a temporary thing. I need to take some time off before I sign on with a large firm." My little white lie is getting easier to tell each time I tell it, but I still feel the tips of my ears heat up with guilt.

Wanda and my mother know each other from their younger days and now volunteer together at the women's shelter. Wanda and her husband, Bruce, also rent one of the slips at the marina.

Wanda has worked at the hospital since she graduated from high school. Mama says Wanda controls all the power levers within the hospital.

"Ms. Wanda"—I've called her that from the time I began speaking as a toddler—"a friend's wife was admitted earlier, and I need to see her if possible."

The woman's casual style evaporates. "Now, April, you know only family is allowed from eight to ten, and it's after nine now."

Yes, I know the rules after Granny's scare last year, and

yes, I can still tell time. "Yes, ma'am. But he wants me to check in on her because he won't be able to tonight."

She looks at me skeptically. Wanda knows me well, so it's not without some justification.

"I suppose we could do a quick visit." She exhales sharply to punctuate the fact she's breaking a long-standing rule for me. "Who is it you need to see?"

"Leslie Wagner."

Wanda's eyes narrow. "The young lady who got roughed up by those two men a few hours ago?"

I try for nonchalance. "Yes, ma'am. That's why her husband wants me to check in on her."

"I don't know, April. How about you come back in the morning?"

"Please, Ms. Wanda. It's crucial." I hate the fact my voice sounds like a six-year-old begging to go to the pool.

Her chin ticks from side to side. "Lordy, I swear. The more things change, the more they stay the same with you, April May. Your mama sure did try."

Busted. I don't know what I was thinking. Ms. Wanda as the gatekeeper is not ever to my advantage.

I don't feel the need to talk to Leslie tonight. If she's at the hospital, she's safe. Anything she can add to the afternoon's events isn't germane unless she followed Vance outside when the shooting began. Yes, waiting until the morning suits me fine, given my stomach is cramping and I'm sleepy, too.

Still, I promised Vance. I really want to keep my word with the first promise I made him for some inexplicable reason.

"I thought I might have seen you at the women's shelter since you were home," Wanda says.

Oh, boy, here we go. "Yes, ma'am. I've had a pretty busy schedule the first month, but Mama and I discussed it, and as soon as I can, I'm gonna come out and help."

"You know we're painting all the rooms on the west wing's second floor this Saturday. We're going to be doing some of the paint with sponge prints. The rooms will be beautiful when we're done." Her face brightens with a wide smile.

She should smile more often. It makes her less imposing.

"I seem to recall a young lady who is excellent at trimming in rooms."

Blackmail by shaming. It's the worst.

"I'm sure I'm too rusty nowadays."

"Nonsense. I'm sure once you get started, it'll all come back to you. You know I used to tell your mama, 'Vivian, that April of yours could make a fortune as a house painter.'" Ms. Wanda wags her finger at me. "You just ask her if I didn't say that very thing to her."

I guess it's helpful to know if this legal career thing doesn't work out for me, I have at least one marketable skill to fall back on. Painting can earn me an occasional dinner, I suppose.

The inevitable horse trade is pitched. "Tell you what, you be at the shelter with your mama at nine on Saturday morning, and I'll have a sausage egg biscuit and some fresh brushes ready for you."

You must understand, coming from Ms. Wanda, that's not a question. It's not even a suggestion. It's a command from one of the women who run the town I grew up in.

There are women in Guntersville who are the Southern, female versions of Don Corleone. They make you offers you can't refuse, and if you do refuse, you wake up with the head of a catfish in your bed informing you of your social outcast status.

I put forth the most pleasant smile I can muster. "You know that would be a lot of fun."

"Fantastic. I'm looking forward to catching up with you some more on Saturday." She runs her finger down the computer screen. "Looks like Ms. Wagner is staying in room three-oh-two. I'll walk you up there."

"Oh, that's okay. I know how to get there."

Ms. Wanda waves her hand. "Nonsense, no trouble at all."

As we ride the elevator to the third floor, Ms. Wanda makes sure to remind me of her nephew, Egbert. He is still quite eligible and seriously looking for the love of his life. This doesn't surprise me. Unless Egbert has transformed from an ugly duckling and gotten better about holding a job, I'm of the opinion he will be a bachelor for quite some time to come.

I follow Ms. Wanda into the intensely cold hospital room. A young woman with wispy, bleach-blonde hair and ivory skin lies in bed. Her raccoon eyes are hard not to gape at as the black bruises stand out more against her fair skin.

Ms. Wanda checks Leslie's chart. She places the back of her wrist on the petite woman's forehead.

Leslie jerks violently to the side rail. Her glare is accusing and promises swift violence.

"It's okay, dear. I need to check that your temperature has come back down." Ms. Wanda draws her hand back and puts it in her pocket. "How are you feeling?"

Leslie opens her swollen eyes wider and thins her swollen, busted lip. "How do you think I feel, you stupid cow?"

Ms. Wanda stiffens her back so quickly it looks like someone goosed her. I contain a laugh of solidarity, as I agree with Leslie that Ms. Wanda's question is absurd.

The large woman turns toward me and nearly catches me laughing. "That's just the pain medication talking."

The woman in the bed sits up. I can tell she is extremely short and not even a hundred pounds.

"Pain medication, my butt. It's the pain of this terrible thirst I have that's causing the issue. Why don't you make yourself useful and go get me a Diet Coke?"

Ms. Wanda turns back to her. "Would you like apple juice or cranberry juice?"

"Are you deaf? I said Diet Coke, woman."

"We can't get you a Diet Coke," Wanda bristles.

"Then what good are you?"

"I'm good for you to heal. The aspartame in Diet Coke is terrible for your health."

Leslie swings her bare legs off the bed. There are visible handprints up and down her thighs and calves. Without even bracing against the pain, she yanks her IV out.

I feel the pain for her as chill bumps cause me to shudder. This little chick is ferocious.

Ms. Wanda stomps toward her, tossing the clipboard to the bed. "What are you doing?"

"What does it look like, heifer? I'm going to get me a Diet Coke."

The two strong-willed women fall into a stare-off. I know Ms. Wanda has the experience and size advantage in spades. Plus, Leslie already looks like she's lost a few butt beatings.

Even so, my money's on the skinny, black and blue, bleached blonde.

Ms. Wanda appears to come to the same conclusion. "Honey, if I get you a Diet Coke, will you let me put the IV back in you?"

The petite woman's tongue slides across her teeth as she considers Wanda's proposal. "If you give me extra ice."

"Sure. No problem. I'll be right back."

Goal obtained, the small woman picks at the welt left on her arm from the IV needle with her finger.

Not gawking is not an option. This woman is the closest thing to a human version of a wet feral cat I've ever met. Her chin jerks up, and she locks her icy blue eyes on me.

"What are you doing here?" she hisses.

"Are you Leslie Wagner?"

She takes an exaggerated glance at the plastic ID bracelet on her left wrist. "Looks like it. Who are you?"

"I'm your husband's attorney, April Snow."

"I done told the stupid po-po. A man has a right to defend his family. There's absolutely nothing wrong with my man firing a shotgun on our property to scare people off."

"Well, if he had fired the shotgun to scare them off, he

wouldn't need me. But since he fired it at them, it gets a bit more complicated."

"I can't believe they're acting like he meant to kill them. It's the stupidest thing I've ever heard. It's a riot gun. It only carries seven shells anyway."

Leslie is agitated, but she is talking. I feel it best to keep her talking. I hope she shares something the police won't get out of her during their later questioning.

"Leslie, do you know how many shells Vance fired at the attackers?"

"Geez, you're not much smarter than the police. Didn't I just tell you our riot gun holds seven rounds?"

Of course, how stupid of me. "How long do you think the whole thing took?"

I can tell she is attempting to piece together the timeline for the entire afternoon. "Just the time between the first and the seventh shell."

Her grin gives me the same chill I got from her husband. "I'd say fifteen, twenty seconds tops. I bet the stupid jerks didn't know what hit them. I feel sorry for the mortuary attendant. Them boys are going to have some soiled britches on them when he strips them down."

"Leslie, did you notice anything odd about them?"

She gives my question careful consideration. "No." She bites her bottom lip. "Their voices weren't right?"

"Like they had a voice synthesizer?" That pops out of my mouth. Still, it's an excellent way for criminals to remain anonymous.

"No, their accents were wrong." She jerks her head quickly side to side. "Never mind. I was so angry, I'm sure I didn't hear right."

I must be too tired and becoming slaphappy since I barely conceal another laugh. It's unbelievable to me a woman barely weighing in at a hundred pounds, who has been slapped around, groped, and tied to a chair shows no sign of being scared or intimidated?

No, she's angry. Yes, if these two women kick off their shoes and start a fight, my money is certainly on Leslie. Ms. Wanda wouldn't have a prayer.

Ms. Wanda returns with a Diet Coke. Her face is set with determination. I'm sure she intends to get her part of the bargain and be allowed to reinsert Leslie's IV. I feel it best to take my leave before another round of their queen bee stare down game begins.

"Leslie, I've got to go now. But I'll see Vance tomorrow. Is there anything you want me to tell him?"

Leslie's bedhead is in such a state she looks like she was dragged across the floor by it, and both her eyes are swollen shut. Her lips look like two ruby-red, overinflated inner-tubes, yet she lights up and says in the sweetest tone, "Tell him I love him and not to worry about a thing. We're gonna be right as rain in no time."

Her words put me in a funk as I walk to my car. How can she be so optimistic when her world has been violated and torn down today by two strangers?

Simple. Leslie is a survivor of the highest order, and more importantly, she is all-in with a man she loves. A man who loves her with equal fervor.

Sure, they're both a scary sort of crazy. I know the type, and you'd be better to mess with a rabid pit bull than cross these two. They can be ruthlessly mean when their "people" are threatened.

Still, I also know that they will be loyal to each other until the end because of their love. They have thrown in lots together, and to folks like Leslie and Vance, "for better or for worse" isn't just a lovely saying on their wedding day. To them, it's a blood oath binding them until the end of their days.

Assuming they somehow make it into their nineties, I'm sure they'll be rocking on their front porch, holding hands as they look out into the woods on their property. They'll share seventy years of memories and inside jokes nobody else in the world will understand.

I'm envious. I want what Leslie and Vance have, and it isn't fair I can't be loved like that, too.

I feel evil for being jealous. Still, I can't help myself.

The steamer twists painfully in my gut and threatens to escape the emergency hatch. I shimmy back into the hospital in a desperate search for a public restroom.

I arrive home before the second round of the steamer terror roils through my intestines, barely. As the cold sweat begins to bead on my forehead and back, I swear off eating processed meats for the rest of my life.

Wait. Is bacon processed?

Shucking my clothes off swiftly, I step into the warmth of a much-needed shower. There's no way I would be able to fall asleep without a shower, considering how many times I have sweated today. The warm water soothes away the last cramps of my stomach.

I know it's not the processed meat causing my irritable bowels. I need to get control of my emotions in the worst of ways. Everything feels like a crisis the past few months, and it's tearing me up inside.

Everybody needs so much from me. I'm not sure I'm even fully qualified to help.

I'm just some rookie lawyer from Alabama who has a mountain of debt, and I live on top of a boathouse down by the river. You're trusting your future to me? How desperate are you folks, anyhow?

Slowing my breathing, I try to calm myself as I pull a worn T-shirt over my head. *Just do the best you can, April May.*

"God won't give you more than you can handle." Granny's favorite adage pops out of my mouth, and I draw another long breath. I've told Granny for years I think God doth overestimate April's abilities greatly.

I slip into bed and go into a full catatonic state from sheer exhaustion. Still, my mind won't shut down as I think about Jared and how someone, most likely me, will have to pull off the Band-Aid and tell him his marriage is over.

Also, I'm concerned about Vance's case. The new law hasn't been tried in court yet. Vance could be spending the rest of his life in jail.

Like a small prayer for distraction being answered, Patrick McCabe's perfect tush appears in my mind. As he digs through the drawers in his service van, he's unaware I have the ideal vantage point to watch him. My breathing slows further as my eyelids relax, and a smile stretches across my face.

Let the rest of the girls view the beauty of priceless Van Goghs and Monets. I'll be watching an American male building something instead. There is nothing more intriguing to me.

My phone dings. I wish it would automatically change to airplane mode when I turn the lights out. I decide to ignore it, but my vision of Patrick McCabe's tush disappears.

I'm staring at the back of my eyelids once again.

My phone dings a second time. I plan to ignore it again.

I do for five minutes, well, two. I groan and lift my phone, desperate for what bit of life-altering information it will treat me to.

The ID on the sender's text knocks my warm, fuzzy mood away. My gut cramps again, even though the steamer has long since vacated the premises.

The text from Lane reads, **Call me as soon as you're in.**

I know it would be professional for me to call Lane immediately. That's what I should do if I want to appear conscientious about my job.

The thing is, I don't want to become more involved with my responsibilities right now. I need rest, and talking to Lane is not going to help with my stress level.

Lane and I have only two available points of conversation: Mr. Raley's anti-aircraft excursion and Vance Wagner's anti-vehicle and anti-personnel event. Unless Lane is looking for some phone sex, he's not going to help me fall asleep.

Eww. Random. Where in the heck did that come from? Lane and phone sex. I'm beyond exhaustion. My brain is short-circuiting.

Punching my pillow, I flip it in search of a cool spot. I turn toward the wall.

I'm sure Lane has dealt with the same sleepless night. Hence the late-night text.

Being a public official, I'm sure it is incredibly stressful. It's a job where he must be continuously second-guessed. The thought of being responsible for deciding which cases to prosecute, which ones to offer a plea bargain, and when it's best to take a pass on a case must be draining.

Suppose I'm fair, though I'd rather not be. In that case, I understand, given the political nature of Lane's position, why he offered Jared an expeditious plea bargain. He'd do anything to keep the stupidity of the case out of Judge Rossi's court.

The civil case I plan to file on behalf of Jared will bring the neighbor's high-flying stupid circus act into Judge Rossi's court despite Lane's best efforts. I know Lane would prefer not to have the prior plea deal be revealed to the judge, but I fully expect the neighbor to bring it up during the trial.

The real concern for Lane is Vance's case. If the number of news vans is any indication, this hometown version of *Walking Tall* is destined to be plastered on the national news for weeks to come. I wouldn't be surprised to see a made-for-television mini-series on the event someday.

It would be a nightmare for Lane and our beautiful lake-side rural town to be scrutinized and judged by every large city in the country. I'm sure a healthy number of the metropolitan population will deem us as dangerous backwoods people.

The Vance Wagner case, as it relates to the "make my day" statute, has all the potential of putting Guntersville on the national consciousness. That's not the free advertising the Guntersville Tourist Committee will appreciate.

I should talk about these situations with Lane. He needs to cut a deal in both cases and sweep them under the rug as quickly as possible. I fully understand the gravity of the situation.

Despite my understanding of his situation, I can't do what he wants me to do. I don't want a fight with him, and I didn't ask for one. Still, it looks like a battle is coming in my direction regardless.

Given everything I expect him to want to discuss, I do the only reasonable thing that comes to mind. I turn my phone to airplane mode and place it face down on my nightstand.

As Grandpa Snow used to say before he passed, God rest his soul, that raccoon will still be treed and angry in the morning. Amen to that.

Chapter 9

It's four in the morning, and I can't fall back to sleep. There is no ghost whispering in my ear or thunder rolling across the lake to keep me awake—only the growing pains of becoming an adult. Personal accountability is way overrated.

My concerns about my career choice are growing. I'm only a part-time lawyer, and I feel like I've aged a couple of years during the last month. If my work is this troubling while working for my uncle and living at home, how will I cope with a mob of cutthroat legal partners where only results matter? I doubt my aptitude for my chosen field at the worst of times.

I kick the covers off my bed and readjust my pillows, but to no advantage. I'll not get comfortable enough to collect on the hour and a half of extra sleep I have allotted. I sit up and slap my feet to the wooden floor as I flip on my dresser lamp.

My phone, lying on my dresser, has all the attraction of an unexploded brick of C4 plastique. A snarl creases my upper lip as I stare in dread knowing I can't delay calling Lane any longer.

"Get it over with, April. You'll feel better," I say.

I reach for the device with impending doom. I know nothing positive can come from the discussion I'm about to have with Lane.

"Forget that. I need some coffee first," I announce as I walk to my vanity. Checking my reflection in my mirror, I pat at my wild hair.

It looks like I caught my hair in a door last night and spun for hours, trying to free myself. Lovely.

The tension in my shoulders releases as I enter my parents' kitchen. The fragrant scent of coffee tickles my nose. The percolating sound of water in the old coffeemaker my parents use has been a mainstay of my life. I sit on one of the stools at the counter and wait impatiently for my caffeine fix.

Chase enters from the interior hallway. He's wide awake, fully dressed, and looks like he's just taken a shower. Some folks are way too industrious in the morning.

He stares at my hair as he grins.

"Don't even," I warn him.

"With any luck, you won't start a trend." He looks away.

I notice a bucket he's carrying. "What do you have there?"

He fills the bucket with water in the sink "A little surprise."

"Come on. You know I don't do surprises."

"Close your eyes and open your mouth."

My face twists. "As if. I'm not closing my eyes."

"I guess you won't find out, then."

I love my brothers. The three of us would do anything for each other, at least after a little cajoling and some begging thrown in for good measure.

Still, it's best not to trust a Snow fully. We're not beyond an immature prank to get a cheap laugh. Chase, of all of us, is the worst.

"Just tell me."

He laughs. "No, the deal is close your eyes, open your mouth, and then you'll know."

"There is no deal. We didn't make a deal."

"Exactly. We don't have a deal because you won't close your eyes and open your mouth. You never want to follow the rules, April."

Ouch. That comment hits a little too close to home. "That's not true."

"My bad, you're right."

I squint my eyes. "I hate it when you do that. That's just rude when you act like you're conceding the point, but you really don't believe I'm right."

"So sue me if I know I can't out-argue a lawyer." He points at me "See what I did there? Sue me."

"You're so not amusing."

"My, oh my." Chase pours a mug of coffee and holds it below my nose. "Does somebody need their caffeine this morning?"

I accept the mug. "Thank you. Now, what do you have in the bucket?"

"You know, for somebody with all your education, you don't listen too well. I said, close your eyes or no deal."

I stand to look in the bucket, and he covers the top with a plate from the sink. He waits until I sit back down to move the cover.

It's stupid. I shouldn't care what Chase is up to, but my curiosity is always wired way too high.

There will be no getting the information out of him. Additionally, Chase knows my curiosity will drive me insane. The last thing I need to distract me today is for me to wonder what my idiotic brother has in his bucket.

"Fine." I close my eyes.

I remember all the times this sort of interaction has gone poorly for me, and I open my eyes. "I swear to gosh, Chase. If you put a slug or an earthworm in my mouth, I'm going to put sugar in your boat's fuel line. And that's after I tell Mama."

His eyes have a dreamy appearance. "I have to remember that one about the slug. But no, honest, this is a pleasant surprise."

As I close my eyes and open my mouth, I know if I end up with a slimy, salty slug on my tongue, I have no one to blame but myself. I know better.

Something the size of a marble rests on my tongue and against the back of my bottom teeth. It isn't squirming, and it doesn't taste salty; both are good things. Right?

It's prickly and rough. The tangy fragrance fills my palate as I identify the item. I bite down, exploding the tart sweetness of the blackberry into my mouth.

"Oh, that's good. Where did you get those?"

Chase lifts a few more from the bucket as he rinses them. "I planted about forty canes up on the front part of the property two summers ago. I've been watching them for the last month. These are the first ones to turn black."

I hold out my hands greedily. Chase dumps a few more onto my palm. "I don't even feel seeds."

"They're there, but they're tiny for blackberries. I think I'll make us a cobbler tonight."

That sounds like a delicious idea. Guilt kneads my consciousness. "I think desserts are my responsibility."

Chase's brow creases. "I didn't know you learned how to bake a cobbler."

I'm sure I can Google it. "Oh yeah. I cooked dessert for my friends all the time in college. They called me the cobbler queen."

"Impressive." His eyes narrow. "You were able to lay the crust over the top and score it? I mean, that's really difficult for beginners."

I wave my hand at him dismissively. "Oh, sure. Everybody said I made the best crust."

Chase bursts into a fit of laughter as he sets the rest of the blackberries out on a paper towel to dry.

"What?"

"Nothing, you're just a hoot." Chase fills his Thermos with the rest of the coffee and rinses out the pot. "I've got to run.

There's a lot to get done at the marina before the Fourth of July celebration."

"Oh, man. I almost forgot about that."

"Just around the corner." Chase stops at the sliding door. "Hey, April. Thanks for offering, but I'll do the cobbler tonight."

"Are you sure?"

"Positive. Just for the record, you don't make a crust for cobbler. You dump the mix in, and it bubbles to the top."

"Serious?"

He laughs. "True story. Look it up." He pulls the glass door shut behind him.

Guntersville is a small town, but its Fourth of July celebration is befitting of the state capital. In some regards, I think the Fourth of July in Guntersville is as popular as Christmas. It makes perfect sense. When you included the opportunity to legally explode things, drink beer, and ride on a boat, Christmas can barely hold its dominance in the holiday hierarchy.

The Fourth means a massive influx of tourists looking to rent boats from the marina so they can join the flotilla in the middle of the lake for the fireworks display.

I've been exposed to a few other Fourth of July celebrations since I left for college. Typically, at the end of the event, I'm left with "that's it?" as my prominent thought. Guntersville is the Mecca for people who like to celebrate Independence Day.

I take my spoils of coffee and fresh blackberries back to my room, trying hard not to think about my ensuing conversation with Lane.

Taming my hair with a quick rinse and dry, I put on acceptably lawyerly clothes. I enjoy the blackberries I stored in a red Solo cup on my vanity and take my time as I'll be well over an hour early into the office.

As I turn onto the state highway outside of my parents' neighborhood, I ride into town on autopilot. On a whim, I pass Snow and Associates. I want to drive out to my parents' marina.

I'm not sure if it's the blackberries or being en route to the marina, but I feel nostalgic. Contrary to what they say, you *can* always go home. What they mean to explain is it will never be the same.

I squish another tart berry on my tongue, and twenty years disappear. I'm seven again, and I am back in the Guntersville that remains static in my mind.

Granny Snow practically raised my brothers and me during the summers. Mama called it her sabbatical. Daddy referred to it as adult time.

Living purgatory is what I called it.

Granny and Grandpa lived on a two-hundred-acre farm off a county road few people ever traveled on. Their house was large enough for the three boys and their parents who once occupied it. My Grandpa built the home himself with the help of one of his brothers. It was indeed a labor of love, which included an aluminum-framed bay window my Granny would clean every day as if it were a jeweled crown.

I thought the house was gross with its concrete floors and short, seven-foot-high ceilings. The shower was a framed concrete block closet with a drain in the center that always seemed to back up, leaving me in murky, ankle-deep water by the end of my shower.

The house also gave me the heebie-jeebies. Nothing dreadful ever happened there, it just always felt off, and during storms, the eaves of the roof would funnel the wind, so the attic screamed as if it were full of banshees.

The boys loved the farm. They were in absolute heaven and always looked forward to our extended visit there.

They had smelly goats, cows, and dogs to play with to their heart's content, acres of pastureland and fields to run through with no adult supervision during the day. If they could sweet talk Granny into packing them a lunch, their exploratory excursions lasted from breakfast until the dinner bell rang.

What I remember the most is it was always hot, and I had a constant grit on my skin I could never wash off. Plus, everything stank. Couple all that with my constant homesickness, and summers were a miserable affair for me.

Granny tried each summer to spark my interest in cooking. Inevitably, she'd come to realize the futility of her attempts after the first week of each visit and exile me to the boys' world.

My brothers did their best to include me and encourage me during the day. My heart was never in it, and I remained melancholy as I pined for the drive home at the end of summer.

The absolute worst was when Grandpa's berry fields began to produce. It was like everybody else in the farmhouse lost their mind. Dusty and Chase would insist on picking berries every day for three weeks while the strawberries and blackberries bore their largest crops.

Heat beat down on my head until my hair felt like it was on fire. My hands, arms, and legs would be covered in scratches from the blackberry thorns by the end of the day. My extremities would remain crisscrossed with small, thin scabs long after the last of the berries were canned.

I hated every minute of it. I loathed being forced to do something I didn't want to do. I despised everybody else enjoying it as if it were great fun. I never even thought Granny's cobblers were as good as the boys made them out to be.

Then, Grandpa would notice my constant scowl and say something like, "Girl, this is the good life. You need to enjoy it while you can."

I'd set my jaw and give him the look of death.

I catch a tear in the corner of my eye before it runs down my cheek and mars my makeup. The tart taste of blackberry hangs on my tongue. So does the vision of the man who always seemed larger than life to me.

Grandpa was a strict man. He was also a pragmatic man. Which means at the time, we were perfectly suited to be polar opposites.

He loved his family with a singular fierceness. He also shouldered any hardship with a smile.

I miss those days of secreting berries into my mouth when no one was looking and crushing their still-warm juice onto my tongue. My heart aches for Grandpa. I wish I weren't such a brat when he was still alive. Tears form freely in my eyes as I struggle not to go into a full, heaving chest sob over a man who died, thinking I couldn't stand him.

Who am I? Why can't I be like my brothers? They fit in their world so perfectly. I'm always trying to be something else and somewhere else. What is wrong with me?

As if I weren't already a wreck. I pass the courthouse on my return trip to the office and stare in terror as I see the RV with the bold letters CNN on the side. The RV is parked prominently between the other four news vans.

A crowd of reporters is congregated at the base of the precinct stairs. They resemble a group of preppie, perky zombies waiting to feast on anyone stupid enough to exit the front door.

The proverbial poop is going to hit the fan now. There is no way I'm getting through the Vance Walker case without getting some severe stink on me.

I pull into my spot—that's what I now call the parking space between the fire hydrant and the crepe myrtle tree. It feels like a safe port as I am turning off the car. I draw an extra-long breath to calm my nerves, hiccup, and break into a full-fledged waterworks exhibition.

What am I doing? This was just supposed to be some easy part-time gig to earn some spending money while I wait for my giant escape. Instead, I feel like the entire world is sitting on my chest, crushing the life out of me. I can't breathe, so

I turn the key in the ignition to power down a window for some fresh air.

The tap on my car window causes me to jump. Lane is doubled over, peering into my car.

Splendid. I wonder how much of the human waterfall act Lane caught.

"Good morning," I say as my window comes down.

"You didn't call me last night."

Really? I didn't realize it. "Yeah, it was really late by the time I got back."

His look tells me he isn't buying it. "Do you have a minute for a conversation?" He makes a show of looking at his Rolex. "I must meet Judge Rossi for breakfast in thirty minutes."

"Sure." Like I have a choice. I close my window as Lane opens the door for me. He leans against the car next to us and crosses his arms. I guess we're not going into the office.

"What did you think about Wagner?"

"He's smart, just like you said."

Lane's lips thin. "I meant do you think he will be agreeable to a plea?"

Yeah, I'm sure Vance, Leslie, and Vance's attorney don't think much about taking a plea bargain. "I suppose, if it meant no jail time."

Lane chokes. "For murder two? That'll never fly."

This is where the old April would fold. I'm not sure if it's Lane's overbearing, cavalier manner, the thought of Grandpa shouldering the world during his life, or the anti-oxidants in the blackberries, but I'm spoiling for a fight. I lean against my car nonchalantly.

The arrogant smile dissipates from Lane's face. His mouth parts as his eyes widen. "Tell me you're joking."

I shrug my shoulders.

"April, he's a murderer."

"I'm sure some people would call him that. But I only need one jury member to call him a human garbage remover, and he walks." I dust my hands off. "No time to serve, no fine, and no parole."

Lane gestures toward the courthouse. "Are you even aware of what has descended on this town? There's a mass of reporters at the courthouse. They're prepared to tell the world a hick town, whose name they can't pronounce correctly, passed a law allowing people to hunt trespassers down and execute them. We are going to look like a bunch of idiots. Do you want that for this community? I mean, maybe it doesn't matter to you since you're leaving, but this can have real implications for your hometown, April."

Implying I don't care how Guntersville is viewed by the outside world rubs my fur the wrong way. "It seems like we will appear more idiotic if we charge Vance with murder and lose the case, DA Jameson," I say through clenched teeth.

He chokes off a laugh. "There is no way I lose this case."

Hoping it conveys I'm serious, I cross my arms and narrow my eyes.

His jaw sets as he shakes his head from side to side. Lane is a man used to getting his way. "Fine, April. Table the Wagner case for a moment. I'll let him cool his heels a little longer in jail. It might do him some good. What are we doing on the Raley case?"

"Moving forward with the civil case, per my client's request."

Lane pushes off the car he was leaning against. "Are you just trying to make my life miserable?"

"No. I'm just doing my job."

"Right. Well, with all due respect, counselor, you have a lot to learn yet on how the law really works. It's not all the theory you learned in law school."

I plan on coming back with something exceedingly creative, but my mind stalls. I'm looking at the heels of the man's expensive loafers as he crosses the street to the courthouse.

It occurs to me I might have poked the wrong bear.

Chapter 10

After making Lane so pleased, I mope into the office. As far as I'm concerned, he can ride his high horse right out of town and leave me alone. I don't care that I've ticked him off. I'm worried that unless I get inspired soon, he will kick my butt in court on both cases. He'll also enjoy doing it.

I don't want to be a loser. Losing these cases will not help me move up in the legal profession. Plus, my clients depend on me for justice.

The thought of climbing the legal ladder successfully reminds me about the applications I sent to advertisements on the job board. I log into my professional email account to see if I've received any responses.

Peaches. I should have known I wasn't going to be lucky enough to escape Guntersville in time to avoid the legal butt-kicking coming my way. I don't have a single response.

I stare at the screen as I allow myself a pity party. It's early in the morning, and I'm in the office alone. Someone has already chewed on me like an old bone this morning. I have two cases on my plate that I'll lose in all probability. Oh, yes, I still don't have a full-time employment opportunity.

Buck up, April. Why are you so sad? You're just living the dream.

What I need on the Wagner case is one or two prior self-defense cases regarding the new law that went in the home-owner's favor when they used lethal force. I seriously doubt I'll find a case where the homeowner literally chased the criminals down and fired a couple extra rounds for good measure.

Still, if I can show it's happened before, it will ease the jury past the incident's violence.

I must continue to remind myself, all we need is one of the twelve jury members to feel Vance's actions were reasonable. I only need eight percent of the jury to disregard the law as it was intended. Now when I put it like that, it doesn't seem so hopeless.

My fingers fly across the keyboard bringing up the legal search database. I know what I'm looking for must exist. Lane will be sorry he ever messed with me on this case.

The front door opens, and Howard steps inside. "Well, good morning. Do you need to get off early this afternoon?"

I almost say no and then think better of it. Since Howard seems amenable to the idea because I came in early, I might as well take advantage of it. "Yes, if you don't mind. I've got a few things I need to take care of this afternoon."

Howard unfolds the *Wall Street Journal* as he walks to his office. "No trouble at all. Besides, from what I hear, you've already managed to tweak Lane's nose out of joint this morning." He smiles over his shoulder. "If your job is to be disagreeable with our main source of income, I suppose your work here is done today."

That isn't even funny. Well, a little funny.

"Hey, Uncle Howard." I follow him into his office and lean against his door. "I've been searching the database, but I'm wondering, do you know of any cases in the last few years where a homeowner defended themselves and the intruder died?"

Howard smooths the newspaper out in front of him. "You mean where the homeowner executes the intruders?"

I roll my eyes. "You're hilarious."

"When the truth is horrific, sometimes the only thing you can do is laugh."

Not helpful. I shake my head and push off from the door to return to my desk.

"Hold your horses. I do recall something about a case down in Dothan a few years back."

That catches my interest.

"It didn't get much coverage. It'll take me a little while to find it." He leans back in his chair. "It wasn't exactly like your case, but I do recall the homeowner was acquitted. The only reason I remember the case is because the intruders were minors and unarmed."

"How's that?"

Howard lays his paper on the desk and straightens the crease. "April, would you say it's difficult to rationalize what people thought when they do something stupid?"

I snort. "There are days I wonder what I thought when I'm faced with the consequences of my boneheaded decisions."

That comment earns me a chuckle from him. "Unfortunately, that makes two of us."

"And the point is?" I move my finger in a circular motion.

"Oh, just that in normal circumstances, it's hard to determine what somebody perceives a situation to be. Like I said, I'll have to find it for you, but in that Dothan case, there was a group of teenagers who took offense to a man turning them away empty-handed when they were trick-or-treating. He told them they were too old. They don't call it "trick or treat" for nothing. The boys didn't get their treat, so they came back later that night to play a trick on the old man.

"One of the boys put a jack-o'-lantern on his head and began beating on a bedroom window. The homeowner opened the blinds, screamed, and opened fire on the haunted jack-o'-lantern."

"You're full of it."

"No, true story. The locals took to calling it the Pumpkinhead case after the movie."

I can't help but laugh. "Pumpkinhead? You made that up." I shake my head and turn back toward my desk. "I don't have time for this."

"Honest, it's true."

"Right, and I rode into work on a dragon."

His story doesn't help me with the Wagner case, but the laugh helps knock some of the stink off the morning. Well, unless there is some truth to the Pumpkinhead story.

I kick out early at three. It's been two weeks since my last manicure, so when Howard mentioned leaving early, it seemed like the perfect opportunity.

Besides, I need some good intel on the cases I'm working on. Lord knows the beauty college is the ideal place to get all the news not fit to print about our locals.

Tiffany hustles me back to the manicure counter as soon as I arrive. She swats an unruly blonde bang from her forehead while grabbing my hands to survey the damage.

"Sorry if I seem in a rush, dear. I've been busier than a stump-tailed cow during the fly season."

"These new girls ain't got no sense," Glenda offers, unsolicited. She adds a loud *tsk*ing sound with her tongue as she continues her work on her client's nails.

Tiffany rolls her eyes. "We were all ignorant when we started."

"Uh-huh. But we didn't start out stupid, too," Glenda says.

Tiffany returns her attention to my hands, and her eyes open wider in alarm. "Have you had a change in your line of work, April?"

That's an odd question. "No. Why?"

"I've seen brick mason hands in better condition than your nails."

I survey my battered nails and fight the urge to pull them back and shove them into my pockets. "It's been sort of a rough month," I say.

"No worries. The doctor is in, and I can work miracles."

Tiffany isn't making an idle brag. I've begun to doze off from her work's soothing motion when she announces we're all done.

I'm surprised our session is already over. I examine my hands and am blown away by the perfect set of nails with thick coats of hot pink shining back at me. I barely recognize my own hands.

My spine stiffens, forcing me to sit straight as I remember one of the main reasons I chose to get my nails done today. I was so relaxed, my intelligence-gathering mission slipped my mind.

"Tiffany, do you know a woman by the name of Crystal Raley?"

Tiffany and Glenda exchange not-too-subtle glances. "Sure. Crystal comes in every Thursday."

I suppose being married to a wealthy business owner has its perks. "Wow, that's a good, steady business." I don't want to appear overly apparent in my effort to pump Tiffany for information.

"Yes. She's a good tipper, too," Tiffany says.

"She'd have to be for me to deal with her," Glenda interjects.

Tiffany glares at her partner "Glenda, AB conversation, so C your way out of it."

"Touchy."

"How do you know her?" Tiffany asks me. "She's a little too old for you to know from high school."

"I don't. Crystal's husband came in the other day. He wants me to file a complaint against their neighbor on behalf of his wife and him."

Tiffany wrinkles her nose. "What do you mean a complaint?"

It isn't clear where the client-attorney privilege in this case begins. But if it keeps Tiffany talking, I think I'll stretch the rules a bit. It will be beneficial to know more about Crystal before I speak to her.

"There was this situation where their neighbor was quite the voyeur with Crystal."

Tiffany tries to conceal a smirk as Glenda lets out an obnoxious snort.

"What?"

"Nothing," Tiffany says as she busies herself, putting her workstation in good order.

"No, there's something you're not telling me."

"Well, I don't like to gossip," Tiffany says.

Seriously? Did she really just say that? Tiffany obviously has never considered what she discusses during the day. Since it's working in my favor now, I'm not going to call her attention to her claim.

"It might be beneficial for me to know. Since I'm working for the Raleys."

Tiffany appears to be struggling to contain her laughter. "I assure you Crystal has nothing to do with that case being filed. It would be all Jared's idea."

"I don't understand."

Tiffany looks as if she will give me the details and then reconsiders.

"If you are talking about their neighbor, Craig West, he'd only be looking at what she is already showing him. That woman has the serious hots for him. She's been talking about him like a cat in constant heat for the last three months."

"Glenda!"

"It's true, Tiffany. You not saying it, don't make it not true."

My initial thoughts are confirmed. The picture Jared Raley showed me of Crystal's lower, "critical to cover" area was not a perfectly timed picture of her adjusting her bikini bottoms. That was her flashing for the camera.

It's nice to have my theory validated. Unfortunately, that means my case with Jared Raley is a loser before we even get to the filing stage.

"Do you think they're having an affair?" I whisper the question in hopes it better suits Tiffany's sensibilities.

She leans in closer to me. "Honestly, I know she wants to, but Craig West is married, too, and I don't think he's the cheating type."

Tiffany's idea of not cheating is obviously a lot more liberal than mine. I certainly believe if I ever found my husband taking pictures of my neighbor's lady parts, I'd consider it cheating.

"I really think she's just baiting him. You must understand, she's one of those women who's used to getting what she wants. If I were to guess, she's made it perfectly clear to Craig what she wants, and the fact she's not getting it would make her just that much more aggressive."

"That actually makes a lot of sense with the information I have. I really appreciate you sharing before I talk to her."

Tiffany's persona brightens considerably. "Really?"

"Absolutely. It's a huge help to have an outside perspective on people before I interview them."

"That's really neat. I'm glad you told me that."

That, in my world, is what I call a win-win. I came in with brick mason hands and will leave with a manicure a New York model would be proud to show off. Tiffany's gossip has been validated as an appreciated community service for conveying needed information to our town professionals. Everybody got something from this bit of trading.

As I get back into my Prius, the red Solo cup that held my blackberries this morning reminds me I meant to ask Chase about Patrick. Since I spent some time with Chase this morning, it will be less noticeable that I'm interested in his buddy. I love it when things work in my favor. Especially when I'm trying to be covert.

After the disappointment of no responses from my interviews this morning, it's apparent my exodus from Guntersville is not as imminent as I would hope. The idea of some male distraction seems like a fair idea. If the male happens to be Patrick McCabe, all the better.

As for the inevitable breakup that'll be necessary when I leave for New York, I'll cross that bridge when I get to it. First, I need some inside information on Patrick from my brother Chase.

Chapter 11

The front yard of the lake house looks like a used car lot as I drive up. I'm momentarily confused until I recognize the cars as those of my brother Dusty's paranormal team. They usually only get together as an entire group when they have an upcoming research excursion.

Nobody has told me they're planning a trip. Am I no longer part of their team? Why would that bother me? The whole paranormal thing gives me the willies, and I darn near got killed on the last trip.

I consider being rude by going straight to my room. Instead, I show real maturity and decide to be an adult. Besides, my curiosity is screaming at me.

I open the sliding door to my parents' kitchen.

Miles turns toward the noise. "Hello, beautiful."

"Can it, Miles."

He shakes his head. "I can't believe you're not attracted to me, April. It's because I'm black, isn't it?"

"I'm not attracted to you because you're annoying and small."

Miles tugs at his belt. "Maybe I should give you a peek, so I can make you a believer."

"You pull that out, and I'll cut it off and feed it to the catfish so fast you're not gonna know what happened." I shake my head. "Honestly, Miles. Does your Mama know you talk like that to women?"

He measures my expression. "You want a beer?" he asks.

"Sure." I take the beer he offers. "Why the called meeting?"

Miles favors me a grin. "It's a hot lead. The Sloss Furnaces in Birmingham just had another incident this afternoon."

I shrug.

"The old pig-iron furnaces," he explains. "There are rumors all the way back from when it went into commission in the late eighteen hundreds that it's haunted. But after it closed in nineteen seventy-one, there have only been a handful of incidents."

"Somebody saw a ghost for the first time in fifty years. That requires an emergency meeting?"

Miles's face creases. "Saw a ghost? No. You don't understand. One of the tourists got shoved off the catwalk."

Now, this is new. "So y'all are, like, investigating murders, too?" I suppose that would explain why they hadn't notified me of the meeting. It's a murder investigation, not a ghost hunt.

"No, silly. Well, I suppose in this instance, we're investigating a murder. Considering the man was pushed over the catwalk by someone nobody saw, it's still technically in our wheelhouse."

Even more interesting. "The staff at the museum are positive the victim didn't just jump?"

"There was a group of twenty tourists going through the factory together. They all report it looked at first like the victim tripped. Then he stood up and flipped over the rail. He hung on with his hands at first while screaming for help and begging someone to stop. He was the only person on the catwalk.

"The tour guide rushed to his aid but didn't reach him in time. The guide reported that as he reached for the man's arms, he heard a loud snapping noise. The victim's fingers bent back violently, releasing his grip on the railing. Then he fell to his death."

Although rare, it's not unheard of for a spirit to physically attack a person. Heck, our team just dealt with such an apparition at the Osborne hotel last month.

I understand now why the team is called together. In their line of work, rare is what sells books.

Taking a sip of my beer, I add, "So y'all are just going to cut me out of this one?"

"Come on, April. You know it's not like that."

"No?"

"It's just... after that last case, Dusty isn't sure if you're up for it."

Dusty has every reason to think I might not be ready for another case. Especially so soon after what happened to James.

If I'm honest with myself, the Osborne case about undid me. Without the intervention from Liza, the expeller from Dusty's team, I might still be the evil twentieth-century spirit's puppet.

Dusty shouldn't be making decisions for me. After all these years, he should know I'm my own woman, and I can take care of myself.

"What in the world would give him that idea?" The words pop out before I realize I'm going to say them.

Miles flashes his extra-white smile. "There you go. There's my favorite Amazon. Come on downstairs and join the group."

Now is the time to bail. As I watch Miles take the stairs to the basement two at a time, I know this is my last best chance to avoid another paranormal excursion. I know I should turn away now.

Unfortunately, my curiosity will not allow me to ignore the challenge. I follow Miles down the stairs in a more subdued manner than him.

"Looks like we've got our ghost whisperer back," Miles announces as we reach the basement.

The chatter in the room ceases. Six pairs of eyes, full of questions, stare at me. I catch myself shuffling from one foot to the other as I wait.

"I think it best for you to sit this one out, April," Dusty says.

Liza steps forward from the shadows. "These boys, always overthinking." She gives me a quick hug, which catches me off guard since Liza is the antithesis of a hugger.

"It's good to see you, April. Don't mind your brother. He's still attempting to shake off the last of his Neanderthal genes."

"Come on, Liza. Be fair about this. April was like a lightning rod for spooks on the last excursion," Luis says.

"Which is exactly why she needs to be included on this trip." Liza turns her attention to me. "You are good, right?"

Am I good? No, I'm about as far away from good as you can get with all this ghost hunting research team. I'm scared and in disbelief that I'm preparing to involve myself again. Paranormal hunting scares the bejesus out of me.

What started as a lark with my brother ten years ago has developed into a thriving business. I can be an asset to his team since I possess a hundred times more supernatural talent than my brother. I love helping my brother, but my "gifts" only get stronger with each paranormal event.

I wouldn't be in this position if it weren't for the boating accident Chase and I were in four months earlier. I had successfully buried my skill for seven years, and the powers had weakened considerably. Then one little boat accident and they come roaring back into my life.

The trouble with my "gifts" are they're like an itch needing to be scratched. No, they're a scab I pick at until I accidentally knock the crust off, leaving an open lesion subject to germs. Bacteria infects the open wound each time, causing the infection to grow in intensity and size.

The worst part is I'm good at paranormal hunting. I like the feeling of being the best at something. Plus, I'm naturally curious about things that otherwise seem unexplainable.

If I had a lick of sense, I'd leave.

"I think I am. I want to learn more about what Miles was telling me."

"I told you not to tell her anything."

Miles frowns at Dusty. "She asked. I couldn't lie to her."

Dusty sets his jaw and seems to consider the situation. He pulls at his beard and grumbles, "Fine. Your skill set will be helpful, but I need you to promise me that it's safety first this time. No more renegade cowgirl."

What the heck does that mean? "I stayed safe last time."

"Right, being possessed is staying safe?"

"Come on now, Dusty. That wasn't her fault." Miles shrinks back in reaction to Dusty's hot glare. "Of course, she could have taken a few more precautions."

You know what, this isn't such a swell idea. Dusty obviously has reservations about me traveling with the team on this excursion. Besides, I don't care to be a distraction to the rest of the group.

"You know it wasn't her fault, Dusty. The blame falls on me, not April. We were paired together, and I was supposed to protect her.

"In my defense, I had no idea her powers were so strong. If you had explained better her energy level, I would've taken more effective precautions. It won't happen again."

I can't believe what I'm hearing. Liza is taking up for me.

"You're killing me. Fine," Dusty says, "in some twisted, perverse logic, the team is safer with your skill at our disposal. It sounds like the apparition remained invisible even as it attacked the tourist. There's a chance that you may be the only one of us who can see this entity."

There. That's why I keep coming back to the paranormal world even though it scares the living daylights out of me. I'm fantastic at it, and everyone knows it. It's as simple as that.

Everybody needs to be appreciated for something in their life. I would rather be a pitch-perfect singer, genius scientist, or—maybe one day—an unbeatable lawyer than a clairvoyant. But we don't get to choose the talents given to us.

"Go ahead and fill her in on the rest of the details, Miles."

"Awesome!" Miles rubs his hands together as his eyes widen behind his Coke bottle thick glasses.

What have I signed up for?

I despise my curiosity. That's the only thought on my mind as I ascend the basement stairs.

I've lost three hours I could have used more wisely prepping for my two cases. I also consumed two beers and half a pizza I didn't need after my earlier stomach issues while committing my entire weekend to the team to boot. At least my curiosity is satiated.

The window is tight for Dusty's investigation team. They want to leave Friday morning in hopes any residual paranormal energies on the railing of the catwalk have not dissipated. Their fast response schedule means I must work out a day off with Howard.

The unmistakable pungent aroma of freshly baked blackberry cobbler tickles my nose as I enter the kitchen. I remember I lied to Chase about my cobbler baking skills this morning, and a hint of guilt flutters across my chest.

But that isn't my fault. Chase set me up. Everyone in my family knows I don't cook.

I search the countertops as I walk through the kitchen toward the glass door, but I can't find the heavenly scent's origin. My mouth is now salivating. Please, like I need dessert.

Being calorically responsible, I reach for the door handle and freeze. I see the light spilling out of the mechanic shed through the sliding glass door, and the roll down door is up. I step onto the porch, careful to remain in the shadows as I focus on the mechanic shed and consider my options.

Chase appears in the halo of light just inside the door. He's laughing while circling in front of the nose of the Corvette.

He forks a bite of something into his mouth from a plate he's carrying. That's just rude to bake a cobbler and take it away, leaving its aroma in the air.

So, now I know where the cobbler is located. My shame from lying dissipates as my sweet tooth's desire increases. That whole caloric accountability thing, it was just sour grapes. I need something sweet.

Besides, this will be the perfect opportunity to ask Chase about Patrick. I love it when a genius plan materializes with no effort on my part.

The gravel walkway crunches under my feet as I step off the driveway and walk toward the mechanic shop. A second male figure, plate in hand, comes into view, and I drop into a squatting position and freeze like a cat burglar hearing a front door open.

Even from this distance, where focused details are scarce, I know Patrick is with Chase. Many conflicting emotions run through me; I become lightheaded and put my left hand into the sharp-edged gravel.

This can work to my advantage. I'll go into the mechanic garage, keep it casual, get a piece of the cobbler, and strike up a conversation. It will be easy to keep it light, nothing serious. I'm the cool and breezy sister enjoying a dessert and striking up a friendly talk to learn a little more about who my brother is hanging out with these days. That's what normal sisters do.

That's my plan. It's a good plan. It's a genius strategy that will give me two birds in the hand, and forget about the bush. I get dessert and an opportunity to catch Patrick's attention as more than just an A/C customer and Chase's younger sister.

Too bad I don't have the guts to implement it.

I sulk as I stay in the shadows and creep silently to my room. I'm such a loser. Not only did I miss out on making a positive impression on Patrick, but my sweet tooth is in full mutiny over missing out on the scrumptious-smelling blackberry cobbler.

My self-loathing does not diminish as I crawl into bed. *It was such a great plan, April. You really snatched defeat from the jaws of victory this time.*

Sleep is elusive. I can only wonder if I will ever get another opportunity to find out more about Patrick.

Chapter 12

Looking in the mirror, I put my hands to my face. I look like ten miles of bad road this morning.

It's all Patrick and Chase's fault. Because of them, I didn't fall asleep until two thirty. Then my eyes automatically opened at four thirty as if being back in the country has turned me into a rooster.

I wash my face. That feels better, but all it did for my looks was to add a bunch of splotches to my face's puffiness.

Bless it. I need coffee before I cover up this mess today.

There's a light on in my parents' house. Good. With any luck, I can bum coffee rather than having to make it myself.

Walking onto the porch, I have an epiphany. I could get a coffee maker for my bachelorette pad. I open the glass door, and the lovely smell of maple sugar engulfs me.

Hmm. That's why I don't make my own coffee.

"Morning, sunshine," Chase greets me before popping a crisp piece of bacon into his mouth.

I struggle not to walk across the kitchen and slap his too happy, perfectly rested face. It isn't quite five in the morning, and he's showered and looking energized. Nobody should look like him this early.

My survivor instincts take me back to more pressing matters. In Chase's left hand, he holds a coffee cup. The steam from it dances in a mesmerizing motion just above his navy-blue Auburn mug.

He has a slice of bacon, standing at full attention, in his right hand. It's cooked to the perfect degree of crispiness—both items I highly covet.

"I wouldn't suppose you made extra?"

"No, but if this is going to become a regular brother-sister thing, I'll make sure to do so tomorrow morning."

I push past him toward the coffee maker. "I can't say for sure. I'm still taking things day by day."

Chase lets out an easy laugh and takes a tentative sip of his coffee.

My blood pressure rises. "What do you find so amusing?"

"Just how hard you work at being miserable. You're really quite accomplished at it."

I miss my coffee mug and burn my hand. "Fudge biscuit!"

"Are you alright?" He moves toward me.

"Leave me alone."

"You should put some ice on it."

"It doesn't hurt," I lie. "It just spooked me."

Keeping my focus on the task, I fill my crimson mug. "For the record, I don't work at being miserable. It just sort of happens."

Chase shrugs. "Sure. Whatever you say."

"What are you so happy about anyway?"

"I don't know. It's Tuesday, I have a cool job, and I was able to work on a classic car last night. What's not to be happy about?"

"Maybe the fact you don't have a girlfriend?" I close my eyes and pray. I hope I thought that and didn't say it out loud. Please, Lord, that just popped into my head and not out my mouth. Right?

"Wow. What happened to you while you were away at Bama? Here I thought you studied law. No one told me you were majoring in ugliness."

My neck tenses as I see the hurt in my brother's eyes. "I'm

sorry I said that, Chase. There was no call. I'm just super grouchy right now."

He studies me so long I become uncomfortable. I wonder if he's trying to determine if I'm sincere or having another bout of sarcasm.

He points at me. "I know what you need."

A jolt of alarm shoots through me. Oh my gosh, my lust for Patrick is so thinly disguised, my brother, who is usually slow with social cues, has picked up on my desires. Chase is about to suggest I need some Patrick loving. I'm mortified beyond words.

"You haven't done it once since you've been back home."

I'm melting into the floor with embarrassment. This is so not a discussion I'm comfortable having with either of my brothers. I'm mortified he's been keeping tabs on my lack of sexual prowess.

Being fair, I started this conversation. Chase may be teaching me a lesson for commenting on his lack of a love life.

He's made his point. I'll never bring it up again.

"I can fix that for you this morning."

My brain glitches so hard I shudder. What the heck? Patrick spent the night—here?

My brother's aura is glowing a golden white and becoming brighter as he continues, "Wait until you see what I did to fix up this toy. It'll drive you insane." He sets his mug down and motions for me to follow him.

Oh, heck no. I stay planted right where I am. "What are you talking about, Chase?" I can't conceal the alarm in my voice.

He tilts his head. "The WaveRunner. You haven't ridden it once since you've been back. You used to love that machine."

Sometimes when I'm with Chase, I get confused. It's difficult to tell if he's a little slow or if he makes me stupid.

This morning I'd say it's the latter. I'm sure it's from my lack of caffeine. Either way, I'm relieved Chase is talking about the WaveRunner and not any of the lurid thoughts going through my mind.

"Chase, I can't worry about recreational things with all the different responsibilities on me. It's difficult for me to get my work done and line up an occasional job interview. There's no time for fun right now."

Chase blows a raspberry. "There's no point in living if you don't work in some fun time. There's also no point in living on the lake if you don't use the water. Now, go get a bathing suit on."

"What?"

"Go get a bathing suit on." he points at my T-shirt. "I mean, you can wear that if you want, but even if I keep us out of the drink, we're still going to get wet from the spray. You might as well be skinny dipping with that on."

My brother is an idiot. If he thinks he can talk me into going out on a WaveRunner with him on a Tuesday morning, he has brain damage from too many high school stunts.

"Move it, girly."

I roll my eyes at him. "I'm not going out on a WaveRunner with you."

"Why not?"

"It's Tuesday, and I have a very demanding day lined up at my job."

"Which is exactly why you need to ride the WaveRunner with me first this morning." He shakes his shoulders and rolls his head. "It'll get you all loose for that highbrow lawyering you got to do today."

"I'm not going, Chase. Stop with it."

I notice the shift in my brother's facial expression and demeanor. Both my brothers and my father have an overdrive to their charismas. It's the ability to go from the normal, likable men they are to someone you simply cannot say no to. It's as if they possess a hypnotic form of magic.

I'm determined to fight his requests. He continues to defend the logic of a quick ride on the lake and all the benefits of clearing my mind by pumping additional adrenaline through me. As confident as I am in my ability to fend off my brother's persuasions, I feel my defenses crumbling around my false bravado.

Kicking off my flip flops, I throw my leg over the Wave-Runner, careful not to lean too far to the left as I straddle the bench behind Chase. I grab hold of the pleather handles on the seat, too small for my hands.

"Seriously, Chase, I'm pushed for time, so this has to be quick."

He ignores my comment as he pushes the craft away from the dock with his foot. "This is an excellent idea. The water is smooth as glass this morning. I haven't been able to open her up all the way since I made the improvements."

A tingle runs up my spine. I know what a smooth lake surface means for speed, and it's both exhilarating and frightening.

Chase turns over the ignition. The water machine glides slowly away from our dock. Our small inlet is a no-wake zone, so he keeps the watercraft slow and steady.

I grin as the cold lake water runs over my feet on the running boards. I narrow my eyes against the mist from the early morning fog as it accumulates on my face.

It's been ages since we've ridden double, and Chase is so much larger than me now I can't see around him easily. Instead, I look to each side and inventory the homes I've known all my life. The neighborhood is a little older than me, but each of the houses is in immaculate condition.

Chase increases the motor, and the noise envelops us as he glides us out of the inlet past our neighbors' boathouses. I readjust my butt on the seat and double-clutch the handles as I attempt to get comfortable for a high-speed run.

For the first time in my life, the idea of putting my arms around Chase feels odd. Because of that, I opt for the hand straps just below my thighs, but I feel less than secure with my hold. I become concerned I'll tumble right off the back of the machine when Chase opens the throttle.

He looks over his shoulder at me and yells over the motor, "You all set?"

No. This is stupid, and I can't believe I let him talk me into it. "I guess."

"Hold on tight, then. Here we go!" Chase's voice barely carries over the motor.

I steal a glance at each side and realize we're entering the main channel. The watercraft releases a thick, throaty scream and pops its nose into the air as we surge forward.

My bare thighs clamp down hard on the seat. I can feel the stitching of the seam bite into my skin. The straps, too close to my legs, quickly prove to be too awkward of an angle to be effective. My fingers are losing strength.

The machine lets out another mechanical scream I've never heard it make before, and I'm looking straight into the sky. I'm struggling to remain seated, but gravity has now combined with momentum. I am seconds from rolling off the seat.

My head jerks hard to the left then the right as the Wave-Runner dances on its tail. I give thanks when the hull levels out and the watercraft begins to skip along the surface like a flat rock thrown exactly right across a calm water surface.

With the threat of gravity gone, I try to readjust my butt, which has slid to the seat's back lip. Fear runs through me as I realize just how close I came to tumbling off.

My stomach muscles fire, tensing my core, as my legs grip so tightly my ankles ache from slapping against the fiberglass body with each skip of the machine.

The wind whips over Chase's shoulder and buffets my face. Spray from the watercraft's nose stings my cheeks, and I tuck my face behind Chase's back for protection.

Then it happens. The fear of pain leaves me, and familiarity replaces it. It's as if I've traveled ten years back in time, and all I want to do now is get as much speed out of this machine as is possible.

The funny thing about speed is it's addictive. Everyone in my family has a natural penchant for speed. I'm no different.

But speed is relative. Maintaining the thrill requires a constant incremental increase in speed.

What gives an adrenaline fix one day will become tomorrow's boring joyride. Hence Chase's work to increase the speed the watercraft can obtain.

As my body continues to adjust to the insane speed, I become appreciative of Chase's ingenuity. He's really done an incredible job fine-tuning our WaveRunner. I never would have anticipated he could get it to travel this fast.

"I'm going to open her up," Chase screams over the onrush of air.

Fear wraps its icy fingers around my heart, squeezing hard. We're gonna die.

The WaveRunner lurches forward. I feel my freshly painted nails being ripped from my fingertips as my thighs get pleather burns sliding backward on the bench. We're at a forty-five-degree angle in the water and hopping across the lake on our tail. The motor screams so loudly, the noise seems to vibrate in my teeth.

My buttocks continue to slide backward on the bench seat, pulling my hands into an awkward pretzel position. My legs and hands are shot. I'm seconds from rolling off the back.

If I fall off at this speed, I'll skip for two hundred yards before I come to a stop. That's if I don't come off and end up in some weird death roll across the water that breaks all my extremities and neck.

As my right hand gives out, I push forward and grab hold of Chase's lifejacket, pulling my hips forward until my vest is flat against his. I lay my head sideways against his vest and pray for the ride's end as my thighs and ankles continue to slap the side with each bump.

The machine settles onto the surface. The violent slapping and bumping are replaced by a smooth slide-and-scoot, slide-and-scoot motion.

The speed normalizes in my mind. With my grip around Chase's torso, I'm able to loosen the hold with my legs, putting an end to the incessant beating they've endured.

I lean forward, ducking my head lower with Chase as we make ourselves even more aerodynamic like we use to when we were kids.

The speed is delicious. Fear turns into exhilaration, and the wind streaming past me seems to strip my cares away. All there is at this moment is me, my brother, and this beast of a machine he has created. There is no stress about my clients' needs or incomplete professional dreams.

Too soon, Chase makes a wide, arcing turn and heads us back in the direction of home. As he slows to near-idle at the mouth of our inlet, the nose dips. A water wake comes across our watercraft's nose as he says over his shoulder, still in shout mode, "I'd say over eighty with two people is booking it."

"You're full of it." We've never cleared over sixty miles an hour with both of us riding.

"No, I wouldn't lie to you. I knew this modification would increase her speed, but I never dreamed it would be that fast, especially with two riders. Of course, you're a lightweight. So, it's more like one and a half riders."

Aww. Now he's just being sweet. Still, that settles it. I'll have to borrow the WaveRunner later and see how fast I can get it to go solo.

I hate to admit it, but Chase was right. A little fear is good for putting things into perspective. It's handy for making you thankful you're alive, too.

Chase and I work in tandem, loading the WaveRunner onto the lift. He doesn't need my help, but he accepts it without a word.

He shows me the new hiding place for the boat and Wave-Runner keys in the boathouse and tells me to feel free to take them out anytime.

We've always been allowed free run of the boats and the WaveRunner at the house. However, it feels good to get permission from one of the equipment caretakers since I still feel more like a guest than family this time around.

"So, did the ride knock some of the meanness off you?" Chase asks.

I can only laugh. Chase is quick to forgive and doesn't hold grudges, but he also never forgets. "Yes, I think that's just what the doctor ordered."

He flashes a smirk. "You might need something else too, but I find speed can be a decent substitute."

"What are you getting at?"

He runs a hand through his blonde hair, leaving it standing on end. "Man, I really don't want to get into my sister's personal business. But I also know you're sweet on Shane, and that didn't work out for you. You haven't dated anyone since you've been home."

"Well, thank you for pointing that out, Chase."

"Don't take it like that. You're just wired differently than Dusty and me. You've always been more comfortable when you're in a relationship."

Really? So, in a roundabout way, Chase was alluding earlier to my present lack of a man. The worst is that now would have been an excellent time to ask Chase about Patrick, except the conversation has morphed into a discussion about my present lack of dates. Even Chase would catch on to my interest in Patrick if I were to ask now.

I'm not ready for anyone but me to know I may be interested in Patrick.

I thank Chase for the ride. I have just enough time to grab a quick shower and make it to work on time if I hurry.

Jogging up to my apartment, I wonder if Chase is right.

Don't get me wrong, I know if I start taking psychological advice from my brother, I genuinely have hit rock bottom. Still, there does seem to be a kernel of truth to his declaration that I'm more comfortable when I'm in a relationship.

The problem is, it's been so long since I was in a committed relationship, now I can't remember how it feels.

Chapter 13

I think it might be time to give Dr. Stanfield a visit. I don't have a fever, and I'm feeling energetic.

All the same, I know something is terribly wrong with me. For a few minutes after my ride with Chase, I consider what life might be like if I were to stay in Guntersville.

The scary part is, this morning, it seems like being close with my brothers and in the community I grew up in would be a good lifestyle for me. Something isn't right. Nobody spends seven years at an accredited college earning an advanced degree just to move back to where they came from.

That's simply crazy thinking. Right?

I pull into my spot in front of the law office with two minutes to spare. I hit the front door at a full run.

Lane's voice is coming from Howard's office. Yay.

I have not forgiven him for being rude the other day. Still, I'll be professional and act like I've forgotten his passive-aggressive transgressions.

Lane's head pops into view. "Have you seen your client on TV?"

My face twists into disdain as if I'm sucking on a lemon— so much for professional mode. I toss my keys onto the desk. "What client? I have more than one client, you know."

Lane paces toward me. "Leslie Wagner. Did you see her

spectacle this morning?"

I'm not going to accept the anger coming my way. "I have no idea what you're talking about."

"Your client, Leslie Wagner."

I sit in my chair. "I heard you the first time. And for the second time, I have no idea what you're talking about. While we're on the topic, let's set the record straight, Leslie Wagner is not my client. She's my client's wife."

"Do you even watch the news?"

Do I watch the news? What sort of silly question is that? Of course, I do. At least once a month. When there's nothing left on Netflix for me to watch. "Yes."

"Then you saw your client—your client's wife—making a fool of herself on the precinct stairs."

Oh boy. I don't like where this is headed. "I'm afraid I missed that this morning."

"I can only hope that the governor missed it, too."

"Lane, April can't be responsible for family members of her client." I didn't see Howard come into the reception area.

Lane's snarls, "Well, someone needs to yank a knot in that little white trash's tail."

"Hey!" I can't believe that came out of Lane's mouth.

"Lane, how about you go cool off, and we'll talk about this later," Howard suggests. "I'll buy you a drink at the Black Angus, maybe have an early dinner around four?"

"Forget it. I've got work to do." He glares from Howard to me. "I want to make sure I do everything I can to bury Vance Wagner under the jail." His eyes flash crazy as he smiles. "Oh, April, I forgot to mention. The arraignment hearing for Wagner is tomorrow morning in Judge Rossi's courtroom at nine sharp. I figure by nine fifteen, his precious wife will know he'll never set foot in their home again."

Tomorrow morning? That's moved a lot quicker than I anticipated. I'm not even close to formulating a good reason to allow Vance to post bail, much less at a rate he can afford.

Lane stops at the exit and turns with the grand gesture of

waving his arm. "Y'all, do have a wonderful day now."

As the front door slams shut, Howard says, "Don't worry about him. He's just embarrassed."

"He's a prick is what he is."

Howard's face turns sour. "Surely you can understand why he is upset. Leslie shouldn't have done what she did."

"Did what? What did she do?"

"She's been giving interviews to every reporter that'll listen to her telling them her husband was only protecting them from a CIA hit."

I'm flummoxed. What's next? The robbers were aliens? "A CIA hit?"

"That's what she claims. She's told the reporters Vance knew they were CIA, and that's why he had to take them out. If he didn't, they would just be back later."

"The CIA works outside of the US," I say.

Howard laughs. "I know that, and you know that, but Leslie and the reporters don't seem to care much about that inconvenient fact. All the news channels have been running the story on state news this morning. Lane received a call from the state attorney general an hour ago."

"That's not good."

He sighs as he retreats to his office. "Uh, no. It's not what Lane is looking for if he ever wants to position himself for statewide office. But this too shall pass."

"I can't control Leslie," I complain.

His voice comes from inside his office. "I'd suggest you figure out a way to control her. Unless you enjoy talking to an angry Lane early in the morning. Every morning."

Now that just isn't fair.

It's one thing to prepare for an arraignment in twenty-four hours. If I really push myself, I can put together a compelling argument.

However, it isn't my job to control my client's wife. Even if it were, after her display with Wanda at the hospital, I know I'm not woman enough for that job.

Fine. I'll go by and talk to Leslie this afternoon and try to convince her to stand down.

I get that she's angry, and she doesn't feel her husband did anything wrong. I'll have to appeal to her desire to help Vance rather than make his case more difficult for us to win.

I'm starting to get more on my plate than I can say grace over. Everyone in my family is a list maker, except for me. If you see me making a list, you know I'm way past my standard capabilities of multitasking and am presently in desperate panic mode.

I look at my fresh to-do list. I choose the most straightforward task to start—a quick update request from our medical examiner.

Doc Crowder explains he's running behind and has already spoken with Lane about the possible delay in completing the autopsies on the two men Vance shot. He promises to call me as soon as he has details.

Doc also tells me not to worry; he has everything on ice. A little medical examiner humor, I suppose. I just roll with it.

Off the phone with Doc and on to the next task. I need to interview the arresting officer. The case was filed by Deputy Gray from the Sheriff's department.

I don't remember a Deputy Gray working with the Sheriff's department. I call Jacob to see if he knows the deputy.

"What's up, April?"

"The Wagner case. Do you know the arresting officer, a Deputy Gray?"

"Sure."

"I need to contact them to walk me through the crime scene. I don't recognize the name"

"Do you want me to meet you out there with the deputy?"

"Not unless you participated in the arrest."

Jacob laughs lazily. His laugh does funny things below my belly button, which aggravates me.

"I make it a point to never use my handcuffs outside of my assigned jurisdiction. At least not in public."

He *so* did that on purpose. Wipe the visuals, April. Jacob's just a friend. "Are you sure you don't mind making the call?"

"No trouble at all. I see Deputy Gray regularly. Our jurisdictions overlap on the east side of town. I'll text you what time to be out at the Wagners'."

"Thank you, I owe you."

Task number three on the list is asking off for Friday. It's lunchtime, and I'm not too proud to attempt bribery. I lean into Howard's office as casually as possible. "So, are you going out for lunch, or do you want me to pick us up some sandwiches?"

"I can eat." Howard lays his credit card at the desk's edge. "I'd like a turkey wrap, no mayo, and baked chips."

I must give it to my uncle. He's hanging in there like a rusty nail on this diet thing. Honestly, I don't see the payoff yet, but if he wants it, I hope it works out for him. I lift the card from his desk and walk toward Jerry's sub shop.

When I first hired on with Howard, he stressed I could take off time whenever I needed to. Even though we cut the deal, I feel guilty asking off because I know it leaves him at the office by himself. Hopefully, before too long, he'll be able to hire some administrative help.

It's still early for the crowd at Jerry's, so they're only partially full. The line is five deep as I queue up, waiting for my turn.

The tall blonde in front of me looks familiar, but I can't place her. I keep stealing looks, trying to remember where I know her from.

She's in her late thirties, so I don't know her from school. She's exceptionally well-kept and oozes sensuality. To say she's out of place at Jerry's would be a comical understatement.

The man standing with her slides the heel of his palm onto the small of her back. His fingers spread over her buttocks. He's ruggedly handsome and a large man, but he does not possess her same Hollywood good looks and sensuality.

I try unsuccessfully not to stare as they place their order. She looks in my direction and seems to stare right through me.

Her eyes are a dead giveaway—Crystal Raley. I'll need to speak to her soon, but now would be unfortunate timing. Especially since she is not presently escorted by her husband, and the man with her is groping her derrière.

Crystal Raley has a lot in common with flashing lights on the highway. You know you shouldn't slow down and stare, but you just can't help yourself. Every movement of her lips, batting of her eyelashes, and slow waving gesture with her long, perfectly manicured fingers promise erotic sexual encounters.

I mean, I'm as heterosexual of a female as there is, and I'm mesmerized by her.

I rack my brain, trying to think why I've never seen her before. There's no way, even if she's ten years older than me, I wouldn't know this woman before now if she's from Marshall County.

She takes a sideways glance, and this time notices me staring. She smiles at me with her lips and eyes as I panic. Like an embarrassed six-year-old, I divert my stare to the floor.

Middle school through undergraduate school, I was the Crystal Raley in the room. I was the flame the boys danced to and around.

One by one, I stole their youthful confidence with simple rejection. It was easy. In some ways, it made me feel powerful.

Don't judge. I know now I was wrong, and if I had the opportunity, I would go back and change things. In some ways, it's a driving reason for me to get out of Guntersville.

I don't want to live in a town where I have a high probability of running into someone I wasn't kind to earlier in my life. Seriously. How awkward do you think it would be for a man if I approach him and say, "Hey, I was a real jerk for turning you down for the eighth-grade dance."

I don't think that's going to fix things between us. It's more likely to rip a scar open.

How's his wife going to feel if she's standing next to him. Most of these men have gone on to marry and have kids. I'm the one whose life growth has been stunted.

Worse yet, what if I marry someone local who turns into a loser, and we must file bankruptcy because he gambles and drinks all our money away. Then I try to numb my shame with copious amounts of fried chicken, chocolate shakes, and macadamia nut cookies and put on an extra hundred pounds. Hence, everyone continually asks when the twins are due.

How much joy would the men I turned away get from that? Would they say, "Oh, poor April May? She's really got her comeuppance." Would I blame them?

No, I wouldn't.

Somewhere along the line, I lost my mojo. It wasn't gradual. It was abrupt. In the last year of law school at Alabama, I couldn't have bought a date if I promised to buy them a steak dinner. Thankfully, I had my best friend Martin. Otherwise, I would have been stuck eating alone all the time. How sad is that?

Things have only gotten worse since graduation. Instead of just an epic dry spell, I'm in the middle of a long progression of "could have been, should have been, and man, why couldn't it have been" micro-relationships. There have been a plethora of attractive, successful, and kind men parading through my life lately, but none of them are mine.

Near misses are more painful than dry spells. Dry spells don't tear your heart out and stomp on it.

Chase was right this morning, even though I'll never admit it to him. I do like being in a relationship. And I'm not ashamed of it.

There's nothing wrong with having someone special in your life. Granted, I'm a serial monogamist. Still, I'm always serious about my relationships, whether they last three days or three months, and I'd give anything to be in a relationship right now.

Grandpa smoked from the time he was fourteen until he was in his forties, according to Granny. There is never a more vigorous critic of someone doing something wrong than a person who used to have the same issue.

To hear Grandpa talk about people smoking, you'd think, "thou shalt not smoke" was the first and most important commandment. He often told me, "Smokers are desecrators of God's temple." A bit ironic considering Grandpa passed from emphysema, but I'm channeling Grandpa now.

I watch men's eyes caress Crystal's ample curves while her pheromones and slight feminine movements tickle their senses. I realize I don't care for Crystal Raley. Women who use their good looks to make men act a fool are enchantresses. They are addicted to their own power to make men act against their own best interests.

I can say this because I'm a recovering addict of that power. I'm honestly ashamed of how I acted when I was younger.

There's another reason for my dislike of Crystal Raley. She has a good-looking, loving husband pining for her at home. Well, he was likely handsome seventy-five pounds ago and prior to losing half a head of hair. Regardless, he loves her.

Here I haven't had a serious boyfriend in the last two years. I can count the number of heavy-petting sessions on one finger. That's extremely sad since I'm in what should be the sexual prime of my life.

Sorrow waves over me as I consider Jared Raley's position. There is no denying he's in love with his wife, Crystal. He can't be naïve enough to think Crystal's friendships with other men are platonic.

Who am I kidding? When he described the drone event, he didn't consider Crystal's lack of action as odd. He didn't think she should have covered herself with a towel when she saw the drone hovering over her. He spoke as if she was totally innocent and an unwilling victim in the event.

I'm convinced she is less of a victim and more of a vixen. Of course, it's none of my concern. However, it does confirm to me my client is blinded by his love for his wife. He's got it bad for what I am afraid may be a bad woman.

How humiliating for Jared. I can't say I even particularly like him, but he doesn't deserve to be played for a fool. Nobody should be so disrespected by someone they've married.

It's beginning to make me ill that I accepted his retainer money. Partly because I know our case is, in all probability, a loser. Jared has been taken advantage of enough. We shouldn't allow him to burn a few thousand on a court case, especially over the honor of a woman who couldn't care less if he's still breathing or not.

Jerry's oldest daughter, Rhonda, calls my number to place my order. As I step up to the counter, I realize I've mostly lost my appetite. I decide to try the same turkey wrap with no mayo Howard ordered. If nothing else, it should count as healthy.

Chapter 14

My master plan is to ingratiate myself to Howard by picking up our sandwiches to make it easier to ask him to let me take Friday off. The scheme is solid. But when I return, he is hard at work on his computer, and I don't want to interrupt him. Okay, I'm chicken. I know he will say yes, but I have rejection issues that prevent me from asking him.

The turkey wrap is worse than I could've imagined. It's like sand wrapped in cardboard.

It looks yummy, but it has virtually no taste. If it weren't for my bottle of water, I would never be able to swallow it because the wrap is so dry it hangs up at the back of my throat no matter how thoroughly I chew.

Watching Crystal act so boldly in public almost made me lose my religion. I know our civil case is a burner. We'll be lucky if Judge Rossi doesn't dismiss it during initial statements.

Still, there must be an angle. There's always an angle to work; they're just elusive at times. I need to find a way to help Jared prosecute his neighbor. There must be a way to bring grief to a man who messed with another man's wife that doesn't require the adulterous wife's help.

The idea of making Crystal's life difficult intrigues me. I have this driving need to teach her the sun doesn't shine on the same dog's tail all the time.

I must set my emotions about Crystal aside for now. With the impending arraignment on the Wagner case in the morning, I need all my focus there.

I'd be lying if I said I hadn't wondered if Lane somehow convinced Judge Rossi to move the arraignment hearing up. He had to know it would catch me unprepared. I wouldn't put it past him. He's been terribly angry I didn't convince Vance to plead to second-degree murder.

Now I sound paranoid. Lane already had the arraignment time before I advised him Vance wanted to fight the charges in court. Besides, I've not met her yet, but I hear Judge Rossi is a hard-charging straight shooter. I doubt Lane could bend a woman like that to his will.

I go through the electronic folder of the Wagner case for what seems like the twentieth time. I take my time flipping through the pictures of the carnage created by Vance, hoping some detail I missed earlier jumps off the screen. I have no clue what I'll argue in the morning.

My phone dings, and I welcome the distraction. The text is from Jake. He lets me know Deputy Gray will meet me at the Wagner house at one thirty. I do a double-take at the time on the top left of my phone. I have twenty minutes to get to the Wagner house.

"Howard."

"Yes." He sounds distracted.

"I need to go out to the Wagners' and meet with the sheriff."

"Okay. Be safe, and I'll see you in the morning."

I grab my keys and leave the office. As I get in my car, I roll my eyes. I forgot to ask off for Friday. It's already Tuesday afternoon, and I still haven't cleared the date for the Birmingham trip. What's wrong with me?

Am I trying to sabotage the Birmingham research trip? It's possible, considering how I feel about my burgeoning paranormal powers. No, that's too convoluted even for me.

I'm just procrastinating.

I pull onto the gravel road off County Nine, which leads to the Wagner home. Fifty feet before the house, a sheriff's cruiser straddles the shoulder on the right side. I pull my Prius behind the large silver car.

As I approach the vehicle, the door opens, and Deputy Gray gets out. Call me sexist, I was expecting a man, possibly an older version of my Jake.

Did I just think, my Jake? Lord, I'm a mess.

"April Snow, I understand you're Vance Wagner's defense attorney?"

Oh my! It's Becky Bucktooth. I freeze in terror and say a silent prayer. *Please, Lord. Please tell me I did not just say Becky Bucktooth out loud.*

Deputy Gray tilts her head as her eyes narrow. "Are you all right?"

Thank you. My treasonous mouth has, for once, remained silent.

Becky Gray had been known from kindergarten through first grade as Bowl Cut Becky for her at-home haircuts, courtesy of her grandmother. At the end of first grade, something incredible happened. Becky's permanent teeth came in, and her two front teeth would've made Harvey the rabbit envious. We're talking significant-sized Chiclets here. They even tilted, so the bottom edges pointed out across her lower lip. They were quite impressive, and her nickname quickly changed to Becky Bucktooth.

She retained her new nickname until sixth grade.

I might've mentioned before, but besides cheerleading and dance, I had to hold my own in the boys' sports, too, because of my older brothers.

By sixth grade, I was a lethal fastball pitcher, which earned me a starting position in two games a week.

My baseball team made it to the playoffs, and eventually, we were paired against the Albertville Armadillos. Becky, like me, was the only girl on her baseball team and a crackerjack pitcher.

I was batting leadoff; my batting was below average, but I was the fastest player on our team, and I could run out an infield hit with my long legs. I stepped into the batter's box, and my confidence immediately left me.

Becky had a huge wad of bubble gum in her mouth, causing her right cheek to protrude as if it were filled with chewing tobacco. Worse, her teeth were poking straight out at me. She was absolutely intimidating, and I wouldn't have been surprised if she adjusted her protective cup and spat tobacco juice.

I ignored my instincts, which were to drop the bat and go tell Coach my stomach hurt. Becky reared back and slung her arm.

I never saw the ball because I closed my eyes when I heard it humming toward me. I swung wildly and was the most surprised person in the park when I heard a loud "ding" ring off my aluminum bat.

There was a solo scream and a collective gasp from the crowd. I opened my eyes to find Becky writhing in the red dirt in front of the mound.

The catcher bumped me hard as he got up to run to his pitcher. "Way to go, Snow," he growled.

In a daze, I followed him to the mound. In my peripheral vision, I saw coaches from both dugouts running toward us.

The catcher pulled Becky into a sitting position. Two pearls glistened at her feet as the sun glared off them at a perfect angle.

Becky will regret wearing expensive earrings to the game, I thought.

Becky opened her mouth as I neared and screamed, "My teeth." My vision went fuzzy from the bleeding, ragged gums inside Becky's mouth to the pearl earrings. I noticed the torn gum and nerve connected to the pearl earrings.

With no warning, I projectile vomited.

Neither team had their starting pitcher for the game.

Becky went to the orthodontist. I sat in the dugout, worried I might throw up again. It was an extra-inning game that we finally won one to zero.

Becky and I were equally scarred by the event. But I didn't have to deal with the pain of getting my teeth knocked out of my mouth.

Odd. Becky doesn't seem to remember me at all as she addresses me. Maybe she's forgotten the event that forever binds us. I know I never will.

"I was hoping to get a better idea of what took place by walking the crime scene," I say.

Becky gives a quick nod, then frowns. "I'm glad to show you, but I'm not sure anyone other than Vance Wagner will ever know what really took place. While we tour, I'll walk you through our theory."

That's not really what I came for. I read the Sheriff's theory of events from the report. "Deputy Gray, if you don't mind, I'm more interested in where we think the shots were fired and what took place with the vehicle."

"Fair enough." She gestures with her finger as she walks toward the front door of the trailer. "Hopefully, Ms. Wagner will remain inside. The woman seriously needs a tranquilizer."

I choke back a laugh. "She definitely seems to be a handful."

"You don't know the half of it." Becky steps onto the front porch.

In my peripheral vision, I notice the curtains of the front window move. The movement reminds me of my next task once I finish the walkthrough with Deputy Gray.

I am relieved Leslie is here to discuss how she can help her husband's cause by parking her crazy at home. I need her to stay away from town until I call on her to appear in court as the small, defenseless wife.

"From my interview with Mr. Wagner," Becky says, "he fired two shells from the top of the porch at the suspect entering the vehicle's passenger side."

I point toward the porch. "Did you collect the shells in the vicinity?"

Becky's eyes narrow. "The site had been scoured by the time I arrived. All I had was two bodies and a burnt-out car. Vance handed me a gallon-sized baggie containing all seven shotgun shell casings. He explained it was a force of habit. He's a former marine RECON, you know."

No, I didn't. But that explains a lot. I get a lift in my spirits from the news the site had been scoured.

"Old habits die hard when they're drilled into muscle memory," Becky says.

"You sound like you have experience." It's helpful Becky considers the rationale for the site being tampered with as reasonable. I marvel at Vance's thoroughness and the plausibility he has constructed. By him clearing the shells, there is no way to reconstruct what took place in his front yard. It's Vance's word against two dead men. Who doesn't like those odds?

"Nothing like RECON, but yes, I was an Army MP."

"That had its own challenges, I'm sure."

Becky lifts her chin to my comment then turns her attention back to the overgrown field that is the Wagners' front yard. She points at the red clay scar cutting through the middle of it, a heavily rutted driveway with drop-off gullies on either side with a few fence line trees.

"Mr. Wagner reported the driver took off in reverse, which trapped the passenger by wedging him between the door and the car. The passenger couldn't get in the car because his legs were being dragged below the car."

Becky walks us down the drive while gesturing with her hands. "Mr. Wagner continued to fire his shotgun. He directed his fire at the driver's windshield after striking the passenger until he struck the driver. The driver lost control of the vehicle when the wheels went off the shoulder. The car rolled from the momentum, pinning the left-hand side of the vehicle against that tree."

Becky points to a misshapen, ancient cedar tree. Its canopy is gone, and the gnarled trunk is heavily blackened.

"The car burst into flames, and the threat was over. Mr. Wagner used his remaining two shells to fire the coup de grâce."

I jerk to attention. That's the first time I've heard anything hinting at these events being an execution. "Vance told you that?"

"Of course not. But I had one perpetrator whose head looked like a plate of spilled spaghetti, and the other perpetrator was extra crispy in the car. My estimation is a close encounter with the end of a twelve-gauge for the one dragged down the driveway. Then another round to the exposed fuel tank of the turned-over vehicle to ignite the fire."

The report did not include her speculations. Still, Deputy Gray is confident her reconstruction of events is what took place.

"Were they carrying?"

"The perpetrators?"

"Yes."

"They were both carrying nine-millimeter Glocks. The one recovered from the driveway had been fired recently."

That didn't make it into the report. "Casings?"

Becky snorts. "In the baggie with the shotgun shells."

"Why weren't they in the report?"

Becky points back to Wagners' home. "No evidence of the rounds. There's no way to know if the rounds were before or after the event. When in doubt, leave it out."

I prescribe to when in doubt, put it in, but whatever. One thing for sure, a lack of rounds in the side of the house doesn't prove anything. I'd venture a guess a lot of folks' aim would become suspect if a former RECON is chasing them down a driveway with a shotgun.

"Anything else you can think of?" I ask.

Becky shakes her head. "No. That's really all we have. I

hope it hasn't been a waste of your time."

"No. And I appreciate you coming out here on short notice." I gesture my thumb toward the Wagners' home. "I need to speak with Mrs. Wagner about her husband's case now."

Becky widens her stance. "Would you like me to hang around just in case you need some assistance?"

"I can handle her."

"Then you're in the wrong line of work. If you get bored, let me know, and I'll find you a job. Of course, I'll make sure they never issue you a baseball bat."

How utterly embarrassing. Becky does remember, and she didn't mention it until now.

I watch her return to her cruiser. She's still built like she was in high school when she was the gymnast who almost made the Olympic trials. She's five foot two and muscular all over with no neck.

Becky pauses before getting into her cruiser. "I'll be just down the road if you need me."

"Thank you." I wave to her.

Who would have thought, Becky, a sheriff's deputy? Still, I must admit it somehow fits her.

As I watch her cruiser turn onto the county road, I understand my procrastination must end. It's time to knock on the door and talk to Leslie about not interfering in her husband's defense. No matter how well-meaning her intentions.

I rap on her front door three times. Each time progressively louder and longer. Still no, Leslie.

Fine, if she doesn't want to talk to me, I don't need to speak to a loco blonde today anyway. If she stays burrowed away in her home, mission accomplished. Surely she knows why I'm here and will stay away from the courthouse until I tell her to show up now.

I make my mind up to leave and see the curtains move again. I holler toward the window, "Come on, Leslie! It's not like I can't see you. Open up."

The silence is deafening. I decide to leave for good. As I turn, the chain on the door rattles. The deadbolt clicks open. Leslie cracks the door open, and I lock stares with Leslie's wild blue eyes.

"What do you want?"

"Hopefully, to get your husband bailed out tomorrow. Assuming you'll help."

She's quiet. Leslie appears to be contemplating her options carefully. The door opens wide enough for her to poke her head through. "What do you need from me?"

Amazing. Leslie is clueless about the damage she did to Vance's case today with her antics.

"I need you to stay at home tomorrow."

Her face contorts into a grotesque snarl. "But Vance's bail hearing is tomorrow. He needs me."

"He needs you to stay home."

"But I—"

Raising a finger, I cut her off. "Did you talk to some reporters this morning?"

Her caginess returns in a flash. "Why are you asking?"

I try to appear as if I couldn't care less, but I'm sure I'm failing to conceal my aggravation. "Because I got a report earlier today that you had a bunch of reporters riled up about a story—the robbers were CIA hitmen."

"I never really said that."

"I wouldn't know. I haven't seen the tape. I'm just going by what the district attorney told me."

Her eyes squint. "That man's the devil."

After seeing Lane under stress this week, I may be in Leslie's camp soon enough. But that isn't going to help Vance's chance of getting bailed out. "If that be the case, you were dancing on the devil's tail this morning, and he's gunning for your husband now. You feel me?"

"Why?"

Oh, to be so innocent about the politics of the world. "Leslie, your interviews with the reporters earned the district attorney a call from the attorney general in Montgomery. It's sort of like having the top boss call you and ask you if you're still able to do your job."

"I didn't say anything that wasn't true."

"Leslie, I wouldn't know one way or the other. What I do know is you made the wrong man angry and, in the process, made it exponentially more difficult for me to do my job."

"I've got a right to talk to the reporters. Free speech. It's like a continental right."

I want to correct her that it's "constitutional," but I don't need the conversation going off on another tangent. It's squirrelly enough as is. "Leslie, I want you to think. Is it more important we get Vance out on bail tomorrow or that you get to tell the reporters what you think is the truth?"

She purses her lips. "Why do I have to choose?"

"You just have to, Leslie." *Please, Lord, get me through this conversation.*

"You have to trust me. If you show up and do tomorrow what you did this morning, we have zero chance of getting Vance out on bail. He will sit in jail until his trial. I can also guarantee you that they will try to put that trial out as far as possible."

"You really think talking with reporters is a terrible thing?"

I squeeze the back of my neck with my right hand. I may have a migraine coming on.

"Leslie, it isn't wrong. But it's not helpful to Vance's cause. The goal is to get Vance out on bail first, and second, we want him not to serve any time. If we get those two things, does it really matter what a bunch of reporters, who don't care about you, think did or didn't happen?"

She looks down at her bare feet. "No, I suppose not." Her head jerks back up, and she locks me with her stare. "But I need to do something. I can't just sit here doing nothing when he needs me."

I have no idea where the words come from that tumble easily from my mouth, but I am thankful as they are precisely what I need to say. "If you need to do something, Leslie, then stay at home and pray. All day, Leslie. Until I call you and tell you he's free. Can you do that for Vance?"

Her face softens considerably. For the first time since I've known her, she appears pretty, not scary.

She nods her head. "Yeah, I can do that, April. That's a good idea. I can do that."

"Okay, then. I'll give you a call tomorrow when it's over."

"April?" Her left eye twitches. "Thank you."

I can sense that "thank you" is not something Leslie often needs to say to a stranger. She offered it to me as if it were a treasured, fragile sculpture from her curio.

Another time I might respond with a flippant "just doing my job, ma'am." I'm not the best at accepting folks' gratitude, but the moment is too monumental for even me to miss.

"You're welcome, Leslie. I'll call you tomorrow."

As I walk to my car, the house door clicks shut behind me as the woman returns to the solitude I'm sure is driving her insane. Vance and Leslie are a team. They're a little intense. Still, I understand they somehow act as each other's anchor in a storm.

I need to get Vance home to her soon. Each of them alone, without the other stabilizing them, is a scary type of crazy.

Chapter 15

Having been so busy the second half of the day, I don't realize how hungry I am until I pull into the lake house driveway. The turkey wrap with no mayo had only enough calories for an hour, and I haven't eaten since.

If I'd been thinking, I would've run through a fast food drive-thru on the way home. But then again, why go through a fast food drive-thru when you live at your parents' house? I'll just forage from their fridge.

The spicy, aromatic smell of taco meat simmering greets me as I pull open the kitchen's glass door.

"Start making some nachos, and all the señoritas show up." Daddy flashes me a smile.

"Is that an invite, I hope?"

"You know we have an open-table policy in this home. If we're eating, everyone's invited." He pushes a bowl of guacamole my way. "To hold you over until I get the rest of the nachos ready."

"Who all is coming tonight?"

Daddy looks puzzled by my question. "It's just you, your brothers, and your mom. Were you hoping for someone in particular?"

"No, just curious," I say too quickly.

"I can always make a phone call and have them appear," he

teases as he turns his back to me to dice tomatoes.

"Who could I possibly want you to call, Daddy?"

"Let me see. It seems to me the other night you wanted to take a Corvette for a test ride."

My face heats so rapidly I'm sure I match the color of the tomatoes. "Hush your mouth."

Daddy laughs. "You might as well have hung a sign around your neck. 'Pick me.'"

My jaw drops. "You're awful."

"Don't throw a hissy. There's nothing wrong with you being attracted to Patrick. It's only normal, and he's a nice guy."

How horrifying. My interest in Patrick is so apparent that even my daddy picked up on it.

That's what bites about being at the house. Everyone is always in my business.

I drag a tortilla chip through a generous serving of guacamole and pop it into my mouth. There is absolutely no advantage to living at home with your parents as an adult.

"Did you go by your granny's yet?"

I stop chewing as guilt squeezes my heart. This is followed by a tsunami of sadness as I remember I promised Daddy I would visit Granny. I'm positive he told her I planned to swing by soon.

Oh no. I can visualize Granny sitting on the porch all day in this oppressive heat, waiting, watching for me to come up her driveway.

I'm officially the worst granddaughter ever.

Daddy looks up from the lettuce he's chopping. "You did go by. Didn't you, April?"

"No, sir," I whisper. "I forgot. I've just been really busy with my cases."

He exhales loudly. "Well, you know she's not going to be around forever, April. She's probably disappointed, too. I know she was awfully excited about the surprise she bought you."

"Daddy, I know." Now I'm whining. I can't stand when my voice automatically changes to whine mode.

"I hope she didn't buy anything that will spoil. The rate you're going, she can give it to you at Christmas."

"Stop it. Just stop it. I already feel bad enough."

He shrugs. "I'm just saying."

I hate the way Daddy hijacked a few adolescent terms and uses them ten years past their shelf life.

"If I promise to visit her tomorrow, can you let it rest tonight?"

"I suppose. But it does seem like you promised last time."

See, that's why I don't want to live with my parents. When I was down at the university, I didn't have to worry about anyone telling me what to do. I took care of my grades and set my own social schedule.

Now that I live at home, I have a "part-time job" that has turned into a high-pressure cooker where I'm trying to keep a man out of jail for murder. Meanwhile, my daddy wants to shame me about not visiting my granny. All because she's bought me a bag of licorice or some old knickknack she wants to give me.

Yes, a rent-free room is helpful right now. Sure, it's convenient not to have to go to the laundromat to do my laundry. Of course, it's excellent to bum an occasional, well a quite often, meal. But it isn't free. It has a cost.

In the end, my parents will get their pound of flesh. It usually comes in the form of guilt.

Now he's done it. He had to keep prodding until I finally threw a hissy fit.

I'm fuming at my daddy's back when the sliding glass door makes a rolling noise. I look over my shoulder and get a case of vertigo as I watch Chase and Patrick come through.

I lean against the kitchen counter as my knees weaken. Why does Daddy have the heat on in the kitchen?

"Do you have enough for one more, Dad?" Chase asks.

"The more, the merrier." Daddy gives the skillet of meat a

stir.

Patrick looks at me, his smile reaching his eyes. "April." He favors me a tilt of his chin.

"Hey," I croak breathlessly.

I catch my brother looking first at Patrick, then at me. A grin crosses his face.

"Chase, let me ask you. When was the last time you went to Granny's?"

"I cut her grass last weekend, Dad. Why do you ask?"

"Oh, for Pete's sake, Daddy. You said you'd give it a rest."

He laughs as he returns his attention to his cooking. He's having way too much fun at my expense.

With the arraignment in the morning, I should go straight to my apartment after dinner. But the food and the company has been too good.

Chase asks if I want to join him and Patrick in the mechanic shed to work on the Corvette. I can't refuse.

Heck, I'm on a roll today. I rode a WaveRunner, weathered Lane's temper, didn't slap Crystal Raley, kept my teeth with Becky Bucktooth, and talked sense into a scary, hundred-pound blonde. If there were ever a day I could impress Patrick McCabe with my exceptional conversation skills, it must be today. Right?

My luck has run dry, though. All good things must end.

Chase and Patrick are more serious gearheads than I could have imagined. They are fully involved in removing the 'Vette engine block to rebore the cylinders and replace all the rings and gaskets.

I have always enjoyed watching the men in my family work on cars. Still, I've limited my car knowledge to pumping gas and turning the ignition on.

That's not true. Daddy taught me how to replace a flat tire, but I convinced a guy to change it for me the two times I've had a flat.

Next to the large metal tool chest, I sit on the wooden stool watching the two big, beautiful men work in concert around the classic sports car. They are a good team. Few words are spoken as Patrick's lack of experience working on vehicles is balanced by his noticeably high mechanical aptitude.

I could have watched for hours if I didn't have more pressing business to attend. After an hour of Patrick-watching, I need to call it a night and get some rest in preparation for my busy morning.

"Chase, I've got the arraignment in the morning, so I'm gonna head up to my room and do a little studying before I go to bed."

He pulls his head out from under the Corvette's hood. "You sure?"

I stand and stretch my arms over my head. "Yeah, I'm beat."

"Okay."

A smirk plays across my brother's lips. He used to get the same look when we were younger and he was about to play a practical joke on me.

He kicks Patrick's leg sticking out from under the car. "Hey, Patrick."

"Hmm?" Patrick rolls out from under the car.

"What was the name of that band?" Chase asks.

Patrick wipes his hand on a grease towel, his eyes narrow. "Band?"

"Yeah, the band you said you wanted to see. Last week you mentioned it. You mentioned they'd be playing in Huntsville. I think at the UAH campus."

"Oh, right, the band. The band I want to see." Patrick stands up from the slide board. "What was their name?"

Chase laughs as he slaps a hand to his forehead. "You're killing me here, dude."

Patrick rolls his left shoulder. "Yeah, I imagined it going a lot smoother."

I think he's asking me out. I don't want to get too far ahead of myself and be disappointed.

Patrick gives me a silly grin. "Well?"

"Well, what?" I ask.

"Man, you two are sad. Do I have to do everything for you?" Chase gestures with his hands. "April, there's a concert in Huntsville next Tuesday that Patrick thought you might want to go to—with him."

I'm speechless. All I can do is gawk at Patrick and back to my brother. I want to scream yes, but my mouth won't work.

Chase picks up a wrench and tucks his head back under the Corvette's hood. "I give. You two are hopeless. There are probably people in the Boaz Retirement Center with more game than you two put together."

"I just don't know what to say. You sort of caught me off guard," I finally manage.

"Yes, would work," Chase grumbles.

I hope the smile blooming on my face does not look as goofy as it feels. "Yeah—I mean yes—I would love to go with you, Patrick."

He looks stunned as he whispers, "Cool."

We stare at each other in a state of mutual stupor until I begin to feel awkward.

"I think you said you had some sort of case you had to get ready for, April. Right?" Chase says.

My brother's voice brings me out of my trance. "Yes. Case. I must go do."

Chase tosses his wrench in the air, and it clatters against the concrete floor as he rolls with laughter. "Who knew we'd have a cameo by Yoda tonight."

I don't do any prep for the Wagner case when I get back to my apartment. I don't concern myself with drones over cheating wives, reporters, or an irate district attorney. I don't worry about what I'll find this weekend down in Birmingham with Dusty on the paranormal trip. I don't even care if anyone has requested an interview from the resumes I sent out.

All I think about is how sometimes things just come together for me like magic. Often when I'm about to suspend hope.

It occurs to me Chase knew early on I was attracted to Patrick, and him to me. Chase had to work with blinding speed to pull his sister and friend together into a date in such short order.

Chase didn't inherit any of the paranormal traits from our grandmothers. Still, he is not without magic. In one day, he's brought me out of a sour mood, solidified our sibling bond, and hooked me up with Patrick.

How lucky am I to have Chase as a brother? Truly fortunate indeed.

I have a real date coming up. I'm so pumped!

This has been the best Tuesday ever, and I want to replay every event as I lay my head on my pillows. Seconds later, I feel I'm melting into the mattress, and the memory reel becomes unfocused.

Chapter 16

No matter how many years of school I completed, I know nothing is quite like doing something for real. For one thing, practicing has never twisted my gut like it feels right now.

As I wait for Judge Rossi to enter the court, my stomach bloats as my blood pressure continues to rise, causing my earlobes to feel unnaturally hot. I flip through the notes on my legal pad for Vance's sake, hoping I appear well prepared.

I need to look like I have my act together for his sake. I must be because, for his part, Vance appears cool, calm, and collected.

Howard offered to sit with me during the arraignment for moral support. I quickly told him it wasn't necessary.

I'm regretting my knee-jerk decision. It will never be anything I say to his face. Still, Howard is a wealth of knowledge about how the legal system works that isn't available in any textbook or legal journal.

Having Howard sit with me would be like having a dictionary in my lap during a spelling bee. It would turbocharge my confidence even if I didn't need to tap into the resource.

I catch movement to my right. I fight, and lose, the urge to look. The clasps on Lane's expensive leather briefcase make a loud clicking noise that reverberates through the silent courtroom. The bottom of his chair makes a loud scratching noise as he pulls it back from under the table. It sends a chill up my spine.

The beast has arrived. I struggle not to run from the courtroom.

Lane looks in my direction. "Good morning, April."

"Good morning, DA Jameson." I grimace. He called me by my first name, and I gave him the respect of his title. The subtle smirk on his face as he turns his attention back to his brief confirms my error.

In my defense, how can I not call him DA Jameson today? Suppose Hollywood agents were looking for new talent to play high-level lawyers on television dramas. In that case, Lane is precisely who they'd want to sign to a contract.

He's a commanding presence with his six-foot, fully filled out broad-shouldered build, pepper gray hair at his temples, and rugged early forty-something face not yet gone "old." He is both handsome and imposing. His physical attributes, coupled with the perfectly tailored suit and the loafers with a shine that looks unnatural, give the appearance of someone who is impeccably prepared for this hearing.

I take stock of the four-year-old skirt suit I'm wearing with black pumps that have seen a few too many nights out on the town. I give the bun at the back of my head a quick pat feeling the individual hairs already escaping from their confines.

As I slide into a dark place, I look down at my hands and see the utterly fabulous manicure Tiffany gave me this week. That gives me a lift, especially when I add the fact I even took a shower this morning.

That puts Lane and me even, or me with a slight advantage in my book. Everyone knows freshly showered with a killer manicure trumps a tailored suit and funky, shining loafers any day.

My triumph is cut short as the door behind the bench opens and the bailiff enters. I stand and lean against the desk to steady my knees.

"All rise," the bailiff commands.

Judge Rossi enters her courtroom, and my lungs quit working. She's five and a half feet tall and rail-thin. Her wiry black—with liberal amounts of gray—hair is pulled back severely into a tight bun. She reaches the bench and acknowledges our presence, offering the briefest of smiles absent of warmth. "Good morning, counselors."

"Good morning, Judge Rossi." My throat feels as if I ate a cup of gravel.

"Please be seated," she commands as she takes her own seat, appearing to wince briefly with pain.

I turn to Vance to take a quick inventory of his state of mind.

He remains too cool for school, but not in a way that makes me comfortable. He appears totally detached, as if he's here to watch a high school play he hasn't much interest in. His eyebrows knit together as he notices I'm watching him.

"Just checking to see if you're still good," I explain.

He leans in toward me and whispers, "I know her."

That gives me a start, although I don't know why. "Okay. Is there a problem?"

The right side of his lip rises with a grin. "I don't think so." He shrugs. "I guess we'll find out in a minute."

Great. What the heck is that supposed to mean? Something tells me the bit of information Vance just shared could become a thing during this hearing. I better be on my toes when we take that sideroad, so we don't get ambushed.

Judge Rossi slides her eyeglasses on and flips through the brief in front of her. She pulls her glasses off, holding them between her thumb and forefinger as she rests her chin on the top of her hand.

"Counselor Snow, your client, Vance Wagner, has been charged by the state with two counts of first-degree murder. How does your client plead?"

I feel a single bead of sweat track down my backside. "Not guilty, ma'am... Your Honor."

Judge Rossi's eyes narrow. "You're Vivian and Ralph's daughter, aren't you?"

"Yes, Your Honor." Her question sets me on edge even further.

Her face twitches into a smile. "I bet you never thought you'd be trying a case in my court when you were down at the University of Alabama."

It was impossible to tell if that is a rhetorical question or if she expects an answer. "No, Your Honor."

A brief cackle escapes her. "Lordy"—she waves a dark bony hand in my direction—"you're too young to understand, but this world is just one big circle."

She turns her attention to Lane. "DA Jameson, if your case against Mr. Wagner is half as fine as your attire today, I am sure he will wish he took a plea bargain rather than take his case to the jury. We will continue this discussion to determine what bail will be set for Mr. Wagner. Unless, of course, you can prove Mr. Wagner to be a danger to the community or a flight risk."

There is a long, awkward silence as Lane and Judge Rossi stare at each other. Judge Rossi breaks the silence. "That is your invitation to begin your portion of the case, DA Jameson."

"Oh, yes, Your Honor. Of course."

I can't help but grin as Lane lays out the facts as he sees them to Judge Rossi. She obviously can intimidate Lane as quickly as she does me.

To Judge Rossi's credit, she listens patiently as Lane explains his version of events that paint Vance in the worst light in full detail. The details are almost identical to the details Deputy Gray told me yesterday in the Wagner's front yard.

Lane takes additional care to explain the timing of Vance freeing himself. He slows his delivery, so it feels like Vance took half an hour to retrieve his shotgun and track the men down while firing methodically until both men died.

The actual timeline is more like thirty seconds.

Judge Rossi points her reading glasses at Lane after he finishes. "DA Jameson, explain to me the thought process behind prosecuting first-degree murder rather than second or manslaughter, please."

Lane shuffles his feet side to side. "Well, as I said, Your Honor, Mr. Wagner freed himself before the victims left the structure. He had ample time to think through how he was going to murder them."

Judge Rossi looks as if she bit into something sour. "First off, the two men were not victims; they were violent thieves. We will refer to them in the future as attackers, not victims. Second, it was not a structure. It is the Wagners' home. In any further discussion, we will call that structure their home. Are we in agreement?"

"Yes, Your Honor."

"Excellent, I like agreement. It makes things run smoother." She puts her reading glasses back on and appears to review her notes. "DA Jameson, I understand your reasoning as explained for first-degree murder, but I have one question for you."

"Yes, Your Honor."

"Do you really expect to get a conviction of first-degree murder if this goes before a jury?"

"Absolutely."

Judge Rossi exhales as she leans back into her chair. "Very well. Still, I think that dog won't hunt, but it's your case."

Lane's face contorts as he raises his hand as if to reply, but Judge Rossi cuts him short.

"Counselor Snow, what good reason can you give me to release your client on bail until the time of his assigned trial date?"

What happens next is nothing short of miraculous. Despite all my apprehension this morning, I'm suddenly hyperfocused and in complete control.

I look Judge Rossi in the eye and give her a complete recitation of the "right to fight before flight" bill commonly referred to in our state as the "make my day bill." I explain the fear Vance felt when he saw his wife Leslie bound and with obvious physical abuse signs on her person. I describe the cuts and abrasions on Vance's hands, which proves he believed if he didn't free himself, the attackers would kill both Leslie and him.

Then I constructed a bit of fiction. Why shouldn't I? There was no way for Lane and Becky to prove the timetable they asserted. Why shouldn't I create an equally plausible chain of events?

See, their attackers were going out to their car to retrieve plastic to put under Vance and Leslie while they killed them. Since they were coming back in, Vance thought his chances were better if he met them outside, so Leslie, who was still bound, wouldn't be struck by gunfire.

The plastic was an impromptu visual that popped into my mind. Of course, deputy Gray didn't find any plastic in the car. It melted during the fire. At least that's my story, and I'm sticking with it.

What I didn't say was the attackers were police officers. Even though this would have given more credence to Vance's violent reaction. My expectation is it could just as easily backfire on us and prove Lane's contention that Vance intended to kill them. Which he did.

I finish and wait in silence.

Judge Rossi's dark face wrinkles into a broad smile. "You have your Uncle Howard's flair for litigation, Counselor Snow. You might want to consider staying under his tutelage a little longer. There's no telling how well it might serve you."

Her eyes slide from me to Vance. "Mr. Wagner, would you kindly stand please, sir?"

"Yes'm."

"It will be Your Honor or Judge Rossi in my courtroom, Mr. Wagner. Good manners never hurt any of us."

Vance stands and nods. "Yes, Your Honor, I didn't mean any disrespect."

"No, of course, you didn't." Judge Rossi frowns. "You know I knew your father and uncle. They were sorry excuses for men. I must have seen each no less than fifty times in this court before they passed.

"But I've never seen you before today, Mr. Wagner. Are you a better man than them, or simply better at hiding your crimes?"

Vance's eyes narrow as his shoulders spread back. "I'm nothing like my father. My Aunt Matilda raised me, and she raised me right—Your Honor."

Something sparks in Judge Rossi's eyes. It's as if Vance just spoke the secret password. The only way he could have answered and had Judge Rossi believe him.

She reviews her notes again, and silence hangs in the courtroom. "Mr. Wagner, it says here you served four years in the military. First, thank you for your service. Second, I want to know if you've ever killed anybody before this event."

"Yes, Your Honor. On three occasions. While I was on tour in Afghanistan."

Judge Rossi leans forward, her fingers lace before her. "Mr. Wagner, do you like to kill?"

My jaw drops in horror. I am shocked the judge has asked Vance that question. I'm too slow in turning to see his reaction.

"No, Your Honor. It makes me sick. The fact is, I can hardly put meat in the freezer anymore because it makes me ill to kill something. L...Leslie and I have gone to mixing store-bought hamburger with what little bit of venison I can take in each year."

Judge Rossi's expression softens as her head ticks side to side. "I sure like me some tenderloin wrapped in bacon."

Vance laughs. "Yes, ma'am. I mean, Your Honor, I'm quite sure that's all they serve in heaven."

"Then, I might quit clinging on so tightly to this life." Judge Rossi's full-face smile sobers. "I hate to hear the war took away something you used to enjoy. I used to enjoy hunting too. Squirrel, dove, or deer, didn't matter what. I'd been hunting almost my entire life since my father first put a shotgun in my hand on Freedom Hill at age eight."

"Old man Lawrence still let people hunt Freedom Hill?" Vance asks.

Judge Rossi shakes her head. "No, old man Lawrence has been dead for at least a decade now. His two daughters own it now, and they don't take to the old ways."

"I never got to hunt there, but always heard it was good hunting."

"It was"—one of her hands leaves her desk—"of course, these old hips with arthritis don't like the cold much anymore. It looks like you and I are in the same boat, Mr. Wagner. The only difference being that arthritis took my joy for hunting, and the war took yours."

She writes something on the case folder. "Mr. Wagner, could you pull five hundred dollars together?"

"Yes, Your Honor."

Judge Rossi peers over her glasses. "In that case, Counselors, we will set bail at five hundred dollars." Rossi brings her gavel down, and the clack reverberates off the paneled walls. "Adjourned."

"But Judge, five hundred dollars for a double murder?" Lane protests.

Judge Rossi struggles to stand. "Lane, I keep waiting for you to grow into your father's shoes. But do you know the main differences between yours and your father's skill?"

It's obviously rhetorical as she cuts him off when he opens his mouth to respond.

"Your father only asked for sentences he thought he could get a jury to agree to."

"But the law has to be upheld..."

"The law does not benefit from you bringing cases to my court, tying up resources trying for convictions that will never be served. If you honestly believe a jury will convict Mr. Wagner of first-degree murder in this matter"—she taps the folder—"then, son, you're not as bright as I hoped."

"But, Judge."

She winces as she takes the first step from her chair and waves her hand at him as she starts down the stairs. "I'll have my office send you the trial dates."

"Judge!" Lane hollers at her back.

Judge Rossi turns, and her dark eyes glare. "Lane, we're done here." Her eyes dip downward. "And don't ever wear those shoes in my court again. That weird shine hurts my eyes."

Ecstatic does not begin to describe my mood as I leave the courtroom. I honestly can't comprehend what all just transpired or what, if anything, I did to positively affect the outcome. The one thing I do know is I'm on the winning team.

It feels terrific! I feel like celebrating.

I think this moment is befitting of a Torino's extra meat supreme large for Howard and me to split. Since I'm feeling like a big dog, I want to buy this time.

As I step out of the courtroom, I look down to do a quick survey of my pocketbook. It's Wednesday, and I'm down to forty-six dollars. I'm not too concerned about cutting it short this week since I know Dusty will be buying the team's meals this weekend.

Oh, no! Wednesday. Howard. I still haven't asked Howard for Friday off. It isn't gonna be just a large pizza coming out of my forty-six dollars. I'll need to buy a six-pack of beer, too.

"April Snow, is it true your client executed two intruders outside his home?"

I'm so deep into my bubble of euphoria and guilt I hadn't even noticed Chuck Grassley sidling up to me with a microphone. I'm sure the expression I inadvertently give him is like I just stepped in something squishy and smelly that I want to wipe off my shoe.

"Is it true that Vance Wagner was let out on five hundred dollars bail? A mere two hundred and fifty dollars per murder?"

I turn on Chuck. "Nice to see you can do the math, Chuck."

"Do you refuse to answer the question, Ms. Snow?"

"My client and his wife were attacked viciously by two criminals. My client defended himself within the confines of the laws of the state of Alabama."

Don't feed the bears, April. I know I've made a dreadful mistake. Chuck's face lights up as soon as I speak to him directly.

"Your case will stand on the merits of the 'make my day' law?"

"You know as well as I do there is no such named law in the state of Alabama."

Chuck is undeterred. "Is your client a flight risk?"

No. But you and I might be a fight risk. I take my own counsel and remain quiet as I push against his microphone and continue down the stairs.

"April Snow, do the Wagners still contend this was, in fact, a CIA hit?"

For Pete's sake, I wish Leslie hadn't done that. Not that wishes ever got me anything.

"No comment." I slide into my car and slam the door.

Chuck follows to the driver's side. He presses his face close to the glass, and I can make out the individual needle pricks from his most recent plug job. I put my car in reverse and back out slowly enough to give him time to clear.

Chapter 17

I feel like a national champion as I park my car in front of our office. I walk into the reception area with a large pizza in one hand and an ice-cold six-pack in the other. "You hungry, sensei?"

Howard's laugh booms from his office, making me smile so wide my face hurts. "I heard a rumor somebody did some serious butt-kicking in court today."

Talk about stealing somebody's thunder. "How did you know already?"

"Small town, news travels fast." He shrugs. "Plus, Lane called. He's madder than a cornered badger."

I set the pizza on my desk. "I suppose he'll just have to get used to it as long as I'm in town."

Howard flips the top on the pizza box. "In Lane's mind, he'll just get even at the trial."

That truth hits home hard. This is just the arraignment. The real prize is an acquittal, and I don't have a solid plan on that just yet—no point in bringing tomorrow's problems into today.

I pop the top on one of the beer cans. "Judge Rossi is awfully complimentary about your litigation skills."

A blush covers his cheeks and ears. "Ms. Margaret is always complimentary. She's absolutely golden."

"Well, maybe. I don't know about that. The judge seems tough to me."

Howard covers his mouth as he talks with his mouth full of pizza. "Tough? You'd be tough, too, if you buried three husbands and your only two sons."

I rock back on my heels. I know better. Both Mama and Granny have always cautioned me about judging people before I know their story.

Here I thought Judge Rossi was hard because she's a black woman in a position of power, living in a white man's world. But as I reexamine the courtroom events that transpired this morning, I understand she took mercy on Vance while prodding Lane to do better.

That's not hard, that's a compassionate teacher. One with a lot of heartaches and physical pain she's dealing with on a personal level.

Howard has the right of it. Judge Rossi is the golden rule personified.

"She doesn't have any family left?"

Howard takes a sip of beer. "She's got plenty of family left. She has two daughters that are frequently after her to come live with them. "

"That sounds like it would be nice. It has to be lonely living by herself."

Howard shakes his head. He takes another sip of beer.

"What?" I know he thinks I've said something stupid.

"One of her daughters has five kids, and the other six. There is no way Margaret has the time or the inclination to have to put up with babies on a full-time basis again."

I want to ask what happened to her sons and her former husbands. I'm sure Howard knows. Still, it seems morbid to ask. Not to mention it's none of my business.

"Oh, I need to ask a favor," I blurt.

"What's that?"

My shoulder tightens as the guilt gorilla jumps on my back again. "I want to go with Dusty on a trip to Birmingham this weekend. They're leaving Friday morning. Do you think you could let me take off?"

He stiffens subtly. "Sure, but before you leave, I need you to do something with the Raley case. Jared has already called twice this morning asking if you have made any progress with his case."

Well, that's a buzzkill. To say I'm regretting taking Jared Raley's money is now officially an understatement. The research I've done on drones hasn't turned up anything of any particular use. Besides, without Mrs. Raley's assistance, there's no way the case will fly. No pun intended.

"I think there may be a fundamental problem with the case," I confide in Howard.

"Well yeah, like there's no real statutes on drones to date."

I wish that were the biggest issue with the case. "It may be a bit more complicated than that."

His brow creases. "How so?"

"I have a suspicion Mrs. Raley wasn't so upset about the neighbor taking pictures of her topless."

"Really? Why do you think that?"

"Umm, because I think they're sleeping together." There the cat is out of the bag.

Howard's eyes bug out, reminiscent of a cartoon character. "Oh! Oh, I see. Do you think Mr. Raley knows this?"

Even if he did know, I'm not sure Mr. Raley would admit it. "I don't think anybody knows for sure yet. I've just seen a few things that have convinced me she's having an affair with her neighbor."

"I see. That would change the complexion of the case dramatically." Howard drains his first beer and pops open a second one. "Still, we'll need to know for sure before we continue."

"How do I do that? I don't even know her. It's not like I can go up to her and say, 'Hey Crystal, are you messing around behind Jared's back?'"

Howard snorts. "Right, let's just say I'd appreciate it if you didn't do that. No, I have a young gentleman in town this week who does some investigative work for me when he can. If he obtains evidence of an affair between Mrs. Raley and her neighbor, the information would be helpful during the settlement phase of Mr. Raley's divorce."

This catches me off guard. "Divorce settlement? That's skipping a few steps, isn't it, Howard? At least a few domestic disturbance calls."

"Where do you think this is heading, April? If she is having an affair, divorce is most likely somewhere in their future."

"I don't think Jared would agree to a divorce. He's still in complete denial. Besides, he's so smitten by her, I don't think he could clear the fog of love away long enough to see the truth regardless of any transgressions on Crystal's part."

"Many men are still in love with their wives when they serve or are served papers. There isn't a whole lot that can be done. Broken is broken. At least if your beliefs are true, we can forewarn him with evidence so the news will be easier to accept, and he can be proactive."

I don't like what Howard is telling me. I don't want to be the one to destroy a man's life, even if it is just a sad delusion.

"It's the best we can do for him, April. It's the responsible thing to do."

"I suppose so," I agree reluctantly. "Responsible reeks."

"I'm not going to disagree." Howard lifts a notepad from my desk and writes down a number. "This is the number for Vander. Go ahead and call him today."

"I have to call him?"

Howard grabs another slice of pizza and tracks toward his office. "It's your commission, April. Besides, you can explain the particulars of the case to Michael VanDerveer better than I can. No need to muddle the details with me being the go-between."

Michael VanDerveer? Just the mention of his name turns

my body into a living dichotomy. The hair on the back of my neck stands up at the same time I get a warm sensation flashing across my chest. I have not thought of that boy in years. Yet, the very mention of his name still has a visceral effect on me.

Michael VanDerveer, Vander as we called him in school, is the template for the good-looking, crazy-eyed Southern boy. His bronze-tinted skin and aquiline nose hint at a seasoning of Italian blood on some days and American Indian on others. He's a few inches short of six feet but perfectly proportioned with broad shoulders and an unnaturally small waist just above his muscular buttocks.

Even though he had movie-star good looks and lots of female friends in school, I don't ever remember him dating.

Most of the guys in school cut him a wide berth. They never talked about him or to him. Their only interaction with him was on the baseball diamond or the football field. Other than that, he kept to himself, and the guys preferred it that way too.

He had a mercurial temperament and a short fuse.

I still remember "the fight" during my sophomore year in high school. I had a thing for Lee Darby at the time, who was a catcher and relief pitcher for our team.

For three weeks straight, Lee had asked me to come to a baseball game and watch him play. It was the last regular-season game of the year. It's a testimony to just how cute Lee was that I showed up.

Guntersville was playing a team out of Huntsville that day. Things were out of hand by the third inning, and the Huntsville team started talking smack.

First, it was cocky, and then it turned vulgar. The batter on deck for the Huntsville team began to make obscene gestures at me and my girlfriend, Brandy Howell.

True to form, I yelled something back at him, real inventive like, "I'm not interested in little boys."

The batter stepped to the chain-link fence and began to

describe to me in vivid details which of my orifices he would put his "bat" into and in what order.

I was facing third base, and I never saw it coming, so I know the Huntsville batter didn't suspect his doom was approaching. One minute he was verbally abusing me, and the next minute, his nose and front teeth were protruding through the chain-link fence as Vander held him against it.

"Do you talk to your mama like that?" The words Vander spoke were irrelevant. His tone and inflection were a threat of further bodily harm to come. "Does it make you feel big to pick on girls?"

I may have missed Vander coming over from third base, but I saw the Huntsville batter who had been on deck running toward Vander with his bat held high. I wanted to scream a warning, but my voice froze. Lee was running after the batter too, but he had gotten a late start, and in his catcher's gear, I knew he wasn't going to be able to stop the first swing of the bat to Vander's head.

With eerie calmness, Vander spun the batter he had trapped against the chain-link fence toward home plate as the other batter swung. The teammate's aluminum bat made a sickening sound as it smashed into the young man's shoulder.

The batter stared in horror as his teammate crumpled into a fetal position and reddish-orange dust puffed into the air around him.

As the recently arrived batter's jaw dropped from his error, his nose flattened to his face when Vander's right hand smashed into it. He cupped his hands over his broken nose as blood flowed freely between his fingers seconds before Vander swept his legs, causing him to fall next to his comrade.

If that had been it, it might've been kinda cool. You know, the smaller guy takes on two bigger guys with baseball bats who are being rude to two of the girls from our school. It's kind of a feel-good story.

There's only one word to describe Michael VanDerveer. If you were to ask a hundred people who knew who he was, I bet ninety-five of them would say the same thing. Intense.

Not just fierce like he likes to win, or he won't quit, I mean a scary, close to out-of-control intensity. The other five folks would just call him crazy.

Both Huntsville batters were on the ground writhing in pain, and Lee was still ten feet away from Vander. Both benches cleared, but they wouldn't arrive in time. Nobody arrived in time to help the downed batters.

Vander proceeded to stomp on both the batters with his steel cleats. Their screams haunt me to this day. As do Vander's eyes. I'll never be able to forget how he glared at them.

I have no doubt he planned to stomp them to death.

Lee arrived and looked like he would pull Vander back, but he, too, saw the murder in Vander's eyes. Lee took a step back from the melee.

The first Huntsville player coming to his teammates' aid, Vander knocked out cold with a vicious right hook. The player collapsed to the ground; his arms held straight out with his elbows locked as he twitched silently in the dust.

The next two Huntsville players arrived at the same time and tackled Vander in tandem. They rolled in the dirt with him until the coaches came and separated the boys and subdued Vander.

The umpire called the game, and Guntersville was forced to forfeit the game. Not a significant loss considering we were well on the way to losing before the fight broke out.

I couldn't help but notice Vander had escaped the melee without a single injury. Well, not escaped totally, as his baseball scholarship to Troy was rescinded the next week. The Troy coach said Vander was a bad fit for their team culture.

Vander graduated a couple months later. I think I heard the next year he joined the service. I remember thinking I'd hate to be the enemy combatant to cross paths with him.

I'm proud of myself after I make the call to Vander. I'm really getting the hang of this professional thing. Despite all I know about the guy, I was able to keep that compartmentalized as we agreed to meet at Hot Mugs to exchange the Raley folder and sign the contract.

I'd never admit it to anyone, but I do find it cool that many of the people I work with, I already know their history. When I relocate to a metropolitan area, the probability of me having already met a private investigator I'm hiring for the first time will be extraordinarily low.

One of the attractions of the big city is your ability to re-create yourself. Nobody knows about your most embarrassing moments. There's no one to remind you of the time you failed. You also get a complete do-over with a new lease on your future.

Yet I've been home a few weeks now, and other than bumping heads with that backstabbing Jackie Rains, nobody has brought up any of my failings.

If Deputy Becky Gray doesn't hold a grudge for me having knocked her front teeth out, people are more forgiving than I imagined. Maybe in small towns, folks let bygones be bygones.

Still, I'm anxious to move on and start my life. I need to earn some serious money and start climbing the corporate ladder.

I must check the job board first thing when I get home. I've been busy the last few days. Still, I can't lose focus that my stay in Guntersville is just a temporary layover on the way to my destiny.

Blast it. I forgot about Granny again. There is no way I can face Daddy if I don't keep my promise and go see her. I call Granny's number before it slips my mind again.

"Hello?"

She sounds distracted. "Hey, Granny, it's April."

"April who?"

I'm speechless. How many Aprils does she know? Oh no,

is Granny getting dementia?

"I'm just kidding, sweetie. Ralph told me to say that when you called."

Well, that's just mean. But it sounds like Daddy.

"I guess you got me."

"When are you coming to see me?"

"I thought I could swing by after work. Say about five?"

"No."

"Ma'am?"

"Oh, not you, April." I hear her breathing heavily, and then she says under her voice, "Stop it."

If it weren't Granny, I'd be wondering if someone was with her. But Grandpa has been dead for a long time, and she lives by herself.

"Did I catch you at an inconvenient time, Granny?"

"I'm sorry, sweetie. What were you saying?"

"That I could come by at five." How is it that suddenly I get the feeling she's doing me a favor letting me come by?

"That'll be great. I have a surprise for you."

"That's what Daddy said."

"Stop it!" She drops her phone. When she picks up, she says with a flustered tone, "April can I call you back? Or wait, no, I'll just see you at five, okay?"

"Okay. Yes, ma'am." I hang up the phone and feel as if I have been dismissed. I mean, I called her. I was told to go visit her. How did this get turned around to where I'm inconveniencing her schedule? And most importantly, what is my surprise?

It sounded like someone kept messing with Granny while she was on the phone with me. I swear, if the surprise is I'm getting a new grandpa, I'm not going to be happy. Not that I wouldn't be pleased for Granny, but that's no surprise for me.

I pull into a parking space in front of Hot Mugs next to a sleek, black Ducati motorbike.

Without thinking, I check my makeup and feel like slapping myself. If there is ever a man in this world and life you do not want to attract to you, it's Michael VanDerveer. Smart people don't attract dangerous things into their lives.

It was interesting talking to him on the phone. He was all business and all about the facts.

Yet there's no hiding the sensuality in the cadence and timbre of his voice. I can't recall ever having had an actual conversation with him in high school. I always admired him from afar. If his voice was the same in high school, it's easier to understand why so many girls kept company with him even when he didn't date them.

My eyes haven't fully adjusted to the dimly lit interior of the coffee shop when he strides out of the shadows. Dressed in black riding leathers, his hair shaved tight on the side and spiked on top, he looks every bit as dangerous as I remember him to be twelve years earlier.

His predatory eyes lock on mine as his lips thin. "Ms. Snow?"

"April," I say on a breathy exhale.

He extends his hand. "Vander."

Accepting his hand, I study his eyes. They're forest green with specs of turquoise and gold. He has a way of setting them on me that blasts to the center of my core. As if I were not only naked in front of him, but my soul laid open for him to read.

I can't resist and push out with my "gifts," eager to glean what I can. I don't care if it's wrong; I'm possessed with a hunger to know.

The slightest hint of a grin breaks his steely gaze. "I'd ask you to dance, but they don't have a dance floor."

"Pardon?" I follow his eyes down to our hands. "Oh, sorry." I nearly shove his hand back at him.

He motions over his shoulder. "I've got us a booth back there if you want to grab a coffee and talk."

That only makes sense, but for some reason I didn't anticipate spending time with him, and his question gives me a start. I don't know what I was thinking. It's not like I would just hand him a folder, have him sign the contract, and that would be the end of it.

He slides into a booth at the back of the coffee shop. I sit across from him.

"Elaborate for me, April. How far do you want this to go?"

I blush as my body considers his comment as a double entendre. "What do you mean, how far?"

Vander leans back casually. His eyes scan me so thoroughly it feels as if my skin is being caressed. "Do you want a verbal confirmation? Pictures?" He grins devilishly. "Maybe a live stream feed of them getting it on?"

"Good grief, I don't think that will be necessary."

Vander raises his eyebrows. "It depends on how much in love your husband is with his wife. Don't underestimate a man's power of denial when he's holding on to the woman of his dreams. I've heard some outlandish explanations. You'd be surprised how a husband will try to explain how a photo of their wife and best friend naked in bed doesn't necessarily mean they were having sex. Videos have a way of squashing those explanations. Especially if you get the money shot."

My jaw drops open.

This is feeling like a tawdry plan. The last thing I would ever want to do is show a devoted husband like Jared Raley, a porn film starring Crystal and his neighbor. Is that what this has devolved into?

"I really don't want us to do anything illegal."

Vander genuinely laughs. Once he regains his composure, he says, "That's so cute. Just remember what they say, it's only illegal if you get caught."

"I just don't think we should take any unnecessary risk by setting up cameras or anything."

"They're already there."

Now I'm confused. "We haven't signed a contract yet. Why would you have already done that?"

His long lashes and eyelids hood over his predatory eyes. "They have smart TVs, laptops, and cell phones. I have all the video cameras I need."

That hangs in the air for a moment while I try to get my mind around it. When I do, my back stiffens. "People can really do that?"

"Well, some of us. I don't know about just *people*."

This is not an easy decision. Especially since I feel one hundred percent sure I'm correct about Crystal. I should tell Jared my suspicions first and see if he acts on the information.

Really? The man has all the info I do, and he thinks he married an angel. I already have my answer.

Maybe if we had a picture or two of Crystal's extramarital activity. Surely, Jared wouldn't be in denial then.

Vander is correct. Jared will explain away anything that speaks negatively about Crystal's devotion to him. It would have to be overwhelming evidence to convince him to drop the ill-conceived lawsuit against his neighbor.

"I guess all the video proof you can get."

"It's best. You don't have to use it, but it's better to have it in case the husband goes into deep denial."

I appreciate the sensibility of his comment. The longer I stay in his company, the more the hairs on the back of my neck ease back into place.

I slide the information folder to him. "Crystal's picture, address, and background information is in there. You said you had a contract for me to sign?"

Vander pulls an envelope from the inside of his jacket. Inside the envelope are two copies of the contract. I sign one, hand it to him, and put the other in my purse.

"You know I know you." That pops out of my mouth, unplanned. "Well, not *know* you, but we went to the same high school."

A smile graces his face that promises untold sexual fulfillment. "I know you, too. I sorta had the hots for you back in high school."

My brain short-circuits. I'm not expecting that newsflash. "You never even talked to me."

"Seriously?" he laughs. "You had so many boys sniffing around you. Nah, I'm the jealous type. I don't share well. Besides, your brother Chase helped me out a lot in baseball when I was a freshman. It's sort of a taboo thing to mess with a friend's kid sister."

What? This is all coming at me too fast. Then again, do I even want to know this? I mean, this is Michael VanDerveer. Danger personified.

He stands and lays down a twenty for the coffees. "This shouldn't take long. I should have you something no later than the end of next week."

Vander walks out of the coffee shop without another word to me. It should have been impossible, but age and the black leather riders somehow have improved his buttocks.

Chapter 18

The best explanation of my attitude while driving to Granny's is "bent." I'm drowning in legal work and need to pack for the paranormal excursion.

The only reason I'm going to see her is that my daddy has shamed me into it, well, and the surprise. So help me, if the surprise is that she has a new lover, I am never going to go see Granny again.

Funny what lies I tell myself when I'm feeling indignant and put upon.

Going to Granny's is an excursion. Her farm is located off a county road that was asphalted back in the fifties. It's two lanes if both drivers are in subcompact cars and a one-way if you're driving a truck.

I turn onto the gravel path that leads up to the concrete block farmhouse. It takes me a few minutes to open the gate, pull through, and close it back.

Driving up the gravel path, I can see Granny out front sitting on the porch waiting for me. She must have run her boyfriend off. Good, I didn't want to meet the wrinkly old cuss anyway.

I give a shudder as a vision of Granny going at it with a stranger materializes in my mind. I struggle to tear it out of my brain before it roots in my mind's eye forever.

Pulling in a deep breath, I shut my car door. It'll only take an hour. That's all that is required. I should be able to do that standing on my head. Right?

"I hope you made enough of that tea for both of us," I say.

She stands and gives me a hug as I top the stairs of the porch. "It's good to see you, sweetie. I'm sorry about the mess. I wasn't able to tidy up before you came."

Granny looks like she has just come from the salon. She has always been one of the most put-together women I know. Honestly, I don't think she'd run down to the grocery store for a forgotten item without her makeup and hair being done.

"Have a seat while I go get another glass."

"I can get it," I say.

"I doubt you remember where the glasses are," she says with a half-laugh, disappearing through the screen door.

Ow. That sort of smarts.

I choose the rocker on the opposite side of the table where the pitcher of tea sits. There's a light breeze blowing across the porch carrying the scent of the pine forest from my right. Two mockingbirds do a mating dance in and out of the dogwoods in the front yard.

My stress magically melts. My shoulders relax, and my lungs become unrestricted as I take a deep breath.

It has been ages since I sat on this porch looking out over the bush-hogged meadow that serves as Granny's front yard. How long has it been? I count in my head.

Whoa. It's been eight long years since I enlisted Granny's help to secure the opportunity for me to travel to Tuscaloosa and go to school at Alabama.

Mama and Daddy wanted me to stay close to home the first year and attend junior college. The thought of not going to Alabama for my freshman year horrified me as my friends were headed either to Tuscaloosa, Auburn, or to work. In my mind at the time, a junior college was for people who couldn't hack the real world or college.

I had a few friends in law school who had started their higher education at junior colleges. I'd never admit it to Mama, but they were right as my first year at Alabama was near-disastrous.

Motion to the left catches my eye, and I see a small black and white kid make its way across the gravel drive. It stops and munches on some wildflowers. I can imagine her funky malodor from here, and my nose wrinkles with the memories of how my brothers smelled after playing with the goats all day. Still, she's adorable.

I scan the adjoining fields to see where the rest of the goats are today. I know from experience Granny doesn't let them run wild in the front lot.

Granny comes out of the house and fills my glass.

"Sweetened, I hope," I say.

"You could say that." Her lips purse as if she's trying not to smile.

"One of the baby goats is out." I point toward the black and white cutie.

"That's Maleficent. She's my current resident diva. She'll start complaining to get back into the pen with the rest of them before too long. She can't ever make up her mind where her place is."

I take a sip of my tea and nearly spit it out as it burns the back of my throat. "What is this?"

Granny becomes so tickled she can't answer me.

"Seriously? What the heck did you put in this Granny?"

"It's a new recipe for tea that your brother Chase shared with me," she says in between giggles.

I sniff the tea and confirm it has enough alcohol in it to put a horse to sleep. Sipping it tentatively, I confirm my fears. "Granny, this is Long Island Iced Tea."

"I'm pretty sure that's what Chase calls it, too." She takes another swig of it. "Beats the tarnation out of sun tea."

"Granny..." Oh, never mind. Chase is such an idiot. If it were Dusty, I'm sure he would've done it thinking it was a joke. The trouble with Chase is, the bonehead might actually think it's a version of tea. I would raise a fuss about it, but she really does seem to be enjoying it, and truthfully, a stout drink might be just what the doctor ordered for me.

I watch the kid work her way closer toward the house. "You don't worry about somebody accidentally running over her?"

"Maleficent?" She shrugs. "I suppose, but the way she's wired, if I try to keep her in the goat pen, she'll just want to get out that much worse.

"Besides, your daddy, uncle, and your brothers are about the only ones that come to visit me. They usually pick her up and put her back with the others when they come down the drive."

It strikes me how lonely it must be to live out on this farm all by herself when four men once occupied the same house with her.

"Granny, have you ever thought about moving in with Mama and Daddy, or maybe Howard?"

She flashes a toothy grin super-fueled by alcohol. "Oh, they offer all the time. I know Howard could use help at his house, but I'm selfish. This is my place; this is where I belong. All the memories of my family are here. I am the curator of those memories for my family.

"Besides, Howie always was a particular boy. We'd get on each other's nerves eventually."

I'm sure to some folks, it wouldn't seem wise for anyone nearing eighty years old to be living secluded on a farm. As I enjoy Granny's company, with a light buzz from our special tea, the breeze wafts the familiar smells of hay and pine across the porch. The orange sun retreats below the far mountain, and it fades to pink as I watch.

Granny's decision to stay on the farm is perfectly sensible to me now. This farm is Granny, and Granny is the farm.

Not to make everything about me, but I can't help but be envious of my Granny. I thought one day, I too would belong to a place. I've always envisioned that place as a grade-A, high-rise commercial building in a large metropolitan business district.

Today I haven't a clue where I belong.

I know my legal talents need the room to grow—room only a large city can provide. Yet my first wins have been and always will have taken place here in Guntersville. The last place on earth I thought I would be right now.

Most disconcerting, and the fact that erodes my sense of purpose, is I've enjoyed the past few weeks at home. To move forward, I must leave all this behind and not deceive myself that I'll be able to have a foot in both worlds.

The legal profession is even more demanding than I ever imagined. It is a jealous god who consumes all your time.

I wish I knew what would make me the happiest.

Stop it, April. Keep to the plan.

See. Small town life is like kudzu. You don't even notice it on the side of the road, and the next thing you know, the vines have tied around your legs and arms, and it becomes difficult to extricate yourself.

If folks stay long enough, the soles of their feet shoot out milky white veins that root into the rich, red clay. Then it's impossible to ever leave Alabama. They stay in that place, die, and become one with the soil. Their blood darkens the clay's shade of red, and their body nourishes the never-ending binding vine that traps the citizens in this small town.

I so need one of my applications to land me a job away from here.

"Sweetie, I can practically smell the smoke coming out of your ears from all that thinking. What do you have on your mind?"

Granny is an excellent listener, but I don't have the faintest idea of how to explain to a woman who is in love with her life what I'm feeling. "Granny, how did you know this was the life you wanted?" The question tumbles out of my mouth before I can recall it.

She tilts her head. "What other life would I have chosen, dear?"

True. Granny's generation grew up when the patriarchal system limited women's career choices. There wasn't an option for her. She knew early on she would be a homemaker after a brief stint as a nurse or schoolteacher.

"Sorry, I forget opportunities were more limited for women in your day."

Granny makes a derisive snort, then empties her tumbler. "What?"

"Sweetie, your granny had a career with the church before and after my children. I didn't quit until your brothers came along. That's while I took care of my first and most important career of running a household and supporting my husband in his effort to make this farm turn a profit"

"I didn't mean to offend you."

"You can't offend me about my career choices, sweetie. Besides, I had a successful forty-year marriage. I also had more excitement than I can shake a stick at." She points to the sunset, now a bruised purple. "And I own a view to die for every evening. What's not to like about my career choice?"

"I know you enjoyed being a homemaker, but don't you wish you could have been a—I meant, like, being a scientist or a doctor or maybe even an artist?"

Granny refills her tumbler. "You know, April, it's good different people want different things. If I wanted, I could spend time wondering why my granddaughter wants to move to New York or Boston away from her family. For the life of me, I don't understand why you want a career where you will often see people at their worst. Yet, if that's what you think you need to do to find your happiness, your family and I will support your decision."

She rocks her chair and closes her eyes. "Child, you need to stop judging other people's life decisions, lest ye be judged."

"I wasn't judging Granny. I'm just saying you didn't have

the same opportunities. You couldn't do anything exciting in your life."

She rolls her head onto her shoulder and cackles. "Exciting? Sweetie, that's why I finally stopped working with the church. That's why I gave it up when your brothers were born. And just for the record, I could've taken the route of my cousin Lily and gone into reporting. But then I may have ended up like Lily."

I have no idea who she's talking about. "Lily?"

She shakes her head as her smile fades. "Another day, another time."

See, that's the problem with having a conversation with the older generations. When you get too close to something they don't want to discuss, they just shut down.

I'm aggravated Granny doesn't understand my point about her generation of women being kept from their full potential. It's common knowledge they were marginalized. Still, I sit with her in companionable silence and watch the horizon turn navy blue. As dusk settles across the field, Maleficent cries out.

"Silly little thing."

I shift my gaze to Granny's silhouetted face.

"Every evening, without fail, she misses the rest of the herd and wants back in their pen."

"Have you ever left her out?"

She laughs. "I'm afraid she would worry herself to death."

I rub my hands over my arms as the temperature drops noticeably and gooseflesh pops up on my skin. "I can put Maleficent up for you when I leave."

"Thank you." She leans forward and arches her back in a stretch. "Are you ready for your surprise?"

I'm already surprised I had forgotten about the promised gift. I can feel a goofy smile claiming my face as Granny stands. "Yes, ma'am."

"Don't move. I'll be right back." She disappears into the house, and the screen door slaps the door frame with a *clack*.

I look longingly at the tea pitcher. I debate how badly my driving would be impaired if I have another serving. I have a warm, comfortable buzz going, but it will end soon.

Surprisingly, self-control wins out as I lean back in my rocking chair. The last thing I need in my life is a DUI on my record while I'm job hunting.

Granny hollers through the screen, "Close your eyes."

"What? No." Never trust a Snow not to pull a practical joke.

"Close your eyes, April May!"

"Fine." I close my eyes and wait for something awful to happen. The screen door slaps shut, and I hear the padding of Granny's Clark slip-on loafers on the weathered porch boards.

There is a weight dropped in my lap. Whatever it is, it begins to roll off my lap, and I clutch at it. I get a handful of fur, and my eyes fly open. "What in the world?"

Granny looks as if she has just been awarded the "best grandmother in the world" award. "Isn't he beautiful?"

I try to steady the squirming furball and lift him to my face. I turn him from tail view to face me. The only thing I can think to say is "Why?"

"Vivian said you were in the boathouse all alone." She points at the silver-and-black furball I'm holding at arm's length. "You need a guard dog. He's a Keeshond. They're excellent guard dogs, and he loves the water."

Granny rubs the top of his head. "He's perfect."

Right. Perfect. Just what April needs is something to take care of because she doesn't have enough to do. I set the puppy on the porch. "Granny, I appreciate it, but I'm too busy for a puppy."

"Nonsense. It's not that difficult to take care of a puppy. Besides, he'll be great company for you. Your mama agreed with me."

"I know you two mean well, but I really don't need anything else to take care of right now."

Something scratches my right leg. I look down and lock eyes with the soulful, chocolate-colored pleading eyes looking up at me.

Good Lord, he's too cute for his own good. He releases a tiny, high-pitched whine as he tilts his head to the right.

"Whoops, looks like he's already claimed you."

Now that's just silly. People claim dogs, not the other way around. I look back down at the four pounds of fur. He lifts his right front paw, taps my leg twice, and then turns his head to the other side.

Well, this puppy seems exceptionally smart for a dog. He is the exception with his extraordinary level of intelligence, and it isn't too much of a stretch to think he's claiming me.

I know I'm beat and make a show of my frustration by sighing dramatically. I lift the little darling from the porch and hold him at arm's length as I examine him from tail to nose. His entire hind section shakes from side to side as he attempts to wag his curled tail.

This is unbelievable. I can't resist the puppy's charm and pull him against my chest as I stroke the top of his head.

"Does he have a name?"

"No, I thought it would be best if you named him."

I shake my head. "What am I supposed to do with him when I'm traveling?"

"Your family has already agreed to take care of him when you can't be at home."

Anger flashes brightly in my mind. "They knew?"

"Sure, they did. They all thought it was a crackerjack idea."

Okay, my dog is, like, the cutest thing I've ever seen. Plus, he really likes me. He also feels oh so good against my hands.

However, that doesn't excuse my family for conspiring to set me up with a dog I don't need. I mean, this is seriously messed up. Dogs are a lot of responsibility.

"I can't believe y'all did this behind my back."

Granny's face crinkles. "Behind your back? It was a surprise, April. Surprises are supposed to be kept secret."

"It's just it's a big life decision. My family shouldn't have decided this for me."

"Oh, stop with the fake indignation, April. It doesn't suit you."

My temper snaps. "I'm not faking it, Granny. I am indignant!"

"Whatevs," she says with a dismissive wave of her hand.

Seriously? Did my granny just dismiss my feelings as irrelevant while sucking down Long Island Iced Tea? This is like some weird time-warped version of Freaky Friday. My family is incorrigible.

I can't name a single friend who deals with the goofy stuff I must deal with regularly. They all have normal, divorced parents who don't care what they do if they just show up for Thanksgiving and Christmas dinners.

Could I be so lucky? No. Everybody in my family has tried to make decisions for me from the moment I was born. They are always in my business and trying to tell me what I need.

"Don't blame anybody else. I just know from experience the area around your parents' boathouse is—let's just say a little murky, and I'm not talking about the water. Given you have the "gifts" from both sides of the family, I thought a loyal guard dog could offer you some peace of mind. Not to mention when you do move to an apartment in a big city, I'll rest easier if I know you have a guard dog."

I continue to stroke my puppy's head as he licks my wrist. As much as I don't want it to, what Granny says makes some sense. The next time the old man in the lake crashes in on my thoughts, having a miniature bear to comfort me might decrease my anxiety.

"You should've asked." My anger has left me, and my voice sounds like I'm whining.

Granny holds out her arms. "My mistake. I'm sorry. I didn't mean to offend you by making the decision for you. Just give me the little rascal back, and I'll take care of him.

He'll enjoy the farm well enough."

I turn sideways as I clutch the furball protectively to my chest. "No!"

"No?" Granny frowns. "April, you're the most conflicted person I know."

"I don't want to break his heart. I mean, he's already claimed me, and if I give him back now, there's no telling what sort of psychological damage it will cause him. That level of psychological trauma at this age, geez, it could ruin him."

Granny smiles. "Indeed. It might just do that."

"It's not like I don't have room for him in the boathouse. And, like you say, living out on the dock separate from the house, it's good to have a guard dog."

"Yes, it's always safer to have a protector."

"Safer is a good thing." I release the silver hair on his back that I'm clutching and scratch between his ears. His eyelids hood as he leans into my fingers. He lays his head against my chest and calms.

Granny sits down. "Speaking of moving, have you had any job offers yet?"

It occurs to me to lie, but I can't bring myself to do it when she just gave me a gift. "No, but I have several good leads. It shouldn't be too long."

"Are you checking out Chattanooga and Birmingham, too?"

She and Daddy must be discussing my options. "No, Granny. I was thinking a good bit bigger than those cities."

She folds her hands in front of her. "I'm not meddling. I'm simply curious."

The puppy abruptly falls to his side as sleep overtakes him. I continue to run my hand idly down his side. The cotton-like texture of his fur is addictive.

"Somebody got hit by the sleepy stick."

"Do you think I should let him sleep with me?"

Granny's lips thin. "I don't know. They can get as big as

seventy pounds. That's a lot of dog in the bed."

I hadn't thought about that. "Yep, gonna be a laundry basket and a fluffy blanket for you, little man."

"How are things with you and Howard at the law firm?"

I give a start, and the puppy nearly rolls off my lap. "Oh my gosh, what time is it?"

"Almost nine."

My heart freezes. Nine o'clock? I haven't even begun packing, not to mention I need to get in early tomorrow to put everything in order before the end of the day.

"I'm sorry I have to run, Granny."

We stand at the same time, and she puts her hands out toward me. "Hold on, I need to bless you first."

For Pete's sake. "Granny, I don't have time."

"Nonsense. Everybody has time for a blessing. Now stand still."

I've been to my fair share of tent revivals growing up. There, the preacher yelled his prayer loudly out to the masses.

Granny's blessings are silent. Which can be worse. Because you never know when she's close to finishing, and she always seems to take longer when she's blessing me.

I'm about to give up and tell her I really must leave when she opens her eyes and smiles. The light is funny on the porch as her face seems to glow like it has a backlight behind her skin.

"So, am I all good now?" I tease.

She shrugs. "Well, I can't be the judge of that. But I do know he will protect you."

"Good to know." I give her a hug and a peck on the cheek. "Thank you for the puppy."

"You're welcome. I hope you two have many happy years together."

I wave to Granny as I turn my car around. Puppy is content in my lap as I traverse the long, gravel drive.

Near the gate, my car lights illuminate Maleficent at the

fence line to the left. I set the puppy in the passenger seat and get out to take care of the wayward kid.

"You want in?" I put my hand on the gate to the goat pen and give her a quick rub on the ear. She pushes her head more firmly into my hand. I can't help but smile. "Silly little goat."

She slips through as I open the gate. I watch as she trots over to two other goats and immediately rubs against them. I guess she had her adventure and is ready to be home.

Chapter 19

My bags are packed for the trip to Birmingham. I have a persistent feeling I've forgotten something. I double-check to make sure it's not bras, panties, or my toothbrush. Check, check, and check—all good with the critical.

I don't know why I'm worrying. We're going to Birmingham, not out into the woods. If I forget something, I can swing by a store and buy it.

My stomach rumbles, and I realize my plans to go immediately to bed won't work. I'm not a little hungry; I have the mega-munchies.

A quick check of my mini-fridge reveals three bottles of water, a half bottle of flat Dr. Pepper, and some questionable French onion dip. No chips.

One thing about me lately, I'm not too proud to beg.

A quick look toward the house reveals I'm in luck. There's a light on in the kitchen.

I slip on my flip-flops as I pick up my sleeping puppy. He makes a small grunt of protest as I pull him to me. He's so stinking cute and feels so good.

The glass door to the kitchen won't open, and I knock on the glass lightly. Mama peers out and narrows her eyes before unlocking the door and sliding it open. "What's the matter?" Her face brightens. "Aww, you finally went to pick up your little buddy."

Well, that confirms Granny was telling the truth. Mama was in on the conspiracy too.

But I'm already past that. "Yeah, I missed dinner."

"Come on in. I think we have some of the country-fried pork chop leftovers from tonight. If you don't want that, there's a container of pimento cheese to make a sandwich with."

She lifts the puppy from my arms. "Let me see this little bruiser."

"Granny said you wouldn't mind watching him while I'm in Birmingham?" I ask as I pull out the pork chops, mashed potatoes, and country gravy.

"I'll just think of it as training for when I take care of grandbabies when you're on a weekend trip. Assuming my adult children ever give me some."

If I stay in Guntersville much longer, I'll be able to lose the fifteen pounds I'm trying to lose. My mother has a way of killing my appetite.

"Look how cute you are," Mama says to my puppy as she holds him close to her face. "When is this Birmingham trip?"

I put the leftovers in the microwave. "Dusty and the team are leaving Thursday night."

Mama looks confused. "When are you getting back?"

"Sometime Saturday evening." Mama's face contorts. "What?"

"Wanda Neil said you were helping us paint rooms all day Saturday."

My hunger is replaced with nausea. I'm so stupid. How did I forget my promise to Wanda? More importantly, how did I get blackmailed into my commitment to Wanda? "Yeah, that was sort of before Dusty told me he had a job for me this weekend."

Mama's mouth drops open. "What am I supposed to tell her?" She closes her eyes. "I even told her how proud I was that you took the initiative to come help this Saturday."

Suddenly I feel four inches tall. If this conversation continues, I'll need a ladder to climb over the glass door running track. "It was Wanda's idea, Mama."

"I see that now. I knew it sounded odd."

Ouch. "Look, Mama, I needed to see the wife of one of my clients. She'd been admitted to the hospital, and only the family could visit. Wanda helped me out, and inadvertently I sorta, kinda hinted I might be there this Saturday to help paint."

"Sorta, kinda might? You're on the worklist, April."

My gosh, either I have the mother of all migraines coming on, or I'm having an aneurysm. I squeeze the bridge of my nose as I shake my head. "I don't know what to tell you, Mama. Can you talk to her for me?"

She shakes her head. "Sure, baby. I'll explain to my fellow volunteer, high school friend, and loyal client of our family marina how my daughter's promises are conditional promises. On the condition, nothing else comes up."

"Aw, come on, Mama. That's not fair."

She holds my puppy up to her face. "I hope they warned you what you're getting into, little man. Hopefully, you'll have better luck keeping her straight than I have."

She holds my puppy out to me, and I accept him into my left hand. She leaves the kitchen without even saying goodnight to me.

Fine. Be disappointed in me. Take a number. I'm a disappointment to everybody lately.

I grab a Dr. Pepper, silverware, and my plate of leftovers with one arm while balancing my puppy on the other. I navigate my way back to my apartment.

Sitting down cross-legged on my floor, I set my dinner and puppy in front of me. I notice my puppy's nose is white from getting a taste of my gravy.

"Hey, you're supposed to ask first."

He wags his entire back hindquarters as he wraps his

tongue around his nose and makes the country gravy disappear.

He's so adorable. His company will do me good, too, since I'm feeling down. It isn't my desire to make it challenging for Mama with Wanda.

When I promised Wanda, I had every intention of keeping my part of the bargain. Or at least I thought so at the time.

It's a miracle with everything I have going on that this is the first time something has slipped my mind. In the past few months, I've had several people's lives in my hands, too many encounters of the paranormal kind, and near-misses with a couple of "almost Mr. Rights." All the while, I'm fighting to hold onto my dream of being a high-powered, big-city defense lawyer.

Sue me if some Sasquatch-sized nurse blackmails me into signing up for paint day at the women's shelter, and I forget. I mean, it's not like I killed somebody.

My puppy tries to edge his way back to my mashed potatoes and gravy. "Hey, no." I cut off a small bite of pork chop and hold it up to him.

His razor-sharp white teeth seem to flash out of his muzzle, and the bite of pork chop is gone.

"Dang. You're like an alien puppy with those teeth."

We finish off the leftovers together. Well, the puppy was satiated at the halfway point, so I had to do the heavy lifting at the end.

I empty my laundry basket and fold one of my throw blankets inside the basket. Lifting my puppy, I hold his muzzle close to my face. "Okay, this is your bed. I'll set it right next to mine, so you won't be lonely. We'll need to discuss what you want to be called in the morning. Try to think about what names you like. You know I can't call you puppy forever."

The moment I turn out the light, he whimpers. I roll over onto my stomach and lay my hand into the basket to rub him. "I'm right here, little puppy. But you gotta get used to your bed."

It's faint at first. So faint, it barely registers with me. But the intensity of the volume continues to grow until I can't ignore it any longer.

"April, April, come swim with me."

The taunt repeats over and over like a broken record in my head. I try to dismiss it as a symptom of the migraine coming on. But the migraine ceased the moment I left my parents' house.

"April, I want you."

Okay, that gives me the creeps. Seventy future pounds of furry dog flesh in my bed sounds like a great defense mechanism against creepy ghosts.

I lift my puppy out of the basket and pull him to my chest. He licks me below my chin twice, rolls onto his back, and immediately goes to sleep. I must've fallen asleep right after him because I don't remember anything after that.

Chapter 20

Howard is focused on extracting one assurance from me this morning. He wants me to confirm that under no circumstance will Jared Raley reach out to Snow and Associates while I'm in Birmingham.

Despite Jared's retainer check keeping the cash flow gears of Howard's firm well oiled, it appears my cuckold client is just that—*my* client.

I don't savor my pending call to Jared. How do I explain to a distraught husband I changed my work scope from his requested lawsuit against his neighbor to preparation for his imminent divorce? Especially considering I pivoted without his consent.

Sure, I tell myself I'm only doing this to protect my client. I try to soothe my angst with the knowledge that Jared is not strong enough to defend himself. While he nurses a bruised ego, he will be incapable of taking the difficult next steps necessary to protect himself from a toxic relationship.

That's what lawyers do. We protect the interests of our clients.

I'm not procrastinating. I'll tell Jared the truth soon enough. I just don't care to destroy his fantasy world before I receive definitive evidence from Vander. Then I'll call my client and explain his marriage's real status and the legal battle that lies before us.

There's no need to rush to judgment. What I observed in Jerry's Deli may be a misinterpretation of Crystal. The man could be Crystal's brother in town for a visit.

No. If one of my brothers ever splayed their hand across my butt in that manner, they'd be gasping for air from the elbow I plant into their sternum.

I force myself to call Jared. My prayers are not answered as he picks up on the first ring despite my sincere hope he is not available.

"Tell me the good news, April. Please, I need something to give me hope," Jared says.

The desperation I hear in his voice puts a lump in my throat. "The courts are backed up at the moment, so we can't get an assigned date yet."

"But you've filed the complaint. Correct?"

I follow up my little white lie with a deflective half-truth. "Jared, I need to let you know I hired a private investigator to do additional research for our case. We should know all we can before we file our complaint."

"That's good thinking. I bet that creep has all sorts of dirty laundry in his closet."

There might be more than one person's dirty underwear in the closet Vander is digging through. Still, Jared doesn't need to know that until Monday. Or longer if I can put the painful conversation off.

"We'll see how helpful it is, but I need to inform you because private investigators do cost money."

"Do I seem like I'm worried about money? Whatever it takes to nail Craig West's hide to the wall, you do it. I trust you implicitly, April."

My stomach turns painfully, "We'll get him, Jared. I want you to take a break from all this and not even think about the case this weekend. You pay me to worry about it. I'll call you Monday with a fresh update. Alright?"

"I don't know if I can just forget about it."

"I need you to try your best. It's important for your health. Can you do that for me?" I use my sweetest voice.

"Sure, I can, April. I'll do that."

"Awesome. Now you enjoy your weekend. Okay?"

"You too, April."

Keeping this charade up is going to ruin my health. By Monday, I hope Vander has some corroborating evidence, so I know which way the Raley case will break. Then I can better manage the situation and get back in my comfort zone of being honest in my conversations.

If it weren't for the insane money Dusty pays me for paranormal excursions, I'd work on my cases this weekend. That is after I pay my dues to Wanda by painting some walls at the women's shelter.

It doesn't feel responsible for me to leave Guntersville this weekend when I have so many commitments I'm forced to slight in order to go on this trip. Still, everyone has their price where they will damage their reputation, and Dusty knows mine.

Howard strolls to the exit. "What time are you leaving?"

"Five, I guess."

"Do you have the Jared Raley issue put to bed?"

"I think I do. He promised to wait for an update call from me on Monday."

"Good. Why don't you go home and get ready for your trip?"

"Really?"

Howard grins. "Yes, I've got this."

I'm not going to belabor the point. I'll take Howard's gift since it means I won't delay the team leaving for Birmingham.

I reach for the Raley and Wagner files. Holding my hand over the folders, I reconsider. Rather than shove them in my backpack, I file them in the top drawer of my desk.

Looking at them twenty-four seven hasn't helped the last two days. I'm hopeful a three-day break from the information will help me look at them with fresh eyes and reveal a better attack strategy for the cases.

"Okay, I'm outta here," I say.

"Promise me you'll come back in one piece."

A tingling sensation runs up my spine, creating goosebumps on my scalp. Why did Howard have to say that? I'm not sure his concerns aren't valid. "God willing, and if the creek don't rise."

He locks me with a stern gaze. "I expect a smart girl like you to leave when it begins to storm rather than wait for the creek to flood."

I know what he means. "Yes, sir."

Opening the front door, I rush to leave before Howard wants to discuss the dangers further. I bump into Lane. "Sorry, Lane."

His eyes narrow. "April."

He steps back and holds the door open as I pass. And to think I once thought he was attractive for an older fellow. His "disappointed" look is highly unattractive. Someone should tell him.

I quickstep to my car and pry open the door. Working for Howard is the best. There's no chance another employer would let me off Friday and early Thursday afternoon so I could run a side hustle.

Wait a second. As I pass the police precinct two blocks down from our office, I realize why Howard shooed me out of the office.

He didn't want me to hear what he planned to discuss with Lane.

Despite my best efforts to tamp them down, my paranoid tendencies flare. The only thing that comes to mind is Howard may be cutting a deal with Lane on the Wagner case, so it never goes to trial, and the news vans leave Guntersville.

I call the office, and Howard answers. "So what does Lane want?"

"April?"

"Is Lane there to discuss the Wagner case?"

"If he were, it would be a one-sided conversation. That's your case, and I don't know the details."

My shoulders relax as I breathe again. Howard's answer suits me, and my paranoia is soothed. "Why is he at the office?"

Howard chuckles. "Well, if it's any of your business, Miss Nosey, we were discussing a wager on the back nine at the Sawmill Country Club. Hopefully, that'll earn me dinner at The Black Angus on Lane's tab when I trounce him."

I hope he does. "When you win, make sure to order the twenty-eight-ounce Porterhouse cut."

"Geez, that would feed me for a week."

"Hey, don't forget. I have a puppy now, and I work for a skinflint. It's hard to afford puppy food on my salary. I'm sure we could put the leftover steak to use. Of course, if you want to spot me a raise so I can afford some puppy food."

"There'll be a pound of steak in the office fridge for your puppy Monday."

I can't contain my laughter. "All right, I see how you're going to be."

"Don't you have a ghost or something to go film?"

"Yes, I'm almost to the lake house. I'll see you Monday."

"Be careful, see you Monday."

Chapter 21

Chet, the two Early brothers, Jason, and Travis are loading equipment into a new large-capacity cargo van when I pull onto my parents' drive. I guess Dusty is still flush with cash despite his divorce if he's adding capital equipment.

I say hello to the guys and hurry inside to check on my puppy. I call his name, Puppy, as I open the door to my apartment. I step inside and holler his name again.

He doesn't come the second time either. It doesn't bother me much that he failed to come to me. He's too young to know his name. He's also uber-smart, so this may be his way of acting out in objection to his new name.

I check for him in my closet and find a chewed-up flip-flop, but no Puppy. Checking my bathroom, I see a roll of toilet paper spun off the tube, still no Puppy. Last, I get on my hands and knees to check under the bed. I spot two half-eaten crickets and no sign of Puppy.

I sit back on my legs. I'm in an absolute panic.

Stupid right? I didn't even want Puppy, and now I'm terrified I've lost him. I know. It makes no sense.

I hit my screen door at a full run. "Have y'all seen Puppy?" I scream.

Dusty is carrying his binders to the van. "I think Dad's got him in the laboratory."

"The laboratory?" I hustle down my stairs and speed walk toward the glass door.

"Have you put your stuff in the van yet?" Dusty calls out to me.

"I have responsibilities I have to take care of first."

"Your puppy?"

I ignore my brother as I slide the glass door and slam it shut behind me. Dusty wouldn't understand. He only has himself to worry about.

My maternal instincts are kicking in hard. I'm visualizing a little fluff ball exploded in some stupid chemistry experiment.

It doesn't even have to be an experimental accident. Puppy will eat anything.

If Daddy drops anything on the floor, Puppy will happily scarf it up in a millisecond. I can't bear to watch the little fellow die a slow, painful death from some poison he lapped up, mistaking it for a special doggie treat.

I swear, for Daddy to be such a smart man, he sure can be stupid.

Opening the laboratory door, I stomp in without knocking. "Where's Puppy?"

Daddy's head whips around in my direction. "April?"

"Where is he?"

Daddy points to the side of his desk. "In his bed. Asleep."

My knees turn loose as I round the corner of my daddy's desk. Relief floods over me, nearly forcing me to sit.

Puppy is lying on his back with his paws crossed over his eyes. He's so blasted cute with all that fur. I want to pick him up, but he looks blissfully content.

"I thought you were leaving town."

"I am in just a little while." Yeah. I'm going to pick Puppy up. Holding him will slow my heart rate down.

"Then let him be. It took him three hours to go to sleep. I'm not sure I can wear him down a second time."

I respect Daddy's sentiment. Still, I have this intense desire to touch Puppy's soft fur.

Compromising, I briefly rub one of Puppy's ears. He responds by brushing a paw over his ear before covering his eyes again.

"You sure you don't mind?" I ask.

"Nah. He's a good feller. A little rambunctious, but a good puppy."

My mind catches up with the surroundings, and I notice the bed Puppy is in. "Where did the bed come from?"

Daddy looks up from his calculations. "I ran out this morning and picked it up for him. I thought it might be more comfortable than the tile floor down here."

I feel awful. Not only am I abandoning Puppy after his first night in a new home, but I didn't even think to get him a bed so he'd be comfortable. Instead, I tried to make him sleep in a laundry basket. No wonder he cried. He thought he was in puppy prison, and Puppy knew he didn't do anything wrong to deserve that punishment. There is no telling what long-term psychological damage I have inflicted on him, and I haven't even had him a full day.

Parenting bites! There are way too many things to worry about and no manual.

I'm torn. I need to leave now. But I have a powerful desire to stay and play with Puppy and at least attempt to patch things up between us.

I must keep my promise to Dusty. Plus, I need the money. I'll try to make it up to Puppy Sunday night.

"Thank you for watching him. I'll be back Sunday night."

"All right. You be good," Daddy says absentmindedly. He measures a red powder into the clear, boiling liquid inside the beaker over his Bunsen burner.

My mini-meltdown over Puppy has me running the team late. I'm the last to load my luggage.

The Early brothers, Chet, and Luis are driving what Dusty now refers to as the equipment van. Miles rides shotgun in the new passenger van with Liza and me, each on our own bench seat in the back.

"I want to warn you this may very well be one big nothing burger," Dusty says.

Miles turns in his seat to face Liza and me. "The witnesses have changed their story, and it's starting to sound a lot more like Steve Bass committed suicide rather than having been pushed by a spirit."

"That doesn't make any sense. How do you change your story after a couple of weeks? You still saw what you saw," I say.

"Two weeks is long enough for a person to rationalize what they saw and replace it with something logical. It's easier for their mind to handle," Liza says in a detached manner.

"Could be. It could also be everyone was so shocked to witness a man killing himself they manufactured a story. His releasing the grip on the bar becomes a ghost prying Steve's fingers back," Dusty says.

Miles pushes his glasses further up on his nose. "We may come up blank on this trip, but the furnaces have an old and ugly history. I'm looking forward to studying it and putting together an outline of the legends. You know not all the spook stories have to be current to make the hair on the back of your neck stand up."

"People prefer to know they can go experience it themselves if they have a mind to," Dusty grouses.

"That reminds me, April." Miles makes the motion of turning a knob in the air. "If you have any way of turning your ghost radar down, you may want to do it. It's been rumored that when the furnaces were in full swing, it was common for them to lose a few men to accidents during each year."

"How many men over the years, Miles? Are we talking two, six, ten?" I shrug my shoulders. "The number of possible spirits count."

"Seventy-three," Miles says. He studies me for a reaction.

"That could be like walking into a cemetery," I say.

"That's why I'm warning you."

Seventy-three souls all taken in sudden, violent accidents could be constant noise for me once on the property. People who die of old age don't tend to hang around. Those who die unexpectedly through an accident often are a little slow to understand they are dead and need to move across the veil.

I'm getting the distinct feeling I've been suckered into this investigation. It would've been helpful for Dusty to have mentioned the number of lost workers.

Miles reads my face and turns his attention back to the front windshield. I appreciate his silence. It isn't like anyone can help me cope. Only I can adjust my sensitivity. I need to focus all my energy on that task before we reach the furnaces.

Liza drapes her arms over the back of my bench. "I've got something for you."

Her voice pulls me out of my dark space. "A Baby Ruth?"

She grins. "Maybe later." Liza lifts my right hand and places something in my palm. "I know you might object, but I would appreciate it if you wore this. For me."

I open my right palm. The ornate, jeweled silver Orthodox cross is on a heavy, serpentine chain. "Good gracious, Liza, I can't accept this. This had to set you back a fortune."

"It didn't cost me anything. It was my grandfather's."

I try to hand it back to her. "I definitely can't accept a family heirloom." It's not just the value of the item that has me refusing the gift. I'm also shocked to be receiving a present from Liza. Our relationship has been improving, but I thought we were on the mutual respect track, not friendship.

"There's no one left besides me. Anyway, I want you to have it." She snorts. "I need you to wear it. Maybe it will keep some of the demons from chasing you."

My upper lip curls involuntarily with doubt. "Liza, you know I'm not religious like that." Even I know you must believe for crucifixes to work.

Liza falls back against her bench seat. "Most of us aren't. We change our minds when we see things we can't explain, and when our lives are in danger. Besides, April, you're more religious than you think you are."

Her comment unsettles me. If I had a dollar for every time someone has told me I have a religious nature, I could buy the team's dinner tonight.

I don't. I'm the opposite. The ghosts and spirits I encounter are, at best, sad, at their worst, malicious.

Why would an omnipotent entity allow such blights on their creation? If I'm religious, why would God give me "gifts" that draw such abominations to me? It makes no sense.

If anything, I believe I'm cursed rather than a blessed religious individual. My burden? Hiding my "gifts" from the world except for this small group and my family.

"Look at me," Liza says.

I turn in my seat, the cross hot in my palm. "What?"

"I wouldn't kid you about these things. I couldn't have summoned the ominous cross in Paducah to battle Les if you weren't of tremendous faith." She frowns. "I had to draw from your energies too to draw it forth. You made that possible, April."

My eyes shift to the large cross on Liza's right forearm. During our last excursion, she cast demons out of me by producing a sizable Orthodox cross from thin air. Later, I realized she materialized it from the tattoo on her arm.

"Liza, what exactly are you?"

She raises an eyebrow lazily. "An expeller. Lucky for you, I'm rather good at it, too."

She's going to avoid my question, but I'm desperate enough for an answer to try her patience. "You're more than that."

She pulls her legs up onto the bench and braces her back against the side of the van. "I have a little clairvoyance, too, but nothing like you. You can make out individual voices. To me, it sounds like a high school cafeteria. I can hear voices, but they're all talking over each other, so I can't make out anything useful. It's just a loud hum."

She's evading my question. "I mean the tattoos, Liza. Where did you get them, and how do you animate them?"

She turns her shoulder away from me and acts as if she'll go to sleep. "It should be enough to know they are there, and I can animate them if I need to. I'm going to take a nap."

She rolls her back to me, and I decide we aren't at the "bare your soul and secrets" friendship stage yet. "Thank you for the cross, Liza."

"Thank you for wearing it."

Friend or co-worker, I'm thankful she has her abilities. Without her animated cross, I'd be dead in a dark basement in Paducah, Kentucky.

I don't know what lies in store for anyone going to hell. Still, a cold cellar in Paducah, Kentucky, sounds like a terrible eternal punishment to me.

Reluctantly, I slip the chain over my head. I hold the heavy cross up and rub my fingers over the rubies and ornate silver. It is a beautiful piece of jewelry. It is a bit gaudy for my taste, but it won't hurt me to wear it during our excursions if it makes Liza happy.

I watch her back, but it's obvious she is done talking to me. I've learned my odd, brave friend can be frustratingly quiet when she wishes.

If I'm smart, I'll follow her lead and catch a nap. Given the late night I shared with Granny, Puppy, and the ghost under the boathouse, I'm exhausted. Still, unlike the first excursion to Paducah, I'm oddly pumped about investigating Sloss Furnaces.

"Miles, tell me about the furnaces. How did so many people die at the plant? I mean, where was OSHA during all that time?"

"OSHA?" He swivels to look at me. "OSHA wasn't even a

regulatory thought when the deaths were occurring. Without OSHA and unions, it wasn't unusual to have fatalities in manufacturing in the early twentieth century. People didn't react the same way to worker's deaths as they do now. But, even then, a series of single fatalities over ten years..."

I can tell he's holding back, and it aggravates me. "Miles, we have to know everything we can to do our jobs. Out with it."

Miles stares pointedly at Dusty.

Dusty sighs. "Just tell her. She won't quit asking until you do."

Miles rubs his hands together as he turns even further around in his seat. "Well, as history goes, sixty-six of the fatalities took place at the furnaces on the third shift over six years."

That's a fast clip. "Miles, that's like once a month."

His smile flashes white as he pushes his glasses up the bridge of his nose. "I know, right? But nobody figured it out until it was too late."

"Too late for what?"

"The third shift foreman was a small man by the name of Lloyd Smith. Now, Lloyd was a real piece of work. There wasn't a single man in that factory who wouldn't have cut him and left him to bleed out if they thought they could get away with it."

"A lot of people work for employers they don't like much." I punch my brother on the shoulder. "I work for Dusty. Maybe I'm crazy."

"Or highly compensated."

I laugh at my brother's quick truism. "And then there's that."

"Yes, but your brother is not a warlock." Miles wiggles his eyebrows.

"C'mon."

"No, true story. Or at least that is the legend. Unfortunately for the workers at the furnaces, Lloyd had completed

185

his curse before they figured out his intent."

Okay, this is getting rich. I bite. "What curse?"

"That every worker's family would be torn apart."

"Why on earth would anybody wish that on somebody else?"

Miles's face brightens. I realize he's been waiting for me to ask that question. He isn't merely good at researching the history and filling in the back story. He has a passion for his work.

"Just like most legends, to understand this one, you have to go back to the start. I said Lloyd was on the third shift, but a little-known fact is that Lloyd was the furnaces owner's illegitimate son. Not only was he the illegitimate son, but he was also the only child of Archie Purvis."

I'm not sure why it matters, but I can't resist asking. "Who was Lloyd's mother to his dad?"

Miles gives an appreciative tilt of the chin. "His mother is the lynchpin to the whole legend. Reports are that Mr. Purvis was married happily to Dolly Lutz for forty years. Despite this, Archie did something totally out of character once during their marriage. He had a brief relationship with Lloyd's mother.

"Her name was Rachel Sutton. She was to Archie what we call a one-night stand nowadays."

Yeah right. I know what that meant in the late eighteen hundreds. "A lady of the night."

"No." Miles shakes his head vigorously. "Rachel was considered a somewhat effective holistic curer among the working class in the neighborhood around the furnaces. She was no lady of the night.

"However, later, much later, after everything transpired, many folks claimed she was Wiccan. A passage from Archie's journal alludes to his belief she may have enchanted him."

"Of course, she did," I say.

Miles smiles. "Not the first man to blame it on the witch."

"Nor the last I guarantee you," I say. "So, the son of the owner, whose mom is Wiccan, worked at his father's furnaces at what must have been a respectable job since he was a supervisor."

I twirl my finger, signaling Miles to speed up with the details. "So what's the conflict? Why would Lloyd do something like put a curse on the workers' families? Assuming he could."

"Like I said, he was the only offspring of Mr. Purvis, so illegitimate or not, Lloyd stood to inherit a thriving business. You must understand, Birmingham at the time was a huge steel-producing town. Certainly, one of the largest in the South. The Sloss Furnaces fed those mills their iron ore. It was highly lucrative."

I can't help but roll my eyes. "Enough with the history lesson, Miles."

"Perspective is important." His lips thin momentarily with a frown. "Lloyd was extraordinarily ambitious and expected to one day own the furnaces. Yet, he had one serious flaw. He was an awful manager, and people hated his guts. A lot was written in the newspaper corroborated by witnesses' firsthand stories. They all reported Lloyd as acting condescending to everyone at the plant.

"These reports filtered up to Mr. Purvis—Archie, unlike his son, was an excellent leader of men. Consequently, Archie demoted Lloyd from plant manager to third shift supervisor."

"That had to sting his pride pretty bad. But I still don't see where that would send a sane person over the edge," I say.

"No, but the demotion didn't change Lloyd's ways. If anything, he became more vengeful toward his crew. This forced Archie to do the one thing that would derail Lloyd's future."

"He disowned him." I take a guess.

"No. He gave the furnaces to the workers. Archie Purvis came into work on his fifty-fifth birthday with three lawyers. He set up a trust fund, transferring ownership of the furnaces to the workers.

"He and Dolly left for California the next day. It seems Dolly had always aspired to be a screenplay writer for Hollywood."

I feel like Miles made the last part up. It smacks too much with the ride off into the sunset cliché from the old Westerns. But when he doesn't crack a smile, I know he has at least read that account in some obscure newspaper report.

"Once Lloyd was cut off from the opportunity to own the furnaces and humiliated by the demotion to supervising third shift, he changed for the worse. He became viler, causing workers not to just dislike him, they loathed him. Also, Archie's transferring ownership to the workers meant he wasn't even guaranteed employment at the furnaces.

"With the new political landscape, Lloyd made a move to the dark side."

"Literally."

Miles grins. "Yes, literally."

"April, I studied the Sloss Furnaces in detail four years ago. I considered including a small section in my third book on the furnaces mainly because it's close to home." Dusty gives me a quick glance. "But nothing. There was no paranormal activity four years ago. It was either a faux legend, or the spirits had moved on sixty years earlier."

"Could've been lying dormant like the Osborne hotel ghost," Miles adds.

"Possible. But then we also have witnesses changing their statements. The recent suicide could be another sad man ending his sorrow."

"Suicide is a private affair, Dusty."

"Then explain suicide bombers, Liza."

Liza rolls her head back onto her bench seat. "That's so totally different, and you know it."

"She has a point. I've heard that too," I offer.

"Yeah, maybe. But it doesn't change the fact it's the first

event in sixty years. Other than people occasionally seeing shadows or hearing odd sounds and getting spooked," Dusty says.

We pull into the motel parking lot on the north side of Birmingham a little before seven. When he comes out of the motel office, he hands Liza a key, and she motions for me to follow her.

"Looks like we're regular roomies now," I offer in hopes of getting her to talk. "I guess it's a good thing there are two girls now."

"I don't mind bunking with the guys." She gives me a frown over her shoulder as she unlocks the door. "Except for Travis. He's a creeper."

Travis Early isn't a creeper, but he is totally infatuated with Liza.

Liza tosses her backpack on the bed closest to the bathroom. She pulls out her toothbrush as I lift the luggage stand out of the closet. I give an audible grunt as I heft my suitcase onto the stand.

"You might want to read the company emails from time to time."

"What?"

Liza looks at me from the reflection of the vanity mirror. "The rest of us were aware this is just a two-night trip."

I shift my view from my bulging full-size suitcase to her backpack. At least I'm prepared in case we need to stay another night—or week.

There's a knock on our door. Dusty's voice booms through the metal door. "Five minutes, ladies, or you'll be eating out of the vending machine tonight."

Yeah, I've done that once before, and I don't care to do it again.

Chapter 22

Dusty's royalties from his last book must be significant. Despite the alimony Bethany is squeezing out of him, he treats the team to Rib Land and opens with an initial twelve-slab order of ribs for us to share.

I briefly consider ordering a smoked chicken breast to minimize the caloric damage to my nonexistent diet but quickly cave to my perceived peer pressure. I up the ante with an order of potato salad.

Hey, there's a lot of truth to that "when in Rome" adage. Rib Land is a culinary Mecca in Birmingham.

We start with voracious appetites, and the bone discard plate soon resembles a dinosaur archeological dig.

But as I halfheartedly shove a small spoonful of potato salad between my lips, I sense I'm in trouble. I reach down with my left hand and undo the top button of my shorts. That doesn't relieve the pressure enough, so I let my zipper down half an inch too.

Dusty leans in toward us. "I need everybody to pay attention for a minute. I have an announcement."

We turn our attention to Dusty. His face, first serious, then blooms into a jovial smile. "I have some exciting news for everyone."

"Who's the lucky she-demon this time?" Luis asks. The

rest of the team laughs.

"Funny guy," Dusty says. His eyes squelch the team's laughter.

"Too soon?" Luis quips.

"Considering the original she-demon has not been cast out of my bank account yet—way too soon."

"What's the news?" Miles prods.

Dusty clasps his hands behind his neck as he leans back in his chair. "Guess what author has been approached by WHY broadcasting for production of a paranormal series."

"You're kidding," Travis interjects.

Dusty raises his hands triumphantly into the air. "True story. And not some eight- or ten-episode deal. They want twenty-two episodes a year, and they guaranteed two seasons with the option for a third."

The decibels at our table go up appreciably. Everyone on the team is bouncing in their chairs while they pump Dusty for more information with their rapid-fire questions.

My vision shifts as if someone has pulled my chair back twenty feet. I'm still in it, but my point of view is further away.

My vantage is what I expect an out-of-body experience to be like if I were dying. I watch the team's moment of celebration. Years of belief and working together toward a common goal are close to culminating into something spectacular.

I'm extremely happy for them. But I'm afraid to participate in the joy. Something inside me tells me that if I join in the festivities, I'm tacitly signing on with the team for the next two years.

I am so not ready for that commitment.

What else was I doing? It isn't like any of my résumés have been answered. I still need a job while I wait, and the paranormal gig pays way better than anything else.

No. I can't afford to get sidetracked by my brother's dream. I need to stay focused on mine.

Someone punches my left arm lightly. Liza is looking at

me. Her lips are moving, but at first, I don't hear her. "... rooming together a lot the next couple of years. It'll give us all an opportunity to set back a nice nest egg, too."

"Yeah. That's great." Despite my best efforts, my voice is flat.

Liza squints. "What's the matter?"

I shake my head. "Nothing. I'll talk to you about it later."

She eyes me suspiciously and appears ready to question me further.

Dusty says, "Now understand, just because we have a contract doesn't mean it's a done deal. They can always back out and just pay the option fee. But I do know they're sending down a crew next week to go over the prospective shooting schedule for this fall."

"I was wondering how we scored that new van," Chet says with a smile.

"Nothing but the best for my team." Dusty raises a beer toward Chet.

My vision closes in, and my chest constricts. Panic laces its icy fingers over my shoulders, pulling me down into a dark place. Somewhere deep in my heart, I knew if I came back to Guntersville, I'd be trapped. Caught and never able to leave even though I hold the key to my chains.

Liza locks the motel door and turns to me. "Okay, tell me."

I don't want to talk about it. Least of all with Liza. The more I consider my concerns after leaving the restaurant, I feel like an ingrate for not being thrilled and joining in on the celebration. "Can we just let it ride? I was just in a mood."

"The only acceptable mood at the moment is happy."

I shouldn't have to explain myself. It isn't like I was raining on the team's parade; I just didn't want to march in it. "My goals aren't exactly aligned with the rest of y'all."

Liza rocks back as if I slapped her in the face. "Y'all?" She wiggles a finger between the two of us. "Forgive me. I thought we were all working on the same team."

I said that wrong. "I just meant that my goals are different. You know, bigger."

"Bigger?" Liza snorts as she shakes her head. "Do you hear yourself?"

What is her problem? "I'm just saying I spent seven years in college to be an attorney. I didn't do all that to go traipsing around the country with my brother chasing after spirits."

"Wow"—Liza marches to the vanity—"just wow."

"What?"

She turns and points her toothbrush at me as if it were a weapon. "So you spent seven years in college, your brother has been working on this for fifteen years, and you can't even be happy for him."

Anger flashes through me, raising my body temperature with my blood pressure. "I'm happy for him!"

"No, I think you're jealous of him. You also think you're better than the rest of us."

"I do not!"

She ignores me while she brushes her teeth.

"I'm extremely excited for my brother. I know he's worked incredibly hard for this. I just know that before too long, I'll be a part of it. I'm not sure I'm ready to commit to that."

Liza rinses her mouth and still says nothing.

"As for me thinking I'm better than everybody else, that's just a total crock, and you know it. Each of you has a skill I don't."

I can't figure out why tears are streaming down my face. "Can't you see, every one of you is getting to do exactly what you want to do with your life. I mean, look at me. I don't even know who I am anymore."

Liza pulls up and stares at me for a moment.

I draw in a ragged breath and wait for what I hope is a

comforting comment from her.

She lifts her right hand to her face, balls up her fist, then mimes wiping tears from her eyes.

My teeth clamp so hard I think I chipped a molar. "Oh, that's mature. Real mature, Liza."

She lets her shorts drop to the floor and sheds her T-shirt and sports bra before pulling back the sheets on her bed.

The expansive tattoos on her back and chest quiet me. I know they're there, but the artwork's intricacy and its beauty leave me in awe. Then it's gone as she slips under the covers. She punches her pillow twice and lays her head down.

I stand in silence for an eternity. "You're not gonna say anything?"

She opens one eye. "Yeah, turn out the light when you come to bed."

Fine. Whatever. I stomp to the vanity and make quick work of removing my makeup and brushing my teeth. I consider brushing my hair and decide I'd run the risk of making myself bald headed if I were to brush my hair with this much anger.

I clomp to my bed, yank back the comforter with a snap, and plop onto the mattress hard enough to make the headboard slap the wall. Reaching to turn off the light, I make sure to hit the lampshade in the process.

The anger that is seething through me mutates into an odd shame. I don't want to argue with Liza. I also don't want to spoil her celebratory mood.

But I'm scared. Scared that my dreams will never be realized.

My shame transforms into sadness, and I know I need to talk through my feelings and make sure Liza isn't angry with me, or I'll be awake all night worrying.

I need Liza to understand I don't think I'm better.

I'm proud of my brother and his team. I'm just not willing to drop my dream for his yet. Liza is a rational person. If she would talk to me, I could put my mind at ease. As I watch her back in the dark, I know she isn't feeling charitable enough to talk to me tonight.

I opt for the second-best thing to closure. "Liza, do you have any chocolate?"

"Yes," she mumbles.

I bide my time and watch the LED display on the clock. "Can I have some?"

"No."

I sigh in defeat. I'm sure I earned that. It's going to be a long, brutal night.

Liza is gone when I wake in the morning. I check the time. We're not due to leave for breakfast for another hour, so I catch a quick shower before applying a little makeup.

A profound sadness settles over me as I sit on the edge of my bed and watch the clock after I dress. In a lot of ways, Liza is a microcosm of all my non-family relationships.

All around me, I see people form bonds of friendship. They remain close to each other for a long time, if not their whole lives, like Mama and Wanda.

Everyone else in the world acts like lunar bodies. Some of them are suns like Mama and Dusty, some are planets like Daddy, Chase, and Miles, and some are moons like Chet and the Early brothers. But they all gravitate toward one another and circle each other in a dance of attraction balanced by space.

I'm April's comet.

I streak through lunar cycles disrupting the gravitational pull. About the time I get used to the idea of others in my orbit, I'm no longer in their solar system.

I like Liza. I like how she is as much of a paranormal freak as I am. She inspires me to learn to control my "gifts" the way she can control her talents.

Now she thinks I'm some stuck-up, privileged princess. Maybe I am. But it isn't like I'm trying to be. It just comes naturally.

Staring at my hands, I haven't a clue how I can make it better. How I can at least take our relationship back to before dinner last night. Back to when she gave me the cross. I reach up and caress the cross under my T-shirt.

The door rattles. "April! Are you coming for breakfast or what?"

I jump up and open the door to Miles. "Sorry, I got sidetracked."

I follow him out, and he climbs into the front passenger seat of the van. When I get in the back, I'm surprised to see Chet. "Hey, good morning."

He raises his chin. "Morning."

"Where's Liza?"

"She wants to see how the new van rides," Chet says as he scrolls his phone.

That might be true, but the insecure side of me thinks she is avoiding me.

At breakfast, any doubt she is avoiding me is removed when she makes a point of sitting as far away from me as possible. It stings.

She isn't shaming me. It's apparent she hasn't shared our conversation with anyone. Still, she is making it a point not to have to deal with me.

I sit between Miles and Dusty. I suppose because, in my heart, I know Miles will always like me no matter what I say or do. Dusty must like me because he's my brother.

The chocolate chip pancakes and chocolate milk should help my mood, but they don't. Truthfully, I'm wondering if chocolate would've even helped last night. Most likely not.

What is it with me? Liza is nobody to me. She's just a coworker at a part-time gig. Some freaky chick with a bunch of tattoos. Why do I care what she thinks? It isn't like we'll maintain a relationship after I've moved to New York and realized my goal of becoming a big-time attorney.

Lies. All lies I'm telling myself. She's honorable, trustworthy, and anything but judgmental. All traits I hope to develop someday.

As for me not having to deal with Liza after I leave Guntersville, that isn't so cut and dried given what I accidentally read off her during our Paducah trip. While fighting for our lives, I accessed her thoughts to pull out a chant I needed to expel a ghost.

Rummaging through another person's mind is a lot like rifling through their dresser drawers. There's no telling what you might find.

In the case of Liza, I learned she doesn't work for Dusty just for the excitement and the great pay. She also has a crush on my brother. I'm positive he's oblivious to her feelings, and I know she would never just come out and tell him.

Maybe if he ever gets Bethany out of his life, he can think about his "next relationship." I hope once the pain of a disloyal wife eases from his mind, he'll notice Liza as more than a valued associate.

I think they'd make a cute, albeit odd, couple.

While I'm dragging part of my chocolate chip pancake in and out of a strawberry syrup puddle, Dusty announces it's time to leave for the furnaces.

As we load up, Liza again rides in the new equipment van. I suppose she hasn't determined if she likes the way it handles yet and needs more test miles.

Chapter 23

Rich Underwood, the curator of the Sloss Furnaces Museum, meets us at the front gate. He's a short man of fifty years of age. He wasn't blessed with good genes and has compounded the issue with way too many fast-food meals.

As he greets us, I shake his proffered hand. His kind nature and genuine grief over Mr. Bass courses through me. I chastise myself for once again judging a book by its cover.

When will I ever learn?

Initially, I assume the museum isn't open on Saturdays. Instead, Rich explains that the recently completed autopsy report of Steve Bass noted bruise marks on his back and on his wrist as well as six broken fingers. The manner of the breaks made it improbable they were because of his fall.

Because of these findings, the case initially classified as suicide has been reopened as a homicide. The police came back on site and did a second sweep for clues and evidence they might have missed initially. They also received an injunction from the local judge to temporarily halt paid tours in case they need to come back and do a third sweep.

"I hope you don't consider this rude of me to say." Rich takes his glasses off and cleans them with a tissue. "There's only one reason I agreed to this research project. Mr. Trufant suggested it would clear the rumors of malicious spirits. Ever since Mr. Bass committed suicide, admissions to the museum have dropped by sixty percent. Now that the police have temporarily closed us, I don't know how much longer we can hold on."

"We?" Liza asks as she continues to look past Rich toward the colossal brick and steel structure.

"Montel and me. I used to have three other maintenance and guide helpers at the museum, but the city reduced our budget even further last year."

"Look on the bright side," Luis offers, "if we document a spirit at your museum, you can start a whole new profit center model as a haunted location."

"I'm not sure how much tourism you're going to generate if you have a spirit that prefers to kill people instead of just scare them," Liza says absently as she walks past Rich.

Rich attempts to smile and accomplishes a grimace. "Like I said, I truly hope you can confirm there's nothing here. At least that would be a start back to recovery."

"The only thing I can promise you, Mr. Underwood, is a thorough job and complete transparency about what we find." Dusty points toward the furnaces. "If you could give us a tour of the grounds now, I'd like to get set up and start work as soon as possible."

Underwood snaps to attention. "Of course. Please forgive me."

Rich leads us through the ancient foundry that covers fourteen acres in the heart of downtown Birmingham. For being a century and a half old, the brickwork is in good condition and looks like it could fire up and produce iron this morning.

The steel ceiling is not in the same good condition and has been tarped over in several places to keep the rain out. Pigeons and doves congregate in alcoves, painting the interior walls white with droppings.

Though dormant for a century, the cloying smell of sulfur released from bituminous coal still permeates the air. The floor, a combination of dirt, dust, and graphite, gives up small clouds of fine particles in protest of each step.

The late-June heat is sweltering. I can only imagine how workers managed to survive in this environment when adding ladles of molten iron into the equation. All I can think is it would have to be like Dante's Inferno.

"This is a huge piece of property you have here, Rich. We have limited equipment and need to get the most bang for our buck. Where are the areas with the highest levels of activity?" Dusty asks him as we circle around to the front office.

The round man gives a quick shrug. "That's just it. Before the incident with Mr. Bass, there really hasn't been anything. Don't get me wrong, there are many dark areas in the plant that aren't open to tours. People have reported odd sounds and voices from time to time, but nothing has ever turned up from that."

"What about the ghost of Lloyd Smith?" Miles sounds as if he is making a counterpoint rather than a question.

"Well, that's extensively documented in our museum library. People feeling pushed in the back and occasionally having burn marks after thinking somebody has grabbed their arms." Rich shakes his head. "All while the plant was open. After it closed in nineteen seventy-one, it lay empty until the nineties. The city took an interest in it and eventually opened the museum. There's been nothing reported since it's been a museum."

I don't like the idea of a dormant ghost. It's just not the natural order of things.

People have a challenging time understanding even things that aren't supposed to exist often follow a particular rule pattern. Typically, when it comes to hauntings, you're haunted from a specific point in time and forward forever, or until the spirit is freed to go to heaven or forced to go elsewhere.

Spirits don't take vacations—especially not vacations

lasting for a century.

As bad as the preposterous idea of a ghost returning from vacation is bugging me, there is something else a little more pressing. I can ask Dusty about it, but somebody else has more juice than my brother, and I want to confirm my thoughts as soon as I can.

I draw a deep breath and put on my best professional face. Hopefully, she'll reciprocate. I move closer to Liza and whisper in her ear, "Do you have anything?"

Her lips thin as she shakes her head. "Radio silence. You?"

"Eerily quiet. I picked up more chatter at breakfast than this."

Liza contains a laugh. "That old man with the Larry Fine hairdo?"

"I thought I was in an episode of The Three Stooges, especially when he shook the ketchup bottle, and the cap was off." I giggle.

"I wondered if you saw that. Why didn't you mention it?"

"Because you're mad at me."

Liza's frowns. "I'm not mad. A little hurt since you don't appreciate what the rest of us are trying to do here. But I'm not mad at you."

Okay, so maybe I don't understand Liza's various levels of mad. But she is talking to me, and I consider it progress. "How many people did Miles say died here?"

"Seventy-something."

"Something's not right, then," I say.

"You can say that again. And I'm looking forward to figuring it out."

"You ladies care to share?"

Dusty is giving us a condescending stare. It makes him appear constipated.

"We were just discussing some of the locations we thought cameras might be most effective," Liza says.

Liza is certainly way quicker than me. I'm thankful, since I never handle Dusty's condescending mode gracefully.

Chapter 24

I help the guys unload the equipment and set up audio and video in the areas we consider the highest probability, given the limited information available. The catwalk that has been closed since Mr. Bass's death receives two cameras, one on either end.

Even though I haven't heard any spirits, it makes me nervous when Travis insists on walking across the catwalk. I'm a nervous wreck as I watch him walk across and then back to us after mounting the camera.

On four separate occasions, I take a break to isolate myself in silence. I constrict everything down to a pinpoint of focus in the middle of my core and then reach out, grasping for anything that wants to communicate with me.

The first three times, I hear absolutely nothing. The fourth time there is a brief vibration inside my left eardrum that lasts only a second. It's so quick I discount it when I open my eyes—the net result of the exercise, nothing.

It's as if the area has been sterilized of spirits—stripped clean of all history.

I can walk down a small-town street, and if I have purposely tapped into my clairvoyance, I'm going to hear a voice or two. Somebody died in a house I pass, or someone who died in a car accident at an intersection—something.

That's why I spend so much of my time with my clairvoyance shut down. I mean, genuinely, if I don't shut it down, I can't hear myself think because every random spirit in my vicinity wants to talk to me.

But here and now, in this place that has seen so much violent death. Nothing? It just makes no sense.

"You want to go up to the furnaces with me?"

I grin like I was asked to go to an amusement park. No, I don't want to go into the furnace area; that's probably where the ghost resides. Still, by her asking, I know Liza's "hurt" really isn't anger.

"Sure. But why?" I ask.

"Why go with me or why the furnaces?"

"Furnaces."

Liza wrinkles her nose. "I don't know. Something in Miles's research notes."

She hands me an EMF meter and turns the one in her right hand on.

What in the world do I need this for? I stare at the meter in my hand.

"I know, I don't much trust them either, but at this point, I figure since we're both drawing blanks, maybe they can at least signal where we should try."

I hand the meter back to her and pull out my phone. "I'm going to use Miles's app instead."

"Suit yourself," Liza says.

I understand why, after our excursion in Paducah, she's not sold on the phone app. I think it gives us more useful information than the EMF meters. I was just inexperienced with understanding the symbols.

Turning on the app, I follow Liza's lead into one of the cavernous archways.

This is a perfect moment to show complete trust in my partner. To just be with her as she follows up on a hunch. That's what friends do. They support each other even when they're not sure what is motivating their friend. Support without a lot of questions or arguments.

The sulfurous smell is more pronounced in here, and my nose tickles, threatening a sneeze. I lift a finger to my nose to try and prevent it and succeed.

Coolness wraps around me, turning the beads of perspiration cold against my body. I look down at my phone app to see if there's a paranormal event in our vicinity.

The screen is still blank. Nothing. Precisely what the sensors in my head are telling me, too. Nada.

"Why do you want to go to the furnaces?" My jaw drops open as I hear my voice. Well, so much for the "unconditional trust of my partner" exercise. How long did I last, all of five minutes?

Liza looks over her shoulder. "Go back if you're scared. But you'll get a zero for being a real part of the team."

My shoulders curl upward in shame. It's as if Liza knows what I've been struggling with this morning. That I need to step up my game in support of my team members.

I failed miserably.

Wait a minute. How did she know I was treating this as a test? "You read me."

"What?"

She did. She's a worse liar than I am, which is saying a lot. "When did you read me?"

"I don't know what you're talking about." She starts laughing nervously.

"That's just messed up, Liza."

Liza turns to face me. Indignation mixes with humor as she gasps. "Like you've never read me."

"By accident."

"As if."

"Seriously, when did you read me? Fess up."

She lets one more laugh roll out before raising her chin toward the ceiling. "Ugh, if you have to know, this morning."

That doesn't make sense. "You weren't even close to me this morning."

"I was this morning before I left our room."

What the heck? "You read me while I was asleep?"

She gives a brief shrug in answer and renews her interest in the yards of red and white masonry.

"Why?" I demand.

She stops walking and turns on me. "I needed to know some things about you."

Now I'm getting angry. The sense of violation is creeping over my skin. "So, like, you couldn't just ask?"

Her facial features soften. "You're the one person I should be able to talk to that would understand people don't always tell the truth."

That hits home. How many times have I struggled not to use my clairvoyance when talking to one of my clients? Clients who I need to be able to believe if I am going to do my job effectively.

My desire to read my clients has always come from my desire to serve them better. I'm a big girl. I know we all lie sometimes. It is not necessarily a big, bold untruth, but we sometimes need to lie to deal with the truth of our compounded actions.

I exhale loudly. "Did you at least find out what you needed to know so badly?"

A huge smile adorns Liza's face. "No, but I learned enough to explain a few things."

I didn't much like being the butt of her secret joke. "What?"

"I learned being in your mind is like being trapped in a laundromat dryer." She makes a rolling motion with her hand as she starts to laugh again. "It's like I can see out the window, but I can't get my bearings."

That is like the rudest thing anybody has ever said to me. I gape at Liza and wonder how she can, first off, live with sneaking a read off me, and then, making fun of the thoughts she read in my mind. It is like a violation with a big helping of humiliation on top of it.

Her assessment of my mind is so accurate it is scary. I'm well aware my mind tumbles continuously from one topic to another.

I've always assumed that it's normal, or at the very least, a female trait. Liza is now confirming that I'm unique. And not in a complimentary manner.

"I'm not sure I know how I feel about that."

Liza holds up her right hand as her eyes narrow. "Did you hear that?" she whispers.

I shake my head, no.

She looks down at her meter, and I check the phone app. No readings.

I close my eyes, quickly center myself, and push out with my energy. I hold my focus for a full minute before letting the breath I'm holding release. "I don't have anything. What did you hear?"

"Chains, maybe?"

Chains? Yes, that would be on my top twenty list of things I don't want to hear right now. My gut tightens in anticipation of impending doom.

Liza enters a hallway to our left. The ceiling is still forty feet above us, but the hallway is only thirty feet across. That's plenty big for two women. Still, I'm getting claustrophobic, and the angst scrapes my bare nerves with the decrease of light.

"You smell that?" Liza says as she presses her hand against my shoulder, halting my progress.

Boy, do I. If I thought the sulfur smell was strong earlier, it was just a prelude to this hallway.

My nose itches furiously. Before I can stop it, I let out an award-winning sneeze. The sound reverberates along the brick hallway.

"Bless you."

I open my mouth to say thank you but never get the words out. A black cloud of movement and shrieks engulfs us.

Instinctively, I squat and cover my head. My arms and

shoulders are pelted. I know I'm screaming, but I can't hear myself for the tremendous ruckus. I close my eyes tightly and squat even lower.

Then as suddenly as it started, it's over.

Cautiously, I open my eyes and turn to Liza. "Please tell me those were bats."

Liza stands up. "I believe they were sparrows. But I've never seen them act that way."

My body convulses with a spontaneous shudder. We haven't even broken for lunch yet, and already, there are too many abnormalities about this paranormal excursion.

Still, Dusty's concerns about the dearth of recent activity other than the suicide appear warranted. The lack of EMF signatures, phone app blips, and voices for either of us using our "gifts" confirms there are no spirits here.

That might be true. Yet there is something off about this place. It's like just the smell and appearance of the site makes my skin crawl.

"You still want to go down that way?"

Liza shrugs. "I figure you cleared everything out with that sneeze. We might as well."

Or I just flushed the first weird thing out of the hallway, and there is still something worse to come.

Reluctantly, I follow her. After a hundred feet, I wish we had brought flashlights, as the extended hallway's lack of openings preclude any ambient light.

When I hear the distinct clink of metal on metal, I freeze. Liza rotates her head to look at me. Her eyes open wider than usual. I give her a brief nod to confirm I hear it too.

In unison, we check our readouts. Nothing. Good, right? Well, that's what I'm trying to convince myself.

Contrary to the excellent thoughts of self-preservation I'm presently having, I follow Liza as she moves forward.

Another clink reverberates down the hallway. I jump into the air as if I were standing on compressed springs that suddenly released.

Liza doesn't bother to ask this time, and she starts forward again. I pull on her shirttail.

"What?" she hisses.

"Liza, go back and get the guys," I plead.

"It might be gone by the time we get back."

That sounds like a bonus to me. The last thing I want to do is corner whatever is at the end of the hallway. Backing out and giving it time to get away sounds like a reasonable proposal.

An idea occurs to me. "We don't have any video equipment." There, that's an excellent point if I do say so myself. I'm positive I just won this debate.

"You don't have to go with me if you're afraid. Go get the rest of the team if you need to, but I want to know what is making that noise."

Great. My present options are to go with "crazy girl" and get eaten by a monster—or turn tail to get my big brother's help and forever be known as Princess Chicken.

Liza pulls her shirt from my grasp and steps forward. I decide a pink T-shirt with "Princess Chicken" screen painted on it might be cute. Who knows, I might start a trend.

A thundering whoosh claps my ears as a blast wave reverberates down the hallway. It's the sound of a thousand gas grills lighting up at the same time on the Fourth of July.

I shake my head to clear my mind as I watch tendrils of smoke lace along the top of the ceiling. They dance across the old sheets of tin in a mesmerizing, uniform manner.

"That's no ghost," Liza declares without looking back to see if I was following her.

"Somebody lit one of the furnaces?"

Liza gives an abbreviated nervous laugh. "We're a couple of dimwits. I bet they keep one of the furnaces operational to show folks on tour."

Her theory has some merit, even if it sounds odd, given there are no tours today. Still, I buy her reasoning. Because I prefer her premise to any of the other plausible explanations that come to my mind.

Liza marches down the hallway with renewed purpose. I am forced to sprint to catch up with her.

We come to a T-intersection. Following the smoke, we take a left and walk by an idle furnace on our right. The hallway makes another turn to the right as we walk past the furnaces' colossal metal doors.

Taking a left at the next T-intersection, I feel heat caressing my cheek. The heavy refracting doors of this furnace have been pulled back, exposing the orange flames inside.

This makes no sense. The staff wouldn't leave the furnace door open, much less unattended.

As I stare nonplussed at the spectacle, the heat bakes my face, and I smell singed hair. I take two steps back.

Liza grabs my arm and pulls me back behind one of the brick walls, breaking my trance.

"Don't stare into it like that again. It's not natural," Liza says.

She's right. I hadn't noticed until she pulled me away, but the fire was drawing me into it. Despite the sweat dampening my shirt from the intense heatwave, I shiver. "It's like it's alive," I whisper.

Liza crosses her arms and searches the hallway glancing side to side. "Who's watching this anyway?"

"Nobody. This is all screwy, Liza. The museum is closed. Why would they be demonstrating a furnace when they're closed?" I don't wait for her answer. "Let's go back and get the guys."

"Yeah, safety in numbers."

I think safety has more to do with location, like outside the gates, rather than numbers. But I'll settle for the company of the rest of the team and am thankful she agrees we need reinforcements.

We hustle back down the hallway, retracing our steps. Breathless from jogging, we turn right a third time. As we approach another brick wall forming a T-intersection in the dimly lit hallway, we pull up short.

The furnaces have become an epic, confusing labyrinth.

"I think we're lost," I say.

"We were lost after the second turn. I was holding out hope we'd double back somehow and find something familiar."

"It all looks familiar. Old red brick with an occasional garage door-sized metal furnace door."

"True," Liza says.

"I'm going to call them."

"Don't. The boys will think we can't take care of ourselves."

I roll my eyes. "Presently, I'd have to agree with them. I don't want to get so lost they can't find us."

"Fair," Liza grumbles, "but I don't think that's even possible." She points at the wall to our right. "It feels like we should be going in that direction."

"I don't remember walking through a wall, so that can't be right," I say as I call Dusty's phone.

Dusty picks up. "Where did you two go?"

"We just wanted to stretch our legs." I force a laugh. "Funny thing is, we got lost. Do you still have that GPS tracker?"

"Are you serious?"

"I'm afraid so."

"Okay." His voice goes up an octave. "Just hold tight while I get the app running."

Liza is chewing on her thumbnail.

"Dusty will have the team here in a minute," I say to reassure her.

"We should have taken pictures of it with our phones," Liza says as she stares into the darkness.

"You've seen one fire, you've seen them all. Although you won't see many burning hotter," I joke.

Liza turns her attention to me and frowns. "Not the fire. The face in the fire."

That raises my hackles.

"April, you're just down the hallway from us."

I shake the icy feeling off me. "We are? Which way?"

"Don't move. I'll bring the team to you." Dusty hangs up.

"He says he'll be here in a minute."

Liza's eyes glaze over. "Let's go back and take pictures."

Reaching out, I grab her by the wrist. "We agreed to get the rest of the team. Let's just wait a minute."

She shakes her head. "Right. Of course."

I hear Dusty's voice and turn. Vertigo threatens my balance. A hallway has appeared where Liza just pointed at a wall. The team is walking down the path led by Dusty and Rich.

Cutting my eyes to Liza, she's shaking her head in disbelief. Good, I haven't lost my mind, or if I have, I have company.

Forget how the wall disappeared. I'm just relieved we are no longer on our own.

"You two were only a hundred yards away from us," Dusty says.

"So close, yet still a big fat fail," Miles jokes.

That's fine. Let the team have their laugh. My radar still isn't picking up anything, but my paranormal senses tell me something is off at the Sloss Furnaces.

My feelings are further confirmed when we tell the rest of the team about the furnace being lit with no museum staff tending to it.

Rich immediately takes exception to our claim. "I'm afraid you're mistaken, ladies. There's not a single furnace in this facility that is operational."

"Well, you have one operating right now," I say as I run a finger over my eyebrow. "I think it singed my eyebrows."

Rich laughs nervously. "You girls are good. You had me biting on that one. I'm glad you're having your fun."

"We don't have time to hang out and pull your leg, dude. You've got a furnace operating down here, and the cupola doors are open." Liza glares at Rich, daring him to dismiss us again.

Rich lifts a hand, hoping to calm her. "Listen, I'm not trying to argue with you. It's just the gas lines to the furnaces were capped in the seventies for safety reasons, and there hasn't been any coal brought in since nineteen twenty-three.

"Without fuel to burn, these furnaces won't operate."

We're at an impasse. I know what we saw, and Rich is speaking to logic about the need for fuel. How can we both be right?

"Listen, we might not be able to explain the process, but you do have a fire burning in one of your furnaces. End of story," I say.

Rich laughs and rubs the back of his neck. "Okay, okay. I'll have Montel check it out. If there is a fire…"

"There's a fire!" Liza shouts.

"Right. I'll have Montel put the fire out. What furnace was it?"

Liza and I look at each other. Right. What was the furnace number?

I concentrate on the furnace until I can almost feel the heat on my face again. Focusing, I search the outside of the door, recalling everything I saw in those few moments.

The number nine is embossed on a large metal plate in an Edwardian-style script just above the door. As I fade out my memory, I see the face silhouetted in flames. I shudder as the heebie-jeebies course through me.

"Nine. It was furnace nine, Rich."

The color drains from Rich's face. "Are you sure," He croaks.

I can't be a hundred percent sure. It's a memory, and I wasn't explicitly looking for the furnace number earlier. Still, my photographic image recall is reliable when I focus. It was number nine.

"Yes, I'm sure."

"Okay. I'll head down there now."

"Would you like some help?" Dusty offers.

The relief on Rich's face is unmistakable. "Yes, please. That would be great."

"Chet, Jason, and Luis, you three go with Mr. Underwood. Take some equipment with you, too, just in case you come across something on the way."

Dusty waits until Mr. Underwood and our entourage clears out. "We're going to take a lunch break at noon. I ordered some fried chicken for us."

I should be too wigged out to eat. But the thought of fried chicken and some mashed potatoes gives me something to look forward to, and my stomach rumbles.

"Did y'all get any readings down there?"

"Reading, no," Liza says as she holds up her EMF meter, "but there is something evil afoot in this old plant, Dusty."

"Anything we can record?" Dusty asks.

Liza isn't volunteering the information about the face in the furnace yet. I suppose that's best. Flames and clouds, you can see anything from demons to teddy bears in them, depending on what's on your mind.

"No, but it might not be a bad idea if the guys were to set up a camera on the fire inside the furnace."

"Okay..." Dusty's brow wrinkles. "Did you see or hear anything? Besides the fire."

"No. But you don't have to be a clairvoyant to know something's not right about this place," I say.

"Unfortunately, without pictures or audio, also known as proof, it's hard to sell books. I see the title of my next book"—Dusty spreads his hands wide in front of his face—"Something's Not Right Here, subtitled, But I Have Nothing to Show You."

Liza clicks her tongue. "The title has a nice ring to it, boss."

Sounds perfect to me, but I'm not going to try his mood by verbalizing my opinion.

He waves a finger at us with a frown. "You two go wash the soot off you before the chicken gets here." He grimaces. "And please check your hair, April. You've got something white in it."

Oh no. Oh no. All I can manage is to stand with my hands shaking above my head as Dusty walks down the hall to join the rest of the team.

"What's in my hair!"

Liza grabs me by the shoulders and turns me as she stands on her tiptoes. "Oh, it's just a little bit of bird poop."

I'm wracked with repulsion. "Birds poop? Get it out!"

Liza takes me by the upper arm and leads me toward the offices. "Come on, princess. We'll go get it out of your hair."

Chapter 25

Liza helps me wash my hair in the office bathroom sink. I squeeze it dry with paper towels as I wonder how badly the hand soap will frizz my hair.

"Did you really get it all?"

"You're all good to go," Liza assures me.

I have no choice but to believe her, but I still feel like I have slime on top of my head. That's the problem with my imagination. Once it gets going in a direction, it hits overdrive, and there's no tapping the brakes.

Chet, Luis, and Jason return from their excursion as we come out of the bathroom. All three of them have long faces and won't look us in the eye.

Dusty comes in the other office door with a cardboard box. He sets it down on an old oak table and pulls out buckets of chicken and boxes of side items.

My spirit bounces back to positive. I earned me a crunchy thigh and a drumstick, as well as mashed potatoes with fake gravy. I'm pretty darn excited about it.

Any further thoughts of the fowl violation of my hair will have to wait.

The best part about Dusty's paranormal team? They like to eat as much as I do. I never feel self-conscious if I overindulge with a second helping of mashed potatoes.

"All right, team," Dusty says as the Early brothers argue over the last few wings at the bottom of the buckets. "As I feared, I'm almost sure this investigation will be a bust. But I don't want us to get too down about it.

"You know from the good news last night we've got way too much to celebrate, and even good teams have a loss from time to time."

"I'm sorry, Dusty. With the documented history, this one seemed legit," Miles says.

Dusty waves his hand. "No. Don't even think about going there. I almost selected this site three years ago. With the recent death, it was too attractive not to investigate."

"Well, what about the fire in the furnace? I mean, there's something weird about a furnace that has no gas or coal lighting up. Right?"

Every man at the table looks down at the chicken bones on their plates. I cut my eyes to Liza. She shrugs her shoulders.

"What aren't y'all telling me?" I whine.

Chet rolls his head back as if it pains him to tell me. "There was no fire, April."

What? Of course, there was a fire. I felt the heat, smelled the sulfur, and now they want to tell me there wasn't a fire. "Funny, Chet."

"No, I'm serious, April. There was no fire when we investigated furnace nine. I'm sorry."

Sorry? This isn't possible. I stood in front of number nine, looking into the flames, looking at him as he called my name. A chill runs up my spine. "Maybe I got the furnace number wrong."

"Mr. Underwood took us to all the furnaces just to be sure. None of them had a fire, April."

"Maybe it went out on its own," Liza offers apologetically.

Jason shakes his head. "No, Liza. I thought about that too, but every furnace door was at ambient temperature."

"Couldn't have been," I say.

"April, I laid my bare hand on every one of the doors." He holds his right hand up. "Do you see any burns?"

This case is becoming more unsettling by the second. I've no idea why I was so pumped to go on this trip. After being possessed by a spirit and surviving on the last trip, why did I assume the subsequent investigation would be less complicated?

Here I am in a situation where all the hard evidence points to no paranormal activity. Yet, I'm creeped out worse than when I was fighting for my life in a Paducah basement.

"All right, now that we took care of that awkward subject, I want to go over the schedule for the rest of the trip. We're going to clear out of here at five this evening. We'll go to dinner and then come back tomorrow morning."

There is a collective groan from the Earlys.

"Hey, you signed up for this excursion. The least we can do is attempt to salvage the historical legend out of it. The piece can be filler for the back of one of the books. Legends debunked are of interest to our readers, too."

"That's what I'm talking about," Miles says.

"Glad you're excited about it, Miles," Dusty says. "You, Liza, and April are scheduled to interview Mr. Underwood and this Montel person who is assisting him. Dig through the archives. See if you can find anything of any interest.

"Chet and Luis, I want you to continue monitoring the crosswalk. It's the one area where we know there's been activity.

"Jason and Travis, head down to furnace nine and set up audio and video there."

"Why?"

Jason's eyes widen. I don't think he intended to ask that out loud.

"Because our host hasn't been truthful with us. When April said it was furnace number nine that lit, the color drained from his face. I didn't press him for more information because he would have just lied. I have no idea what it's about. Hopefully, Miles and the girls can unearth the clues we need tomorrow."

Dusty claps his hands together. "All right, team, everybody has their assignments. We have a three-beer limit tonight instead of the usual two. So, there's something to look forward to."

The team breaks into a happy chatter as they leave the table.

I can't help it. I'm grinning from ear to ear.

It's no wonder my brother is such a success. I fully expected him to chastise Liza and me when no fire was found in furnace number nine. Instead, he is already a step ahead and noticed the change in Mr. Underwood's body language. He might not be able to hear spirits like I can, but he sure can read people.

"Ready to hit the company archives, ladies?"

"Geez, I'm almost over-titillated, Miles," Liza says with a roll of her eyes.

Miles chokes as he blushes a darker shade of black.

Rich Underwood sets us up with newspaper articles and two books written about the furnace. One of the books delves into the legend of the ghost of Lloyd Smith.

Rich also pulls out of storage the legal documents created during the plant operation, including the final transfer of rights to the plant workers. Lastly, he provides us several accounting ledgers from the last five years of plant operations.

Miles immediately immerses himself into the articles and books. Liza takes over the ledgers, as she has a bookkeeping background; who knew. Which means I'm left combing through the legal documents.

As I approach the second hour of reviewing contract after contract, I'm quite sure I never want to be a contract lawyer.

By the time we call it quits at five o'clock, I'm not sure I even want to be a lawyer anymore.

I've never been so bored in my life.

Stepping into the shower at our motel is a spiritual event. I can't believe how much grit is stuck to my skin. I mean, under my clothes. How did it get under my clothes?

"You're up," I say to Liza as I come out of the shower room.

Liza strips in the room on the way to the shower. "Excuse me." She reaches to the side of my legs to pull out two towels and a washcloth.

"Sorry."

"No worries," Liza says as she closes the door behind her.

I rewrap my hair in a turban, pick up my lotion bottle, and pop the lid open. Slathering myself in fragrant lotion soothes the last irritations from my skin.

Even the dust of Sloss Furnaces has a "not quite right" feel to it. It's as if my skin is begging me to get as far away as possible from the old manufacturing facility.

If I could, I would. Unfortunately, my curiosity is already spinning. With each hour spent at Sloss today, I came away with more questions. It's not in my nature to be satisfied with an unsolved mystery.

Pulling on my shorts and shirt, I work on devising a plan for tomorrow. Our remaining time in Birmingham is limited. It's a challenge to determine which activity will yield the answers I crave.

Should we spend more time in the archives in hopes of finding some invoice or journal entry that points us in the right direction? Or would my time be better spent trying to draw out the eerie face in the flame?

I shudder as fear slides up my spine like an icy dart, causing my scalp to tingle. Hopefully, Dusty will put me back in the archives tomorrow. I'll just learn to live with the unsolved mystery.

Liza steps out of the bathroom, rubbing her hair vigorously with the only towel she carried to the shower. She stops and tosses the towel into the corner as she turns on the hairdryer.

Initially, I thought Liza's propensity for nudity was meant to intimidate me. If it was her intent, it worked well.

I now believe it's just Liza. She's that comfortable in her own skin.

I've always thought of myself as relatively confident. I know, especially around men, I can channel my "Warrior Chick." Still, that's just a poor acting job compared to Liza's boldness.

Trying not to stare at the verses, archaic symbols, and weapons tattooed across her back, I adjust the towel on my head. I don't care to be rude, but the colorful ink contrasting against her milk-white skin unfailingly draws my attention. The many intricate details of the artwork would require hours of study to fully comprehend.

What is each item's meaning, and what makes it significant enough to cause Liza to use her skin as a canvas for the items? Questions. Everywhere I look in life, there are so many questions.

"It may not be a ghost, but there's something supernatural in that foundry," Liza says abruptly as she turns off the hairdryer.

"Yes. I don't have an explanation for the fire."

"It's not just the fire, April. Those walls changed, and if you didn't notice, we kept being forced to turn in the same direction. As if we were rats in a maze, and were only being given the option to return to where the furnaces wanted us to go."

The thought makes me uneasy. Why hadn't I noticed that?

Because it speaks to a more manipulative entity. Something not just possibly evil, but actively able to design a strategy.

"Dusty is giving up on this too soon. He's got us tucked away in that office. We can't figure out anything in there."

Liza is dangerously close to blowing up my plan of hiding out safely in the archives and running out the clock on this excursion. "Maybe we'll find something. I do agree with you. It doesn't seem to be a ghost."

Liza's lips thin. "But, then what? I kept having this odd clicking noise in my head when we were in the hallway. Like when your ears pop. It was the weirdest sensation."

Yeah, I'd had that, too. I dismissed it as the start of a migraine or an allergic reaction to the foundry dust. "The key is, what can toss a man from a catwalk and start a furnace with no gas but isn't a spirit."

"I've been thinking about that. What I keep coming back to, in my experience, this is too chaotic in nature. It's as if something is playing with us. Demons don't play; they act out violently and swiftly."

I jolt to attention at the mention of demons, which had not crossed my mind. I'm glad they hadn't.

Liza gestures with her hands. "And if it's not a demon or a ghost, the only other thing I can think of is some sort of Wiccan."

Nana comes to mind, and I grin. If Nana is indicative of all Wiccans, Liza is mistaken. They have some interesting beliefs, and their veil to the other side might be as thin as hyper-stretched gauze, but they're not evil. The idea is preposterous.

"That doesn't make any sense either. A powerful Wiccan could kill a man with an invisible push and create the illusion of a furnace burning." She sighs. "But for what purpose? That's the real question if we go down that path."

An epiphany washes over me. My law career layers over my paranormal gig, and I set my impressions of Nana aside.

Spirits, ghosts, and demons, they are all predictable in their own rights. Once you know what you're dealing with, you know what to expect. Nothing really surprises you.

But Wiccans are human. Humans with pumped up skills, mind you, but humans all the same. There must be a motive and opportunity for humans.

Liza is correct. We've all but proven this is not a ghost or demon issue. If there is the possibility this is Wiccan, we must treat it like any other human case. We need to determine who has the opportunity and a motive.

My mind immediately targets Rich Underwood. But then I remember the reading I inadvertently lifted off him this morning. That rules him out.

Great. Another dead end for this case that makes no sense.

If Dusty is upset about the case being a bust, he's not showing it. The three-beer limit grows into four, and he even allows Liza and me to opt out of beer for wine. A rare concession on his part.

Cutting my eyes to Liza, I note she's staring at her glass. She has become quieter the more she drinks.

The odd sensation of being outside looking in on my brother and his team takes me over.

My mind wanders to home. I wonder how Puppy is handling his abandonment and if he will remember me when I get home. I feel guilty for leaving him. I'm not much of a mom.

I hope Uncle Howard's Friday wasn't too hectic. He's run the firm for years by himself. Still, I did ditch him on short notice.

To prepare for the upcoming week, I should call Doc Crowder tomorrow for an update. If he has any information on the autopsies, that'll give me a jump on Monday.

Vander said he might have something for me by the end of the week. He may have already talked to Howard. Especially if he obtained video proof of Mrs. Raley's affair.

How will I break the news to Mr. Raley? That's going to bite.

As I finish off my glass of wine, I scan the team. I watch the six men's mouths move as they gesture wildly, but I can't hear their words or laughter.

It's as if the pressure in my mind has built up to the point it pushes everything else out. I have so many things in my mind that my ears won't let the team's conversation enter my brain.

I must seat somebody in the jury for the Wagner case who will vote him innocent. Lane's too quick to let me place a former frontline serviceman like Vance. I'll have to be creative.

Regrettably, Judge Rossi is trying the case. Given her sudden affinity for Vance, she would be more useful on the jury.

Why hasn't anyone called me back on my résumés? Am I doing something wrong? Do I need to change my résumé format? Change the fonts? I need to add some civic volunteer information.

Oh man, civic work. Mama is going to be sore when I get back home. She probably assumed I'd cave and cancel my trip with Dusty.

I'll have to hide in my apartment for a while and let it blow over. I better stock up on noodles and soup when I get back since I won't be eating dinner with the family for a while.

That's not cool. I'm becoming accustomed to the family dinners. I want to enjoy as many as I can before I leave.

At least I won't have to hide in my apartment Tuesday night. I have a hot date with Patrick. Free dinner and some good eye candy. That'll be fun.

Who knows, there might be some flaming kisses for dessert.

Why not some heavy test kissing? I might as well use the taster spoons before I commit to a full scoop, right?

Liza has joined in the conversation with the boys. The entire team laughs, and I feel the warmth of their energies flow over me like the heat of a fireplace on a cold winter's day.

Yeah. Life is hectic but surprisingly good right now. Things are looking up in April May Snow's world.

Chapter 26

My life so sucks. I've been at these contracts for ages now.

Well, three hours this morning, but contract review is like dog years. One hour of contract review is like seven hours of everyday office work.

I don't remember contracts being so boring during law school. Publishers must have picked out the most exciting papers in the world for textbook examples because they were riveting thrillers compared to this pile of stodgy legalese. It's like reading one of Daddy's *Engineers of America* magazines he leaves in the bathroom.

The old documents are so dry the paper crunches with brittleness on each turn of the page. My hands are coated with some unidentifiable funky dust layered on top of the journals. The grime caused my hands to break out with a rash, and I've accumulated three nasty papercuts.

I'll probably bleed out from the cuts, contract some ancient blood disease, or suffer a case of early-onset dementia caused by extreme boredom.

If I were one of those souls who find solace when others are equally miserable, I would have a better attitude. The chatter over the walkie talkies Miles, Luis, and Dusty carry confirms the entire team is bored senseless.

Well, except for Miles. He is seriously in his element. He

best not relay one more useless factoid he's gleaned from an article. If I again hear his tone of expectation, for me to agree how captivatingly interesting the information is—I'll hit him in the mouth. Partly because he's annoying me, and I want him to be quiet. Mostly because I'm frustrated and want to go home.

"Whoa! I found the holy grail," Miles exclaims.

"Again?" Liza asks without looking up from her ledger.

I'm thankful. Liza's sarcasm is the only thing that keeps me from hauling off and slugging him.

"No, seriously." Miles lifts the stack of articles he's tilled through yesterday afternoon and this morning.

"All this is documentation on the accidents that took place on the third shift while Lloyd Smith was the supervisor. Then about the hauntings. How workers felt something invisible pushing them in the back and about weird burns blooming on people's arms and shoulders."

"Yeah. I believe you've relayed every single fact to us by now." I'm not feeling charitable.

Miles is unphased. "But what was the one thing that none of these reports mentioned. The one thing that would unlock the mystery?"

"Miles, I sure hope that's a rhetorical question. Otherwise, you're going to be waiting a long time for an answer from me," Liza says as she turns another page in her ledger.

I don't wait for his answer. I really don't care anymore.

Instead, I return my glazed eyes to scanning the contract in front of me. I'm done humoring Miles. That's not part of my job.

What exactly is this contract about?

"Furnace number nine. Why Rich Underwood looked like someone walked over his grave when you two reported it was burning yesterday."

That gets my attention. I notice Liza has stopped reviewing her ledger as well.

Miles continues grinning like an idiot. I suppose the little turkey thinks he's building suspense. I know if he doesn't hurry up and tell me something interesting, I'm going to clip his wings.

"Guess how Lloyd Smith met his untimely demise?"

I snap. I don't realize I threw the pen until it bounces off Miles's left ear.

Miles grabs his ear. "Ow!"

"Sorry, it slipped."

Liza erupts into laughter.

"What? It did." I shift my view from Liza to Miles. "Seriously, I'm sorry about that."

Miles lights up with excitement again after one last caress of his ear. "Lloyd Smith was murdered in furnace number nine."

"In?"

"His team pushed him into the furnace. He would have just disappeared if one of the workers hadn't had a guilty conscience and turned himself in to the police later that month."

I want to scream. This case totally blows.

Suppose I were anywhere other than Sloss Furnaces. In that case, I guarantee if a furnace lit where someone had been murdered, I'd have some spirit squawking in my ear about the injustice of it all. If not the ghost, I'd get replays of the victim's last living moment.

But not here. No. My skills are useless here.

Get over it, April. I need to keep perspective. It's only a short chapter in Dusty's book. It's not like the world cure for stupidity has eluded me. It's just a debunked legend about an evil man who never was a ghost.

"April, that's just too weird," Liza says.

"I don't want to talk about it."

"We should go back down there. We must have missed something."

"Knock yourself out." I know we didn't miss a single detail in the furnaces. The case is majorly cattywampus—an outlier. I'm done with it.

"You're seriously not going with me?"

I don't know what makes Liza think she can shame me into going. "Right. Why wouldn't I want to get all gritty and sweaty again, or get more bird poop in my hair? No, I think I'm good right here in the air conditioning."

"Well, I'm not ashamed to say I'm seriously disappointed in you," Liza says as she slouches back in her chair.

Take a number. Disappointing people is my specialty.

Liza turns another ledger page. "They probably could use our help."

"Tens of thousands of dollars of the top equipment available in the industry, and they need our help. I don't think so, Liza."

"They can walkie-talkie us anyway," Miles says.

I force myself to focus, and I can understand each paragraph of the contract on the first read instead of reading it two or three times. The stack I started with has dwindled to only a few thin remaining legal documents. I check my phone. We have an hour and a half before lunch break.

"Hey, Miles, do you still have that full-moon cheat sheet you made last year when we were investigating the shapeshifter?"

"Yeah. You need it?"

"Maybe." Liza covers her mouth with her hand. She appears to be considering her hypothesis.

"You think it might be a shapeshifter?" Miles presses.

Liza shakes her head. "No." She stands and carries her ledger to Miles.

I wasn't invited, but I'm too curious to not be included. Besides, I need to give my eyes a rest for a minute.

"All right, Mr. Big Shot, it's your turn to play 'guess what I found.' Unlike you, I'll give you a solid hint." She leans over his shoulder and points at the ledger. "See these payment entries here?"

"FBI?"

"How far apart are they?"

Miles turns several pages back and pauses. "Roughly every thirty days, a little less."

"Sound familiar?"

They might as well have been speaking Portuguese. I'm still back on the FBI entry trying to figure out why the iron ore foundry needs to pay the FBI every month.

Miles pulls out his phone and scrolls. He appears to check several of the dates against the information on his screen. "No. None of these are dates of full moons."

"Of course, they're not." Liza crosses her arms and leans against the conference table. "Policies take a couple days to payout. But I bet if you backtrack the timetable, you'll find a corresponding death plus a set amount of days afterward before each of these FBI entries."

Miles pulls his stack of accident reports closer to him and carefully compares the dates against his phone. "Well, I'll be," he whispers.

"Crazy, huh?"

Miles looks dazed. "How in the world did they not figure this out."

"I'd say they did eventually. I don't think Lloyd ended up in furnace nine just because he was verbally abusive."

"But so long. Why could the workers not notice earlier?"

"Couldn't see the forest for the trees, I suppose," Liza says.

I'm lost in the forest and can't see a single, blessed tree.

Sometimes I'm great at connecting the dots and figuring stuff out. But there are times when somebody else explains a hypothesis, and I have difficulty following their logic. This is one of those times.

Miles sobers. "But how does that help?"

Liza giggles as she points to Miles. "Did I get you?"

"Aw, come on, Liza."

"Say I got you. Tell me my deductive reasoning is superior to yours."

"All right. You got me. But I'm not saying all the rest. It

would be a lie."

"Okay, I'll take that because I know how tough it is for you. Lloyd Smith wasn't just a jerk of a supervisor. Like the legend says, he was a warlock, and he was sacrificing men on each full moon."

"Dude, that's an insane blood debt." Miles shakes his head.

"I know. Makes you wonder what Lloyd got in return."

"So, was he paying off the FBI to keep them from investigating?" I ask.

Miles rubs his temple as his gaze shifts to me. "No, honey. It doesn't work like that. FBI stands for family burial insurance. Back in those days, people couldn't afford insurance to set a spouse up for life if they died. They were more worried about practical things like being able to put their loved one in the ground without having to give them to the government to put in Potter's field."

Okay. For the first time, things are making sense. The legend of Lloyd Smith being a warlock probably isn't bunk. All interesting points to know, but I fail to see how that information helps our cause.

I didn't plan to ask it, but I can't help myself. "So, how does this help us with today's ghost?"

Liza favors me a smile. "As far as I know, it doesn't. It's just really cool to confirm the background information."

Cool to me would be figuring out what the heck is going on here. If I fail to do that, the next coolest thing would be to get in the van and go home.

Miles's walkie-talkie crackles to life. "Liza and April, do you read?"

I start to reach for the walkie-talkie, but Liza beats me to it. "Go ahead, Dusty."

For some reason, I just know they finally saw what we witnessed down at furnace nine. I wait for Dusty to describe the face in the flames.

"I was going to keep it simple for lunch today and just order pizzas. Any preference?" Dusty asks.

"Pepperoni and mushroom for me." Liza glances in my direction.

"Supreme," I grumble.

"And a supreme."

"Good deal. I'll get the pizzas ordered. I'm sure they'll arrive within the hour."

"Why didn't he ask me what I want?" Miles asks.

Liza's forehead wrinkles. "Because he knows you'll eat any kind of pizza, as long as it only has cheese on it."

"That's the best kind. All that other stuff detracts from the pizza," Miles says.

Not only am I becoming better at focusing for long periods, but I'm also improving my ability to block out the stupid.

Don't get me wrong, short of being at the stage of wearing a sign that says "Will do legal work for food," I'm positive I don't want to be a contract lawyer. Still, I do have a small measure of pride in how efficient I've become at searching for the flecks of information gold hidden among the moldy yellowed papers. Info that, when put together, will tell me what I need to know.

Searching for a contract with pertinent information is similar to playing a video game. Only instead of run, run, shoot—it's more like skim a long, dull sentence, squint at small scribbled numbers, read the confusing sentence twice —wait. I read that last sentence one more time and highlight it before setting it on the "golden" pile.

I lift my last unread contract from the scarred oak desktop. I'm filled with a sense of accomplishment, which is quickly extinguished. Dread suffocates me as I wonder what dreadfully boring task I'll be asked to complete next to kill the remainder of the time allotted for our investigation.

The document in my hand is the transference of ownership of the plant to the workers. The contract itself is straightforward. All profits from the plant's operations were divided among the workers at the end of the fiscal year.

Workers were eligible for profit sharing if they completed a full year of employment. The payout was based on a matrix which weighed average worker salary times years of service.

How special of a man Archie Purvis must've been. To build a successful company in and of itself is a monumental accomplishment. But to decide to leave it all behind to encourage the love of his life to follow her dream... isn't that the sort of man we all hope we partner with? But rather than cash out the business he created, which was entirely his just due, he effectively gifted the company's profits to the men who did the work.

Archie Purvis had not been like today's new-age, high-tech moguls with a penchant for virtue-signaling the world of their incredible charity. Instead, he commissioned his lawyers to draw up the contract, quietly gifted the plant to his employees, and left for the Pacific coast. The truly altruistic nature of Mr. Purvis does not escape me.

Sure, you can judge the man on his weak moment. He had an extramarital affair, which produced an illegitimate son. Yet Archie Purvis must have rectified the error of his way with his wife sufficiently to salvage their marriage. That couldn't have been an easy task, even if Dolly Lutz Purvis were a forgiving woman.

As for his son, Lloyd Smith, Archie attempted to take care of his needs. Unfortunately, the devil had already laid claim to Lloyd's soul.

The contract continued with several contingencies. Mr. Purvis was not a man to assume things would always remain static.

Stipulations in the contract dealt with the liquidation of the furnaces. If the business produced a loss two consecutive years, the facility was to close.

All property rights on the first option reverted to the city of Birmingham. The city was required to transform the industrial plant into a museum. If they declined to open a museum, all property rights passed to Mr. Purvis's surviving heirs.

Interesting. I slouch in my chair and consider the implications of the clause. Lloyd Smith was the sole heir of the furnace. Did he know about this contract?

Surely he knew.

Lloyd was shrewd enough to understand it would behoove him to ensure the plant failed. Were his actions driven by the lust for ownership of the foundry rather than the sinister dark magic ritual Miles's research indicates?

When the plant closed, Lloyd would be a step closer to owning the property. The city of Birmingham still had the first right of refusal. The city's option would be a difficult obstacle to overcome.

Unless Lloyd Smith had the mayor and most of the city Council ready to do his bidding.

No, people like Lloyd Smith have a challenging time being political long enough to curry favor. Even if he knew about the contract, I don't believe he would've thought he would ever benefit from it.

Man, they should've called this place the Dead-End Furnaces. Whenever I think I have a lead, I end up staring at another soot-covered red brick wall.

The walkie-talkie crackles. "April, Liza."

I beat Liza to the radio and press the side button. "What's up, Dusty? If you're going to ask thin crust or deep dish, I want mine thin and crispy."

"I don't know about the thin, but I've got the crispy for you."

Turning to Liza with a grin, I circle my finger around my temple. "You keep telling the girls you're that hot, Dusty, and they'll all think you're conceited."

"No, seriously. Are you two where you can break away?"

His tone concerns me. All my muscles tense. "Yes, what's up?"

There's an uncomfortable pause before he answers. "Furnace number nine lit itself."

A laugh escapes me. "Come again. It lit itself?"

"Yup. That's what I said."

That's not good. My mind swims with a myriad of possibilities. The most probable candidate being a haunted object, with the thing being the furnace.

That would be believable and easy to solve. If it weren't for the fact there was no paranormal activity at furnace nine yesterday—any furnace for that matter.

I pull at my ponytail. It's possible I had an off day and missed the paranormal energy from the furnace. Still, that would mean Liza missed it, too.

"Tell them we're coming, April." Liza gestures to the walkie-talkie dangling from my hand.

"We're on our way, Dusty."

Chapter 27

Five minutes in the foundry and my skin is coated with sand sticking to my suddenly cold perspiration. The discomfort of having to ride home without the opportunity to take a shower first is creeping into my mind.

I think it's self-defense because I don't care to think about what we may encounter at furnace nine. As far as I'm concerned, we've already done our job. We have a decent story with enough eerie details to make a decent short read in Dusty's next book.

So, we don't have pictures or an actual sighting. What do Dusty's readers expect?

It's not like we can summon supernatural beings.

Well, most likely, we could. Still, our job is to report on the paranormal. Not create it.

The sulfur in the air bites at my nose. Whisps of smoke crawl across the top of the archway. I hear the roar of oxygen-fed flames as we take the last turn.

Dusty, Chet, and Jason have a camera angled, allowing a brick wall to block most of the heat spilling out of the furnace. The cupola doors are open. Flames leap out from the gaping maw of the furnace.

I point to the doors. "You left them open from yesterday?"

Dusty shakes his head. His face has a hard, stoic set. To an outsider, it might appear like determination. I know it to be Dusty's "I'm seriously wigged out face."

Oddly, that calms me. I close my eyes and marshal the energies around me. As I pull them in, it's difficult to center them, and I fear the mass I have formed will slip away from me.

I force a smile, and the positive vibes allow me to bracket the energy. Slowly, I pull the orb of energy into my sternum, then push out in a large arc.

A stabbing pain assaults my left eardrum. I cringe as I cover my ear.

Fudge biscuit that hurts!

"Please tell me you have something because I've got a big zero," Liza says.

Her eyebrows rise as she looks at me. "What's the matter?"

I pat at my ear. "I've got some sort of ear infection going on here."

"Just now?"

"I guess." I shrug. "I didn't have it earlier."

"That's bad timing. Weird, too."

"Tell me about it." I gather myself to try again. I'm not going to lie. I'm scared of another round of the icepick through the eardrum routine, and I'm not entirely focused on the task.

The sharp pain forces me into a crouch. I nearly lose my balance. "Agh!"

This is so stupid. I hate this about my life. I'm always fighting to conceal my "gifts" from the world, but when I really need them, they're not available to me. Usually because of something miniscule like swimmer's ear, and I can't remember the last time I went swimming in the lake.

My life blows.

The light on the opposite wall shimmers like a mirage. Dropping my hand, I step back. I tilt my head, concentrating on the spot on the brick.

The wall shifts again. It's like watching a film where someone bumps the projector.

I grab Liza's arm. "Do you see that?" I point to the spot where I saw the shimmer on the brick wall.

"See what?" Liza squints.

Her lips part. "What is that?"

"I know what it's not."

"Invisibility mirage?" Liza asks.

"I don't know anything about spells. I'll have to follow your lead on this one."

Liza starts toward the glimmer.

When I said I'd follow her lead, I didn't mean literally. But for support, I reluctantly follow her.

"If it's not spirit or demon..." she says as she's six feet from the wall.

I'm an uncomfortable fifteen feet behind her and thinking we should have stayed put.

"Then we are looking at a simple illusion, cloaking a real person."

It doesn't appear to be so simple of an illusion to me. It does seem like a handy skill to possess. I can think of countless times I would have loved to have been able to disappear from people's sight. How handy would that have been when...

Liza lurches forward with two quick steps and dives at the brick wall.

I recoil, knowing she will knock out her front teeth when she impacts the brick wall.

Liza flies backward, narrowly missing me.

As she hits the dirt floor, back first, and orange powder puffs into the air. She's unconscious.

"What the devil!" Dusty yells, drawing my eyes away from Liza.

A man engulfed in flames stands at the wall. He takes four steps toward Liza then stops. He thrust his hands out, and spheres of fire twirl in his palms, gaining size with each rotation.

Kneeling, I put my hand on Liza and feel the movement of her lungs. Good, she's alive—for now.

The spheres in Flame Man's palms have grown to the size of bowling balls. He rears back like the bully in dodgeball who lived to hit other kids in the face and glares at Liza, his target of choice.

I dive in front of Liza. Screaming, I thrust my hands toward the abomination as he releases the first sphere.

My universe is rocked by an explosion of sound, light, and heat, forcing me to my knees. I'm hardly aware of the gray-blue light in the air inches from my outstretched hands.

"April, get out of there."

Dusty's voice is muffled. It reminds me of talking to him through the wall yesterday.

Flame Man glowers before rearing back with the second sphere. The bully throws so hard this time he even kicks with a follow-through.

The flaming bowling ball explodes against the gray-blue air in front of my hands. Shrapnel ricochets, gouging the old red brickwork. The smell of sulfur roils in the air.

My enemy screams as he moves toward the translucent bubble surrounding Liza and me.

I don't understand how Liza is creating the shield around us, especially while she is unconscious. More importantly, I have no idea how long it will last. I'm just praying it will hold up through this onslaught.

I'm also clueless about the flaming entity yelling at me. I know nothing about its powers or motives.

Think April, think!

Dusty and Chet run past me. Jason attempts to pull me back toward the equipment. He jerks his hands back and tucks them against his stomach. When he unclasps his fists to inspect his hands, they are bright red as if he has touched a hot stove.

Dusty and Chet charge Flame Man in an attempt to tackle

him. As they close in on him, he pushes his fists out, flinging both team members across the room.

Obviously, they didn't learn that lesson from what Flame Man did to Liza, or they thought their testosterone would make the difference in that failed strategy.

While his attention is on my brother and Chet, I seize on the only idea that comes to mind. "You are not welcome here. Leave us now."

Flame Man laughs wildly.

It's lame. I know.

But it isn't like I have a weapon or magical tattoos I can animate like Liza. I do what I can do and push out violently with my mind.

Either he's arrogant enough not to care if I read his mind, or he hadn't anticipated it. I came loaded for bear and hit a pigeon. He hasn't the slightest barrier set around his consciousness.

I overshoot my mark and fall deep down into the core, reptilian thoughts of the young warlock. The brutality, perverseness, and visions in the man's mind tear at my sanity. I scream, wrapping my arms protectively around my chest.

He pauses as the revelation settles in his mind. I hear him debate if I might be of use to him in the future.

Well, that sure as heck isn't going to happen. I'm enough people's girl Friday already. I don't need some newbie warlock pushing me around, too.

There must be something useful in this twisted mind. I push out of the primal core of his brain, into the madness where cerebral thoughts should reside. He obviously was holding the door for everyone else when God handed out the skill of logic.

His thoughts slam into mine as he attempts to drive me out.

Success! Thank you for letting me know I was getting warmer.

I worm around the synapses of his mind and clutch with

all my energy in preparation for his next attempt to drive me out. Simultaneously, I open my mind to soak in everything I can access. I don't concern myself with sorting relevant from useless. I want it all. I take all his thoughts with no regard to what I was lifting or if the evil would corrupt me.

I just know he must have a weakness—a fear. I need his thoughts to identify it.

"Die Wiccan," Flaming Man commands.

I'm not sure about the "Wiccan" comment, but if he's telling me to die, I must be getting too close to what I need to quench his flames for good.

It would be helpful if someone could distract him. I'd kill for Liza to shoot him with an arrow tattoo or lightning bolt, so he doesn't turn his attention to the battle outside his mind and cook me with one of those flaming dodgeballs.

A quick glance behind me confirms I'm on my own. Liza, Dusty, and Chet are down.

Jason is clutching his burned hands. His face white and contorted in pain, he appears on the verge of passing out.

I snarl at the warlock. "I'm going to fry your brain from the inside out, flame boy!"

I made that up on the fly. It sounds hardcore; very *Dirty Harryish.*

I wish I really knew how to fry his brain.

"It doesn't matter. I'm going to kill all of you in the next three minutes."

There is nothing I hate worse than a boastful man. In my experience, men that tell you what they're going to do either can't really do it or never get around to doing it.

He raises his hands to the sky, and flames swirl around his wrist and hands. He crashes his fists into the side of the protective bubble Liza created.

The bubble vibrates and pales from the strike.

Great. I would find the one boastful man who's the exception to the rule.

He rears back to lash out again.

My shoulders ride up to my ears. I flinch as fiery fists come down. Our protective bubble pops with a resounding snap like a rubber band pulled beyond its limit.

The warlock laughs as he draws his fist back for another attack. I can hear the certainty in his mind. He will kill me with the next blow.

Instinctively, I throw my hands out. It's pointless, I know, but there's nothing left to do. All I have left is a feeble attempt to block a flaming sledgehammer of a blow with my hands.

Snowflakes float down from the pitch-dark ceiling. Floating down lazily into the flames engulfing the warlock, the flakes sizzle and hiss.

I'm not sure what Liza is thinking by selecting snowflakes. If she were to cast a spell for something to fall on him and asked my opinion, I would have picked boulders or cars.

To be fair, he knocked her silly, so I'll have to cut her some slack. I'm thankful for the distraction and moment of reprieve from my imminent demise all the same.

The warlock looks up at the snowflakes, and I feel his amusement as I cling doggedly to his mind. He sticks out his snake-like tongue. Over a foot and a half long, it ripples with fire as he whips a few snowflakes from the air and is delighted as they sizzle on his tongue.

"Now, that's down right cool," he cackles, amused by his own dad joke.

Nothing. I'm finding nothing of use and know the warlock tires of our game. He prepares to eliminate me in short order, and I have no means to prevent him.

The warlock opens his hands wide and makes a hugging gesture toward me. I feel my ribs constrict as the air rushes straightaway out of me. My arms are clamped to my side, and I can't move.

The pain is excruciatingly unbearable. It must stop.

My bottom jaw keeps dropping to draw in a breath of air,

but I can't. Please let me pass out. Please stop the pain.

For mercy's sake, if this is dying, let me die already!

I watch but am in too much pain to be terrified any further as the flaming warlock creates two more spheres of fire. He holds one up to his face and blows on it. As if he is blowing on kindling to increase the flame.

Flames spew from the sphere, simulating a flamethrower and catching the brick on fire. The warlock rotates in a semi-circle, starting with his back to me. He turns until our eyes lock.

The flames are inches from my ear. The heat is so close to me, it brings a flood of sweat from my brow. I refuse to flinch.

He will have to kill me without that satisfaction.

He stops blowing on the sphere and glares over the top of the orange ball. Snarling, he commences juggling the large spheres in a deadly taunt.

"Some like it hot." He laughs.

My vision is closing in, and what little I see is blurring. I can't inhale, but inconceivably the tremendous sharp pain, still present, has dulled to a throb.

My life can't end this way. Why spend seven years in law school if you're going to get offed during a side gig that doesn't even require a degree?

It makes no sense.

Flames lick up all four walls of the cupola hallway now. Sulfur, thick in the air, burns my eyes, causing them to water and me to lose the last of my sight. I know it's only a matter of seconds before the bricks of the furnace begin to glow and cook the flesh from our bones.

Think, April. Concentrate. If you don't think up something in quick order, this nut job will cook everybody alive.

"Wow. You're so hot," he mocks.

This guy is a total jerk. On top of the fact he's killing us.

I want to take him out so badly I can taste it. Not to mention his bad jokes are annoying me to no end.

Clamping down on the last of my consciousness, I try to focus. There is something in the warlock's mind he doesn't want me to find. Something that terrifies him. I know I'm out of time, but just maybe I can locate it before it's too late.

My skin feels like it's peeling from the heat. Along with no oxygen, I now have no moisture left in my body.

The team is cut off from the exit. This is it. Either I find the information now, or we will perish.

It's no good. My mind is slipping.

"Free me!"

My left eardrum rings fiercely from the demand.

Fantabulous. The ghost wouldn't talk to us the whole weekend when we searched for it, but now it decides to become talkative. Isn't that simply the way it goes? Just when some madman gets on the verge of killing me, everybody wants to channel their chatty Cathy.

"Free me. I am your hope."

Well, that sounds more promising than anything my oxygen-starved brain has managed to formulate. What do I have to lose?

Besides, if I remain in the twisted mind of the young warlock a second longer, I'll need to die to clear the detestable visions from my mind. I wrench my energy from the warlock's mind, uncoupling us.

My life fading, I desperately reach out with my energy, feeling for the voice source in my mind—the voice offering hope.

The warlock, now just a shadow in my failing vision, lifts both fireballs to his lips. I hear the crackle of the whoosh of the flames as he begins to increase their intensity with his breath.

I should have done this earlier, but I believed I could get us out of this situation until now. With death imminent, I make the decision most difficult and drop all the partitions in my mind in one massive crash.

I force my unprotected mind out to the voice and hope for

the best. With no barriers, I am vulnerable and open to all manner of mischief.

My choices are to burn to death while being crushed, or be possessed. I can't come back from being burned to death.

The spirit of the voice comes to me in a rush. I feel its hunger. Not hunger to be heard, the actual need to eat.

My heart skips, and regrets course through me as I smell fetid breath blowing on my neck from behind. Lord, what have I done?

My skin heats from the fire. If the flames get any hotter, my face will melt from my skull. I'm going to die. Flames from a fireball or in the belly of some invisible beast, I'm done for.

"Free me!"

"Yes, how? I don't know how to do that," My dry, cracked lips don't move. The instructions flow into my mind. Despite my skin baking, a chill slides up my spine.

I know I shouldn't. I know what it asks is incredibly reckless and may have terrible consequences.

But it's far too late for thoughtful decisions. If anyone cares to second-guess me after the fact, they can kiss my grits. We are in a desperate situation here.

"Dominus liberate! Dominus liberate! Dominus liberate!"

The flaming warlock drops his spheres. "What have you done!"

I fall onto my side. I'm too concerned with extracting oxygen from the sulfur-laden air as Montel's hold releases me. His name was revealed to me by the same entity who convinced me to free him despite his energy's evil composition.

Monstrous darkness slides out of the furnace, and I have other regrets. All I can do now is grimace and hope I'm not about to be a snack. If I am, I'm too tired to fight it.

The black shadow's tail finally flicks out of the furnace. The ghastly creature straightens its posture. Its sharp-edged face is lost near the top of the thirty-foot foundry ceiling.

The warlock screams. Montel turns to run from the cupola area.

The flames Montel created along the walls vanish. The heat that never was is gone in an instant, and the air clears. I gasp and choke on the fresh, clean air streaming into my oxygen-depleted lungs with each greedy gulp.

The giant apparition reaches down as Montel scrabbles to clear the exit. With a quick flick of his massive hand, the shadow pinches the warlock between his oddly prolonged thumb and forefinger. Several ribs crack in succession, sounding like dry sticks. The young man cries out a long howl of pain followed by a sob.

"No. Please, no. I'll set it right."

The shadow says nothing to the man as the abomination, my savior, stalks back to furnace number nine. But I can hear its thoughts reverberating in my mind. As it sticks the first of its long legs into the furnace, I come to understand what has transpired.

People are forever saying stupid things. One of the most foolish things I hear is, "Well, he got what he deserved." It would be easy for me to say Montel Bryant got precisely what he deserved.

If I didn't have to watch his brutal death. Nobody deserves to die in that horrific manner.

I stare in a paralyzed stupor as the vast shadow pulls Montel into the blazing furnace.

Montel's eyes are wide and wild with fear. His voice cracks and fails him as his mouth remains open in a perpetual scream. The fantastically evil spirit pulls Montel legs first into the flames.

That must be the worst imaginable way to die. My personal fear of being eaten by a great white shark one limb at a time is nudged out of first place by this new worst death ever.

A truism plays over in my mind. Nobody dies pretty, and death is a uniquely individual experience.

The flames from old number nine, like Montel's screams,

dissipate. I force myself up onto all fours and then to my knees.

Immediately, I wish I hadn't, as a sledgehammer of pain hits both sides of my ribcage.

"What was that?"

I'd forgotten Jason was still conscious. I debate how much to tell him and decide now is not the time to start keeping secrets from the rest of the team.

"That was one incredibly powerful dead warlock and a not-so-powerful young warlock who happened to be his great-great-grandson."

Lines crease the edge of Jason's eyes. "How do you know all that."

Because my mind is scarred.

I can only imagine how long it will take before I'm not haunted by what I've seen in their twisted minds. They were filled with perverse destruction of humanity for the sake of sadistic pleasure. Things I can't wrap my mind around. Visions that could throw me into a pit of despair if I weren't ecstatic for my good fortune. I can draw a breath, and my skin isn't peeling from my body.

"Just idle chatter I heard from their minds."

"That's some pretty detailed chatter." Jason raises his hands. "Look, my burns disappeared."

"Yep. We got lucky. The illusion was broken before it was complete." I push off my knees to stand and notice my pain is easing, too. "Come help me check the guys, Jason."

"But it couldn't kill us, right? It was just an illusion. A trick."

He's nervous about what just happened. Maybe it is better to keep things from the team. At least the team members without any paranormal "gifts." I don't want to be the one to explain to Jason how close we came to death today.

"I'm not really up on the whole 'spells and curses' thing, Jason. I'm sure Liza can fill us in once she's coherent."

I kneel with difficulty and put my ear to Liza's chest as

I check her pulse. She has a pulse, but I'm not sure she is breathing, so I lay my hand on her sternum.

She begins to stir. I relax and realize I was holding my breath.

"Hey, sleeping beauty. How do you feel?"

She pushes up from the orange dirt floor. "Like a monster walloped me."

"Close enough." I steady her as she pulls into a sitting position. "Take it easy. Just sit here for a minute for me. Can you?"

"I'm not going anywhere anytime soon."

Good thing. Liza is a definite candidate for the concussion protocol.

I better check on the rest of the team. I look back to the now-dark gaping mouth of the furnace.

As the adrenaline deserts my body, I shake all over. I realize without the intervention of the abomination that stepped out of the furnace, all of us would be charred husks sprawled across the floor of the Sloss Furnaces.

Dusty is stirring as I reach him. Shocking surprise. All the Snows have hard heads.

"You cleared it out?" he says as he rises to his knees.

"Not exactly." I frown.

Dusty tenses to full alert as he scans the room quickly.

"April, like, summoned this huge dark demon, and it grabbed the flaming dude and pulled him into the furnace," Jason gushes.

"What? You summoned what?"

I'm going to make Jason wish Montel fried him. "I didn't summon anything. There was this ghost talking to me, and it wanted to be helpful."

Jason snorts. "Biggest ghost I've ever seen."

Perturbed, I move to check on Chet. Kneeling next to him, I feel for Chet's pulse. It's strong, but I can see a grotesque bump rising at the top of his skull.

"We need to get Chet to the emergency room. He's got this

cone head look going on over here."

Dusty crawls to Chet and examines him. "Well, at least it's coming out."

"Yeah. But I'm sure it will smart for a long time."

"Oh, hey, the film." Jason disappears around the corner.

Dusty frees the walkie-talkie from his hip and calls Miles and Travis. When Miles answers, Dusty asks him to call for an ambulance.

"Yes!" Jason sprints toward us with a camera in his hands. "Look, dude, we got the man on fire, and that freaky blue bubble April made."

"Liza made," I correct Jason.

"You made." Dusty takes the video camera from Jason and examines the display. "Man, this is top-shelf footage!"

I stare at my brother. My mouth opens and closes. I must have misunderstood him. "Dusty, Liza cast the protective bubble."

Dusty stops reviewing the film and locks eyes with me. "Liza was out cold. You cast it."

No, no, no. It can't be. I can't cast spells, and more importantly, I don't want that "gift." Since I don't wish for it, it's not real. That's right, everybody is mistaken, and when Liza is fully cognizant, she'll explain it was her and clear this misunderstanding up for us all.

"April, you've got to see this," Jason says.

Yeah, well, I've already seen it up close and personal. I'd rather forget it, but that's an impossibility.

The world best be thankful the camera couldn't catch what was inside Lloyd's and Montel's minds. There's nothing the boys captured on the recording half as scary as what I witnessed.

My legs are unsteady. The room tilts and spins slowly like a merry-go-round shifting in a brisk breeze. I'm just coming down from the incredible adrenaline rush, and I'm exhausted from the stress of everything that has transpired.

I plop onto my butt. Whisps of burnt orange dust twirl

around my legs. The world fades to black.

Chapter 28

I mourn the supreme pizza left behind at the foundry with my name on it. It's five in the afternoon, and I'm starving. I consider slipping down to the cafeteria to see what they are serving on the buffet. I'm desperately hungry.

It's time to be a good teammate. I attempt to ignore my hunger.

We're waiting on the doctor's decision about Chet. The doctor prefers to hold him overnight for observation.

With a fear of hospitals, previously unknown to the rest of the team, Chet insists on leaving immediately. I get the feeling the first time the nurses leave him unattended, Chet will make his escape good, released or not. The Lamberts are a wily bunch.

The doctors finally acquiesce with the promise someone will stay with him during the night and wake him up every hour. The Early brothers eagerly agreed Chet could stay at their house. They grinned when the doctors reiterated the need to wake Chet every hour.

Poor Chet. There's no telling what means of torture those two numbskulls are devising.

Since Chet is well cared for, I duck out of his room and walk down the hall to the emergency room. Old memories from Atlanta come back to me as I watch nurses and doctors moving through the halls and hear conversations behind curtains drawn.

I don't miss Atlanta at all. I've even marked it off my list of "suitable big cities" to begin my career.

I've no issue with the vibrant city. There are just too many ghosts there for me now. Ghosts that make me sad. Memories of my first monumental failure, the loss of a close friend, and the pain of being in love for the first time—with that love unrequited—all reside in that city.

Emergency rooms remind me of Atlanta, and Atlanta reminds me of bourbon. It still hurts.

I peek around the curtain and grin at Liza. She looks to be her usual wired, mean self. My heart skips as my eyes turn liquid with relief.

"What? Did the test show stage four cancer or something?"

I catch a tear at the corner of my eye and sniffle. "No, stupid. Only glad to see you're okay."

"Please don't go all soft on me."

"No one stayed with you?"

She curls her lip. "They've all stopped by, and I sent them away. They're so clingy."

"No, they're worried. We were all worried."

"I'm not made of glass." Liza looks at the floor. "Thanks for pulling us out of the fire. No pun intended."

I make a wet, snorting sound. "You'd have done the same."

"Probably. That just means neither of us has a bit of sense."

We stare at each other. An awkward silence fills the space between us. I feel the need to hug her—but don't.

"Hey, I was going to see if the cafeteria had anything worth eating. Do you want me to bring you something back?"

"Yeah, I'd really like a chocolate nougat candy bar."

I grimace as I stare at Liza.

She laughs. "I'm kidding."

"I was wondering. For a moment, I thought you were permanently brain damaged, or one of those spirits possessed you."

"No, same old moody Liza in here." She gestures to her heart.

"Considering some disembodied spirits were floating around at the end, I'll take the original moody Liza any day."

"I am sorry I left you in a bad spot. There's no way I would've gone to tackle that Wiccan if I believed he had enough power to toss me through the air like a ragdoll."

Now is the perfect time to broach the subject. "I'm just thankful you were able to form the protective shield. Without it, I wouldn't have had enough time to locate what I needed to save us."

The sides of Liza's lips twitch up, forming a faint smile. "Shield?"

I'm about done with people messing with me. "It's not funny, Liza. Dusty's already been playing games with me, so you need to stop."

"April, I'm not. Mainly because I don't even know what you're talking about."

"The shield." I'm talking with my hands. They're waving wildly in front of me. "The shield that prevented the fireballs from hitting us."

Liza laughs while shaking her head. "I hear you fine. I just honestly don't know what you're talking about." She gives a quick shrug. "I remember charging the mirage and the sensation of flying through the air. Then you were calling me by a princess's name. That's it."

"Sleeping beauty," I mutter.

Liza snorts and falls back against her pillow. "As if."

I don't care for Liza's version of events. This is not what I want to hear.

Okay, April. Just hit the brakes a minute before you go into full panic mode. This isn't like your clairvoyance.

Let's suppose, and this is strictly hypothetical, if I can cast spells, and I'm not saying I do; it's different because I don't have to unless I want to. Since I don't want to cast spells, I don't have to worry about it interfering with one iota of my future life.

This is just a one-off—an anomaly.

So what if I made a giant-sized blue bubble? Is there any harm in making it snow indoors? What if I did accidentally summon a shadowy Tyrannosaurus rex-like humanoid who killed a man? It's not like I "appeared" a nuclear bomb and accidentally detonated it.

Dear Lord, how do I control this?

No. I'll just ignore it. If I don't tap into this power, I'll be fine.

I realize Liza is studying me. "You manifested a shield?"

"Somebody did. If you were knocked out, I guess it was me."

"That's awesome, April." Liza leans forward.

"That's not my thoughts on the matter."

"Tell me about it."

Reluctantly, I fill Liza in on everything that happened while she was unconscious. I explain, the best I can, the thoughts and visions in the young warlock's mind. Then I described the different and even more horrifying experience of melding into Lloyd Smith's residual energy and freeing him from the magic locks that bound him inside the furnace.

Out of breath and detail, I stop. Liza is staring at a point above my head.

"That's so insanely sad," she whispers.

"I know, right."

Liza won't look me in the eye. "You do know that brand of magic is hereditary."

"I told you he was his great-great-grandson."

She rolls her eyes. "No, Princess Avoidance, I'm talking about your power. I'm just mentioning this to you since you're not comfortable with the idea of having that power.

Still, there must be someone in your family who has the same skill. Seek them out. Let them help you with it, April."

My gut turns as the probable family donor comes to mind. Nana Hirsch.

Seek out, Nana? Just the thought of her tutoring is more unnerving than the danger of the newly discovered "gift."

I prefer my idea of ignoring the issue much better.

The doctors release Chet to us at seven in the evening. By eight, we are in Blount County on Birmingham's north side and pull into a fast-food drive-through.

We're back to our original seating arrangement. Dusty is driving, Miles is shotgun, while Liza and I have our own bench seats. Which is perfect for my plan of eating two shamefully large hamburgers and curling up on my bench seat for a nap.

Dusty has other designs as he continues to pump me for information. He's irritating the stew out of me. Not just because I'm exhausted, but since what I found in Lloyd's and Montel's minds are beyond any perversion I can comprehend.

It will take years, if not decades, to cleanse my mind of their obscene thoughts. Rehashing the details with my brother is not helpful to the cause of forgetting.

That's not fair. I know I need to share the details with Dusty for the sake of his book. After all, I have the unfair advantage of having information he's not privy to that connected the dots for me.

Besides, recounting today's events to Liza earlier took some of the sharp edges off my shock. Telling it a second time may put me on a quicker path to filing it away in a deep corner of my mind. If I'm exceptionally fortunate, I'll forget where I put it.

In detail, I explain the deed transfer I found in the archives this morning and how if the museum were to cease operations, the fourteen acres reverts to the surviving heirs of Lloyd Smith.

Montel Bryant was the great-grandson of an illegitimate daughter born to Lloyd Smith six months after his death. Montel had learned about the contract's existence from his mother.

The family legend of the contract was enough to spark the young man's ambitions. He latched onto the plan of closing the museum by causing the deaths of tourists. He would use the one right of inheritance he had already received from his ancestor—black magic.

With his great skill in the dark arts, he was confident he could cause many unfortunate mishaps while remaining anonymous.

For his first, Montel used a cloaking spell to hide while he pushed Steve Bass off the catwalk. When the man caught hold of the steel platform, the invisible Montel wrenched Steve's fingers free, causing him to fall to his death. It was the same cloaking spell Liza and I saw through by furnace number nine.

The stories of Sloss Furnaces being haunted by Lloyd Smith meant a ghost would be blamed for the deaths. Since there's no such thing as ghost exterminators, the museum would have to close or face being sued into bankruptcy.

The plan was perfect, or so Montel believed, right until the moment Lloyd pulled him into the fire.

The ghost of Lloyd Smith had been dormant since nineteen twenty-nine. Dormant because of his mother, Rachel Sutton.

At first, she mourned the death of her son as much as she swore vengeance against the men who ambushed him and pushed Lloyd into the cupola.

To remain close to her son's spirit, she visited furnace number nine daily. Every day she came, and every month another man died a fiery death.

At first, she denied the events had anything to do with her lovely Lloyd. But as the months went by and always a man died on the full moon, she could deny it no longer.

She implored him to stop his reign of terror. He wanted to obey, for his love for his mother was incredible. Still, he had been so wronged!

The plant should have been his. These men had killed him. Worse, his father treated him like the bastard he was and humiliated Lloyd by demoting him from his foundry manager position.

Then, if his hatred were not enough to keep his reign of terror in a continuum, there was his mother. The blood sacrifices sustained the incredible power he had become and allowed him the freedom to move as he pleased in the foundry. Without the moon cycle sacrifices, he would lose his strength and eventually fade away. How would he hear his mother's soothing voice then?

Rachel's grief weighed heavily on her broken heart. She became even more wretched as she realized her son's demise stemmed from her failure to educate him properly. When instructing him in the craft, she had failed miserably in instilling the creed "An' ye harm none, do what thou wilt."

Her love blinded her to his true nature. Blinded her to his insatiable self-study of text that did not belong to their creed of magic.

Now the blood of scores of innocent, hard-working laborers, men with widowed young wives and fatherless, hungry children, stained her hands in her dreams and sometimes in visions during the day. She could not wash the stains from her hands. In the summer, when the humid nights came and the breezes stilled, Rebecca could smell the pungent copper odor of their spilled blood.

She told him these things. It was the only sorrow I found during my brief stint in Lloyd's mind.

But she didn't tell him of her plan—the plan to stop the cycle of death.

Rachel could not bring back Lloyd's victims, but she could end his future killings. It was one last act of love by a mother. The greatest sacrifice she would ever make. She would stop her son, who could not stop himself.

Rachel completed a binding spell as the next full moon broke the horizon. A potent dark magic spell that would hold her son until he was to be called on for a single act of good.

The spell had to be sealed with the blood of a high priestess. Rachel slit her throat open with her ritual dagger at the door of furnace number nine. She was Lloyd Smith's last blood offering.

Until Montel today.

Eighty-seven years of solitude and the suicide of his mother had been enough to reform Lloyd Smith's spirit. Today Lloyd Smith decided enough blood had been sacrificed in the never-ending quest for increased magic. He refused to stand idly by and watch his descendent create the same pain and suffering. "An' ye harm none." Or, in this case, eliminate the one who would do harm.

I finish the story and stare out the front windshield as headlights cut through the dark. The hum of the tires on the asphalt is the only sound.

It feels good telling the entire story, not the abbreviated version I gave Liza earlier. The second time it was more comfortable. Less nightmarish. Sharing the information with Dusty is surprisingly therapeutic.

Dusty breaks the silence with a long exhale. "Well, I'm darn glad we captured some excellent video. As good as your findings are, we would be called out for speculation if we used it." He rotates to look over his shoulder. "Sis, you have sick skills. There is nobody who could have pulled that read off a malevolent spirit. Much less have the intestinal fortitude to do it while everyone else was out of commission."

Turning his attention back to the road, he scoffs. "And you were seconds from death. Unbelievable. You've got grit, girl."

Oh my gosh. Is that my big brother paying me a compliment? Not just a "hey, your hair looks nice," but a real "you have nerves of steel" compliment.

"Thanks," I whisper.

"Thank you. I'm not sure we would be driving home if it weren't for you."

Miles, who has been watching me intently the entire time, blurts, "Yeah, thanks. I mean, I wasn't there, but that's crazy brave, April."

I can't help it. I sit up straighter and smile. April May Snow, Crisis Conqueror. Yeah. That has a nice ring to it.

Chapter 29

Puppy and I sleep all day Sunday. Well, I sleep, Puppy tugs, rips and scratches everything that isn't nailed down in my apartment. I'm exhausted from the trip, but I'm also hiding out from Mama. I can stare down a ninety-year-old spirit from the hot underworld, but not Mama.

I can't get Liza's voice out of my head. Her advice to seek out other Wiccan, if I own being a little Wiccan, in my family. The other Wiccan would mean Mama's mama, Nana Hirsch.

The idea horrifies me. Of all the women in my family, it would be my luck I'd take after Nana Hirsch.

I know Liza is correct. If I created those things under duress, though I'm still not convinced, I could just as easily create something terrible. Which means I need to understand what is happening to me, and heaven help me, practice, so I know how to keep a blue ray from shooting out my finger if I point at something. I'd just die.

I roll out of bed as the sun begins to set and fix me a can of soup in my microwave. As I wait, a thought comes to mind, and I giggle.

Sitting down at the table, I grab the empty soup can. I'll train myself. I'll practice rolling the can with my mind.

The empty soup can remains stationary on its side, mocking me. A bit of yellow liquid slides out the open end.

I redouble my efforts by pulling all the available energy into my core, and I focus with all my might. I am stronger than the can. The can will not win.

While I have no luck getting the can to budge, I did manage to give myself an awesome migraine. Just peachy.

I toss the can in the garbage and pull my soup from the microwave. Cold.

Checking the clock, I'm surprised I concentrated on moving the can for ten minutes. Wow, that's impressive. If only I had that sort of mad concentration skill during college. I also wish I could get back the ten minutes I wasted trying to move the can and get rid of this headache.

I eat three-fourths of the soup and give Puppy the rest. My appetite is shot since I'm having difficulty getting the evil visuals out of my head from this weekend.

The idea of going back to work at Snow and Associates in the morning relaxes me. The busyness of the law firm will help put some distance between me and the paranormal.

I'm done with the paranormal. The pay is excellent, but I have to think about my long-term health.

Eager to get the paranormal flushed from my life, I arrive thirty minutes early to work Monday. Surprisingly Vander is sitting on the hood of a two-door sedan when I pull into my parking space.

A thrill flutters through my belly. Vander isn't dateable, but he's fun to look at.

Vander is not Hollywood good-looking. Still, there's something about him that demands I watch him. As if he's about to do something incredible, and if I don't stare, I'll miss it.

While everything below my eyes watches him and reacts, my brain screams, "Danger!" I'm not concerned. We're just high school acquaintances. Besides, we have well-established boundaries.

"Good morning, Mr. VanDerveer."

He slides off the car hood removing his sunglasses. He's too cool for school.

"Ms. Snow."

"I take it you have information for me. A video perhaps?" I think it best to go straight to business as I unlock the front door.

"I told you I'd have something for you by the end of the week. But Crystal couldn't wait."

He says the last bit with a flirtatious tone. I shoot him down with an icy glare.

Well, I tried. Vander is apparently impervious to such hints as he continues to smirk at me as I open the door.

"So, was I right?" I ask as I toss my keys on my desk.

"Yes and no."

"Hmm, binary question, Vander. Cheating is a yes or no. Like my daddy says, you can't be kinda pregnant. Either Crystal Raley is boinking her neighbor, or she isn't."

Vander flashes a devilish smile that tickles me just below my belly button again.

"Boinking?" he says.

"Sex."

He laughs. "I know what boinking is. I've even been known to participate in it once or twice. It's just cute the way you say it."

I think that stupid air conditioner may be broken again. I'm starting to sweat. I notice the flash drive in his hand. "Tell you what, Vander. Just leave me the drive, and I'll figure it out myself."

There's that smile again.

"I don't know, it's pretty hard-core. Parts of their sexual encounters, I'm still scratching my head over. Maybe if I stay, we can help each other figure it out."

If I'm not the color of an overripe tomato right now, I'll be surprised. I've never blushed this much in my life.

I cock my head to the side and give him the meanest look I can muster under the circumstances. It's a waste of time. He's unaffected.

"Then, she is having an affair with the neighbor."

"Yeah, the neighbor, her pool boy, barista at Hot Mugs, pastor, and the three guys who do her landscaping once a week."

"All three? Like, how could they not know she's sleeping with all of them?"

Vander burst into laughter.

"What?"

"They know because she has sex with all three of them at the same time."

"The same time! What kind of freaky-deaky is she?"

Vander shrugs. "She's a very sexual woman. Sadly, in the last five days, the only male she's been around she hasn't had sex with was her husband."

"Are you sure about this, Vander?"

He hands me the flash drive. "Video doesn't lie."

I examine the flash stick in the palm of my hand and frown. It represents the hard conversation I'll be forced to have with Jared soon. "I appreciate it, Vander."

"Glad to be of assistance. Do you need me for anything else, April?"

Bless it. Who knew your scalp could blush, too? I break eye contact so I don't melt into a puddle. "The checkbook is locked in Howard's office."

I watch his shoes swivel on the floor and go in the direction of the exit. "I didn't come by to get paid. I'm going away for a while, and I wanted to give you what you need before I leave. Just have Howard drop me a check when he gets the chance."

"Okay. Thank you again."

He waves and pulls the door closed.

I plop into my chair, exhausted.

Vander is not my type, but I swear it's not fair that every word he says sounds like a double entendre. Then how every move he makes drips with sexuality. You can practically smell the pheromones blowing off him.

I check the air conditioning thermometer, and it reads seventy-two degrees. No way. I'm sweating like a hog. I crank it down to sixty-five.

I'd prefer to take Vander's word and skip viewing the evidence. It feels voyeuristic and wrong now. Because I care about Jared's feelings, and even though I don't like what Crystal is doing, I've seen her. She's a real person to me now.

What happens next is easy to predict. There will be no winners in the events to come. Both Jared and Crystal will be miserable during the divorce proceedings.

Fudge. To talk with Jared, I must watch the evidence.

Reluctantly, I connect the flash drive to my laptop. There's only one file, and when I open it, Crystal immediately appears in a hot embrace with her neighbor.

I marvel at the clarity of the recording. It's as if Vander were invited into the bedroom to film them for their own private porn movie.

Given Crystal's reported propensity for unconventional sexual encounters, I wonder if they did ask Vander to film them.

That's just silly. I'm letting my imagination run wild now.

Besides, I remember he said he could get this sort of footage off their household electronics—items like their smart TVs, phones, and laptops.

I'm suddenly extremely uncomfortable. I cross my arms over my chest and scan the room while Crystal screams breathlessly where she wants it next.

I return my attention to the video as Crystal has a medical emergency. Or at least I think she's having a seizure until I realize she's in the middle of a monumental orgasm. I'm in awe. I was unaware the female body could do that.

It makes me envious. Apparently, there's a grade "A" orgasm I didn't know existed, and I've only experienced the "B" version. Occasionally.

I'd honestly kill for a "B" grade and be content with a "C" after the last six months.

Vander needs to work on his editing skills. The scene changes abruptly from Crystal lighting a cigarette in bed to her sprawled across the steps of an outdoor pool.

A young man, waist-deep in the water, pumps his hips furiously like a motor piston. He has the most excruciating look on his face. I suppose it's good Crystal is facing the concrete steps. If she caught sight of her lover's comical expression, she'd have to laugh.

I've been told laughing at an inappropriate time can cause a man's ego to flag and force a premature stop to sexy time.

The scene changes with another jolt, and I blush.

Lord, I'm already desensitized to this voyeuristic, homemade porn. The first two scenes didn't embarrass me, and last week I would have been tomato red while viewing them.

Crystal lounges spread eagle on a plush, emerald green carpet. Above her, with white-socked feet on either side of her hips, stands a creepy-looking old dude. He must be eighty years old if he's a day.

Bending over her naked body, the man smudges two perpendicular lines forming a cross on her belly before standing and unzipping his black trousers. I try not to look, but it's too late. He pulls an insanely long and thin member from his pants.

In a quick motion belying his apparent age, the man drops to his knees and cries out as he enters Crystal. My lips tighten in disgust as sweat dribbles off the old man's forehead, splashing onto Crystal's bouncing bosom.

Vander pulls the shot back from the couple. Are those church pews? Peaches, that's the floor of a sanctuary. That's so wrong!

The preacher mews like a cat as his body convulses. My

stomach turns. I taste vomit in my mouth.

I grab my mouse and begin to click the video off. Instead, I manage to enlarge the video to full screen, making the situation decidedly worse.

Before I can line up the cursor to close the video, the scene changes.

This is like a twenty-car pileup, and I can't quit gawking. Alright, I'll watch one more scene.

We're back in what I now consider to be Crystal's bedroom. It's far too beautiful of a room to be any hotel. Besides, I can see a pool outside her French doors.

Loud music with a great beat hammers my speakers. I smile as my shoulders sway.

"Oh my." I'm glad my curiosity forced me to watch one more scene.

Crystal is surrounded by three men in various stages of undress. The men are beyond hot. Each man has chiseled muscles, dark eyes, and rich mahogany tans. Their striptease to the sultry music mesmerizes me as much as it does Crystal.

Wow. I lean in for a closer look.

"I didn't know you were into telenovelas."

I jump so high my right thigh slams into the bottom of my desk. "What are you doing here?"

Howard chuckles. "I work here."

Rubbing my bruised thigh, I attempt to regain my composure. Poorly. "I didn't hear you come in. You scared the living daylights out of me."

"I see that. What's with the porn?"

All four actors in the homemade video are nude. I slap my laptop shut. "It's not porn."

"Why'd you close it? I thought the blonde was attractive."

It's obvious he finds the situation funny, and he's trying to make me more uncomfortable. It's working.

"You and about a hundred other men. That's Crystal Raley."

"Oh." He squints. "Vander does incredible work. It's as if he were in the room with them."

"I know. It's sort of disconcerting."

Howard pushes his lips outward with a puff of air. "There's nothing private anymore. Ever since the patriot act, the government films every one of us. Even when we take a leak."

Now I know where Dusty gets his conspiracy theories. "I don't know how to break this tragic news to Jared. It's going to devastate him. There doesn't seem to be the right time to tell him."

"A right time?" My uncle looks at me as if I've lost my mind. "Now, April. You tell him now. It's best to rip that Band-Aid off."

"Maybe Crystal is just in a phase and she'll change," I plead, not sure why I'm coming to Crystal's defense.

"I've heard of attorneys catching delusionality from their clients. I've just never seen it first hand."

"But..."

"No, ma'am." Howard takes an unusually assertive stance. His eyes narrow as he points his finger at me. "We will do our job. You are not a social worker; you're an attorney. You will prepare your client and his case to the best of your abilities."

He's right. I hate when Howard is right.

From my limited experience with him, Jared is a sweet guy. The video indicates that he provided a beautiful home for the woman he loves.

It's too bad the woman he loves, loves all men.

What really bites, allowing me to feel equally sorry for me, is I hold proof positive of Crystal's extramarital activities. The unenviable task of pulling my delusional client into reality falls to me. I'll be forced to keep his lying eyes to the video evidence until he accepts the truth.

I hate Crystal Raley. I hope I never see her in Jerry's sub shop again. If I do, I might plant my size nine sneaker in the middle of her butt.

After making a copy of the flash drive, I toss it in my purse. "Wish me luck."

"You'll need your communication skills, dear. Not luck."

Turning, I give Howard a nonplussed look.

He waves his hand. "You've got this. You're a professional. And April..."

"Sir?"

"The 'no drinking on the job' rule doesn't apply today. If you need a couple glasses of wine before you come back, you can expense it. Just be safe."

That brightens my outlook on the day, marginally.

I phone Jared on the way to his office. He is excited to hear from me.

As he pumps me for details, I know he thinks we have evidence that will help in our case against his neighbor. I can't tell him the real purpose of my visit over the phone, so I keep the information vague.

The dealership has expanded since I went to Tuscaloosa. Business must be profitable. The lot has three times the cars in inventory from when I was in high school.

There's an internal war waging inside of me despite Howard's pep talk. I see things a little differently than some of my family. Well, all my family.

I was raised with the conviction that friends don't let friends fool themselves. If a friend has a drinking issue, you confront them about it. If they're rude to other people, you ask them to not be a jerk. Lastly, if someone is taking advantage of a friend, you explain to your friend the actual lay of the land. From a morality point of view, I suppose that's the right approach.

Then again, who am I to strip away someone's perfectly comfortable delusion. Suppose someone is being duped but are happy in their ignorance. Who am I to interject myself and ruin their excellent fantasy?

I park my car, letting the motor run as I process my right

to destroy Jared's false reality. It feels so cruel.

That dog won't hunt. I would want to know.

Besides, if I found out someone kept information pertinent to my marriage from me—they better hope somebody's around to hold me off. Because I'll be looking to cancel their birth certificate.

This is going to blow.

Resigning myself to the inevitable, I turn my car off and trudge to the palatial office. Jared walks through the tall glass doors before I reach the entrance. He's grinning like a kid at Christmas. My heart breaks for him.

He looks professional in a starched white shirt and a red power tie. I accept his proffered hand, and he proceeds to pump my arm vigorously.

Cut to the chase, April. "Jared, is there somewhere private we can talk?"

"Oh, yes, for sure." He leans in conspiratorially. "We can't be too careful. There's no telling how many spies he might have at my dealership."

I was thinking of how many lovers Crystal might have at his dealership. Thankfully, my mouth stayed shut for once.

The walk to his office on the bright waxed floor gives me the impression of a dead man walking. Yeah. I was right. This is really gonna suck.

Chapter 30

I need a shower. Something about watching porn featuring a man's wife with him sitting next to you is a bit too surreal for me.

The absolute worst was when he burst into a snot bubble-filled crying fit. Well, when the blood vessels in his nose ruptured, deluging his starched white shirt with bright red blood—that was unexpected and awful, too.

I tried my best to console him. Still, what do you say to a man when his world is knocked off its axis, and there's nothing he could have done to prevent it.

True story. I feel I know the Raleys well enough to judge.

Jared is and always will be madly in love with Crystal. I concede, but it's not easy; I believe Crystal thought she could be happy with Jared because of his financial success. Unfortunately for the couple, her sexual itch is too powerful for her to contain.

Briefly, I considered asking Jared if Crystal would get some help for sexual addiction. But after having seen the evidence, my gut says she might be a little too far gone for therapy. I decide to let Jared have that discussion with her if he decides he wants to attempt to save their marriage.

That's right, save their marriage. Jared refused to give me a firm commitment on the divorce contract because he wants to think about it.

He's more forgiving than me. I suppose it is a lot to take in all at once, and he may require a few days of thought to get his mind around the unpleasant situation.

I have nothing but awe for my uncle's level of understanding and experience. I wonder how often he had to break life-shattering news to a client. More than what he would care to recount, given he mentioned it was acceptable for me to get a drink afterward.

It's only ten in the morning. That leaves me two options for alcohol.

I could bum a bottle of wine from my parents' cupboard. Which comes with the risk of running into Mama since she has the home office.

What's wrong with me? I can inform a man that the wife he loves is unfaithful. Yet, I can't face my mama about missing Saturday's workday at the women's shelter. I am beyond pathetic.

I'll have to settle for my second option—Jester's, which never closes.

At ten in the morning, the riffraff from the night before must have cleared. The workers from the dog food factory and the boisterous motorcycle bikers shouldn't arrive until later in the afternoon. I'll be hitting Jester's at the optimal time.

Gravel crunches under my tires as I pull into the roadhouse lot. I survey the lot as I walk to the door. Besides a dumpster with garbage bags spilling out from it and two tractor-trailers, I look to be the only thing in the lot.

Tugging on the heavy wooden door, I'm assaulted by the smell of stale beer, sweat, and Pine-Sol covered vomit. I cringe and step in.

The day is overcast, but the interior of Jester's is so dark my eyes struggle to adjust. A huge man wipes down the bar counter with a towel so stained a gallon of bleach couldn't help it.

The man stops and scans me from head to toe before his jaw drops open. I can empathize. Our looks have changed a lot in the last seven years.

"April May?"

"Walter Enoch?" I shoot back with a smile.

Walter Enoch, Winky, and I went to school together since kindergarten. We never ran in the same groups in high school. He was a gearhead, and I played the part of a blonde airhead while I hid the fact I made straight A's. But our bond, albeit random, remained tight.

Winky was my first boyfriend. He's never told me if he was attracted to me or too afraid to tell me no when I asked him to be.

In first grade, I sent him a note asking him if he liked me. He was to check the box indicating yes or no. He checked yes on Wednesday, I tried to kiss him on Thursday, and we were broken up by the weekend.

Young love can be mercurial.

It may not have worked out for us as lovers, but we remained loyal friends throughout school. My friends knew if they ever said anything condescending about Winky, I'd scorch their ears.

I never told him I knew, because I know it would have embarrassed him, but twice in high school, Winky was suspended for popping a guy in the face because they commented on my butt in his presence.

"Somebody told me you were back in town." He points at me with the filthy rag.

"Guilty as charged." I make a quick scan of the bar. "Your daddy still working with you?"

His face darkens. "You know Jester is too mean to die."

"Probably afraid to leave you unattended in this world."

He favors me a good-natured laugh, and the dimple on his right cheek appears. "I know you didn't come in here to catch up with me. What flavor are you drinking today?"

"I'm trying really hard to stay away from the rum and the

tequila, so how about you set me up with a nice red wine."

He crosses his thick, muscular, tattooed arms as he narrows his eyes at me. "Wine?"

"Sue me, I'm trying to be good. It is only ten in the morning."

"Mornings call for a tequila sunrise."

I point my finger at him. "Don't tempt me. I've still got more work to do today."

"All right, I think I might have an old Cabernet in the back and some fruit I can maybe use to whip up something tasty. It won't be all fancy like you're used to. Watch the bar for me."

"Extra brandy," I call out.

He waves his hand over his head as he disappears into the back.

I spin my stool around and prop my elbows on the bar. There are two truck drivers in the corner sharing a mound of nachos and Cokes—breakfast of champions.

Jester's is one of those places that doesn't change. It looks the same as when Jester threw Jackie Rains and me out when we snuck in on a Saturday night when we were juniors in high school.

He threatened to call the police on us. I was relieved he didn't want to give our parents a call.

Jester made us promise not to come back until we were twenty-one. Funny, I'm six years past the invite.

But it's not the same. Not really.

Everything looks a little older. The signed pictures on the wall are yellowed, and Winky runs the bar now.

For so long, I've run away from this town because nothing ever happens here. I need change and excitement in my life. Still, change has come to this quiet corner of the world, too. Slower than the rest of the world, but if you quiet yourself and pay attention, it's there.

My thoughts disturb me. A sense of melancholy colors my mood as I inventory the things that changed while I was away.

It's as if, while I was busy running away, the steadiness of my hometown was there as my constant. It was my touchstone when the world occasionally overran my abilities to cope.

But it's not steady at all. It's always changing. It seems Jared is not the only one struggling with a fictitious reality.

"All right now, this sangria is just a step above Mad Dog 20/20, and the pineapple is a tad overripe, but the extra brandy should cover it nicely."

"As long as it's strong, we're good." I grab the straw and suck a mouthful of the burgundy-colored liquid into my mouth. My sinuses catch fire. I manage not to cough the drink from my mouth as I struggle to force the liquid down. It burns a trail all the way to my navel, where it sits like a bonfire.

"Good?"

I slam my fist against my chest. "Perfect," I say, an octave lower than usual.

"Hey, I want to tell you I heard what happened with your job in Atlanta. That's messed up." He shrugs. "I always knew you would make it big. I was excited for you, and I know it must be tough having to come home to wait for your next opportunity.

"I mean, I'm glad you're here. If everything had gone to plan, you'd be in big Hotlanta, and I wouldn't be catching up with you. But you deserve what you want. Just know I'm always rooting for you."

The shy way he looks down at the bar reminds me why I thought he was so darn cute in first grade. Tears well in my eyes. "Thank you, Winky. That's really sweet of you to say."

His eyes raise to mine. "Well, you always were the most resourceful girl I've ever met. If you wanted something, you always got it. And I know you want that big-time job."

I'm resourceful? I'm collecting compliments in droves this week. First, Dusty and the team compliment me on my crisis control abilities, and now I'm the most resourceful girl. Take that, Wonder Woman.

"I have some feelers out to a couple of different firms. With any luck, I'll get an interview in the next few weeks."

"You will. And when the firm interviews you, they'll be like, 'Wow, where has this one been?' and hire you on the spot."

His encouraging words remind me why Winky and I were so tight in elementary school. I was often apprehensive and full of angst. Still, Winky believed in me unequivocally. It was as if he allowed me to borrow his courage temporarily to jumpstart mine whenever I faltered.

What did he get out of it? I guess a friend he could talk to about how sad he was since his mom died. Someone to tell in confidence how his dad's renewed obsession with weight training and drug use scared him. How with the noise of the heavy metal music, dropping weights, and punching bag chain jangling below his room early into the morning, he couldn't catch a wink of sleep.

We joked about his dad's anger issues. As children, it was the only defense we had for the scary situation we were powerless to improve. From one of those discussions, the nickname Winky was born, and it stuck.

There was scant advice I could offer my friend as he fought the familial demons that invaded his home. The last person to have died in my family was Grandpa Snow, and although that made me sad, I knew it wasn't on the same magnitude as if it were Mama who had died. None of my family members had a drug abuse issue or were even heavy drinkers.

All I could do was listen. And I did.

Winky's grades continued to decline, and his constant optimism was extinguished. He remained my friend, but we had transformed into entirely different people by the time high school began.

I have a thought. "Hey, Winky, does Chase still come

here?"

He lifts his chin. "Sure, your brother came in with a crew and ran the jukebox for a couple hours last Tuesday. All-you-can-eat taco night is a big hit with the guys who like to eat."

"That would be most guys."

Winky pats his stomach. "Guilty as charged."

"Chase has a friend, Patrick McCabe. Do you happen to know him?"

"Yeah, Pat was with your brother Tuesday. Why?"

My stomach flutters. "I have a date with him tomorrow night."

"Really?" Winky rests his forearms on the bar. "Have y'all known each other for a while?"

"No, I just met him a week ago. Chase is helping him fix his daddy's car."

Winky scratches the back of his neck. "Yeah, that was pretty rough on Pat."

"I want to get your opinion on something."

"Shoot, Tink."

My brothers called me Tinkerbell when I was little. Winky latched onto the nickname early and abbreviated it to Tink. It was only fair I had a nickname, too.

"He seems to be a really nice guy."

"He's great. He's a real stand-up guy. I can see you two together," he says with a wistful smile.

"The only thing is—well, you know my long-term plans. I may not be here in a few weeks. Still, I could really use a distraction right now from work and job hunting—and living back at my parents'. I swear, Winky, I think I'm about to lose it. It's like, if one more crazy thing happens, I might just snap!"

I notice my hands are waving wildly, and I clutch onto the edge of the bar. "But he does seem like a nice guy, and I don't want to be that girl who leads him on when long-distance relationships never work. I'd absolutely hate myself if I used him for my own selfish needs when I can't be committed to a relationship right now. I really don't want to break his heart. Am I awful? Oh Lord, I'm the worst person ever."

Winky's expression remains neutral. He slides my drink closer to me, and I grasp it. The chilled glass against my sweaty palms feels terrific.

"I'm awful, aren't I?"

"No."

I take a sip of the sangria. The brandy brings tears to my eyes. My lips tremble. "I'm a Jezebel."

Winky laughs.

"Don't laugh at me." A tear traces down my cheek, landing in my drink.

Winky's hands cover mine on my glass. "You are no Jezebel, Tink. In fact, you're the opposite."

"I really don't want to hurt him, Winky."

"I understand, but did you ever think you might hurt him more if he didn't have the opportunity to know you."

Narrowing my eyes, I snort. "You're being silly now."

"I don't think so," he says. "Pat's a smart guy. I'm sure he understands your goals and how that would impact the relationship. If it counts for anything, I fully approve. For both of you."

My nerves calm, and I breathe deeply. "So, Patrick is a good guy."

"You know he is, or Chase wouldn't be hanging out with him. I can tell you he's one of the most grounded guys I know. He has to be."

I feel so much better I risk another sip of the fire sangria Winky made me. The earlier gulp must have singed the capillaries in my esophagus. There's no burn pattern to my navel this time.

Winky clams up. He wipes down the counter again. I wait for him to continue the conversation, lose patience, and prod him.

"What aren't you telling me?"

Winky frowns and continues with his work.

Dang, it. This is poetic justice. Wasn't I the one debating if I should tell Jared the truth about his wife this morning?

Winky knows something about Patrick, and he doesn't want to tell me. I need this date something fierce. Still, I don't need a new crisis in my life. Especially if Winky has information that will keep me from being blindsided. "You need to tell me."

"There's nothing to tell. I'm just surprised—is all. I didn't think guys who have to do what he has to do would be on your list." Winky turns to the sink.

I talk to his back as he rinses tumblers.

Is that all? I had already gotten over Patrick's career choice. "I take offense that you'd be so shallow as to think I'd not be attracted to a blue-collar guy. Patrick is nice, and he's good-looking—besides, he asked."

"Well, hey"—Winky leans against the sink, crossing his thick arms across his chest—"when you set the bar as high as, 'He asked,' I'm surprised anybody gets a date with you."

I pick up his rag and throw it at him, hitting him in the face. "You're the worst friend ever."

"And yet, here you are," he says with a grin.

After my straw quits working, I turn my glass upside down to drink the last of the sweet wine. I contemplate ordering a second sangria. Howard said a drink or two.

My phone rings.

Doc Crowder shows on my phone display. "I have to take this, Winky."

Winky waves at me, and I head for the door. The sun temporarily blinds me when I step outside of Jester's. The morning's clouds have burned off.

"Hi, Doc, what's going on?"

"April, can you come to see me? Now."

I would be drinking in the middle of the day when I receive this critical call. Doc's voice inflection sounds more like an implied command than a request. "Yes, sir. Do you mind me asking what's up?"

"No, doll. I don't mind you asking. But it is going to be a lot easier to explain when you're looking at it. Give me a call when you're at the front door, and I'll come up and let you in."

He hangs up before I can ask my next question.

I trot back into Jester's to settle my tab with Winky. I lay a twenty-dollar bill next to my empty glass. "Thank you for the talk, Winky."

He looks up from his wash and wipes his hands quickly. "Wait. Do you still like that sweet wine, the pinot noir?"

"Yeah." What in the world is he getting at now?

"Hold on a second." He disappears into the back room.

I check the time on my phone and assess if I'll be a hundred percent buzz-free when I arrive at Doc's. Who am I kidding? Fully sober, I'll still smell of cheap brandy and wine.

I dig through my purse for an elusive stick of gum.

Winky reappears, holding out a bottle to me. "For you."

I must have the stupidest grin in the world on my face since Winky feels obligated to explain.

"This bottle was in the latest delivery from my supplier. I reported it to them, and they told me to keep it. Something about the paperwork to take it back would cost more than the bottle."

He gestures at the tables in his roadhouse. "You can imagine there aren't too many requests for pinot noir in here. Even if someone did like it, they wouldn't be crazy enough to ask for it."

I dig in my purse for more cash.

"No, April. I'm giving it to you."

"You sure?"

"I insist." The dimple appears on his cheek as he smiles. "It would sit back there forever, otherwise. If it makes you more comfortable, consider it a welcome-home gift."

"Thank you, Winky. That's so sweet of you."

He blushes hard. Which is quite comical given he looks like an MMA fighter. "No worries. Now you be careful wherever you're off to. And don't you forget about old Winky."

"My first love? Impossible."

He rewards me with another blush of red across his face.

Chapter 31

Even if I weren't coming off a pleasant buzz, I would be concerned about finding Doc's place. I'm surprised when I see the chain-link roll-away gate on the left, just like my GPS reports. I follow the gravel drive up to his home and park in front of the large porch.

I text Doc letting him know I arrived.

Before I get out, I check for Bubbles, Doc's Rottweiler. My cop friend, Jacob Hurley, swears she's a sweet dog. I'm not convinced.

Deciding Bubbles is not on the loose, I sit down on one of the white, cane-bottom rocking chairs. Doc has a good front porch. Granny's has a better view, but Doc has better rocking chairs.

The front door cracks open. "Good, I'm glad you're here. Come with me."

Doc is acting odd. Even by his standards.

We exit the elevator and enter his downstairs laboratory. Both stainless steel tables hold what I assume to be human remains. Yes, I meant to say assume.

One assumed "body" resembles a long, dried-out chunk of charcoal carved into a rough facsimile of a human in the fetal position. The second "body" has a six-inch diameter indentation in the middle of its chest and is headless above the bottom jaw.

"April, I want you to meet Derek and DuWayne Colbert of Muscle Shoals, Alabama. These are the two men Mr. Wagner put out of commission after the home robbery."

My eyes shift from what is left of Derek to DuWayne's disfigured remains. One thing is for sure, I need to keep pictures of the deceased from being entered into evidence during the trial. The horrific condition of the bodies could sway a juror's opinion.

"Now, Lane is under the impression that both men were killed by buckshot from Mr. Wagner's shotgun."

"Yes, sir."

"The challenge here, my job, is to discern whether Derek died from buckshot or if he was cooked to death."

Doc Crowder puts an ungloved hand on DuWayne's leg. "And determine whether DuWayne was killed by buckshot or if Derek, having carelessly ran over him during their haste to escape, precipitated his demise."

"Yes, sir."

"Let me explain my predicament. Derek was shot seconds before his car flipped and caught on fire. DuWayne was shot but ran over by a three-thousand-pound vehicle. The tire caught him in the groin and crushed everything from his pelvic bone to his clavicle."

The thought of what that must have felt like makes me cringe.

"What do you think is the probability I can accurately determine whether a buckshot pellet killed them or if the ensuing accidents killed them?"

I'm hoping that's a rhetorical question. Doc continues to stare at me with an expectant expression. "Not likely?"

Doc grins as he bounces up on his toes. "By golly, you'll win the understatement of the year award, young lady."

"To determine if a gunshot wound killed a man when he has traumatic injuries or burns shortly after that is impossible."

My heart sinks. I just knew somehow, someway, Doc would pull a rabbit out of his hat for me. If his report is inconclusive, I'm positive the jurors will assume Vance killed them with the shotgun.

I hang my head in defeat. "I understand, Doc. I appreciate you doing this for me."

He smiles, exposing his yellowed teeth. "No, doll. I don't think you do understand."

If he can't confirm the resulting accidents killed the men. What can he be smiling about? "I don't understand."

"Of course, you don't. Because I withheld something from you, April."

He gestures for me to follow him. "Come here and take a look at this." He leans over what remains of DuWayne's head.

I follow his lead. Odd, DuWayne is such a mess his injuries aren't even repulsive. He resembles a poorly done zombie model from a haunted house.

Lifting a pair of forceps, Doc points to one of four welts on the side of DuWayne's neck. "What are these, April?"

I focus on the large, puckered mound, red with a whitish, almost clear, top. "A really disgusting zit. Maybe a boil?"

Doc laughs so hard he goes into a coughing fit. He regains his composure and starts to work with the forceps. He squeezes at the base of the zit. I step back in anticipation of something nasty happening.

My face elongates further in disgust. I struggle not to turn away. I'm afraid the zit or boil will explode, sending a pussy core in my direction. Doc may be old, but so help me if something lands on me, I'll jerk a knot in his tail.

Doc pauses, puts the tip of the forceps to the top of the puckered mound, and pulls gently. He holds the forceps' tips in my direction.

I don't care to see the core of a boil. If I do, I'll hurl.

"Look at it, April."

Oh no, please no. I don't want to. Somehow I'm able to be

a professional and turn my eyes to the forceps.

The boil core looks more like a rock. That must have hurt to have under his skin.

"What do you see?" Doc coaxes me.

"Besides nasty? I'm not sure, Doc. Maybe a chip of gravel?"

His eyes light as if he's revealing a closely guarded secret. "Salt."

That's a new one on me. "Zits make salt?"

"No. Zits make puss." He raises his eyebrows. "Come on, April, use that deductive reasoning."

Doc obviously has a higher opinion of my deductive reasoning than I do. I haven't a clue where this is going.

His smile melts as he realizes I'm coming up empty. "I'll give you a hint. Look, it's under the skin."

I dutifully examine the other three welts. It is, as Doc says, under the skin. Nothing. I have nothing.

Doc exhales in defeat, which makes me feel like a complete loser. "You know what I didn't find on either of the victims?"

I look from table one to table two. "Faces?"

With a groan, Doc rolls his eyes. I don't have to reach out and read his thoughts to know he's disappointed in me. That's okay. Disappointing people is my specialty.

"I didn't find a single buckshot pellet," he announces.

I let that sink in for a second, and it still eludes me. "Vance missed with the shotgun?"

"Oh no, he hit them all right. But the shotgun shells were loaded with rock salt.

"I didn't think rock salt could kill you."

Doc grins. The twinkle is back in his eyes. "It can't. It's nonlethal. Might shoot your eye out, and it stings like a hive of hornets, but you'd be hard-pressed to kill anybody with it."

He did it. Doc pulled a rabbit out of his hat for me. I was right for having a good feeling about this visit from the start. Always trust your gut.

"What are you going to list as the cause of death?" My client's freedom hangs on his decision.

Doc removes his glasses and rubs his eye. "If I were to be truthful, I'd list the cause of death as their own stupidity and meanness. Still, since those aren't approved causes, I'll be forced to list smoke inhalation and crush syndrome, respectively."

"No gunshot wound." I lean forward.

"No GSW."

Golden! I'm not optimistic it will be enough to convince Lane not to try the case. Still, I like my chances better at trial now. Instead of praying one juror holds out, I bet there will be three or four jurors unwilling to convict Vance considering the case's circumstances.

I can't contain my happiness. I give Doc a bear hug. "Thank you so much."

"You don't have to thank me for doing my job, doll."

"Well, thank you for doing your job well. I have to get back to town and convince Lane to drop the charges against Vance."

"Good luck with that. You know Lane has a tendency not to ever want to change his mind."

Yeah, that's a diplomatic way of saying he's hardheaded. I nod in agreement and move toward the elevator.

"Oh, April?"

"Yes, sir?"

"It's none of my business, but take it from an old pro. If you plan on drinking during work hours, develop a taste for vodka."

I start to explain myself and stop. "Good to know, Doc. Thank you for the tip."

"Anytime, doll."

Chapter 32

I have no intention of going straight to Lane or Uncle Howard with Doc's findings. This chick might be new to the game, but I catch on quickly. I'm going to dot my I's and cross my T's on this case and hold the new discovery like an ace up my sleeve.

Doc examined the bodies for me, but it occurs to me what applied with the bodies should apply to the burnt-out car as well. Also, I need to talk to Vance about his shotgun shell load and why he didn't share information so critical with me earlier. If I had known at the start, it might have been enough to exonerate him.

Something else itches at the back of my mind. I already decided it wouldn't be beneficial to bring up Vance's suspicion that Derek and DuWayne Colbert were police officers. But were they? And if so, how did they get involved in a robbery with a man they didn't know?

I know it's a tangent unrelated to exonerating my client. Unfortunately, my curiosity has a habit of overriding my common sense.

I call Officer Jacob Hurley as I drive back to town. "Hey, baby, whatcha wearing?"

"I'm at work. I'm wearing my uniform."

He sounds agitated. Which makes me want to press his

button again. "Ooh. A man in uniform always gets me hot."

Jacob laughs.

Man, he has a sexy laugh.

"Alright, April, what can I do you for."

"The perps' burnt-up car from the Wagner case. Is it in your impound or the Sheriff's?"

"As I remember the details of that case, Mr. Wagner is the perp."

"Semantics. Who has the car?"

I hear him blow on the receiver. "We do. Why? Do you need to see it?"

"I would like to, if you would be so kind."

"Tell you what, my shift ends at four. Meet me at the impound lot, and I can get you in."

"You rock."

"You mean I'm a pushover. Okay, I'll meet you out there."

"Wait!"

"I'm sort of covered up here, April."

"I'm sorry, I just need one itsy-bitsy little favor."

"You mean another favor."

Technically, since he'd already committed to the other request, this is like a clean slate. But whatever. "I need two little names run through the database."

"No."

What? "Why, no?"

"Because the database is for police use. If you need information, you know how to requisition it."

"Well, I'm sort of like pseudo-police."

"Like pseudo-renegade."

I break into a wide grin I'm thankful Jacob can't see. "I resemble that remark. Come on. Nobody would think twice if you ran two names for me. Besides, if I requisition it, you know I'm going to get it anyway."

"Yes, but legally. And I wouldn't be on the hook."

"You're not going to get in trouble."

There's an uncomfortable silence on the line.

He groans loudly. "Fine, I'll run them for you. I'll never understand why I do stuff for you I wouldn't even think of doing for a woman I was sleeping with."

That gives me an unexpected jolt of heat in my tummy. My car's air conditioning isn't working very well. I turn it on maximum air and direct the registers at my face.

"I'll bring a printout to you when we meet at the impound lot."

"Wait, I didn't tell you who I needed the searches run on."

"Seriously? If nothing else, you are predictable. I'll be at the impound lot at four; don't keep me waiting."

He hangs up on me.

I'm not predictable. I'm the least predictable person I know. That was mean of Jacob to say.

I call ahead to Vance to make sure he's home. No answer.

Pulling up Vance's long dirt drive, I see him sitting on his porch steps. He stands up as I park.

"I'm so glad you're home today," I say as I reach his porch stairs.

His expression is stern, and there are dark pouches under his eyes. He looks nothing like the jubilant man who made bail last week.

"You'd be the only one happy about it," he grumbles.

I'm still not entirely comfortable with the client-attorney relationship thing. I know I should keep everything businesslike and my clients at arm's length. If I become too familiar with them, I'm liable to do or say the wrong thing and make everything awkward.

Then there's the real driver of what I do. My insatiable curiosity has me butting into the most personal details of other folks' lives.

My life would be so much easier if I could stay in my lane and let others handle their own business. The struggle is real.

"Come on, now. The clouds have burned off, making it a beautiful day, you're out of jail, and you obviously have the day off."

His jaw flexes, and he stares at me as if I just said the stupidest thing. "I have the day off because I don't have any work. Three of my four homebuilders have dropped me."

"What! Why in the world did they do that?"

"Because of the case."

That is so idiotic. "Vance, it's innocent until proven guilty. Not the other way around."

He gives me a rude snort. "Maybe in your world, April. But out here, it's all about relationships. In business, relationships are always built on protecting your own."

"You're in construction, Vance. I didn't realize that contractors were such a pinnacle of morality in the community."

"You just don't understand how it works, April. I manned up to all four of my builders the day after the shooting. Every one of them was supportive. Every one of them said they would've done the same thing."

"So?"

"Most of the homes I do are the big custom ones on the lake. You know, like your mom and dad's."

My impatience is kicking in. Miraculously I hold my tongue.

"A lot of the folks that buy those homes, they're not from here. You know they're from Huntsville or Birmingham, city folks. Big-money folks.

"Some of them have never been in a fistfight. Never felt threatened, at least not physically. Understand, I'm not downing them; I'm just saying some of them have no clue how the world operates."

"Vance, tell me what happened. Maybe I can help."

"No, you can't help, April. I mean, you can help by making sure I don't go to jail." He laughs, but the humor doesn't reach his eyes. "But the business side, only I can fix that. That is if I can stay afloat long enough to fix it."

"There has to be some legal recourse. The builders can't

drop you for something you're only accused of."

"April, don't you go sounding like one of those big-city folks now. You've been raised better than that. You know the world ain't fair for those of us trying to scrape our way up from the bottom."

Honestly, Vance's tone is so dark it gives me a rash of goosebumps. "You still haven't told me why the builders changed their minds after verbalizing their support."

"The builders didn't change their minds. The home-owners building the lake homes changed their minds for them. Someone took the time to call every one of the home-owners on every one of my builders' projects. The caller told them their drywaller was some NRA gun freak who gunned down two innocent men the week before in cold blood. All the homeowners demanded their builder change the dry-waller subcontractor."

"They did that without checking into the validity of the claim?"

"Rich people don't have to check into things, April. They all do what they want because they have money, and we want some of it. My builders did what they had to do to protect their families. I'll own the consequences because I did what I thought I had to do to protect mine. They might be able to bankrupt me, but nobody's burying L and me this week, now are they?"

Well, that's a positive. I guess? "So, what are you going to do?"

The screen door opens, and Leslie walks onto the porch. "I thought I heard someone out here. Everything okay, April?"

If it's possible, Leslie looks as if she's lost more weight. The bruises under her eyes have turned to a stormy green color.

"Vance is explaining to me what he's doing to rebuild his construction dynasty."

"Build it from the ground up like I did the first time. A lot of that depends on you, though."

I'm surprised he's looking at me. "Me?"

"Sure. Whether or not you can get me off. I can't rebuild it if I'm in jail."

"That reminds me. I've got a bone to pick with you, Vance."

"Okay."

"You had to know that the shells being loaded with rock salt instead of buckshot was important. I can't believe you didn't let me know that detail."

Vance's eyes tighten until they are slits. "Rock salt? Why would you think I'd have rock salt in a home protection shotgun? That's just stupid, April."

I'm at a loss for words. I've spent enough time with Vance now that I know he's convinced his shotgun shells held buckshot.

I might doubt Doc Crowder's findings if I hadn't stood over DuWayne and watched Doc pick salt out of the dead man's neck. But surely Vance can't be wrong. For Pete's sake, it's his shotgun.

Leslie takes a step back as she bites her lip. She already looks pale, but now she's taking on a green color to match her healing black eyes.

I hate to put her on the spot, but I need answers. "Leslie, can you help clear this up?"

She puts her hand to her chest. "Me? I don't know nothing." Her voice is high and strained.

Vance looks over his shoulder at her. He rotates on the stairs, leaning on his right arm as a brace. "What is it, L? You look like something has you spooked."

She chews on a fingernail, catches herself, and shakes her hand as if she's scolding herself. "There might've been rock salt in the shotgun, Vance honey."

A nervous laugh gurgles out of Vance. "No, it wasn't L. That would be silly. We only load your four-ten with rock salt. To scare away critters."

"The four-ten is only a single shot."

"L?"

"We've always got raccoons and opossum trying to get in our garbage. You don't know, you're never here, but I get tired of taking a shot loading a shell, taking a shot loading a shell."

"What are you telling me, woman?"

"It was just a lot more convenient with the twelve-gauge since it holds seven rounds."

Vance stands. He's trembling uncontrollably. "You put rock salt in our home protection weapon?"

"We haven't ever had to use it before."

Vance points toward the yard. "I chased down two armed men with a shotgun full of salt. Salt!" He shakes his head. "All so you wouldn't have to be bothered with reloading your shotgun?"

Leslie looks set to cry, but I know Leslie well enough now to bet that wasn't going to happen. "It can be a really cool story to tell your cousins?"

Vance glowers at her with such intensity, even I step back. Leslie stands her ground with her chin stuck out.

I flinch when Vance frees a maniacal laugh from deep inside.

"You are one crazy chick. Get over here." He opens his arms to Leslie.

She rolls into his arms and tucks her head under his chin. "You're one bad dude."

I can only stare. I may be in shock.

Their relationship tops out the odd meter. But as I watch them clutch each other, a pang of envy hits me again. The Wagners are two strange birds that are perfectly matched. I only hope someday I'd be mated to my own odd bird.

Chapter 33

It's three in the afternoon when I make it back to town. I'm starving.

I call Howard and ask if he wants me to bring him something from Ms. Bell's. He tells me he's already eaten lunch.

Ms. Bell's is crowded even though it's only a few minutes before they close for the day. I stand close to the register and wait for a table.

Eating alone always makes me feel like a social loser.

Someone taps my shoulder. I turn and am gifted with the pleasant surprise of the "easy on the eyes" face of Patrick McCabe.

"I guess great minds think alike."

I begin to sweat profusely. I watch Patrick's sexy smile turn awkward, goofy with my silence.

"Are you meeting someone else for lunch?" he asks.

Patrick's short-cropped dirty blonde hair is mussed. He's sporting a three-day beard shadowing the sharp ridges of his jawline. The Cool Breeze HVAC T-shirt he wears is stretched across his chest.

I hadn't seen him in a few days and had begun to wonder if I accepted his offer for a date because he was kind and I hadn't been out in forever, or if I was genuinely attracted to him. Oh, I likey.

Patrick is the equivalent of Thanksgiving dinner when Mama puts the pecan pies in the center of the table as decorations, and all I can think about is dessert.

I want dessert, and I want it now. Forget about the date.

"April?" His eyes squint with concern. "It's okay if you're meeting someone else. It won't hurt my feelings."

I shake myself to life. "No. I would love some company."

I'm a firm believer in the laws of averages. That is that all things being equal, over a period, everything sort of norms out. Nobody stays on top forever, just like you can't have a never-ending streak of bad luck.

Today is a special day. Today everything is coming together as if April has laid out the perfect master plan.

Meeting Patrick by chance at Ms. Bell's is a blessing. Neither of us has the awkward pressure of a first date. The companionable conversation flows smoothly between us.

We talk about the progress he and my brother have made on his father's Corvette, what it was like going to college in Tuscaloosa. We cover him growing up in Huntsville. We even touch on the career opportunities I'm pursuing.

The last is a relief to me. Patrick fully understands that I'll leave town for good when the offer comes from the right firm. It feels good to set boundaries and expectations in a relationship at the start.

I check my phone. It's three forty-five. I tense so hard I pull a muscle in my buttocks. "Crud muffin! I gotta go!"

"What's the matter?" Patrick stands as I do.

"I forgot I'm meeting the police at four. Oh, I can't believe I did this!"

"I'll get these." Patrick picks up both our checks.

"You don't have to."

"You can get the snacks when we go to the concert."

"That was the deal for the price of the tickets."

"Was it?" He hands the cashier cash for the meals and tip.

"You know it was."

He holds the door open for me. "I might have expensive

taste in snacks."

"As if."

We reach my car. Patrick turns me and kisses me on the lips.

My knees turn to jelly as I lean into his kiss. What started as a nibble turns into a fire-starting lover's kiss. I wrap my arms around his waist and pull him tighter to me as I savor the tingles that run across my skin.

Oh my. Oh wow!

"I can't tell you how fortunate I feel that I had a job in Guntersville today," he says with his arms still enveloping me.

"Me too." My pulse is racing. It is impossible to catch my breath.

"I don't want to let you go. But I'm glad we'll be spending more time together tomorrow at the concert."

"Me too." I want to say something more, but I can't think clearly with all the physical stimulus overload.

He releases me, and my body screams, "No!" I want dessert. I need dessert.

"Okay, I'll pick you up at the lake house tomorrow at six."

"Okay." I continue to stare at him.

"Police appointment?" he says.

"Huh?" I jolt to action. "Fudge nut!"

Chapter 34

A text comes in on my phone as I pull into the impound lot. The pleasant ding makes me smile as I know Patrick has sent me something sweet about our date tomorrow.

Jacob's police cruiser is parked in front of the impound lot office. I pull in next to him and steal a look at the text on my phone.

It isn't Patrick. It is the law firm from Boston I sent my résumé to last week. They have an opening for an attorney and want to interview me this week.

My heart stops. Boston. Oh my gosh, how awesome would it be to live in Boston? The history, the market, the Patriots football team, what a dream come true.

A knock on my window startles me so badly I drop my phone. Jacob is bent over, looking in my driver's window.

Okay. Be professional, April. It's just an interview. In the meantime, you need to do your job.

Jacob takes a step back as I open my car door. "Sorry, I just got a message from one of my clients."

"No worries, it's just Randall likes to close a few minutes before five, and I want to make sure you get to see what you need to."

I follow Jacob's long strides as he walks to the back of the lot. "I want to tell you again how much I appreciate you doing this for me."

"Well, I'll share a secret with you. And I'll deny ever having said it if you repeat it."

"I'm good at keeping secrets," I say.

Jacob pulls up and looks at me with a dubious smirk. "You believe that?"

Well, I'm good at keeping secrets when I don't accidentally say something out loud. "Just tell me, all right?"

The left side of his lips twitches into a grin. He turns and continues to the back of the lot. "It's not just for you. It's the whole situation with this case. Call me a caveman, but I feel if somebody has the nerve to violate the sanctity of your home, you better take them out. Otherwise, they're just going to do it again."

That statement from Mr. Boy Scout, "do it by the book" Jacob catches me by surprise. I feel Lane has made a severe error in judgment for bringing the case to trial. If someone like Jacob feels this way, Vance's chances of winning the case are sky-high.

Jacob stops and points. "Lot three forty-two. There is what's left of the Colbert ride."

The vehicle is burned down to metal and aluminum. I step forward and examine the most probable area I can think of the passenger door being. I squat to get a better look.

"What are you looking for anyway, April?"

"Buckshot holes." I scan the door thoroughly. I don't see a single slug, shot, or bullet hole. There are a few random indentations that look more like hail strikes. I take a few quick photos with my phone.

I stand and examine the hood of the car. It's clear as well.

The driver's door is also free of bullet holes. I try the door handle, but the door is welded shut. I look up to ask Jacob to check the roof for me, but he already is examining it.

"Randall must have given me the wrong lot number."

"No, he didn't."

Jacob's eyebrows raise. "Yes, he did. There are no rounds in this car. He must have it confused with a different burned vehicle."

"The Wagners' shotgun was loaded with rock salt."

"Say what?" I can tell Jacob thinks I'm joking.

It's my turn to arch my brow.

"Really?" He shrugs. "That's like chasing down someone with a BB gun."

I step back and point at the car. "And yet, that's what happened."

Satisfied that I'd done my due diligence in confirming Doc's theory, I walk back to my car. Jacob remains silent until we approach the office. He pulls up next to me.

"You got to get him off, April."

"That's the plan. Do you have the printout on the brothers?"

"Yeah. Back in my cruiser. April, I'm serious. This can't stand."

"I think I have this now, Jacob." I'm not blowing smoke, either. I'm gaining confidence by the hour.

I'm convinced Lane had overplayed his hand. He might —might, mind you—have been able to get a manslaughter charge. Still, there is no way he will ever get a second-degree murder charge to stick, much less a first-degree murder charge in this county.

Jacob hands me the file.

"Did you read it?" I ask.

"Of course not. I'm not assigned to the case."

I glare at him with my "you're so full of it" look.

He cracks a smile. "Alright. You were right. Both brothers were former Military Police in the Army who were dishonorably discharged. They got caught with a stupid money-making scheme where they shorted liquor shipments to the commissary."

"So, Vance was right!"

"Yes, he was right." Jacob's brow furrows. "I'm not sure

sharing Vance's suspicion of the Colbert brothers' background is wise. I feel it lends credence to the DA's theory it was premeditated on Vance's part."

I wave Jacob's question off as I get in my car. "I know that, silly. I was simply curious."

"I risked my career to get you their printout to satisfy your curiosity?" He rocks back on his heel. "Seriously?"

"Looks that way. Thank you again."

Chapter 35

I drive straight home, let Puppy out for a pee break, then barricade myself into my apartment. I have some serious strategizing to do, and can't afford to be drawn into any family drama tonight.

Dinner is accomplished with dry kibble Daddy purchased for Puppy and ramen noodles for me. Puppy is satisfied with his dinner. He promptly plops into another one of the plush beds Daddy bought him. He rolls over onto his back, legs straight up in the air, and commences to snore.

I'm still hungry. But, I don't have time to clear the air with Mama and join the family dinner.

I review the original case file from Deputy Becky Gray. This time I'm more interested in how the Colbert brothers knew about the money at the Wagners'. Vance made it clear he had never met his attackers before the day of the shoot-out.

How could they have known Vance doesn't use a bank for his quarterly taxes and worker's compensation insurance payments? How could they have become privy to that personal information?

I call Vance. "Vance, did I catch you at an inconvenient time?"

"No. L and I just finished dinner. What's up?"

"I'm going over your case, and something isn't making sense to me. You told me the Colberts knew about your worker's comp payment being in the house. How are you so sure? How can you be sure they didn't just guess that you might have it at your house?"

"April, they said they knew it was there. When they put the gun to L's head, I could tell they were cocksure of themselves by their eyes. That's the only reason I told them where it was hidden. I would have bluffed if I thought they were fishing for clues. But I knew they wouldn't hesitate to put a round in L's head to prove the point they weren't leaving without the cash."

A chill runs up my spine as Vance describes the Colberts putting a gun to Leslie's head to me for the first time. Why doesn't he understand details like that move a juror's opinions on these cases?

"Who knew, Vance? I need you to think who knew that you kept cash at your house.?"

"Nobody. Just L and me."

He must be forgetting someone. I push again. "Vance, I need you to think hard on this. Who might you have told in passing or in conversation?"

"April, I'm not going to talk to somebody about money just as a conversation point any more than I would what L and I do in bed."

I believe that, but there must be someone. "Okay, Vance. But someone knew. When you think of it, make sure to give me a call."

"Well, there's not. But I'll call if I think of something."

The Colberts' printout is a treasure trove of petty crimes, stupid schemes, and failed extortions. There's also a pattern of intensifying violence over the years.

It's a wonder the two managed to elude anything longer than a couple of months in prison at a time. They must have had a guardian angel.

Until they messed with Vance's wife.

In my mind, he did the world a favor. Unfortunately for Vance, the law doesn't take kindly to vigilantes. The judicial system prefers to reserve the right to punish criminals, and they value their job security.

The idea to check social media pops into my head. It's a big zero with Derek. However, DuWayne was a veritable social butterfly. He posted pictures and memes daily.

I peruse his posts and pictures, getting the impression of Dixie Mafia wannabe and a large extended family. He called North Alabama his stomping grounds.

Did these smiling people taking selfies with DuWayne know what was in the man's heart? That he would kill a woman for twenty thousand in cash.

Does anyone know what is in someone else's heart? What they are capable of doing.

I do. I've never thought of it that way. In a pinch, if I really need to know, I can scan what is in a person's heart.

My phone rings. "Hello?"

"Hey, April. This is Vance. Listen, I wasn't trying to be short with you. It's just that it's been eating at me, too. The fact I kept the money here because I don't trust the banks caused all this mess. It got L hurt and almost killed."

"I understand."

He exhales loudly as if the next thing will pain him to say.

"I used to have this project manager, Stacy Deaton. I trusted him like a brother, and we worked together for about five years. We would go and get a beer or two after work regularly."

"Did something happen between the two of you?"

"Not really. I mean, I don't think we ended on bad terms. The last year Stacy was with me, he kept pressing me to make him a partner. Well, I'm just not cut out for partnerships. In the end, he took a project manager position with Jay Able's company, Perfect Walls of Alabama. I had mentioned to Stacy my distrust of banks and that I kept back important payments like my quarterlies and worker's comp."

His strained voice tells me the event is tough to recount. He's regretting the slip of privacy.

"Thank you for calling me back with the information, Vance."

"I just don't see Stacy being behind this. He was like a brother."

"Vance, it may be nothing. But it's my job to check out every angle and make sure I'm not missing anything."

"Yeah. I guess you're right. Like checking the tape before you plaster even though you know you have a good seal. A good craftsman checks their work even when they are sure it's right."

"Yes. That's all it is."

"Okay. I'll let you get back to your work, April."

"Good night, Vance."

His praise is the cherry on top of a perfect day. I suppose lawyering is a craft, too.

Puppy whimpers at the door. I put down my notes and laptop so I can take him out to do his puppy business. He's got to get settled in for the night, so I can do more social media stalking. This time my targets are Stacy Deaton and Jay Able.

Chapter 36

Despite not going to bed until two in the morning, I unlock the office door five minutes before seven. That's two days in a row where I beat the boss into work. Scary, right?

If life has taught me anything, it's when you have a hot hand, keep rolling those dice.

It's eight in Boston now. Which means it's time to roll the dice again. I call the law offices of Lester and Mays in Boston.

After the male assistant puts me on hold, I run through my canned speech in my head one last time. The assistant comes back on the line and patches me through to Bree Manning, the personnel director who sent me the email yesterday.

"Bree Manning, human resources."

That little speech I had in my head? It evaporated. "Uh, Ms. Manning, I'm calling about the email you sent me."

There's an uncomfortable pause. Bree says in a clipped tone, "And you would be?"

My word. I'm bungling this, and my brain is closing down the longer I stay on the line. "Yes, ma'am. My name is April Snow."

"I'm not old enough to be your mother, so you don't have to call me ma'am. Ms. Manning will be fine."

While I listen to her fingers click on the keyboard, I

strongly consider hanging up. Some things are just not meet to be. Right?

"Yes, April Snow. I see here you recently graduated from the University of Alabama law program, and you are scheduled to take the bar in July. Correct?"

"Yes, ma'am... I mean Ms. Manning."

"You are sure about the authenticity of both the transcript and your seat registration for the bar?"

The question strikes me as odd since I sent in a PDF copy of both with my application. "Yes."

"I only ask because we will investigate to confirm before any offer of employment is extended to you."

Are you kidding me? What sort of country bumpkin does she take me for? I feel my redneck bubbling up despite my best efforts, and know I must get off the phone call as quickly as possible. "I understand."

"All right?" Her voice is condescending, as if I lied to her. "I'll go ahead and set you up a Zoom meeting with Mr. Bailey tomorrow."

"Sure. What time tomorrow? I have several client appointments."

"I'm sure you do," she snips. "I'll propose three in the afternoon to Mr. Bailey and send you a confirmation email."

"That will work. Thank you."

"Oh, I forgot to ask, you do know how to navigate Zoom, don't you? I mean, I should've asked what technology you have available to you in Alabama."

I live in Alabama, not Angola, you condescending witch. "Yes, Bree. The other firms who extended offers did their initial interviews by Zoom or Teams as well."

"Oh, good. I'm so relieved."

"Yes, I'll be looking forward to the confirmation email." I disconnect before she can say anything else to rub my fur the wrong way. Before I say anything I may regret later.

There's no option for me. To be a big-time lawyer, I must relocate to a large, metropolitan area. Still, being honest with myself, I'll miss the "No politics" aspect of working with Uncle Howard.

All my ducks are in a row, and I'm eager to contact Judge Rossi. But I want to take advantage of reviewing everything with Howard before I commit the first move in this chess game. I trust him to identify any blind spots in my plans.

Reviewing my notes one last time on the Wagner case, my phone rings. The ID reads Jared Raley. "April Snow."

"All right, we're gonna do it," Jared slurs.

"Do what, Mr. Raley?"

"We're gonna nail that two-timing, lying slut's butt to the wall."

I can barely understand him, and I minored in drunk friend languages in college.

"Mr. Raley, have you been drinking?"

"Don't you judge me."

"I'm not, sir. I want to make sure you are aware today is a workday, and it's only eight in the morning. I know you have a business to run, and eight in the morning is a little early to start drinking by anyone's standards other than alcoholics and master brewers."

"She told me she loved me." His voice cracks.

Not today. I'm not in the mood to hear a grown man cry. Plus, I don't want him to cool off my hot hand.

"And I'm sure in the future some other woman will tell you the same, Mr. Raley."

"You think?" His voice rises an octave.

He sniffles so loudly I pull away from my phone, revolted. Swallowing hard, I attempt to put a bandage on the situation until I can deal with it later.

"Sure, they will." And why not? He's loaded.

"Crystal. I should've known better than to marry a woman who goes by a stripper's name."

That tweaks me for some reason. "Mr. Raley, regardless of any other issues she has created, she didn't choose her name."

"She most certainly did."

"Come again?" This stupid conversation is hurting my head. I feel a migraine coming on.

"Her real name is Paulina. Her stage name was Crystal. She just prefers Crystal."

My Goodness. If that doesn't explain a whole heck of a lot. I feel like whacking my head against the top of my desk. "Maybe strip clubs aren't the best place to find your future wife, Mr. Raley."

"Ha! You've obviously never been to one. That's where the world's hottest women are."

Alrighty then. I'm not gonna win this one. "Mr. Raley, I'd prefer you to call me back when you are sober."

He laughs, which turns into a wet cough. "Shoot, I might not be able to call you back for a year or two, then."

I wonder how quickly I can relocate to Boston. "I tell you what. We'll compromise, Mr. Raley. I'll go ahead and pencil you in for a divorce consultation next Tuesday. There will be a twenty-thousand-dollar retainer due at that time if Snow and Associates agree to take the case on. But we will not accept the contract unless you are sober at the time. Do you understand?"

"Man, you bust my balls as bad as Crystal does."

"Yes, and I'm not half as hot. Do we have a deal or not?"

He lets out a disgusted breath. "I'll be there."

"Good deal. Between now and then, take care of yourself."

As I hang up, I realize the dice bounced high on the rim of the table with that roll threatening to fall to the floor, but I came up a winner again anyway. We'd have another twenty-thousand-dollar retainer on Tuesday.

Whoop! Whoop! Cash flow is always a good thing.

Howard walks into the office carrying a paper sack. The large grease bloom on the bottom of the bag causes my mouth to water. It can't be. Nobody can have this long of a lucky streak.

Howard lifts the bag. "Guess who's working at Ms. Bell's

today."

"Return of the grill master," I tease.

"I got you two just in case you pulled an all-nighter and didn't eat. Or if you want to set one back for lunch later."

"Have I told you lately how much I love you?"

"Not necessary. I know I'm impossible not to love." He sets two steaming biscuits on my desk.

My elation turns to suspicion when he turns toward his office. The sack is still quite full. "Hey, what happened to your diet?"

"Diet?" He shakes his head quickly as if he has no clue what I'm talking about.

"The diet, Ms. Mobile, super fun time, remember?"

"Oh, that thing. It's no longer a thing."

Well, that sort of bites. "Really? I hate to hear that. How come?"

"You'll have to file for discovery on that one, Counselor." He disappears into his office.

"Wait! I need to talk to you about the Wagner case." I brace my arms on the frame of his office door. "I think I have grounds for dismissal."

Howard points at the greasy sack on his desk. "April, I don't believe you fully understood me. These are tenderloin biscuits."

I could argue about priorities. That a man's freedom should outweigh tenderloin biscuits. But I would lose the debate. I compromise and bring my biscuits into Howard's office and discuss my points for dismissing the Wagner case.

Chapter 37

Judge Rossi is less than pleased when I call her and request an appointment. She explains she plans to be off the rest of the week for personal reasons. The only time slot she has available is three thirty this afternoon, right after she finishes traffic court for the week.

Vance sits next to me in dirty blue jeans and muddy boots. Drywall dust still clings in his hair, giving him an older appearance. He found work for his crew today and left straight from the job site for court. I'm not sure if the hard-working young entrepreneur's look will help or hurt him with Judge Rossi.

According to Howard, my argument and the evidence I will provide should be grounds for dismissal. He used the phrase "slam dunk."

I wish I could convince my body that Howard is right. My hands are so wet with sweat, they feel like I'm holding a palmful of lotion in them. It's not just my hands that are slick. Perspiration builds up on my scalp under the uber-professional bun I put my hair into this morning. It's not going to look entirely professional when sweat begins to trickle down my neck to stain my royal blue dress collar.

Get it together, April. Just the facts. The facts speak for themselves. You've done the hard part and found out the truth.

My breathing slows. I may have succeeded in calming myself.

I look to my right. I know it's a mistake.

Lane is sulking. I figure this must have cost him a tee time with one of his buddies at the club.

Finishing the last dispatch of court-ordered community service, Judge Rossi asks the bailiff to clear everyone except Lane, Vance, and me from the courtroom. She makes a clicking noise with her tongue as she leans forward. "Counselor Snow, what is so important it requires me to cancel my trip to Metropolis this evening?"

"Your Honor, I have uncovered several pieces of evidence I believe will exonerate my client of the charges of first-degree murder."

"I object, Your Honor. If Miss Snow has uncovered some monumental information, surely we can review it at the time of the trial. The state has compiled a persuasive case against Mr. Wagner. We would like the opportunity to present our evidence to a jury since he is not inclined to take the second-degree murder plea, we so generously extended."

Judge Rossi angles her head. "Lane, what do I have on?"

"Excuse me, Judge Rossi?"

"I said what do I have on, son?"

"Under your robe?"

"No, not under, but yes, a robe. Do you think I wear it because black looks good on me?"

Lane struggles for an answer. "No, Your Honor?"

"I wear it as a symbol of justice and impartiality. My point, Mr. Jameson, is there is no difference between presenting your information to me or the jury. We both can decide. Now, if you find it acceptable to follow the laws of the great state of Alabama in this courtroom, I would like to proceed. I have been sitting in this chair for way too long today."

"Yes, Your Honor." Lane shifts his stance.

"Counselor Snow, you may begin."

"First, I would like to reiterate the fact the DA has decided to charge Mr. Wagner with first-degree murder. With the new evidence I have unearthed, there is absolutely no way for the state to prove first-degree murder in this case. The state of Mr. Wagner's mind when he pulled out his riot gun cannot be proven to be filled with homicidal intent. In fact, he repeatedly stated that he feared his attackers would return to his home and inflict further injury or death on him and his wife. To show premeditated murder under the circumstances will be impossible."

Judge Rossi cuts me off by waving her hand in front of her. "Counselor Snow, you sure have a nice voice. I truly do like listening to you talk, and you look beautiful up on your soapbox and all. Still, I sure hope you didn't have me cancel my Metropolis trip to hear you regurgitate what we already know. You promised me additional information. I suggest you get along with it. Otherwise, I'll be inclined to agree with the DA and decline your dismissal request."

I hide a smile. "Yes, Your Honor. My intent was to reset the facts of the case before I mention the autopsy reports reveal neither Colbert brothers' death resulted from buckshot injuries. May I approach the bench?"

Judge Rossi motions me forward.

"For Pete's sake, Judge, I haven't seen the autopsy report yet."

"Perhaps you should've waited until Doc got done with them before you filed your charges, Lane," Judge Rossi hisses.

I present copies of the death certificates Doc emailed me last night. "As you see, neither brother died from GSW. The deaths are crush syndrome and smoke inhalation."

"Because they had been shot by a crazy man chasing them down the street, which caused their accidents," Lane protests.

I smell blood, and I'm going in for the kill. "The crazy man was the victim of a robbery and an assault in his residence.

He wasn't chasing them down the street. He was chasing them down his private driveway."

"Lane, you might not want to use the word 'accident' when trying a defendant for first-degree murder."

Judge Rossi refocuses on me. "I don't know, Counselor. While this is compelling, I still believe your client was protecting property at the expense of human life."

"My client had no intentions of hurting those two men." I had to hurry through my big fat lie before I blush. "He did want to scare them away. Mr. Wagner was afraid they went to their car to retrieve what they needed to kill him and his wife and dispose of their bodies."

Judge Rossi frowns. "According to Deputy Gray's report, they already had the cash."

"Yes, but they also had held a gun to Ms. Wagner's head. They threatened to pull the trigger. My client simply took the men at their word. He had every reason to believe the Colbert brothers would kill them to eliminate any witnesses."

"Again, Counselor Snow"—Judge Rossi crosses her arms —"unless you have some proof for me, this is best left up to a jury trial. You are attempting to establish a state of mind just as the DA attempted. The jury will have to determine your client's intent. I can't do that in this forum."

"What my client intended to do was scare the criminals away so he and his wife would be safe. I know this because his shotgun shells were not filled with buckshot. They were filled with rock salt."

Judge Rossi's eyes narrow. "Salt?"

"Yes, Your Honor. If he meant to seriously injure them, surely he wouldn't have used rock salt-filled shells. That goes doubly if he intended to kill them."

Rossi turns to Lane. "Did you know about this?"

"No, Your Honor, I didn't."

I'm on a roll. I'm really feeling it.

"Judge Rossi, we also know the Colberts were there to

commit a murder." I pull out the social media photos I printed last night. Handing the photos to Judge Rossi, I again force down a smile.

As she flips through the stack, I explain the significance of the photos.

"The photos were taken during the Easter holiday at the home of Jay Able. The house is in Huntsville. As you flip through the pictures, you will see the Colbert brothers. It may be a little tough to tell from the autopsy photos, but trust me, it's the Colbert boys."

"Judge, what does this have to do with the trial?" Lane complains as he looks pointedly at his Rolex watch.

"The Colberts are nephews, were nephews, of Mr. Able. The same Mr. Able who hired away one of Mr. Wagner's top project managers a year ago. The project manager who is aware Mr. Wagner hides large sums of money in his house right before making his quarterly tax and insurance payments."

Judge Rossi puts her reading glasses on. "You believe the Colberts and this former project manager..." She points at the pictures in her hand.

"Deaton, Stacy Deaton."

"This Deaton and the Colberts, they cooked this up?"

"No, your honor. I believe it had little to nothing to do with the money and everything to do with Mr. Wagner's business. You see, Mr. Able and Mr. Wagner are competitors."

The judge's facial features pinch. She points at Vance. "Mr. Wagner. Is this true? Are you and Mr. Able in competition?"

"Yes, Your Honor."

Judge Rossi shakes her head. "I told you I thought you were outkicking your coverage on this one, Lane. There's a case here, but Mr. Wagner isn't it. Your team should be investigating if the Colberts were operating on their own or if they were hired."

"Judge, I still have a solid case for manslaughter."

"And then what? If you can't prove manslaughter, are you

going to try and hang weapon charges on Mr. Wagner?"

Lane frowns. "He was in the county. So, it's not really..."

"That was a rhetorical question, Lane. For heaven's sake, son. Let it go. Just give thanks that we caught this before it went too far, and you had the embarrassment of an appeal process."

Judge Rossi stacks the information I gave her and taps the edges of the paper on the top of her desk. "Excellent work, Counselor Snow. I will be dismissing the case against Mr. Wagner today. Your client is free to go."

Even though I believed we would get a dismissal, hearing the words from her gives me such a rush I'm forced to steady myself against the judge's bench. "Thank you, Judge Rossi."

"But the state attorney general has given this case a high priority."

"That's political, Lane, which makes it your job. Mine is seeing justice is served in this county."

"But, Judge, surely we should be able to follow up with a manslaughter charge."

Judge Rossi flicks her wrist at him as she stands. "Lane, it's a tie right now as to what's aggravating me more, my hemorrhoids or you, son."

She turns her back and steps down as the bailiff opens the door for her. She stops and focuses her gaze on Vance.

"Mr. Wagner, I understand your reservations regarding banks. Still, I think in the future, you might want to reconsider holding cash in your house. The Guntersville Credit Union is local, and I believe they have a fair rate of return for business accounts. You might want to check them out."

"Yes, Your Honor. Thank you for the tip."

"My pleasure, son. Good luck with your business."

It might only be Guntersville, but I'm one "Big Gun" defense attorney. I now am two and oh on capital murder trials.

Well, neither of them went to trial, but that is a minor technicality. I got my clients off in both cases and saved innocent people from going to jail. I'm a success, and more importantly, I feel like a success.

Vance and I stride out of the courtroom together. It's like being an Olympic champion as we open the oaken double doors together.

It's all too fitting that as we clear the doors, a slight blonde jumps on Vance and wraps her legs around his waist. He laughs joyfully as Leslie plants quick kisses all over his face.

I realize I've never heard him laugh before now. I was able to give him his laughter back. There is something profound and special about that.

Stepping back, I watch the couple until I feel voyeuristic. I make to slip away unseen when Leslie grabs my arm.

"I don't know how I will ever repay you, April. But don't you dare hesitate to call if there's something you need me to do for you."

The intensity of the stare from her blue eyes is slightly unsettling. "I was just doing my job, Leslie."

"And you're extremely good at it, April. Don't let anyone tell you differently."

Seeing them in their embrace wakes my memory to events outside of court. I check my cell phone and panic. Patrick is due to pick me up in an hour.

Bless it! I still must pick out an outfit, take a shower, no... I also need to shave my legs. Or do I leave them hairy as an insurance policy? In case I get too carried away on our first date.

Am I overthinking this?

I tell the Wagners goodbye and hustle out the judicial building's glass doors. I know it sounds silly when people say they're floating on air, but everything feels lighter as I jog on the balls of my feet to my car.

Chapter 38

As I give in to my hair's desire to be wild and crazy this evening, there is a knock on my apartment door. Puppy goes into full intruder-alert mode, barking and snarling as I insert my last earring.

"Calm down, Puppy. Save some for the bad guys." I bend over and pull him back from the door.

I open my door and smile. Oh yeah. I'm glad I agreed to this.

"Hi."

"Hey, come on in. I just have to grab my purse."

"For a woman as beautiful as you, I'll wait all night." He steps inside.

It's corny, but it still makes me warm inside. "Careful, you never know what flattery might get you." I'm pleased to see a blush color his cheeks.

That's what I thought. It took Patrick all day to work up the boldness for that opening line.

"I hope you don't mind riding in my dad's 'Vette this evening. We still haven't replaced the upholstery, but I thought it might be fun since she's running well."

"That sounds fun." I'm glad I didn't opt for the super-tight skirt I considered wearing tonight.

He's scratching Puppy's head. Puppy rolls over, and Patrick obliges him with a tummy rub, too. I'm not sure which one of them is cuter.

"I have reservations at Santiago's in Huntsville before the show. We can change it if you don't like that," he says as he opens the door for me.

"Santiago's? You spoil me this much on the first date, what are you going to do for encores?"

Patrick has a pleased smile on his face. "I'll worry about that when the time comes."

It's been too long since I went on a real date. That's what I think as we ride out to Santiago's, where we relish a fabulous Italian meal with expensive wine. Then we dance until we collapse into our seats at the concert, holding hands on the way back to his car.

I haven't been on a date like this since my freshman year in college. The last six years have been a series of double dates, groups of friends going out together, hanging out at apartments with guys I'm interested in and hooking up for brief encounters. Nothing as intimate as tonight with Patrick.

That's the word, too. Intimate. And mature.

The intimacy builds a fire in me going well beyond my usual lust for the skin-on-skin contact. Driving back from dinner, I swear I can feel the tips of my fingers and toes tingling with anticipation.

The saddest part is my life goals are out of sync with my immediate desires. I need this now. I must have this man who has connected with me on so many levels. Not just on a physical level, either.

Sue me. I'm even wondering what it would be like to be married to Patrick. I'd love to be on a journey with him. Not just to Santiago's and a show, but a journey through life.

I know it's crazy. Right? But everything we do is so simpatico, and this is only our first date. Just imagine!

But I'm not staying in Guntersville, and he hasn't mentioned leaving North Alabama. There is no way all my pretty visions of marriage can come true. It won't work with me working eighty hours a week at a major law firm on the East Coast while he's back in Alabama fixing air conditioners.

It's a childish dream. It could never happen.

That in mind, the responsible and kind thing would be to let him take me home, thank him for a spectacular night—which it was—and never see him again. That way I won't be leading him on, and nobody would get hurt.

"Hey, take that right coming up." I'm such a terrible person.

"Isn't that just a dead end?"

I press the nail of my forefinger against my teeth and grin. "Maybe."

Patrick certainly isn't stupid. He returns my smile and turns right.

I've lost track. Out of breath and fully satiated, I tuck my head against Patrick's chest.

Shifting, he whispers, hot against my neck, "I wish we had a bed."

True. A Corvette is my last car of choice for a make-out session. Still, I can't complain. I've had two orgasms and never made it out of my panties.

"Maybe we skip dinner next time and get a room."

"We could get a room now," he offers.

"If the concert had been on a weekend night. I have work in the morning."

Patrick groans as he pulls away from me. "It's so unfair the tour manager scheduled Huntsville for a Tuesday night. Why?"

"I know. Of all the rotten luck. Didn't they know?"

We laugh. We stare at each other by the light of the crescent moon.

This is special. It feels so right.

"I'm afraid to start the car. I worry this will all melt away like a wonderful dream. I don't want this night to end."

"I don't want you to take me home, either. But I'll live knowing we'll have more nights like tonight."

"You promise?" I see his eyebrows raise.

"I do."

"Good. But know I'll hold you to it," Patrick says as he turns the key and the motor rumbles to life.

I'm proud of myself when we drive up to my parents' driveway. We passed two hotels on the way to their house, and I kept my willpower.

Patrick walks me to the door and presses me between him and the front door as he freely takes a kiss from my mouth, leaving me feeling like jelly all over again.

He pulls back inches from my face. "I have to see you tomorrow."

My brain is addled, and my legs have lost all power. I'm debating what it would mean if I invite Patrick inside my apartment. "Okay," I manage to answer.

"I need to introduce you before we go any further. I'll cook dinner at my place."

He's old-fashioned. It suits him. I suppose inviting him in tonight would be a mistake.

There was a time when it would've offended me if a man thought he had to introduce me to his mom before we got serious. My mind is changing regarding a lot of things lately. "Okay," I whisper.

He kisses me hard again, and I don't care if he is old-fashioned. I want him tonight.

He pushes off the door with his hands. My body objects to the coolness of the seventy-five-degree air and laments the loss of his body's pressure against my chest.

Patrick gets in his car and waits for me to go inside. As I lean over to pick up Puppy, who bum-rushed the door to greet me, I hear the big motor of the Corvette rumble to life.

Chapter 39

I'm a hot mess this morning. I have the interview with Lester and Mays this afternoon, which I will nail. Which means I'll be going to Boston and starting my high-power law career in short order.

Tonight, I'll meet the mom of a man I'm convinced I could spend a long time with and be happy. I don't know if I love him. Whatever that means.

I do know I'm intensely attracted to him. I can talk to him for hours without ever becoming bored, and I get these giddy, warm, and fuzzy feelings every time I think about him. Heck, I even debated whether I prefer April May McCabe or April Snow McCabe. So, I guess I'm in serious "like" right now.

"Hey, April?"

"What!" I cringe at my aggravated tone.

I'm further embarrassed when Howard steps out of his office. "Are you okay?"

No, I'm a train wreck. "Yes, sir. I guess I'm just a little nervous about my interview this afternoon."

"Why don't you take the rest of the afternoon off. Maybe relax on the dock for an hour," he says. "Work on sounding less like a tyrant."

"That bad?"

He pirouettes and walks back into his office. "Oh, yeah."

Working in a small town, I won't miss it. Working for my uncle, I know I'll miss terribly.

I take his advice and sit on my parents' dock for an hour tossing bread to the catfish while Puppy barks at them and eats his own fair share of bread.

Going into my apartment, I sit at my kitchenette and set up my laptop. I paste in the meeting address and receive the cue that the meeting will be starting momentarily.

Howard's advice worked. I'm not the least bit nervous about this interview.

The face of a younger man, only a few years older than me, appears on the screen. I read the name Hunter Bailey, who is the partner Bree told me would interview me.

Initially, I'm taken aback by a partner being so young. Still, that could bode well for an aggressive young attorney like me to make partner at the firm in short order.

"April Snow?"

"Hello, Mr. Bailey."

"My. Bree said you were sharp. Here I thought she was talking about your intelligence."

I'm confused by his comment. I'm not sure how to respond, and there is a long silence.

"Are you interested in moving to the East Coast?"

I try to recover. "I hear you need to go where the opportunity is."

He laughs. It sounds practiced, oily, and void of humor. "That is true. We have plenty of opportunity at Lester and Mays for the right kind of girls."

Girls? Maybe he's one of those men who just say everything wrong.

"Tell me your favorite part of law school, April."

Besides graduating? "By far, litigation. I feel I have a natural ability to communicate the facts of a case and be persuasive while I do it."

"Yes, I could see you being very persuasive while you do

it."

Are you kidding me? Is this dude, like, for real, or is he just testing me?

"It also says here that you've defended a capital case?"

Oh, I didn't update my resume. "Two capital cases. I successfully defended a second client this week. I'm no beginner, Mr. Bailey. I'm more seasoned than most any of the candidates coming to you directly from law school."

Hunter's facial expression tightens. "Winning in a small-town court is less challenging than our demographics."

What a prick. I come close to telling Hunter what I think of his small-town court comment, but I know he holds my ticket to the big market.

"How do you feel about contract law, April?"

"Like, litigating contract law?"

Hunter fake chuckles as if I asked an absurd question. "Of course not. I meant like proofing contracts before authorizing signatures."

"Isn't that work you would normally have a paralegal do?"

Hunter shrugs. "You don't have any real-world experience, so until we get you trained, you are a paralegal. But I like the way you look. I think you have the potential to add some pizzazz to this firm."

Pizzazz? I'm a paralegal?

My thoughts return to this weekend, combing through the mind-numbing contracts from Sloss Furnaces. I'm sure I can deal with the East Coast's wintry weather, the long hours, initially small paychecks, and even Hunter's inappropriate references to my appearance. The one thing this girl knows she can't handle is contract law review.

"Mr. Bailey, I apologize, but when I spoke with Bree, I didn't understand this was a contract law position. I thank you for your time, but I have no interest."

"You need to be clear on this, April. If you turn this opportunity down, it will preclude you from ever interviewing for another position at Lester and Mays."

I'm amazed Hunter can say that and look as if I'm tearing up a lottery ticket.

"I understand, Mr. Bailey. Again, thank you for your time." I disconnect the Zoom call before he can comment further.

I lean back on my chair and consider what just happened. I all but had a ticket to Boston and threw it away over a preference.

Still, there is the possibility this happened for a reason. Wasn't it just today I told myself how much I would miss working with Howard?

Plus, I'm pulling down some sick money with my brother on the paranormal book investigations for a part-time gig. Maybe I'm supposed to stay here. Perhaps the whole reason everything has been falling through on the job front was to bring me home to find Patrick.

I'm not sure how I feel about that if it's true. One part of me feels giggly and free. Everything below my brain thinks it's a fantastic idea.

My brain, the other part of me, believes I'm compromising my dreams. Exactly what I have always said I would never do.

I'll just do what I do best. Work my plan but be prepared for contingencies.

Chapter 40

Since I am meeting Patrick's mom, I dress in a conservative, knee-length plaid skirt and ivory blouse.

I type his address into the GPS of my phone. It looks like I should arrive at his house in Huntsville fifteen minutes early.

I like that. Patrick's mom will consider me punctual but not overly eager.

As I pull into his neighborhood, I realize we must be eating at his mom's house. The homes in this neighborhood are all-brick and pushing five thousand square feet.

The McCabe home is a large, gray French château style complete with an acre of backyard behind a wrought-iron fence. I also make out a water slide, presumably to their pool.

I have a moment of empathy as I consider the laughter that must have once filled the home while Patrick was growing up. The pain of losing his father must weigh on him while visiting. Even if introducing me to his mother should be a "happy" event.

I chastise myself as I look at the doorbell. I should've thought to bring a gift—a bottle of wine or something. Standing on the enormous house's front porch makes me self-conscious for not remembering that small bit of etiquette.

Too late now. If Patrick's mom ends up hating me because I didn't bring a gift, that will just have to be assigned to fate also.

I ring the doorbell.

Patrick opens the door. He has a griller's apron on and wipes his hands on a towel. He looks adorable. His face lights up, making me feel like the most special person in the world.

"I can't tell you how glad I am you're here."

I want to return the favor from the other night, pin him against the wall, and plant a hot kiss on his lips. I opt for a more subdued kiss, with the flick of the tip of my tongue promising more for later.

"I'll show you how glad I am to be here later tonight," I say in my "sexy" voice.

Patrick laughs as his face flushes red. He gestures me inside. "Thank you for doing this. I'm so glad you understand the importance of family, too."

I visualize my family, and it brings a smile to my face. "I do understand."

The smile lines of his eyes deepen. "I love the fact we both feel that way."

I hear footsteps behind us, but I can't take my eyes off Patrick's handsome face. He is so in his element. His joy is so great he has a glow about him that, impossibly, makes him even more attractive.

"Robert, this is the lady I was telling you about. Miss April."

"The one with the puppy?"

Patrick laughs. "You have to excuse that, April. He's been after me for the last year to get a puppy, and we're still in negotiations."

I turn to my right, belatedly taking notice of the boy standing next to me. I'm not the best at guessing children's ages, but I'd put him at eight. His hair is slightly darker and longer than Patrick's, but there is no denying they are related.

Leaning over, I extend my hand. "I bet my puppy would love to play with you. Maybe your big brother will bring you over next time he comes to my house."

He giggles. "You're silly. I don't have a big brother."

"April, Robert is my son."

There is no oxygen in the room that has begun to spin. Someone has turned the heat up to ninety degrees.

I'm not stupid or deaf. I heard what Patrick said. I look from Patrick's smile, which is slowly fading, to the miniature version of him named Robert and back to Patrick.

The walls are moving in on me.

This is beyond any humiliation or embarrassment I can recall. Five minutes ago, I was all but married to Patrick. But a kid?

What do I know about kids? The little boy would end up hating me. Then Patrick would hate me.

No. This is all wrong. This isn't how the dream went.

I pull back and backtrack toward the door without turning.

Patrick reaches for my hand, his face suddenly panic-stricken. "April, stop."

I keep backing up toward the door, reaching for the knob behind my back.

"I'm sorry I didn't tell you sooner. I don't like to introduce my family to just anybody. You're special to me."

I know I'm shaking my head vigorously, side to side. I want to stop, but I can't. My hand clutches the doorknob. Relief washes over me as I turn it in my hand.

"April, don't!"

"I'm sorry, Patrick. I just don't—I didn't—" I wave my hand between the two of them— smile at the adorable little boy. "I'm sorry—" I turn and run to my car.

Patrick taps on the driver's side window as I put my car in reverse. "April, talk to me." His voice is muted through the glass.

I can't look at him. I focus on the rearview mirror until I'm in the street. I slap the car into drive and speed away.

The tears are streaming so hard down my face they blur my eyes, making it difficult to see. I hurt all over.

Fudge!!!

What have I just done?

My chest heaves uncontrollably. I can barely steer my car safely to the curb for the shaking of my hands.

I release a prolonged wailing mew until all the air is expelled from my lungs and my stomach muscles burn.

I'm a foolish—foolish girl. What have I done?

I've ruined everything. That's what I've done.

Struggling for control, I take short quick breaths. The warm salty streams continue down my face, but I have slowed the shuddering of my chest to a tremble.

I can go back. That's it. I'll go back and say—it was a joke. Right. I was playing a joke. Little boys like pranks.

Lord, I'm so stupid. There's no going back. This was a one-time opportunity, and once again, I blew my chance right at the finish line.

My life is a joke. Everything I've held as a belief is wrong. Who knows, I might actually be good with kids. It's not like I have any experience to know one way or the other.

I visualize Robert's smiling face as he talked to me about Puppy. The fact he was playing an angle to persuade Patrick to get him a puppy of his own makes me laugh, forcing a snot bubble out my nose.

Smart kid. I love his moxie.

My jaw stretches open, and I lean forward, resting my forehead on the steering wheel as another wail works its way up from my gut. As the decibels in the car rise, it's as if all the hope and love that could have been mine is purging from my body to leave me the hollow shell I was before I met Patrick.

Eyes blurring with tears, I stand in front of my apartment door and curse the fact I have no comfort foods. When you're having a crisis of this magnitude, ramen noodles don't cut it.

I need chocolate ice cream.

Wrenching open the sliding door to my parents' kitchen, I fumble for the light. I make my way to the deep freezer and rummage until I find a half-gallon of ice cream. Rocky road, how apropos. It'll do just fine.

I toss the container's top into the sink and grab a serving spoon from the silverware drawer.

Five spoonsful in, my waterworks have stopped, but I can feel depression blooming through my soul.

I feel so awful. It's as if somebody took the giant spoon in my hand and scraped all the happiness out of me, leaving me a hollow shell.

And who did that? I did.

"April?"

My lower lip trembles as Mama looks at me inquisitively.

Her glance goes down to the ice cream and back to my eyes. "Baby, what's the matter? What happened?"

My throat tightens, and my nose tingles fiercely as the waterworks threaten to begin again. I can't speak.

Mama is across the kitchen, putting her arms around me in one quick movement. "Talk to me."

The tears and the words pour out in equal measure.

"It's just I don't understand why I can't move forward, Mama. I try to do better. I really do. Still, nothing ever goes right.

"The interview went badly today, but I don't even care about the interview. I really like Patrick. I think I may even love him. But he's got a son. He's cute.

"But I didn't *know* Patrick had a son. He never told me." I lock eyes with her for affirmation. "He should have told me. *Right?*"

"I suppose."

My chest starts back with the annoying shaking, and I can barely croak the last of my rant. "If I had known, I would have been prepared and not done anything stupid."

"Stupid?"

Leaning my head back, I open my mouth wide in an effort to stop the sobbing. What's done is done. "I ruined everything. When I saw Patrick's son, I panicked and left."

Mama's eyebrows come together. "—after dinner."

I shake my head slowly from side to side. "No, Mama. Right

after Patrick introduced him."

"April—"

"I know, Mama." I look away from her. "I feel awful. I really do. It just happened. One moment I was in their home, and the next, I was driving down the street."

Mama's warmth engulfs me as she pulls me into an embrace. "I'm so sorry. I know you really liked Patrick."

Mama is stroking my hair like she used to when I was little. It helps me breathe.

"Everything will work out in the end," she says.

I pull back from her shoulder and wipe my nose with the back of my hand. "You think if I explain, Patrick will understand, and we can start again?"

She winces. "No, baby. Those eggs are already broken. You'll have a mess to clean up in the morning. But it will be to set things right. You have to remember, Patrick is a good friend of your brother, too."

I hang my head. "Chase is going to be so mad at me."

"Lucky for you, Chase has a short memory, and he loves you."

I nod my head as I draw a deep breath. There will be a couple of tough conversations for me in the morning. Still, it won't be the first time I've had to pull my big girl pants on for having done something foolish.

Mama favors me with a sympathetic smile. "You're in transition right now, April. I don't know why but you still have a lot of growing up to do."

I burrow my face tight against her chest. "I'm sorry I'm so much trouble."

She chuckles as she rests her chin on top of my head. "You're no trouble—a challenge maybe—" Mama laughs. "I am so proud of you. Think of the people you have helped since you've been home. You're special—a special kind of infuriating some days. Still, you have a lot of heart and, most of all, grit. Unfortunately, tonight you were anything but the strong woman of grace I raised you to be."

"Not helpful, Mama."

She laughs and hugs me tighter. "You're still my foolish girl."

"I'll try to do better."

"I know you will. Your time is coming, April May. Mark my word, your time is coming."

I hope Mama is right.

The End

April's story continues with,

Foolish Cravings

Have you read the prequels? *The Gifts Awaken* stories are the prequel series to the *Foolish* novel series of April May Snow.

Click to get your copies today!

The Gifts Awaken Prequel Series

Throw the Bouquet
Throw the Cap
Throw the Dice
Throw the Elbow
Throw the Fastball
Throw the Gauntlet
Throw the Hissy

M. Scott lives outside of Nashville, Tennessee, with his wife and two guard chihuahuas. When he's not writing, he's cooking or taking long walks to smooth out plotlines for the next April May Snow adventure.

Dear Reader,

Thank you for reading April's story. You make her adventures possible. Without you, there would be no point in creating her story.

I'd like to encourage you to post a review on Amazon. A favorable critique from you is a powerful way to support authors you enjoy. It allows our books to be found by additional readers, and frankly, motivates us to continue to produce books. This is especially true for your independents.

Once again, thank you for the support. You are the magic that breathes life into these characters.

M. Scott Swanson

*The best way to stay in touch
is to join the reader's club!*
www.mscottswanson.com

Other ways to stay in touch are:

Like on Amazon

Like on Facebook

Like on Goodreads

You can also reach me at mscottswanson@gmail.com.

I hope your life is filled with
magic and LOVE!

Made in the USA
Monee, IL
14 September 2022

14030509R00184